in

Island heat – the s........ ....ne seduction!

By Request

Passion in Paradise

A DEVIOUS DESIRE
by
Jacqueline Baird

THUNDER ON THE REEF
by
Sara Craven

CARIBBEAN DESIRE
by
Cathy Williams

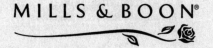

MILLS & BOON®

*MILLS & BOON and MILLS & BOON with the Rose Device
are registered trademarks of the publisher.
Harlequin Mills & Boon Limited,
Eton House, 18-24 Paradise Road, Richmond, Surrey, TW9 1SR*

PASSION IN PARADISE © by Harlequin Enterprises II B.V., 2004

A Devious Desire, Thunder on the Reef and *Caribbean Desire*
were first published in Great Britain by Harlequin Mills & Boon
Limited in separate, single volumes.

A Devious Desire © Jacqueline Baird 1995
Thunder on the Reef © Sara Craven 1994
Caribbean Desire © Cathy Williams 1991

ISBN 0 263 84068 9

05-0304

*Printed and bound in Spain
by Litografia Rosés S.A., Barcelona*

Jacqueline Baird began writing as a hobby when her family objected to the smell of her oil painting, and immediately became hooked on the romantic genre. She loves travelling and worked her way around the world from Europe to the Americas and Australia, returning to marry her teenage sweetheart. She lives in Ponteland, Northumbria, the county of her birth, and has two teenage sons. She enjoys playing badminton, and spends most weekends with husband Jim, sailing their Gp.14 around Derwent Reservoir.

Don't miss Jacqueline Baird's next sexy read: Coming soon in 2004, in Modern Romance™!

A DEVIOUS DESIRE
by
Jacqueline Baird

CHAPTER ONE

SAFFRON flopped back down on the plastic chair at the roadside café and grinned at the elderly lady seated at the opposite side of the table. 'I've paid the bill and asked the proprietor to call us a taxi. It's half six and we have to be back on board by seven.'

'Don't fuss, child, and finish your wine.'

'Your wish is my command,' she quipped. 'But remember that is your third glass. Don't blame me if your arthritis plays up later on.' And with a wry smile tugging her wide mouth Saffron picked up her glass and sipped the sparkling wine. She hadn't the heart to deny Anna a few moments longer at the café in the ancient walled town of Rhodes. A café Anna had spent hours trying to find!

'What was so important about this particular place?' Saffron asked for the umpteenth time, but not really expecting an answer. Anna had been very secretive about the reason behind her search for this café, but Saffron wasn't complaining.

A month ago she had been working as a beauty and aromatherapist for a London agency that provided a personal service to clients in their own homes, and also to a few of the more enlightened city hospitals, when a request for a home visit from Anna Statis's doctor had arrived. The lady had had a fall and badly bruised her shoulder, which, combined with arthritis in her knee, had left her in a little difficulty with mobility. He had considered that aromatherapy might help her. Saffron was given the job. Ten days later she had a six-month contract as Anna's personal ther-

5

apist, and for the past week they had been cruising the Greek Islands on the liner the *Pallas Corinthian*. Life could not be more perfect. Saffron sighed in contentment, and raised her glass to her lips.

They had just spent an enjoyable afternoon walking around Rhodes, discovering the Street of the Knights and marvelling at the inns that housed the Knights of St John. Then finally they had found this small bar, much to Anna's delight and Saffron's relief; she did not want the old lady overtired.

'My son was conceived here.'

'What?' Saffron jerked upright and swallowed the wine, almost choking with laughter. 'You're having me on. In a pavement café?' Her sparkling green eyes clashed with misty blue ones.

'It is true. I was a dancer on a cruise ship. Very daring for a well brought up English girl in my era. The ship visited Rhodes regularly and I met and fell in love with a handsome Greek, Nikos Statis, and in a room above this café my son Alexandros was conceived forty years ago this week.'

Saffron glanced at her employer, not sure whether to believe her. In her mid-sixties, her once blonde hair, now white, was swept up in a loose chignon, revealing the delicate features of a still beautiful face, but a sad, reminiscent smile hazed her blue eyes.

'And now you're back again. How romantic,' Saffron murmured. But privately she had her doubts. Within a week of taking up her live-in job as Anna's therapist she had watched in awe as the old lady had persuaded her doctor that what she needed to make a quick recovery was a cruise! Anna might look fragile, but she had an amazing ability to get her own way.

'Romantic! I thought so at the time,' Anna continued softly. 'But I was wrong—so wrong.'

Saffron was intrigued and, eager to hear more, prompted, 'Wrong…?'

'Some day I will tell you my life story. I feel the need to tell someone, and in the short time we have been together I feel closer to you than I have to anyone in years. Probably because you have been on your own and lonely most of your life and so have I.'

'But you have a son.' Anna was always talking about him, but he neglected the woman shamefully. As far as Saffron was aware he had never so much as called his mother since she had started working for Anna.

'Yes, true.'

Obviously they were not close. A typical selfish male, Saffron thought, but at that moment a taxi drew up at the kerb, and she knew any further revelations would have to wait.

Anna drained her glass and in a lightning mood change grinned. 'Finding this place today has helped me to lay some ghosts. But now we'd better make tracks, hmm?'

'Yes,' Saffron agreed and, standing up, she added with a smile, 'I'm glad we found your café. You do look more content.'

'Content! Yes, do you know I really think I am? Thank you, Saffy.'

With a tender glance at her boss, Saffron swung her shoulder-bag over her shoulder and gently put a hand under a frail elbow, helping Anna to her feet. She waited and watched as the other woman gave one last lingering look at the top floor of the building and was just about to help her into the car when to Saffron's astonishment someone yelled, 'Get the hell out of the way!' and grabbed the strap of her bag, hard fingers scraping her bare flesh.

Her hand slipped from Anna and she cried a warning. 'Look out! A thief!'

Years in an orphanage, and looking after herself for most of her life, along with classes in self-defence, had taught Saffron something, and with lightning reflexes her arm shot up, her finger and thumb nipping the front of her attacker's throat while her knee crashed up and into a very male groin. Spinning on her heel, she gently pushed Anna back into her seat. 'Don't worry, Anna, I've got it under control.'

Saffron shot her a worried glance, and was amazed to see that Anna was not in the least fazed by the unpleasant incident. In fact she was smiling, then chuckling, then laughing!

'It's not funny—we were nearly robbed.'

'Oh, Saffy, dear, if I ever had any doubt about your suitability for the job, I don't now!' Amid much laughter mingled with very masculine groans she went on, 'I have never seen anything so funny in my whole life.'

Saffron, adrenalin still pumping, had no idea how magnificent she looked. At five feet five, with her red-gold hair a wild tangle about her lovely face, and dressed in neat white tailored shorts, braless under a navy strapless tube-top, her green eyes flashing fire, she looked like some avenging Valkyrie.

'What is so funny?' she demanded, and then spared a glance for the man she had felled. 'This man was trying to attack us.' She could not see his face, but she could hear his moans. He was folded double and clutching a very private part of himself.

They had gathered quite a crowd, including the proprietor of the café, who asked, 'Shall I call the police?'

The police... Saffron hesitated. They had to be back on board soon; if they were delayed by the police they would miss the boat. She glanced at Anna, only to see the other woman wiping the tears of laughter from her eyes with one hand while waving the other frantically in the air as she got out over her amusement. 'No police, no police.'

'Then let's get in the taxi and go.' Saffron was suddenly conscious of the crowd and being the centre of attention and she did not like it. She hitched her bag more firmly on her shoulder and cast an uneasy glance at her assailant, who had dragged himself to the seat she had recently vacated, and she saw his face...

Night-black hair fell in tousled curls over a broad forehead; perfectly arched brows framed glittering black eyes. The nose was large and slightly hooked, the jaw square, and wide mouth completed the rugged features, but the lips were pulled back in a grimace of pain. Her gaze dropped to his broad shoulders; a plain white T-shirt clung lovingly to a broad chest, the faint trace of dark body hair showing through the fine fabric, and brief denim cut-offs exposed the considerable length of tanned muscular legs, also with a downy covering of black hair. He looked dangerously tough, and suddenly Saffron had serious doubts about what she had done. Her legs felt weak, and she was amazed at her own success in overpowering him. If she had got a good look at him before, she would never have tried...

Odd! He also looked vaguely familiar, but he couldn't be... Dismissing the uncomfortable thought, she said quickly, 'Come on, Anna; get in the taxi. We don't need to bother with his sort; the police will catch him soon enough.' She opened the car door and put her other hand under Anna's elbow, urging her up and into the taxi. She was desperate to get away. The man looked as if he was getting his wind back and Saffron did not want to be around when he did.

'No, no, Saffy, you don't understand,' Anna said, still chuckling. 'This is my son Alexandros. Alex.'

'What? Your son!' Incredulity widened her green eyes to their fullest extent. 'I don't believe you. He can't be…'

'But he is. Honestly…' Anna, finally controlling her amusement, answered seriously.

'Thank you, Mother. I'm glad you found my distress so hilariously funny.' A deep rich voice broke into the women's exchange.

Saffron felt as if she had been pole-axed, then her lips began to twitch in the beginnings of a smile as she thought that actually it was the man who was pole-axed, and by her! She knew it was completely the wrong time to find the situation amusing but she could not help it—a snort of laughter escaped her before she could control herself.

'And as for you, whoever you are,' the deep voice continued harshly, 'I would not laugh if I were you; if anyone is calling the police around here it will be me for your completely unwarranted attack upon my person.'

'Oh, for heaven's sake, Alex, listen to yourself! You sound like a pompous ass,' his mother responded, and, grabbing Saffron's arm, she added, 'I think you're right, dear; let's get in the taxi and go; we don't want to miss the boat.'

But their escape was not to be so easy. With a speed that belied his great size and his recent injury, Alex was on his feet and ushering his mother and Saffron into the back seat of the cab. Sliding in beside them, he then issued instructions to the taxi driver in Greek, and they were on their way.

'Now, Mother, perhaps you will tell me what you are doing with this red-headed devil—' he cast a venomous glance at Saffron who was squashed between them, and then looked past her to his mother '—on a cruise ship touring the islands.'

'Having a holiday,' Anna said bluntly. 'Saffy is my new

companion—and before you say another word Dr Jenkins thoroughly approves.'

Saffron felt the dark eyes fixed on her, but she kept her head bent, hiding her face. After the excitement of the past half-hour, she was slowly beginning to realise just what she had done. Assaulted her employer's own son. So much for the job of a lifetime, she thought morosely. She had been counting on this six-month contract with all living expenses provided to boost her bank balance to the magical amount that would enable her to set up her own beauty clinic. She could see her dream disintegrating before her eyes. Burnt to ashes by the heat of anger that shimmered between the taxi's occupants.

Suddenly Alex aimed a torrent of rapid-fire Greek at Anna, and as if to punctuate his words he stretched a long arm along the back of the seat to touch his mother's shoulder. At the brush of his arm against the back of her neck Saffron almost jumped out of her skin, a tingling awareness making the small hairs on her neck stand on end. Immediately she was shockingly conscious of his powerful masculinity and bitterly resented the fact.

She had met his type before—hard and ruthless. Even his mother had hinted that they were not very close, and she was lonely. Now Saffron could understand why, given the autocratic way he had bundled them both into the taxi like so much unwanted baggage. 'Arrogant pig!' she thought, then to her horror realised that she had spoken out loud, and the full fury of glittering black eyes was turned on her red face.

'Woman, if you want to live to see tomorrow I suggest you keep your mouth shut. You have done quite enough harm already. Kidnapping Mother, attacking me... One more word and you will be in a Greek gaol so fast your feet won't touch the ground—'

'That's enough, Alex,' Anna cut in sternly. 'A taxi is not the place to argue, and in any case we have arrived.'

Alex, without another word, got out of the car and walked around the other side, opening the door for his mother. Saffron slid out on to the dock and glanced up at the cruise liner, then rather warily over the top of the taxi at the other two. As she watched she saw Alex smile and bend down to brush a light kiss on the top of Anna's head before paying the taxi driver then gently taking her arm and leading her up the gangway.

Saffron hesitated. Perhaps she was wrong. Maybe Alex did not neglect his mother. As she thought back to the scene at the café it struck her. For a woman who said she hardly saw her son, Anna had not been in the least surprised when he had suddenly appeared. In fact she had thought it a huge joke. Odd. Very odd...

A soft sigh fluttered past Saffron's lips. What did it matter? She had little doubt that in a very short time she was going to be out of a job. It would have been nice to finish the cruise but if the murderous expression on Alex Statis's face earlier was anything to go by she would probably be on the next flight out of Rhodes back to England.

But in that she was mistaken...

Once back on board she deemed it wise to give mother and son some time alone and grasped the chance to speak to a fellow traveller, a nice American gentleman who was travelling alone. She listened to him wax lyrical about the beauty of Lindos—the destination of the shipboard excursion that day—then slowly made her way to the cabin.

As soon as she walked in the door she immediately sensed the tension in the air. Anna was sitting in an armchair, her lovely face composed, her hands folded neatly in her lap, while Alex paced up and down the cabin like a caged tiger.

'Don't hurry, will you, Miss Martin?' He fixed her with piercing black eyes, and she shivered at the force of his anger.

'I wasn't aware there was any hurry,' she snapped back. 'After all, we are on the boat for three more days.'

'You are not.' Saffron's heart sank at his words. So she was to be sacked! But to her astonishment he continued, 'You are to pack for the pair of you, and be ready to leave as soon as possible. I will arrange with the captain to delay sailing until you are ready, but hurry—every extra minute over departure time is going to cost me dearly.'

'What?' Saffron wasn't sure she had heard him right. They were leaving the ship, but to go where? 'Where?' she exclaimed.

'My yacht. And I have no time for questions. Mama insists you fulfil the six-month contract; she seems to think you are invaluable to her.'

His eyes swept over her from the top of her red head, lingering for a moment too long on the proud thrust of her breasts beneath the brief top she wore, and on down to her narrow waist, slim hips and long legs, then back to her face, his expression saying it all. He couldn't see why! Then, with two lithe strides, he was beside her.

Her hands curled into fists as she fought down the instinctive urge to push him away; he was much too close. She stiffened, banishing the blush that rose to her cheeks with a mighty effort of self-control. There was something about the man that threatened her in ways she didn't understand. Sexually, she freely admitted, but it was more than that. On some deeper, darker level he threatened her. She knew it instinctively, but not why. She raised her eyes to his harsh face and searched the rough-hewn features with the growing conviction that somehow—somewhere—she knew him. Then suddenly his words penetrated her puzzled mind.

'I have met your kind before, and I am not so sure you're of any value,' he drawled cynically. 'More likely a costly mistake.'

Saffron gasped in outrage at his comment, and raised her hand to slap the swine's face. But he caught her hand in his and continued insultingly, 'However, against my better judgement I have agreed to allow you to stay for my mother's sake.'

Saffron felt the electric shock the length of her arm as his strong fingers tightened on hers deliberately. 'Smile,' he hissed, and added loudly for Anna's benefit, 'We have a deal, Saffron. Shake on it.' And she was forced to comply with the social nicety before he finally let go of her hand.

She was still reeling when he bent his head and murmured, as he brushed past her through the open door, 'But don't think I've forgotten what happened earlier; I'm going to make you pay, you green-eyed witch,' and left, slamming the door behind him.

Anger and fear mingled in her eyes. The arrogant devil! How dared he threaten her? For two pins she would walk out now, but, catching Anna's expression, she fought down the impulse. The appeal in the older woman's eyes was unmistakable.

'I apologise for my son; he can be rather domineering, I know, but he does have my best interest at heart. You will still come with me, won't you? I need you.'

'I'm not sure it's a good idea,' Saffron said drily. 'Your son and I are obviously not going to get on, especially after I nearly crippled him.' A fleeting smile curved her mouth as she remembered his discomfort earlier.

'That wasn't your fault; I'm sure he won't hold it against you, Saffy. In any case the yacht is huge and if I know

Alex we will rarely see him; he always brings one of his women with him, if not more than one, and of course the *family*.' She frowned, adding cryptically, 'That is the main reason I wanted to come on a public cruise. It's much more fun with strangers around.'

Saffron's heart sank. How could a son treat his mother so cavalierly? Take her on holiday, then leave her to her own devices while he enjoyed himself with his latest sex object? She was sure that was all women meant to such an aggressively macho man as Alex and his own mother had more or less confirmed it.

'But the doctor did say you had to have no stress. Maybe it would be better for you if you told your son the truth. You fell and got a nasty shock, but soon you will be as good as new.' Anna had sworn both her doctor and Saffron to secrecy over her accident, insisting that she did not want her son to know and fuss over her. Personally Saffron thought it was way past time her son fussed over her, instead of leaving her in London all the time while he apparently based himself in Greece when he wasn't jetting around the world. 'I'm sure if he knew he would stay with you, and you won't need me.'

'You don't understand, dear. I can't tell Alex; I know what he will say—that I'm too old to live on my own. He will insist on my giving up my London home and staying with the family. I would hate that. I like—I need my independence. Please say you will stay…'

Saffron sighed inwardly. She could not desert her charge, however much she might dislike the poor woman's son. But 'poor woman' was not really accurate. She smiled to herself. Even the mighty Alex Statis had bowed to his mother's demand and allowed Saffron to stay. Anna, despite her delicate old lady act, was obviously a wily old bird.

'Yes, of course,' she answered a touch wryly, and moved to the wardrobe, adding, 'I'd better start packing.'

Saffron turned restlessly in the bed, and pushed the light satin cover down to her waist. But she knew it was not the heat keeping her awake—the yacht was fully air-conditioned—nor the low throbbing of its powerful engine as it ploughed through the Aegean Sea in the middle of the night. It was the intervention of the frightening, sinister figure of Alex Statis in her life.

With an efficiency she could only marvel at he had whisked her and Anna away from the cruise ship and, after a brief taxi ride, into a waiting helicopter; by ten o'clock the same evening, to her amazement, the helicopter had landed on a helipad on the top of a luxurious ocean-going yacht, anchored off the Greek mainland.

With a minimum of fuss a very correct steward had shown Saffron to her cabin on the top deck, and what a cabin! A large circular bed in a mahogany-panelled room with a matching *en suite*, the bathroom and toiletries all sparkling white with brass and mahogany trim. Anna's quarters were even more luxurious, with a private sitting-room.

Saffron had tried to quiz her boss while unpacking, but for some reason the older woman had not been very forthcoming. However, while Saffron had gently brushed Anna's hair, before settling her for the night, she'd begun to talk.

'I guess I was being irresponsible to go off on my own that way—at least, Alex thinks so,' she murmured softly, almost to herself, and then, looking in the mirror, she fixed Saffron with pleading blue eyes. 'But you understand, don't you, dear?'

Saffron didn't, not one bit; her head was reeling at the

events of the evening. Dinner had been an informal buffet, not because of the lateness of the hour—Greeks were used to eating late—but in deference to the fragile health of her charge, she was sure. After the meal Alex had taken one look at his mother and then told Saffron to see the lady to bed. Saffron had been only too happy to comply; for the last few hours she had been all too conscious of Alex's eyes following her every move, studying her as if she were something the cat had dragged in, and the feeling had been unsettling to say the least.

She smiled at Anna's reflection in the mirror. 'Not really,' she confessed simply.

'No, I suppose not. It was an old lady's fantasy to re-create the past. The *Pallas Corinthian* was the boat I worked on, you see, the one I later found out Nikos, my husband, owned...'

'You mean you got me to book a cruise on your own shipping line?' Saffron had wondered, when Anna had asked her to book the cruise, why she had insisted on the one particular ship. Now she knew.

'Not exactly. Alex is in charge of the business, has been for ages, and he sold the liner to another company years ago. He has no time for sentiment. That's why I couldn't tell him what I wanted to do. But I'm glad we had our little holiday, Saffy; seeing Rhodes and the café today was enough, and thank you again, dear, for pandering to a sentimental old fool.'

Instinctively Saffron put down the brush and gave Anna a hug. 'I don't think you're an old fool; I think you're wonderful. And now do you want me to massage your shoulder before bed or not?'

'No, not tonight. I'm tired enough to go straight to sleep.' Rising, she touched Saffron's cheek. 'You're a good girl to put up with me, but there is one little thing I would like you to do.'

'Yes.' Saffron realised that in the past few weeks she had grown to really care for Anna and, arrogant son apart, she would do anything for her.

'Please don't mention to Alex why I wanted a beauty therapist as well as a masseuse. I would hate him to know I can't even lift my arm high enough to comb my own hair. He is an astute man, and would soon guess there was something more wrong with me than arthritis, and it would only worry him.'

Personally Saffron thought it was about time the globe-trotting swine did worry about his mother, but not by a flicker of an eyelash did she reveal her dislike of the man; instead she promised to say nothing.

Tossing and turning in the luxurious bed, Saffron tried to tell herself that nothing much had changed from this morning. They were still cruising but simply on a private yacht. So why did she have this weird feeling of foreboding? It didn't make sense. She still had her job, in a week or two she and Anna would return to Anna's comfortable mews house in the heart of London and Saffron would rarely, if ever, see Alex Statis again. All she had to do was keep her mouth shut and out of his way; that shouldn't be too hard; she was just the hired help after all...

She closed her eyes and once more tried to sleep, but the vivid image of Alex leaning against the door-frame as she'd walked by him to follow Anna to her cabin seemed to be imprinted on her pupils. Casually elegant, his black hair swept back from his broad forehead, grey wings curling around his ears betraying his thirty-nine years, and a wide, sensual mouth that had hissed cynically as she'd passed him, 'You can leave now. But I haven't forgotten I owe you.' That parting shot lingered threateningly in her mind.

Her eyes flashed open. 'You can leave now,' he had said, and something niggled at the back of her brain, a sense of *déjà vu*. Had she met him before? No, it wasn't possible; her mind must be playing tricks, or—perhaps the most likely explanation—she must have seen a photograph of him in his mother's house. Yes, that was it—of course. And, closing her eyes once more, she finally fell into a troubled sleep where a tall, dark man stalked her dreams...

A knock on the door broke into her restless sleep and, slowly opening her eyes, she yawned widely.

'Coffee, madam,' she heard the steward announce, and responded.

'Come in.' Hauling herself up into a sitting position, she blinked drowsily, wondering if Anna was awake yet. Then it hit her, the events of the previous evening, and her eyes widened in horror on the approaching man, a gasp of outrage escaping her. 'You...'

Alex, dressed in a brief white towelling robe belted loosely around his waist, revealing a wide expanse of hair-roughened chest and inordinately long, muscular legs, strolled to the bedside, a tray bearing a coffee-jug and cup on it in his strong hands. 'Good morning, Saffron.'

'G-g-get out of my room,' she stuttered. The man wasn't conventionally handsome, but he possessed a lethal attraction few women could resist, herself included. His tanned skin, the early morning stubble darkening his jaw gave him the rakish appearance of a swashbuckling pirate.

'Now is that any way to greet your employer? Especially when he is delivering you sustenance.'

'You are not my employer,' she retorted, but his remark had reminded her of her duties. 'But if you get out of my cabin I can dress and go and see Anna,' she said, suddenly wide awake, and wary. She had no idea how lovely she looked, her red-gold hair tumbling in disarray around her shoulders, one long strand with a will of its own curving around the fullness of her breast, the skimpy spaghetti-strapped cotton nightie she was wearing barely covering her high, firm breasts.

'You're not a morning person... Pity, because you look absolutely delectable.'

How dared he flirt with her? Saffron's angry eyes flew to his face and she was horrified to realise that his gaze was fixed rather lower on her body. Grabbing the luxurious satin sheet, she pulled it up to her chin. Just in time, as Alex sat down on the side of the bed. He was much too close, the bedroom was much too intimate, and he had no right to be here.

'Will you get out?' she cried, her temper rising.

'Don't look so terrified. You must have had dozens of men in your bedroom, a girl as beautiful as you.'

She had never had any man in her bedroom, and she was damned sure she wasn't about to start with this over-poweringly arrogant specimen of the male sex. 'Out,' she snapped, indicating the door with her free hand.

'Don't flatter yourself, girl,' Alex drawled cynically, his dark eyes sliding insultingly over her flushed face and rumpled hair. 'I only want to talk before you see Mama. Why else would I wake you at seven in the morning?' he asked mockingly.

Saffron could do nothing about the blush that suffused her whole body.

Alex slowly shook his head, one dark brow arching sardonically. 'What a naughty mind you have, Saffron.'

The man delighted in teasing her, but she had promised to try and get along with him, so, ignoring his comment, she turned to where he had placed the tray on the table beside the bed and filled a cup with coffee. She took her time adding milk, before she dared turn back to face him.

'Tell me, why Saffron? I always thought it was a spice. Are you spicy?' he queried, a wicked glint in his dark eyes.

She slanted him a glance from beneath thick lashes then quickly looked down at the cup in her hand and took a long swallow of the hot coffee, before responding curtly, ignoring his innuendo, 'Saffron is a plant that when dried yields a deep yellow, orangey dye. When I was born my parents took one look at my ginger hair and called me Saffron.'

A large hand reached out and picked up the loose curl that framed her breast. Alex twisted it around his long fingers, his knuckles brushing the tip of her breast. 'Your hair is not ginger, it is gold, red, blonde, a collection of colours creating a living flame.'

Her breast hardened at the brief touch and embarrassment at her instant reaction brought hot blood to her cheeks. Saffron knew that Alex was aware of her response and suddenly she felt helpless, as if she had lost control of the situation. Yesterday she had been a mature, efficient professional doing her job to the best of her ability. In the past twelve hours her life had quickly become entwined with this sophisticated man and his jet-set lifestyle, and she wasn't sure she liked it. She pulled her head back, freeing her hair from his far too familiar fingers, and quickly lowered her eyes, afraid of the predatory look on Alex's harsh face.

But the following view was even more disturbing as her gaze dropped to where his robe fell apart, revealing a tanned muscular leg in stark contrast to the white towelling. A startling erotic image flashed through her mind as he moved slightly, his taut thigh pressing against her leg, only the satin sheet preventing their naked flesh touching: Alex, naked and golden brown all over, reaching for her, his deep brown eyes smouldering with passion…

'Coffee. Good.'

Horrified at her wayward thoughts, Saffron tore her gaze away from his legs and, shocked by her sexy fantasy, kept her head lowered to hide her blushes. She mumbled, 'Yes,' then breathed deeply and exhaled slowly. Her reaction to Alex Statis was getting ridiculous. What on earth was happening to her? She prided herself on her self-control but she had an awful premonition that around this man she would have to fight for every ounce.

'Cabin OK?' he asked.

He knew very well it was the height of luxury; he was deliberately goading her, but she would not rise to the bait. 'What do you want, Mr Statis?' she demanded firmly, pleased at the even tenor of her voice.

'It is not so much what I want but what you want, Miss Martin.' All trace of teasing was gone. His eyes, hard and dark as jet, caught hers. 'My mother is a wealthy woman. I don't know who persuaded whom to go on a holiday cruise which was totally unnecessary in the circumstances.'

'I didn't…'

'Maybe you're telling the truth. Mama can be very devious,' he said drily.

Anna devious! Well, maybe a little, Saffron admitted honestly, but compared to this man Anna was innocence personified, and she listened in mounting anger as Alex continued.

'I've checked with her doctor and apparently it is all above board. My mother likes you, she tells me you are good at your job, and I know to my cost—' his lips thinned in a tight grimace '—you are more than capable of looking after yourself and her. But what worries me is where you learnt such talent, and why you needed to. So take this as a warning if you have any notion of fleecing my mother, or getting involved with any more of her madcap plans; I advise you to forget it—understand?' He got to his feet, his dark eyes boring down into hers, a threat explicit in the black depths. 'I will leave you to enjoy your coffee—oh, yes, and welcome aboard.'

Saffron had never been so insulted. The nerve of the man! Madcap plans indeed! And as if she would cheat an old lady. The temper that went with her red hair exploded, and she threw the half-full cup of coffee straight at him. The cup bounced off his chest, spilling coffee all over him.

'Why, you…' Two strong hands caught her upper arms and dragged her off the bed and against his hard body. She was suspended in mid-air, her feet dangling inches from the floor, but she did not have time to dwell on her predicament as a dark head swooped, Alex's mouth capturing hers in a brutal grinding kiss that drove the breath from her body. She tried to struggle and felt herself falling…

CHAPTER TWO

SAFFRON fell back on the bed and felt the full weight of his huge body follow down on top of her; she tried to lift her knee, but Alex wasn't the sort of man to be caught twice. His naked thigh pushed firmly between her legs, and as she tried to claw at his face his hands caught hers and pinned them either side of her head.

'You damned hellcat,' he swore. 'Yesterday you got lucky. For the first time in twenty-odd years you caught me off guard. But it was also your last, sweetheart. It is time someone taught you a lesson, and I am just the man to do it.' His deep brown eyes had darkened to black and the flame leaping in their depths sent fear scudding through Saffron's body.

'Says who—?' Her last word was all but swallowed by his mouth once more closing over hers, his tongue gaining entry to the moist interior with devastating results. Suddenly she was conscious of his naked thigh between her legs, her short nightie rucked up somewhere round her waist; his towelling robe had fallen open and their lower bodies were naked flesh on flesh... Her breasts pressed against his muscular chest, hardened with inexplicable need and straining against the fine cotton of her nightgown.

To Saffron's dismay, heat fierce and totally unexpected flooded through her veins. Her heartbeat accelerated like a rocket, and the kiss she had fought so furiously turned into a passionate seduction of her senses. She was aware of his powerful, virile body through every pore in her skin. His

24

heavy thighs moved restlessly against her slender limbs, and something else...

Well, I certainly did not injure the man yesterday, she thought wildly, just as Alex's mouth left hers, and she burst into terrified hysterical laughter.

'What the hell...?' His dark head reared back and he looked down into her flushed, laughing face. He let go of her abruptly and stood up.

Whether he recognised that it was fear more than humour that had brought on her hysterical reaction Saffron didn't know; she only knew that, with a savage glance at where she lay tumbled on the bed, he snarled, 'Cover yourself, woman; I'm not caught that easily,' and pulled the sheet up over her.

Caught? What did he mean? She gazed up at the dark figure towering over her, and all trace of hysterical humour left her. He was virtually naked; his robe, hanging loosely off his broad shoulders, hid nothing of his magnificent body, or his obvious state of sexual arousal. Her earlier fantasy was fulfilled. His powerful body was tanned all over, except for a pale strip across his lean hips! Mesmerised by the stark beauty of his virile form, she could not look away...

'Remember, you've been warned,' Alex said coldly as unselfconsciously he folded the robe over his chest and knotted the belt around his waist. 'Now I suggest you do what you were supposedly hired for and look after Mother.' And with that he strode out of the room, slamming the door behind him.

Saffron lay where he had left her, completely shell-shocked. Nothing in her life so far had prepared her for such a lightning attack on her senses. Her body still pulsed with unfamiliar heat, her breasts felt heavy, the tips aching for she knew not what, and the lingering scent of Alex hovered in the air around her, seducing her even in his absence.

It was incredible—no, impossible, she told herself. She did not like the man, and yet for an instant she had wanted him in a shockingly sexual way. She who could count the men she had kissed on the fingers of one hand!

Slowly, as her breathing reverted to normal, she justified her reaction. It must have been a mental apparition; her response was not real, just a figment of her imagination. She was twenty-five years old and knew herself well enough to realise she was not a sexual person. Two unfortunate events in her teenage years had quickly squashed any real interest in the male sex.

At the age of ten she had lost her parents in a car crash and, left alone in the world, she'd been placed in an orphanage. It was quite nice, the staff friendly, but it could never make up for the loss of her home in Surrey and her parents. She had been thirteen, her body beginning to develop, when one of the older boys had caught her and forced her to the ground, his hands grabbing at her breasts. But Eve, her friend, had stopped him.

Saffron sighed and swung her legs off the bed. A soft film of moisture glazed her eyes as she stood up, remembering the past. Eve, two years older than Saffron, had been her best friend at the orphanage. Even after she'd left, she'd still called back occasionally to see Saffron. Eve's untimely death not many months ago had affected Saffron deeply; she still wasn't over it. She brushed the moisture from her eyes and headed for the *en suite*.

Memories were best left where they belonged—in the past. She stepped out of her nightie and into the shower; turning the tap on full force, she tossed her head back and let the reviving water wash over her.

The sensible thing to do was to pack in her job as soon

as the boat docked and return to England. She would miss Anna, but common sense told her that the older woman would have no problem getting someone else to fill her role, and if she stayed she would have a problem with Alex Statis. He was a powerful, dangerous man, and he made no secret of the fact that he thought she was after something from his mother. It would be difficult; she had given up her room in the apartment she had shared with two others, Tom and Vera, and they had been quite happy to see her go as they had decided to marry, and quite naturally preferred to have the place to themselves. She supposed she could stay in a hotel or hostel until she found somewhere else, but it would certainly cut into her business fund, she realised sadly.

Then she recalled once more Eve's last message to her.

You have it all, Saffron—the looks, the character and the expertise to make it on your own. Not like me. I was born a loser. Promise me, Saffron, you won't let some bastard of a man get at you. Stick to your dream. Start your own business, be your own boss. Do it for me. You show them.

Squaring her shoulders, a new light of determination in her lovely green eyes, she turned off the water and stepped out of the shower. Wrapping a large fluffy towel around her slender body, she walked back into the bedroom. She would not allow Mr Statis to frighten her out of her job. Anna had employed her. Anna was happy with the arrangement, and in any case once they got back to London she would not have to see the man. But her salary for the next few months would be enough to fulfil her dream. Ten minutes later, neatly dressed in navy shorts and a plain white T-shirt, she opened the door of Anna's suite.

'Oh, you're awake!' Saffron smiled at her employer, sitting propped up in bed, her glance going to the tray beside her. 'And already at the coffee, I see,' she chided gently; if Anna had one weakness it was that she drank far too much coffee.

'Yes, my dear. I received the same service as you, apparently. Alex delivered it.'

Saffron felt the colour rise in her face. Anna certainly had not been attacked by the great brute as she had! Walking to the dressing-table, she busied herself with the case that contained her oils and other supplies. Trying to hide her blush, she said, 'Would you like me to order breakfast or would you prefer a shower and massage?'

'The massage, but make it quick. I have been instructed by Alex to meet him on the deck for breakfast at nine-thirty, and I don't dare argue. I have already wasted three days of his time, he informed me.'

'Wasted!' Saffron's temper rose at the comment. 'Surely it's his own fault? We were perfectly all right on the *Pallas Corinthian*. This was his idea.' She flung out an arm, gesturing around the luxurious room.

'Well, not exactly. I have a confession to make.'

Saffron spun round to stare at her charge.

'You see, dear, we always cruise in June for a week or so. But with Alex being in Australia and not sure when he was coming back I decided I wanted to cruise on my own...well, with you. The poor boy arrived in London last weekend and didn't know where I was and so he spent three days tracking us down, instead of working. Ordinarily I would have joined the yacht at the weekend along with Alex and the rest of the relatives.'

'If that's so, why are we moving now?' Saffron glanced out of the window at the vast expanse of clear sunlit water.

'We could have waited in port for the other guests and your son could have stayed at work.'

'That's my fault. I insisted we set sail straight away because I was frightened that with a couple of days in port you might change your mind and go back to England. I know what a pain my son can be, and I didn't want to lose you. This way you can't get off the boat and I've told Alex he has got to make friends with you.'

'Why, you conniving lady,' Saffron opined, with a wry shake of her red head.

'Yes, but you know my secret. In any case no one can do my hair or make-up as well as you. Not even me when I was fit,' Anna said with blunt honesty.

An hour later Saffron put the finishing touches to Anna's hair and then followed her along the passageway down the companionway, through the staterooms and through large glass doors to the poop deck where Alex was waiting for them.

It had been dark last night when they had arrived, but Saffron had been awed by the luxury of the cabins, the elegant main lounge and equally stunning dining-room, but the deck was something else again. Under a plain white awning were arranged three plump-cushioned long sofas covered in William Morris shades of blue and green printed cotton satin, a couple of over-stuffed armchairs and one large low table plus a handful of smaller ones discreetly stacked beside one of the potted vine trees that dotted the area. Beyond the seating area, on the open deck, was a circular swimming-pool. Through the sparkling water Saffron saw the outline of dolphins patterned in the tiles; the effect was as if they were swimming in the pool and completely magical. Around the pool was scattered a dozen sun-loungers, and a few more tables with gaily patterned beach umbrellas in the centre.

How the other half live! Saffron thought, bemused. She had realised Anna was wealthy, but it was slowly dawning on her that Alex Statis must be extremely rich. No wonder he was worried about his mother being ripped off by some unscrupulous companion. But it still gave him no right to suspect her, she thought grimly. He didn't know her, and was never likely to. She was way below his social circle and she knew it.

Subdued, Saffron sat down in one of the armchairs, avoiding looking at where Alex lounged elegantly on a sofa opposite. But to her surprise breakfast was a pleasant meal. The same steward who had shown her to her cabin the previous evening placed a wide variety of cereals, croissants, bread and accompanying confections on the large table, along with jugs of coffee, tea and various fruit juices, before asking if anyone wanted a hot meal.

The conversation was general. Saffron made an occasional comment but after a while she left mother and son to do most of the talking, content to admire her surroundings. It was early June, and the hot morning sun sparkled and danced on the deep blue sea, dazzling on the brilliant white of the boat. Paradise must be a lot like this, Saffron mused as she spread thick honey on a second warm croissant. Heaven help her weight if she kept eating like this…

'Is that all right with you, Saffron?'

She jumped at the sound of her name, her glance flashing between the other two. She felt that some comment was expected of her, but hadn't a clue what had been said.

'Tell her again, Alex,' Anna said with a grin.

Saffron reluctantly looked across at Alex. He was lounging casually back on the sofa, with his long legs stretched out in front of him. His hard, dangerously masculine body was briefly clad in a sleeveless black T-shirt that moulded his broad, muscular chest in loving detail. A pair of white shorts exposed his long legs, tanned to a golden bronze and rippling with muscles. He was all male, all-powerful, and he made her head spin...

'We will be arriving in Mykonos in a couple of hours. Mother wanted to see the island again, but she does not feel up to going ashore in the tender.' He hesitated and Saffron raised her eyes to his questioningly.

'She suggested I take you.' His sensuous mouth curved mockingly, his dark eyes raking suggestively over her slender frame. Saffron felt the colour rise in her face at his *double entendre*, before he added slowly, deliberately, 'For a few hours.'

The lazy smile, the long body stretched out only feet from her were having a totally alien effect on her. She opened her mouth to say no, but was horrified at the odd constriction in her throat. She swallowed hard.

'Yes, of course she will,' Anna answered for her. 'Mykonos is not to be missed.'

'I don't know,' Saffron heard herself murmur; she knew intuitively that being alone with Alex Statis represented a danger she was not sure she could handle.

'Of course you will, dear,' Anna insisted.

Saffron glanced across at Alex; the amusement in his eyes was obvious; he knew she wanted to say no, and was daring her to... 'Yes, that would be lovely,' she heard herself gush, and missed the flicker of cynicism in Alex's dark eyes.

'Good. Well, if you will excuse me, ladies, I have work to do.' Rising to his feet, Alex smiled gently at his mother. 'Round one to you, Mama.'

His austere features relaxed in a genuine smile that took years off his age and, though his comment puzzled Saffron for a brief second, she saw the man behind the ruthless mask. She sucked in her breath, her green eyes wide with wonder; he looked almost beautiful. But as he glanced briefly at her the tenderness vanished, to be replaced by a glittering predatory glow that turned his deep brown eyes almost golden.

'I'm looking forward to showing you Mykonos. I want to see your reaction to the place.'

A frisson of some nameless emotion slid down her spine. Fear! No. Anticipation of a day out, Saffron told herself sternly, nothing more! She refused to acknowledge her inexplicable violent attraction to Alex. 'I'm sure it will be delightful,' she offered with a cool smile, but had to turn her head away to stare at the sea. In her mind's eye the sight of him standing so tall and broad, scantily clad in shorts and shirt, was doing something very peculiar to her breathing.

Saffron stood leaning on the ship's rail, Anna beside her, as they watched the crew lower the gangway and the boat that in a few minutes would take Alex and herself ashore. The island of Mykonos looked everything Anna had told her as they had lounged around the boat all morning, relaxing and chatting.

The yacht had dropped anchor in the bay of Mykonos Town, and the view was spectacular—sparkling white houses, the blue-topped domes of the small churches the place was famous for dotted among them, along with the impressive row of windmills, six marching in a line along the horizon. Tearing her gaze away from the beauty before her, Saffron tried once more to persuade Anna to accompany them.

'I'll help you down into the boat, Anna. You will be all right, I promise. It seems a terrible shame for you to miss going ashore.'

'Rubbish! I can see all I want from here. Don't forget, Saffy, I have been here countless times.'

'Well, if you're sure.'

'Positive. I want you and Alex to forget about me and don't come back until you have seen the sunset from Little Venice.'

Before Saffron could reply Alex was at her side. She glanced up at him and her heart jumped. He had changed from the morning into a pair of navy shorts and a navy and white patterned silk shirt, and he looked devastatingly attractive.

'Ready, Saffron?' He drawled her name like a caress, sending tingles down her spine. 'Got your bathing suit?' he demanded, his dark eyes gleaming knowingly down into hers. He knew exactly how he affected her and obviously found it amusing.

'Yes,' she said frostily, swinging her beach bag, and would have preceded him down the gangway but a hand on her arms stopped her.

'Gentlemen first in this instance, then if you fall I am in front of you to prevent a hasty descent into the sea,' he explained, before releasing her arm and stepping on to the ladder.

The small boat reached the shore in minutes. A hire car was waiting for them and moments later they were speeding out of the town and into the countryside.

'I thought we were going to see the town,' Saffron prompted, a bit miffed that Alex appeared to have a different idea.

'We will later; first we will drive around the island, go for a swim maybe. There are some magnificent beaches. One or two nude ones if you prefer.' He shot her a wicked sidelong glance.

'No way,' she snapped back.

'Why not? It will be nothing we haven't seen before after this morning.'

A telling tide of red suffused her face as for a second she saw in her mind's eye Alex as he had been that morning in her room—almost naked.

Alex laughed out loud at her obvious discomfiture. 'OK, you win; bathing suits it is.'

It was like a day out of time for Saffron. After that one bit of teasing in the car Alex set out to be charming company, and Saffron found her antagonism vanishing in a puff of smoke.

They lunched on succulent fish on a bed of rice and fresh vegetables, at a small café alongside an almost deserted beach. Afterwards they lingered over their wine, and eventually strolled along the beach.

She found Alex an informative and amusing conversationalist as he told her something of the island's history. Apparently not that long ago it had been just another tiny Greek island inhabited by shepherds and fishermen. But the stylised form of building all white with the distinctive blue touches had been seen as so picturesque that a crafty local had decided they should cash in on the tourist trade. Now it was extremely popular with all the cruise liners, but was never overrun, simply because the bigger ships could not dock. The only way ashore was by tender.

By mid-afternoon the sun was much stronger in the sky and Alex suggested that they rest for a while. From the small duffel bag he was carrying he withdrew a towel and spread it on the golden sand, and Saffron followed suit, cautiously laying her own towel a foot away from his.

'Spoilsport,' he murmured as casually he slipped out of his clothes and stood before her clad only in tiny black swimming-trunks that left little to the imagination.

Saffron gulped and dragged her gaze away from such a

blatant display of sheer masculine perfection. He might be nearly forty, she thought, but not a spare inch of flesh marred his tall, muscular frame; he had the body of a man in his prime, and she was beginning to wonder at the wisdom of being alone with him.

'Race you to the water,' Alex challenged, and she had to look up at him.

'You go—I'll catch you up.' She needed a couple of minutes alone to still her erratically beating heart. She watched as with a casual nod he turned and began to run down to where the turquoise water met the silvery sand. He was as enticing from the rear as from the front, his broad tanned back tapering down to gorgeous lean hips and long, muscular legs. God! What was she thinking of? In a rush she slipped off her plain denim skirt and the neat short-sleeved shirt she had worn over her swimsuit.

She glanced down at herself, and wondered if the suit had been such a good idea. She had bought it for the cruise, thinking it was more conservative than a bikini, but now she had grave doubts. In jade-green, it was a simple figure-hugging Lycra suit with high cut-away legs almost to her waist, strapless and slashed straight across her breasts. Suddenly she saw just how provocative it was. How come she had never noticed before? she groaned silently, but it was too late to do anything about it now, and, taking a deep breath, she ran down and into the water. She could see Alex's head bobbing in the distance; he was a magnificent swimmer, but she had a sneaky suspicion that he was the kind of man who would do everything magnificently.

Saffron did not bother to try and compete; she could swim but was no great shakes, so she stayed near the shallows and floated for a while, enjoying the soothing stroke of the water against her sun-warmed flesh. Occasionally she glanced at Alex, who appeared to be heading determinedly towards an outcrop of rock that to Saffron looked miles away. He swam with a rhythmic determination that she could only marvel at. Slowly, with a sigh—it wasn't disappointment at Alex ignoring her, she told herself firmly—she made her way back to shore.

Collapsing flat on her back on the towel, allowing the sun to dry her, she closed her eyes. The hustle of the past two days, the food and wine at lunch, and the warmth of the sun all combined to make her fall asleep.

'Saffron!' She woke up with a start, for a moment completely disorientated and wondering where she was. Alex was leaning over her, his body damp, drops of water glistening on the dark hair of his chest and taut, flat belly. He frowned down at her. 'Don't you know it is the height of stupidity to fall asleep in the sun?' His hand reached out and with one finger he traced the soft curve of her breasts revealed by the straight bodice of her swimsuit. 'This flesh is far too fair and tender—you will burn,' he opined huskily.

'Alex,' she murmured dazedly; his touch was doing unreal things to her pulse-rate. She wanted to ask him if he'd enjoyed his marathon swim, but he was quite openly studying the soft swell of her breasts, his finger tugging lightly on the taut fabric, lowering it slightly. She shivered as his finger dipped down almost to the crest of one breast. She knew she should object, but had not the will to stop him, hypnotised by the sensual gleam in his eyes and his throatily voiced comment.

'So silky and voluptuous. A perfect combination.'

He smelt of sun and sea and sky and a lingering masculine scent that was all his own. He moved, and she felt the length of his leg move over her thigh, entrapping her slender limbs, as his dark head lowered, blocking out the sun.

'Saffron...' he rasped. 'You drive me mad.' And deep down inside her Saffron felt something spring to life—a matching madness. Perhaps...

She knew she should move, get away, but instead her tongue licked nervously over her suddenly dry lips as she anticipated his kiss. The hot brush of his lips over hers made her gasp; his hand cupped the round fullness of her breast and gently squeezed as his mouth moved more determinedly against hers, his tongue thrusting inside, arousing a response in her that she had never experienced with any man before. She felt his instant reaction, his length hard against her lower body, and he broke the kiss with a groan of frustration.

There was no 'perhaps' about it, she thought helplessly as, wide-eyed and trembling, she stared up at him. He looked dark and threatening, his eyes narrowing as they scanned the pale oval of her face.

'God, Mama has surpassed herself this time!' he exclaimed almost angrily. 'How old are you, Saffron—nineteen? Twenty?' His fingers deftly readjusted the top of her bathing suit, and his leg slid off her body so that he was lying on his side. Propped on one elbow, he stared down at her with an expression of disgust twisting his harsh features. 'I must be crazy,' he muttered.

Finally finding her voice, Saffron responded in what she hoped was a steady tone. 'Flattered though I am, I happen to be twenty-five, almost twenty-six.' And why he should mention his mother she had no idea...

'Thank God for that. I don't seduce young girls.'

'And you're not seducing me.' Saffron sat up abruptly, shoving at Alex's chest so that he fell on to his back. 'I think it's time we left here; I've had enough sun for one day,' she babbled as it sank into her bemused mind just where his question about her age was leading.

A strong hand curved around her shoulder as she tried to stand up. 'Wait, Saffron. I know we started off on the wrong foot yesterday, though you have to admit that was not solely my fault. But we are two consenting adults; surely we can be sensible about this?'

Saffron turned her head to gaze down at Alex. His deep brown eyes were fixed on her face, the residue of passion still lingering in their depths. 'Sensible?' she queried.

'Yes. I want you, more than I have wanted a woman in years.' He cast a rueful glance down his long body, and Saffron's eyes followed his and then quickly looked away. The man had no shame, she thought furiously; he was quite blatantly aroused. 'It's been a long time since a woman has got me this way so easily, and I think we should explore the possibilities. I know you want me—you tremble every time I touch you. So how about it?'

It was the very matter-of-fact way in which he stated his case that infuriated Saffron. Springing to her feet, she looked down at where Alex lay. He looked like some basking killer shark, about ready to devour its prey. And she was it… Snatching up her towel, she shook it over his supine form, covering him in sand. 'In your dreams, buster!' she scoffed and, grabbing her clothes, she stormed off down the beach, his deep laughter ringing in her ears.

Of course five minutes later she had to walk back, but at least she was fully clothed, she told herself. Just let him try anything else and she would flatten him, she vowed.

'Perhaps I didn't put that in quite the most flattering of terms,' Alex began as he pulled on his shorts and slipped his shirt over his broad shoulders.

'I am not interested in any of your terms, Mr Statis,' Saffron responded stonily. 'Now, can we leave? I did want to see the town of Mykonos—that's what we came ashore for. Not your sleazy suggestions.'

Alex shot her a quizzical glance. ' "The lady doth protest too much, methinks." You wanted sex as much as I did, only you're not prepared to admit it,' he told her casually as he caught her hand. She tried to pull free, but Alex, with one glance and a dry, 'Don't be childish,' quelled her revolt and side by side they walked back to the car.

Saffron was determined not to speak to him again, and on the drive back she kept a stony silence. Eventually, when they arrived in the town, Alex turned to face her and said quietly, 'OK, I apologise. Truce, pax, friends…' and held out his hand. 'I promise, no more teasing.'

Saffron felt the colour scorch her cheeks. What a fool she had been; twice in one day she had melted in his arms, while to him it had been a huge joke. Calmly she put her hand in his and agreed, and she told herself she was not disappointed. Of course Alex could not seriously want a girl like her. His own mother had told her he had women galore.

Soon the charm of the town, and an apparently reformed friendly Alex, swept the earlier episode on the beach to the back of her mind. No one could fail to be delighted with the tiny streets, and the windmills that even Alex didn't know the reason for. Finally, as the sun began to sink lower in the sky, he led her to Little Venice. The buildings were right on the edge of the sea and the upper storeys hung out over the water in marvellous timber balconies. They walked up a tiny winding flight of stairs to a delightful bar which Alex insisted was the best on the island, with a perfect view of the sunset and classical music in the background. Sitting by the window at a tiny table for two, Saffron had never experienced anything so romantic.

'What would you like to drink, Saffron?' Alex asked quietly; it was as if even the great Alex Statis was affected by the atmosphere.

Saffron turned glowing green eyes on his rugged face. 'Anything—you choose. This is just perfect.' She could not contain her delight and, stretching out her hand, she touched his arm fleetingly. 'Thank you for bringing me here.'

'The pleasure is all mine.' Alex smiled back, and for an instant Saffron could only stare; his dark brown eyes gleamed with a rare tender warmth, and the effect on her senses was electric.

The waiter arrived with a whisky and soda for Alex and some fabulous red concoction for Saffron, with an umbrella and a sparkler burning in the glass.

'Cheers,' she toasted Alex as she removed the sparkler and took a sip. 'I said "anything" but I didn't expect to get a flaming potion.'

They laughed together, and then in unspoken accord turned their attention to the view from the balcony, as the sun turned to brilliant scarlet and slowly sank towards the horizon.

The music changed and Saffron recognised it immediately; the opera was a secret passion of hers. 'Rossini—my favourite composer!' she exclaimed. 'The overture to *The Thieving Magpie*, I think.'

'You like his overtures?' Alex's dark eyes lingered over her fine features, taking note of the mass of hair that rivalled the sunset in its colour.

'Yes, I adore them,' she said, slightly uneasy at his unwavering scrutiny. 'I have quite a collection.'

'Yes, I can see why. You're a romantic and as impetuous, pulsing and sometimes as abandoned as Rossini's music. It's all there in your cat's eyes and your magnificent hair—your passionate nature.'

Saffron was about to deny his reading of her character angrily, then realised that what Alex had said about the music was true. Did her love of Rossini disguise an impulsive passionate nature? The thought worried her... She was here on a Greek island with a man she hardly knew... And, lost in her own thoughts, she barely heard his cynically murmured comment.

'Let's hope the title does not accurately reflect you as well.'

She glanced warily across at Alex; his dark eyes caught and held hers. For a long moment the sunset, the surroundings disappeared; they were the only two people in the universe, and something deep and compelling seemed to flow between them.

'You agree with me,' Alex husked softly, and she did not think he was talking only about the music.

She forced herself to look away and, picking up her glass, drained it, making no response. She couldn't...she was terrified. After one day with Alex, a few kisses and now a glance and a simple observation on her choice of music, the man had made her recognise her own sexuality in a way she had never considered before. She had always thought of herself as a passionless sort of girl, if not frigid. Sex and romance played no part in her life. With a sense of shock she realised that the be-all and end-all of her life for years had been her burning ambition to succeed on her own. She had no close friends, except perhaps Eve, who was now dead...

She turned and gazed at the sea; the Statis yacht, aptly named *Lion Lore*, rode at anchor and as she watched the coloured lights from prow to stern flashed on, as the sun sank below the horizon in majestic glory, turning the sea blood-red.

'You must visit the outdoor opera in Verona; it is an experience not to be missed.' His hand covered hers on the table. 'Will you let me take you, Saffron?' he asked in that throaty, sexy voice of his, his thumb teasingly stroking her palm.

In that second she realised she wanted to say yes! But she knew he was asking for a lot more than an evening at the opera and, snatching her hand from his, she jumped to her feet. 'It's time we left. Anna will need me.'

'She's not the only one,' Alex taunted softly as he led her out into the balmy night air. Stopping at the edge of the water, he turned her to face him, linking his hands loosely around her waist.

Saffron tensed. Why did his words sound like a threat, she wondered, when his every look and touch promised her delights she could only guess at, and secretly longed for…?

'Funny. For a girl with a passion for overtures…' he bent and brushed the top of her head with the lightest of kisses '…you are very slow on picking up on them.' His dark eyes smiled teasingly down at her.

Saffron grinned, her tension vanishing. 'God, that was a terrible pun, Alex!'

'It worked—it made you smile.' And, holding hands, they made their way back to the yacht.

CHAPTER THREE

DINNER was again an informal affair; Anna had arranged for a hot and cold buffet to be served, unsure at what time Alex and Saffron would return.

Once more in the company of the older woman, Saffron sighed with relief, and the tension of the afternoon and her complete capitulation to Alex's sexual charm faded to the back of her mind as the three of them partook of a leisurely meal on the rear deck beneath the star-studded canopy of the night sky.

Saffron sipped her wine and cast a speculative glance beneath her thick lashes at Alex. He and his mother were discussing some people they knew and Saffron was quite happy to let the conversation wash over her as she secretly studied him. He wasn't really handsome—his features were too hard-cut and there was a certain ruthless hauteur about him that said, Watcher beware!—and yet he fascinated her as no other man she had ever met had.

Why was that? Why did she find herself wondering what it would be like to lose her virginity to a potent, sensual man like Alex Statis? Under her dress she felt her breasts go suddenly heavy; she trembled and folded her arms defensively across her chest, sitting straighter in the chair and fighting down the colour rising in her throat.

Why did he affect her so intimately? And, more important, why did she think she knew him? she asked herself for the hundredth time. He was way outside her sphere of experience, and yet there was something…! He was dressed as casually as usual in cream trousers and a blue knit polo shirt, his bare feet slipped into a pair of navy loafers, and yet the feeling of leashed power just below the surface was blatantly apparent. She'd bet he was a dynamic business-man, and she wondered just what kind of business he was in. Anna had told her the cruise line was now only a tiny part of Alex's business interests. He kept it going in def-erence to his late father, but he had expanded into a host of other projects.

'Sorry, ladies, but I have work to do.' Saffron was jolted back to awareness by the sound of Alex's voice. Startled, she looked up as he rose to his full height—well over six feet—and for a moment his dark gaze settled on her up-turned face.

'Don't keep Mama up too late, will you, Saffron? We have guests arriving tomorrow.'

'Hmmph!' Anna's inelegant snort prevented Saffron from answering. 'It's time you got yourself a decent wife and presented me with a few grandchildren, instead of fool-ing around.'

'I might surprise you and do just that, Mother.' He held Saffron's gaze even as he responded to Anna. 'What do you think, Saffron? Would I make a good husband?' he asked with mocking amusement.

'I wouldn't know; I don't know you,' she said coolly and, turning her head, she caught the oddest look on Anna's face.

'Then I'll have to make sure you do,' Alex murmured, before moving to drop a brief kiss on the top of Anna's head and adding, 'You promised to behave yourself, Mama, so make sure you do.'

Saffron's puzzled glance slid between the two of them. 'What was that about?' she asked when Alex had gone. 'You always behave yourself.'

'Yes…well…you haven't seen the guests yet,' Anna replied with dry irony, and Saffron could get no more out of the woman, though she did try as she saw her safely to bed.

By seven o'clock the following evening Saffron was beginning to see what Anna had meant. The boat had docked earlier in the day at an exclusive marina on the Athenian riviera some half an hour's drive from the centre of Athens. She hadn't seen Alex since breakfast that morning, when to her astonishment, on leaving the table, he had kissed his mother as usual and then bestowed a brief kiss on her— Saffron's—softly parted lips as well, with the muttered comment, 'As set-ups go, you're the best yet.'

Blushing fiery red, Saffron had glanced at Anna to see her smiling like a Cheshire cat. 'What was that about?' she'd asked suspiciously.

'Forget it, Saffy; Alex is a law unto himself.'

Forgetting had not been so easy, but they had seen nothing more of him until a couple of hours ago, when three long black limousines had drawn up and he'd appeared with his guests.

'Give me your arm, dear, and let's get the greetings over with,' Anna had commanded as the party had trooped up the gangway.

'You don't sound very enthusiastic.' Saffron cast a worried glance at her employer as she took the older woman's arm and walked along to the foredeck and main reception area.

'I'm not,' Anna whispered in an aside before turning to the woman approaching her with a social smile. The woman was obviously Greek, and about the same age as Anna, but still very attractive.

'Katherina, how lovely to see you.' Kisses on both cheeks were exchanged and then Anna turned to a younger woman. 'And Maria—how nice. And who is your friend—

or is it your friend, Alex?' She eyed her son, who brought up the rear of the group with another, older man.

'Allow me to introduce Sylvia, who for the past three years has been the very efficient director of our health and leisure chain.'

Saffron's head jerked round in surprise. So Alex owned a string of health clubs. Now why should that bother her? But it did. There was something niggling at the back of her mind, and if she could just remember... But she did not have the chance as she was swept into a flurry of introductions.

Sylvia, the only English member of the party, was about thirty and stunningly attractive, with black hair, dark eyes, a perfect figure and face, and a smile that would have floored Casanova himself. She dismissed Saffron with a contemptuous glance once she realised she was only a companion. As did Katherina and her daughter Maria. The older man, Spiros, was apparently Katherina's husband.

Saffron shot a worried glance at Anna, who seemed to have gone very quiet among this crowd of confident relatives, and, edging her way to her side, she asked, 'Are you all right?'

Alex caught her whispered question and responded for his mother. 'Of course she is; she is with her family.' But Saffron wasn't so sure. And now, Saffron having just finished massaging Anna with a reviving mixture of aromatherapy oils, the pair of them were relaxing for a few minutes over a very English pot of tea, delivered by the steward a few minutes earlier.

'So what do you think of the family?' Anna asked with a cynicism that Saffron had never seen in the other woman before. 'You can be honest; I won't mind.'

'Well, I...I don't really know them; I mean, first impressions can be…' She was digging herself into a pit, but she was no good at lying. 'They're very Greek…'

Thankfully Anna's light laugh stopped her babbling. 'Exactly. Do you know, dear, sometimes I even forget my son is half English? He has such a Greek outlook on family. He insists every year that the relatives holiday together, and he has no idea of the agony it is for me.'

'What's the matter? Don't you get on with them?' Perhaps it was because she was English, but Saffron dismissed that notion immediately. The Greeks were very friendly on the whole, and had a particular liking for the English. No, something else was bothering Anna.

The older lady replaced her teacup on the small table, and dramatically let her head drop back against the soft cushions of the sofa. Then she looked at Saffron, her blue eyes serious.

'You remember on Rhodes when I showed you the café and I said I would tell you my life story one day? Today is the time, I think.'

'You don't need to.' Saffron was worried by the strange quality in Anna's voice. But, as if she had never heard her, Anna continued.

'I must; like all Greek tragedies it needs telling. My husband was an honourable man and he married me because I was pregnant. I loved him, and was happy. His elder brother was married to Katherina and lived in New York. My son was twelve years old when they first came back to stay with us. I saw my husband look at Katherina and I knew they were more than friends. At a party held in their honour she told me quite openly that my husband had always loved her, that she married his older brother because he was wealthier at the time, but she could get my husband at the snap of her fingers.'

'My God! That's awful.'

'Worse! She was right. I faced my husband with it and he admitted he had known her before his brother but he swore it was over between them years ago. I tried to believe him. His brother and family went back to America, holiday over... Alex went to school in England and for the next six years we carried on as before, except I knew I had never been first choice with my husband.' Anna's blue eyes burnt with a brilliant intensity on Saffron's shocked face.

'He must have loved you—' Saffron began, but was cut off.

'Katherina and her husband returned when Alex was eighteen and she brought her daughter with her—we even holidayed together in England. And then a few weeks later her husband died and she became the grieving widow, and of course stayed with us, as is the Greek way. After a few months of having the woman share my house, I gave my husband an ultimatum. Alex was at university in England by this time and we had bought a house in London. I told my husband I was staying in London, and he had to decide either to get my sister-in-law and her daughter out of our home or get a divorce. I could not live with the situation. I had been in London two months when I got a call from Heathrow airport. He had arrived and wanted to talk. But, as in the best Greek tragedies, he was killed in a car crash on the way from the airport.'

'My God!' Saffron exclaimed, horrified, but she could not help noticing a glint of mischief in Anna's blue eyes.

'What could I do? I couldn't tell my son his father had been going to divorce me and marry his aunt; I didn't want to disillusion him about his father. Consequently my only son cannot understand why I'm not crazy about my Greek relations, and it drove quite a wedge between us.

'Ironically Katherina did set up in a villa in Athens just weeks after the funeral, but I stayed in London and Alex chose to spend most of his time in Greece. He dropped out of university and took over the business. Katherina married again five years ago, and my relationship with Alex has improved quite a lot over the past few years. I visit the villa on the island of Serendipidos every year. Actually it's my island; his father left the property to me. But now you can see why this annual cruise is not my favourite holiday.'

Saffron had never heard anything so appalling. For Anna to entertain year after year the woman she thought her husband had loved. If it was true; Anna was a great one for romancing, Saffron qualified to herself. But still, the stress it must create in the poor woman... 'But why on earth don't you tell your son? Surely it must be better than...?'

'No. Much as I love him he is more Greek than a true Greek—family is everything to him. At eighteen I could not disillusion him, and now it does not bother me that much.'

If the man weren't such an insensitive clod, Saffron thought privately, he would have realised himself years ago how his own mother felt. 'I still think you should have it out with him.'

'No—no way, child. I wouldn't have told you if I'd thought it would upset you.' She sat up straight, her quavering voice suddenly remarkably firm and strong. 'Just be sure you make me as beautiful as is humanly possible this evening. We eat in the dining-room at nine. I'm going to miss our casual buffet meals on the deck.' And, rising, she crossed to the dressing-table and sat down again. 'Come on, dear. Do your best; I want to outshine Katherina.'

And she did. Anna looked as beautiful as Saffron could contrive. With her long hair swept up into an elegant chignon, diamonds glittering at her ears and throat, and a classic designer-label full-length soft blue silk crêpe de Chine dress, cleverly cut to enhance Anna's still youthfully slim figure, she looked like the lovely lady she was.

Saffron had dressed with care in her one formal gown, a second-hand purchase from a small shop she knew in London. The Ralph Lauren design was a simple black sheath with black embroidery around the bodice and hem. It fitted her slender figure like a glove, and a thigh-high split enabled her to walk freely. The neckline slashed diagonally across her breast to leave one arm and shoulder bare. Her long red hair was swept up on top of her head in a mass of curls, a few stray tendrils curling around her face and the nape of her neck. She never wore much make-up but tonight she had gone all out, eyeshadow, mascara, blusher, the lot, and she knew she looked good.

With Saffron firmly supporting Anna, her hand under the older woman's elbow, they entered the dining-room together—late! But on purpose. Anna had not wanted to have to sit and sip pre-dinner drinks with the rest of the clan.

Alex was standing near the top of the table deep in discussion with his aunt and Sylvia and two men Saffron had never seen before. His dark head shot up as they entered, and he smiled across the width of the room.

'So glad you could join us, Mother; we were beginning to wonder.' His dark eyes flashed to Saffron and widened slightly before deliberately raking her from head to foot, a derisory smile curving his firm mouth. Saffron knew he was doing it on purpose and fought down the blush that threatened to overwhelm her.

'Charming, and no doubt time-consuming,' he drawled silkily. 'But if the job of looking after Mother as well as yourself is too much for you, Miss Martin, you only have to say.'

'Not at all, Mr Statis,' she snapped back. Gone was the teasing friendship of the past two days and his use of her surname put her firmly in her place, she thought cynically. A servant! But how dared he be so sarcastic with his own mother? she fumed, and was still fuming as Alex curtly introduced the two new arrivals. She had heard the helicopter earlier but had thought nothing of it.

Alex's PA was a tall blond Englishman in his late twenties called James. The other man, the company accountant, was much older, a Greek named Andreas. It made the party up to nine, and Saffron gave an inward sigh of relief; as the odd one out, she could sink into the background, do her job, and be ignored. But it didn't work out that way.

They took their seats around the large rectangular dining-table. Alex, of course, was at the head, his mother on his right hand and Sylvia on his left; next to Anna was Andreas and then Katherina and her husband while next to Sylvia was Maria and then James and lastly Saffron.

'We seem to be one man short,' Spiros chuckled.

'One good one is worth a dozen others,' Sylvia simpered, with a flirtatious look at Alex as she curved her red-tipped fingers around his arm.

Saffron could not help the contemptuous curve of her full lips as she saw the little scene enacted before her. Now she understood his reversal to her surname. His girlfriend had arrived and he did not want Saffron spilling the beans about his amorous flirtation with her.

She watched as Alex, looking stunning in a white dinner-suit, patted the hand on his arm and said, 'I'll take that as a compliment, Sylvia, darling.' His dark eyes lifted and caught Saffron's derisory glance and for second something flicked in the deep brown depths, but was quickly squashed as his cousin Maria spurted out a torrent of Greek.

Saffron took little interest in the conversation—she could not speak a word of the language anyway—so she was reduced to twiddling the cutlery through her slender fingers to still the nervousness in her stomach. She wished the meal were over with and she could leave. High society held no appeal for her, and there was something about Alex in a tailored white jacket as opposed to his usual casual clothes that she found irrationally threatening. So she was surprised when she looked up from the table and found all eyes on her, as though awaiting her comment.

Anna leapt into the silence. 'Maria was bemoaning the fact that her cabin is on this deck when usually she has your cabin. Alex was explaining that the four state cabins are occupied, Katherina and Spiros in one and Alex in the main cabin and naturally I need you next to me.'

'There is no need to explain, Mama; the matter is settled,' Alex said curtly, and Saffron felt her anger rise again at his abrupt treatment of both his mother and herself, completely ignoring the fact that he had defended her against his cousin.

Luckily the steward served the first course and in the ensuing chatter the matter was dropped. But it wasn't an easy meal. James made no secret of the fact that he found Saffron attractive and when he discovered that she lived in London and liked to wander around the London art galleries in her free time they got into a long discussion about the National Gallery, only to be interrupted by Alex.

'James?' Saffron glanced down the table, her green eyes clashing with Alex's suspicious brooding gaze, which quickly shifted to the man beside her. 'You are not here to seduce my mother's companion, but to work. Kindly remember that.'

Silence! A giggle from Maria broke the tense moment but Saffron felt her face turn scarlet. As for James, he turned astonished eyes on his employer and like a true English gentleman responded, 'My intentions towards Saffron, or any other woman for that matter, are always strictly honourable.' He then spoilt his gallant reply some-what by adding ruefully, 'If one values one's health in the present dangerous sexual climate, they have to be.' The ensuing laughter set the meal back on course and Saffron sighed with relief yet again, sure that the worst was over, but it was not…

The first course, a light pâté, was delicious; the next, lobster, with all the accompanying sauces, was perfection. But for the rest of meal Saffron never looked once at Alex, though she was aware of him in a way she had never ex-perienced before. The deep resonance of his voice, his oc-casional laughter grated on her over-sensitive nerves. She'd never felt such an instant attraction to anyone. So why him? She wasn't sure she even liked the man, and bitterly re-sented his peculiar effect upon her, making it impossible for her to enjoy the sumptuous meal.

His deliberate sexual teasing of the previous day and her shocking reaction to it still rankled. He was so damn sure of himself! It was obvious that he had been making fun of her, filling in time until today, and the arrival of the lovely Sylvia. She noted that it had been Maria, not Sylvia, who had complained about her cabin—probably because Sylvia knew she would be sharing with her boss.

'Isn't that so, Saffron?' Alex's distinctive drawl cut in on her musing. He was back to calling her by her Christian name. Was she supposed to be honoured? she thought sourly. She looked up and saw once again that all eyes were on her.

'Yes, Saffron, do tell us,' Sylvia demanded. 'I can't be-lieve anyone could get the better of Alex.' And she smiled, but Saffron, looking at the beautiful face, saw the spite in the hard eyes.

She had no idea what they were talking about, but help came from an unexpected source: Spiros.

'Did you really mistake him for a thief?' he asked, and she guessed what he was referring to.

Deliberately replacing her fork on her plate, she faced Alex down the length of the table. She could see the amusement sparkling in the depths of his brown eyes, and it enraged her.

'I wouldn't necessarily call it a mistake,' she opined with dry sarcasm, holding his gaze and delighting in the flash of anger in his dark eyes, 'but yes, I caught him by the throat and kneed him in the groin.' She said it with relish, and, pointedly turning her gaze on Sylvia, added, 'I'm sure the ladies in his life will have nothing to worry about—I doubt he suffered any permanent damage.'

Spiros's shout of laughter broke the tension. 'Damn! I wish I could have seen it—the great Alexandros brought to his knees by a slip of a girl.'

Everyone joined in with a comment and Saffron stroked one up for her then quietly withdrew from the conversation—or tried to, but James appeared to have other ideas. She had half expected him to ignore her after Alex's earlier comment, but with brave disregard for his employer he did no such thing, but continued to include her in the conversation at every opportunity, much to Saffron's rising embarrassment. She could feel Alex's dark eyes on her, watching her like a hawk.

Later, sharing a sofa with Anna and sipping coffee on the canopied deck, she was congratulating herself on having got Anna and herself through the evening reasonably well when to her horror Katherina began reminiscing. Saffron was convinced that the woman was doing it deliberately.

'It seems strange that Alex is the only male of the family left. Do you remember, Anna, when our first husbands were alive they were such loving brothers? And, incredible as it seems, it is seven years since I lost my own brother. All relatively young men, and so much sadness, and yet here we are, still a family.'

What a bitch! Saffron thought, casting a worried sidelong glance at Anna, but surprisingly she was smiling. What courage Anna had to put a brave face on something that, true or untrue, was still obviously hurtful.

Without a second thought Saffron got to her feet.

'Excuse me, everyone, but it has been a long day.' She saw Alex's head snap round to where she stood. 'Coming, Anna? It's getting late, and I have to massage your shoulder.'

'What?' Blue-eyed astonishment was quickly masked with a gentle, 'Yes, dear, of course.'

Saffron helped Anna to her feet.

'Shoulder?' Alex queried, his dark eyes spearing Saffron's with speculative scrutiny. 'I understood the arthritis was confined to Mama's knee.'

Saffron could have kicked herself; she had not been thinking clearly or she would not have made such a mistake. 'Yes—yes, it is, but…'

Anna came to her rescue.

'It's not important, Alex, simply a touch of rheumatism in my shoulder, and Saffy has the most soothing hands; I exploit her talent shockingly. If you will all excuse me I am tired.'

'I'll see you to your cabin, Mama.'

Saffron followed behind mother and son, up the stairs to the door of Anna's stateroom, and hesitated as the couple in front were talking.

'Is there something you're not telling me, Mother?' Alex asked quietly, a gentle arm around Anna's shoulder. 'I know how secretive you can be, but you know I love you and I only have your best interests at heart.'

Saffron was surprised by the wealth of caring in Alex's

eyes as he watched his mother. Perhaps Anna should tell him the truth about her accident; this caring Alex might just possibly understand. But with his next words the illusion was shattered.

'Heaven knows as a family we see very little of each other—two or three times a year at most.'

'I know, darling, but you know me; I like London and the others don't.' Anna raised her hand and stroked his rough cheek in a gentle caress. 'Goodnight, son,' she murmured before opening the cabin door and walking inside.

Saffron moved to follow, but was stopped by a large, strong hand grasping her upper arm.

'Just a moment, Saffron.'

Reluctantly she halted. He was so close that she could smell the clean, tangy fragrance of his cologne, and the door shutting behind Anna seemed to leave the pair of them cocooned in the dimly lit passageway. 'What do you want?' she managed to ask levelly.

'You, Saffron,' he murmured sexily, and deep down inside her she felt her body's treacherous response and did nothing to evade his lowering head; she could almost taste his kiss. But instead he said, his deep voice close to her ear, 'But I can wait...' his warm breath touched her cheek '...until I discover exactly what you and Mama are up to.'

She trembled as his breath caressed her skin. She had felt desire before, but never anything like this... Yet she knew Alex was not serious. He was back to his sexual teasing of yesterday, and she had almost succumbed again. Stiffening her spine, she responded flatly, 'I have no idea what you mean. Now if you will excuse me Anna needs me.' And with her free hand she found the door-handle and turned it.

'So do I. Oh, so do I!' Alex husked, and with a swift bite on her earlobe that sent shivers down her spine he slowly relinquished her arm, his long fingers sliding down the slender length to her hand; his thumb stroked over her palm and his husky chuckle was enough for Saffron to snatch her hand away.

'Go tease Sylvia,' she grated between clenched teeth. He was not making a fool of her again. 'She will appreciate it—you're two of a kind.'

'Maybe!' His eyes narrowed on her flushed face. 'But don't make the mistake of thinking you and James are two of a kind. I will not allow it.'

His arrogance was incredible, she thought angrily, but was in no mood to argue. Hadn't she decided to get through this holiday with the least possible aggravation? She needed the money and as long as she remembered that and kept out of Alex's way she would succeed. Pushing open the door, she slipped into Anna's cabin, without a word, and closed the door behind her.

Anna was sitting at the dressing-table mirror, but turned as Saffron entered, a worried frown marring her gentle face. 'Do you think Alex is getting suspicious about my accident?' she asked immediately.

'No, of course not. He has probably just decided to keep a closer eye on you.' After neglecting you for months on end, Saffron added silently, but didn't say it, though she wanted to.

The next few days were a mixture of heaven and hell for Saffron. The yacht sailed majestically on through clear blue waters, the sun continuing to shine with the temperate heat of early summer that was just about perfect. They cruised around the group of islands known as the Cyclades from the island of Kíthnos to Sérifos, Sífnos, Kímolos and Páros.

Saffron did her best to avoid Alex, and Anna helped by insisting that they breakfast in her cabin. Saffron used her fair skin as an excuse not to join the rest of them around the pool for morning coffee. Instead she took to creeping out at seven in the morning and enjoying the pool by herself. But on the third morning that was also ended as the tall, dark figure of Alex appeared, his broad, muscular frame virtually naked except for black swimming-trunks.

Saffron gulped and almost swallowed half the pool when she first clapped eyes on him, but worse was to follow. His bronzed body executed a perfect dive into the water with an elegance that belied his huge frame, then surfaced where Saffron was holding on to the side of the pool. His brown eyes searched her face with an intensity that made her tremble. He lifted his hand to where her usually riotous curls were plastered to her head, and said, 'I know you from somewhere. We have met before, I'm sure of it.'

'That old line…' she snorted, but was stunned to realise that he was only vocalising what she herself had been thinking since the first time she saw him at Rhodes.

'Maybe we were soul mates in another life,' he murmured, his hand stroking over her head and down to her throat, 'and the desire has lingered on.'

'Please…' She gulped as his hard thighs brushed against hers beneath the water; his hand slid lower, curving around her waist, then eased upwards to cup the underside of her breast.

She trembled. 'Stop that!' she gasped. 'Your mother will be here any minute.'

'So?' he mocked. 'I'm a grown man, and anyway I'm sure she'd be delighted if her plan worked.'

'Plan…?' Saffron was lost.

'Don't look so worried. This is not the time.' A steward walked past with a loaded coffee-tray. 'Too many distractions, but I am going to have you, Saffron, so stop trying to avoid me, hmm?'

*   *   *

Saffron locked the cabin door behind her and marched straight to the bathroom, shedding her dress and underwear on the way. She turned on the shower tap and stepped under the soothing spray, silently cursing Alex Statis. Thank God the boat was docking in the port of Piraeus tomorrow morning; she couldn't stand much more.

Since the morning in the pool Alex had gone out of his way to make her life hell. At every opportunity he touched her—an arm around her shoulder, even a kiss on the cheek, and, if he caught her alone, a kiss anywhere else he could reach. She tried to stop him, but her own foolish emotions seemed to leave her paralysed in his presence. He had the uncanny ability to enthral, entice and terrify her all at the same time. The others had noticed, of course, and Sylvia had actually stopped her earlier today by the pool and told her in no uncertain terms just what she thought.

'Really, Saffron, throwing yourself at Alex won't get you anywhere. He's used to your sort, and like all men he's not going to refuse something so blatantly offered. But make no mistake—I am the one he always comes back to.'

Speechless with anger at the utter unfairness of it all—it was Alex chasing her, or more exactly teasing her, not the other way around—Saffron had walked away without answering.

But tonight! She groaned out loud, recalling the scene at dinner. Anna had been sitting next to Saffron at the table and she had quietly repeated the request she had made earlier that day for Saffy to make the job permanent.

Green eyes gentle, Saffron had tried to explain her reluctance. 'I intend to start my own salon, Anna, by the end of the year; it's always been my ambition. But I promise you can be my first customer.'

'But what about my shoulder? I need you every day,' Anna whispered so that the others couldn't hear.

'In another few weeks you will be back to normal.'

'But I like having you...'

'You won't need me...' Saffron hadn't realised her voice had risen, and she shot a startled look down the table, her green eyes caught and held by Alex's devilish brown ones.

'Need you, Saffron, darling? Maybe Mama doesn't, but you know I do,' he prompted mockingly.

Complete silence greeted his comment. Horrified, Saffron glanced around the table and seven pairs of eyes were fixed assessingly on her flushed face. The eighth pair—Alex's—were lit with laughter and something deeper she didn't recognise.

She attempted to laugh off his outrageous statement, but her dry mouth would not let her. Angry at herself and him, she shot back, 'Yes, well, you would say that, Mr Statis.' Her fingers crossed beneath the table, and praying that Anna would forgive her, she added insultingly, 'After all, if I look after your mother it saves you the bother.'

His dark brows drew together, his mouth tightened to a grim line ringed with white in his tanned face and his eyes darkened to jet, his fury at the insult implicit in her comment barely contained. Saffron thought he was about to explode, but help came from an unexpected quarter: Sylvia.

'You did not have to put it so bluntly, Saffron. We all knew what Alex meant, and it is only natural that he wants his mother cared for, and I must say you and Anna do seem to get on remarkably well.'

Normal conversation resumed almost immediately, the social niceties preserved. But Saffron felt the force of Alex's anger beating down on her all through the meal, and she didn't dare look at him.

Stepping out of the shower and briskly rubbing herself dry with a large fluffy towel, she padded barefoot back into the bedroom. She stopped suddenly, her eyes going to the door. The handle was turning, and then was violently rattled.

'Open this door, Saffron; I want to talk to you,' came Alex's unmistakable deep voice.

No way, she thought, a broad grin curving her lovely mouth. She had locked the door and left the key in. Not even the master key would do any good.

Thanking God for her foresight, she crawled naked into bed, a self-satisfied smile on her face. Stroke another one up to her...

Early the next morning, as Saffron quietly opened her cabin door prior to going to Anna's, she halted in her tracks.

Sylvia, dressed in a diaphanous black négligé, her hand curved around the handle of the door opposite, held a finger to her lips and whispered, 'Shh. Alex needs his sleep; it was almost dawn...' Her lips curled in a smile; she looked like the cat that had swallowed the canary. 'Well, you know what I mean, Saffron, dear. But, with his mother on board, propriety dictates that I return to my own cabin...'

CHAPTER FOUR

SAFFRON was stunned. She closed her eyes for a second, fighting to subdue the pain spreading in her chest. She tried to tell herself it was heartburn—perfectly natural; she had not eaten yet. But she knew she was only fooling herself. She hated to admit it, but for the first time in her life she was suffering from the green-eyed monster—jealousy.

Dazed, she made her way to Anna's cabin and walked in, horrified at her blind stupidity. She was jealous of Sylvia and Alex. How had it happened? She had told herself that Alex just liked teasing her, his attentions weren't genuine, and anyway she didn't care a hoot about him even if she did enjoy their verbal sparring. But seeing Sylvia leave his room had shocked her to the core, and she was forced to admit that somewhere deep down inside she had nursed a secret hope, ever since Mykonos, that perhaps Alex did care for her.

'Good, dear, you're early. I wanted to talk to you before we have to join the others.'

Saffron raised dazed green eyes to where Anna sat propped up in bed, a tray with a coffee-jug and cups at her side. 'Talk'; she had heard that much.

'Yes, come and sit down and have a coffee.' Like a robot Saffron did as she said, taking the proffered cup and sipping the hot brew thirstily. 'About last night, Saffron. I think I might have misled you slightly in the past weeks. Actually my son and I have a very good relationship, and I do see him a lot more than I led you to believe. But the accident made me feel down. Alex was in Australia, and I was wallowing in self-pity.'

Saffron's head shot up and she saw the guilty smile on Anna's face. 'Misled me?'

'Yes, well, ordinarily Alex is in London every month; he has his own place but he calls to see me or telephones me almost daily. Plus in the autumn we holiday together at the villa on Serendipidos. He really is a very caring son and would not shunt me off with just anyone.'

Saffron wasn't even surprised! Now she knew why Anna had not been shocked when Alex had appeared at the café in Rhodes. But, frightened by her own reaction to him, she wanted to believe the worst of him.

'I know, Anna, and the comment I made last night was more in self-defence. Your son seems to delight in teasing me, I realise now.' Especially after seeing Sylvia this morning, she thought sadly. 'He doesn't mean anything by it.'

'Oh, I'm so glad you understand, because Alex is really quite soft-hearted beneath that hard exterior of his, and I don't want you to think badly of him, especially as he seems to like you.'

Like her? What a joke! He liked anything in a skirt, Saffron thought, and it gave her no joy.

'Plus I want you to come with me to Serendipidos in the autumn. It's a beautiful place; you will really enjoy it. You convinced me last night that you don't want a permanent job, but it will only mean extending your contract by a week or two.'

Saffron's face fell. Weeks in the vicinity of Alex was not something she could look forward to with equanimity. Her body reacted in the strangest way whenever he was near, and yet there was something about him that subconsciously repelled her. She didn't understand it at all.

Anna, as if sensing her disquiet, added, 'Well, it is a

long way ahead, but think about it. Sun and sea—a lot better than autumn in England.'

Saffron held up her hand. 'OK, Anna, you've convinced me.' The shock of this morning had cured her growing fascination with Alex once and for all, and by the time she had spent the summer in London with Anna she would have got over her peculiar attraction to the man, she told herself sensibly.

Breakfast was a buffet on the poop deck, a kind of casual chaos. In the middle of it a car arrived to take James and Andreas into Athens, and hasty goodbyes were exchanged. Alex coolly instructed Saffron to have everything ready for Anna and herself to depart by helicopter for the airport, where a private jet was waiting to take them directly to London. He intended to accompany the rest of the party into Athens; his head office was there, and he needed to work.

Following the steward carrying their bags to the helipad on the top of the yacht, Saffron was feeling slightly piqued. The least Alex could have done was to be around to say goodbye to his mother, she thought, not for a second admitting that she was peeved because he hadn't seen fit to say goodbye to her either.

The blades were already in motion on the big black insect-like machine as she and Anna waited while the steward loaded the luggage.

'Mama, I almost missed you. Have a good flight and I'll be in touch soon.'

Saffron turned her head at the sound of Alex's voice. He had stopped on the opposite side of Anna, his dark head bent to kiss the older woman on the cheek. Saffron's eyes widened in amazement as he straightened up and looked directly at her. Gone was the casually dressed man of the past week and in his place was a sombrely dressed businessman. He was wearing an expensively tailored navy three-piece suit, the jacket fitting snugly across his broad shoulders, the trousers elegantly tracing his long legs, a white silk shirt in stark contrast to his tanned complexion and a conservative navy and grey striped tie at his throat. A black leather briefcase in one hand completed the picture of a ruthless tycoon. Her whole body clenched in shock.

'You can leave now,' Alex drawled, but she did not hear him say that the pilot was waiting or that he would see her in London, and, like a thunderbolt, it hit her.

She did know him! Had done for seven years... She must have said something that passed as goodbye, she thought distractedly as she urged Anna towards the waiting helicopter. She did not see Alex's frowning glance or the intense scrutiny in his dark eyes as she climbed aboard. She could not get away fast enough...

She was intensely grateful for the noise in the helicopter that prevented her having to talk to Anna. She needed the time to collect her own thoughts...

Seven years ago, the first day at her first job after finishing college that also turned out to be her last day at the supposedly exclusive health club. The man standing in Reception saying, 'You can leave now,' and her own furious anger and embarrassment as for one long moment she had stared at the owner of the place. A tall, dark man in a navy suit, briefcase in hand, and contemptuous black eyes that burned into her skull. She had not said a word but had run out never to return. A bitter, cynical smile curved her soft lips; Alex Statis was that man. She would stake her life on it.

A tug on her arm by Anna, and she realised that the helicopter was circling to land at the far side of the airport. But Saffron was in no position to take in her surroundings; as if in a dream she helped Anna from the helicopter and followed the pilot across to a waiting jet some hundred yards away. Still in a state of shock she sank down into the seat beside Anna and barely spoke as the jet took off.

Luckily for Saffron, Anna slept almost the whole journey, only rousing to eat a perfectly prepared meal and then dozing off again. By the time Saffron sank down on the familiar white-lace-draped four-poster bed in Anna's London home late that night, alone at last, she felt sick to her soul.

How she had managed to hide her distraught state from Anna for the past few hours was a miracle, she thought with a grim smile. In fact she was not sure that she had, because over dinner Anna had asked her if anything was wrong. She had quickly reassured her that she was fine, just a bit jet-lagged, but had felt an absolute fraud when Anna had insisted that she go to bed and forget about her massage for tonight.

Private yacht, private airplane, this lovely house, dotted with antiques, a whole island for heaven's sake! She ground her teeth in sheer rage. Some would say she was lucky to be living in such an environment. Except that Saffron knew where some of the money had come from, and a few questions to Anna had convinced her that the older woman didn't.

Over dinner Saffron had deliberately turned the conversation to Alex's business, and finally asked the question that had plagued her all day.

'Does he own health clubs in London? I seem to remember hearing of one in Wimbledon,' she'd said, and had mentioned the name.

Anna's response had confirmed what Saffron already knew. 'I vaguely remember hearing the name somewhere but I really have no idea, Saffy. When Alex took over the family shipping business it was in a sorry state; he had to work like a slave to make it profitable. He has expanded into all sorts of things over the years. I can't keep up with him; I'm hopeless at business—much prefer the arts. But Alex is quite famous in his own way. The gossip columns seem to enjoy reporting his numerous affairs, unfortunately.'

Now, sitting on the bed, Saffron let her head drop into her hands. She thought about Eve, her one true friend who had died so pitifully young; it was Alex Statis and men like him who had driven her to it. She rubbed the moisture from her eyes and, stripping off her clothes, took a quick shower in the adjoining *en suite* and then crawled into bed, her mind in turmoil.

Who said crime doesn't pay? she thought scathingly. It had certainly paid for Alex. Anna had told her earlier, when waffling on about their coming trip in the autumn, that only a few years ago Alex had completely demolished the villa on Serendipidos and replaced it with a much grander one... On the proceeds of his ill-gotten gains, Saffron thought, hatred and loathing for the man swamping her tired mind. She closed her eyes and prayed for sleep but it would not come. Instead she was eighteen again...

Saffron glanced once more at her gold wristwatch—eight-thirty—then back again to the entrance door of the small pub in Covent Garden. Eve was already half an hour late; she resolved to give her five more minutes then leave. It was sad but true; the two girls were drifting apart. It had to happen, she thought sadly. Eve had left the orphanage long before she had, and gone to live in an apartment with another girl, somewhere in the East End. Whereas Saffron, on leaving the orphanage, had taken up residence at the YWCA.

She had finished college in June a qualified beauty therapist and aromatherapist, and for the past two months had been looking for a job in a health club, salon, anything, but so far without much luck. When her parents had died so tragically young, the house had been sold, but after the debts and expenses had been paid there had not been much left to be put in trust for Saffron. On her eighteenth birthday she had inherited almost two thousand pounds and her mother's gold watch. But her nest-egg was quickly diminishing while she looked for work. Her only social life was a once-a-month meeting with Eve.

'Saffron, darling, sorry I'm late but we couldn't find a parking place.'

Saffron lifted her head and smiled. Eve was a tall, well-endowed blonde, and tonight she looked flushed and happy.

'Sorry I can't stop but Rick, my new boyfriend, is parked on double yellow lines. He's gorgeous, Saffron, and, better yet, rich. I only called in to give you this card. It's the address of an exclusive health club in Wimbledon, Studio 96—Rick has a share in it. Go tomorrow at eleven, mention Rick's name and the job of masseur is yours.' Eve blew a kiss, called, 'Ciao!' and left.

If only it had been that simple, Saffron thought as she tossed restlessly on the bed. With hindsight she realised she had been terribly naïve, but at the time it had seemed like a gift from the gods.

She had attended the interview the next day with a rather hard-faced women who was the manageress. As soon as she had mentioned Rick and produced the card she had been given the job, and told to start the next day at twelve. Saffron had had no qualms; the building was in an excellent area and was elegantly furnished, and a conducted tour had shown her a gym and spa, sauna, and the various individual cubicles for massage. The manageress had even warned her that any employer found offering sexual intercourse to the

patrons would be immediately dismissed. It was a club favoured by leading members of society, from aristocrats to
Members of Parliament, and they came expecting to relieve
their tension and relax—nothing more!

The following day she was shown to a cubicle and told
that her first client would be arriving at twelve-fifteen for
a full massage. Slipping on her overall and with her personal belongings stowed in a small locker, she greeted her
first client, a rather overweight middle-aged gentleman.

Slightly nervous, she instructed the gentleman to remove
his robe, wrap a towel around his waist and lie face down
on the bed while she went to collect the required oils. On
her return the man was lying down, and she began the
massage as she had been taught by her tutor. In most reputable establishments when massaging a man one only did
the back, the arms and shoulders, and the feet and legs as
far as the knee. Anything more and male masseurs were
usually employed.

Fifteen minutes later all hell broke loose, when the man
turned over and said brutally, 'Hurry up, girl. You know
the muscle I want relaxing and it sure as hell isn't my
back.'

To Saffron's absolute horror he grabbed her small hand
and forced it towards a very personal part of him. She did
the only thing she could think of: picking up the dish con-
taining the remainder of the oil, her eyes closed, she hit
him with it.

He gave a howl of outrage. 'What the hell do you think
you're playing at? I paid good money and I'm not being
fobbed off with a bloody back-rub.'

Saffron flung the robe over him, grabbed her coat and
bag from the locker and shot straight out of the cubicle,
heading for the exit, her face flaming.

'What on earth…?' the manageress exclaimed. She was

standing at the desk, a tall, dark-suited businessman standing beside her, a briefcase in his hand. 'Where do you think you're going, girl? You have a client.'

'I thought this was supposed to be the *crème de la crème*.' The fat man, a robe pulled over his nakedness, had followed her. 'Your prices certainly are.' He was all bluster and Saffron could only stare at him, numb with horror and disgust. Then the tall businessman turned around and she saw his face. It was Alex Statis...

'Maybe I can help you, sir.'

'You the owner? Well, for the money I paid, I expect expert service, not some bloody little amateur who hasn't a clue.'

'Why, you...!' Saffron's short, platinum-blonde hair, like a silver cap on her small head, did not prevent her true red-headed temper from flaring out of control even though she was terrified. 'You fat blubber of lard, you're a disgrace...'

She got no further as the tall stranger caught her arm and ushered her towards the door.

'You can leave now.'

She never heard what else he said. Her terrified green eyes clashed with contemptuous black for a long moment, before she took to her heels and ran.

Three days later Eve appeared at the YWCA to ask how the job was going. Saffron told her the place was no health club, but a very up-market massage parlour only one step removed from a brothel as far as she could see. A grey area in law maybe, but very lucrative for the owners. They finally ended up roaring with laughter about it, Eve declaring that her years in the orphanage and then working for a living in a supermarket must have blunted her instincts, and they both knew what she meant.

Eve had been taken into care because her parents were drug addicts, and had killed themselves with an overdose.

The social services had moved in and put Eve in the orphanage. Saffron could only imagine the horrid childhood of her friend, but her loyalty to Eve was one hundred per cent, had been ever since the day she had saved her from the boy groping her.

Saffron stirred uncomfortably on the wide bed as the black bile of sheer hatred rose in her throat, threatening to choke her. She hauled herself up into a sitting position, her small hands clenched in fists, as she fought down her rage. If the incident had ended that day at the YWCA, Saffron might have been able to forget the part Alex Statis had played. But it had not... To think that she had allowed Alex to kiss her, touch her; it made her flesh creep. Alex Statis deserved to pay for the lives he had helped destroy as part-owner of that sordid club.

She remembered Eve as a teenager, large and laughing, loyal and protective of her friend. Over the next year Saffron had worked in a small beauty clinic and had seen less of Eve as the other girl's relationship with Rick continued. Then Saffron had got a live-in job at a health spa in Scotland and had left London. They'd kept in touch by letter until the day Saffron's latest letter was returned address unknown.

Saffron had stayed three years in the Highlands before returning to London and starting work at the home beauty agency. She'd shared a flat with two others, and spent her spare time improving her craft. Doing voluntary work in a local hospital, she'd developed a special interest in clinical beauty therapy. She'd loved showing women, who for various reasons, from birthmarks to those who needed to use a prosthesis as result of face cancer, how to use make-up to cover their disabilities.

Then ten months ago a policeman had arrived at Saffron's door with the information that Eve was dead. She had left a letter for Saffron, and the police had traced her through her income tax returns. In the letter Eve had explained how she had, at Rick's insistence, ended up working in the massage parlour Saffron had run out of, fulfilling the demeaning task of massaging fully the male clients, who then went smugly home to their wives in the belief that they had not technically been unfaithful... Eve had hated the job and had started to drink and take drugs to get her through the day. Rick had dumped her, and she'd felt she had nothing left to live for.

But the final paragraph had been an exhortation to Saffron to succeed.

You have it all, Saffron—the looks, the character and the expertise to make it on your own. Not like me. I was born a loser. Promise me, Saffron, you won't let some bastard of a man get at you. Stick to your dream. Start your own business, be your own boss. Do it for me. You show them.

Saffron had been devastated. She had attended the inquest the following day, and the only slight relief had been that the coroner had returned an open verdict, not prepared to say that Eve had deliberately overdosed on drugs and alcohol. Saffron had arranged the funeral and she had been the only one at the ceremony.

She groaned out loud and slid down into the bed. Here she was, living in the house, eating the food, taking the pay of the diabolical fiend who owned the club... What was she going to do? She could not blame Anna; it had nothing to do with her; of that Saffron was sure. But she hoped and prayed that she would never have to set eyes on Alex Statis again as long as she lived.

Anna would be hurt, but Saffron had no choice. Much

as she liked Anna she would have to leave, and with that thought worrying her mind she tossed restlessly all night and when, finally, dawn broke the sky, she still had not found the comforting oblivion of sleep. But not for a second dared she admit that the thought of never seeing Alex again hurt even more than the knowledge of the despicable lengths he would go to make money.

A few hours later, heavy-eyed, she completed Anna's massage, and mentioned leaving. 'I know my contract is for six months, Anna, and I've only completed a little over one, but I…'

'What is it really, Saffy? Something is bothering you; You've been quiet ever since we left the boat. Is it me? Am I too much trouble for you?'

Saffron felt an absolute heel. How did one tell a woman that her son was the lowest of the low, and you couldn't bear the thought of ever having to see him again?

'I could increase your salary.'

'No, no, you're more than generous. It was just I— Oh, nothing! Anna, forget I mentioned it.' She couldn't hurt her, and if that meant having to stay here and run the risk of seeing Alex again then so be it. She would just have to bite the bullet and disguise her hatred of the man.

The only trouble was, she thought grimly a few hours later, she had not expected to have to do it so soon! Anna had been lying down in her room, resting, and Saffron had taken the opportunity to do some hand-washing at the sink in the utility-room, when the telephone had rung. She'd known that Mrs Chambers had gone shopping, so, quickly drying her hands, she'd nipped into the kitchen and picked up the wall-mounted telephone.

'Mrs Statis's residence,' she intoned breathlessly.

'Saffron. I was hoping you would answer.' Even over

the telephone there was no mistaking Alex's deep drawl. 'Are you missing me, green eyes?'

Her first thought was to slam down the receiver but she stopped herself just in time. Fighting down the rage that just the sound of his voice invoked, she replied coldly, 'I'm afraid your mother is sleeping at the moment, Mr Statis; perhaps you could call back later.'

'I did not ask for Mama, I asked if you missed me,' Alex corrected her in a teasing tone. 'Why the frozen air, Saffron, sweet? Sulking because I'm not there with you?'

'No. Thanking God you're miles away! Goodbye.' And she slammed down the receiver, her hand trembling with the force of her anger. The man's conceit was only surpassed by his enormous ego. Bitter hatred consumed her. If there was any way on God's earth she could make him pay for what he had done, she would. The telephone rang again. She was torn between letting it ring and possibly waking Anna, or answering it and hearing the hateful voice again.

Duty won. 'Yes?' she snapped.

'No one puts the telephone down on me. Do I make myself clear Saffron?' His former easy amusement had vanished; he was now back to being a hard-voiced autocrat.

'Mr Statis, I have told you, your mother is sleeping. I have no wish to speak to you, not now, not ever. Do I make myself clear?' she drawled with icy cynicism.

'Something has happened; you sound different.'

She was different; she was no longer the naïve innocent, helplessly surrendering to his practised seductive charm. Just the sound of his voice, which she had once thought deep and rich, now filled her with loathing.

'Saffron! Are you still there?'

'Yes, sir.'

'Cut out the sarcasm and tell me what has happened. Did you discover Mama is a fake? Is that it?'

'I see no point in this conversation, and unless you have a message for your mother I really must go.' The only fake Saffron had discovered was Alex Statis and the rage was like a festering sore inside her.

'Yes, OK, I'll be in touch.'

Not if I can help it, she thought grimly, replacing the receiver.

Saffron strategically placed the lounger in the back garden of the house to catch the sun's rays and settled down to soak up the sun. She had driven Anna to her Friday afternoon bridge game and the next few hours were her own. Who needs foreign holidays, she mused, when late June in England is just about perfect? Warm days and long light nights.

By a bit of judicious questioning she had established from Anna that Alex was not expected any time in the near future, and she remembered her telling her that when he did come to London he had his own apartment, so her fear of seeing the man had abated over the past two weeks. She knew he telephoned every day but she had found it relatively easy to vanish when he called.

Anna had improved in leaps and bounds and her shoulder was completely better. In fact Saffron felt that she was taking her salary on false pretences but Anna would not hear of her leaving. Plus there was the small problem of having nowhere to stay. She didn't want to waste any of her savings on an apartment when very shortly she would have her own property.

To Saffron's surprise, she had discovered that Anna was a much livelier lady than she had first thought. Together they had attended various art exhibitions, the theatre, an outdoor opera. The woman was a committed culture buff. At last night's poetry reading in Anna's elegant sitting-room Saffron had hardly been able to contain her amusement as the latest 'darling boy' waffled on about 'Chopsticks', the symbolism escaping Saffron completely.

A smile on her lips at the memory, she closed her eyes and gently dozed.

'Perfect Sleeping Beauty waiting for her prince.'

Saffron's eyes snapped open and she was horrified to find Alex Statis standing staring down at her. She hauled herself up to a sitting position, stiff with outrage at his unheralded arrival. 'And instead she gets the toad,' she drawled, her head high, her eyes blazing hatred.

One dark brow arched enquiringly at the biting sarcasm in her tone. 'I had hoped for a more enthusiastic welcome after deserting my office simply to come and look after you and Mama.'

'You shouldn't have bothered. Your mother and I can manage perfectly well on our own.' She glanced up; over his tall frame he was still wearing a business suit, and the last lingering doubt vanished from her mind. It was the same man.

'I'm sure you can, Saffron,' he agreed as he shrugged off his jacket and dropped it on the ground. With one hand he deftly loosened the tie at his throat and flicked open the top three buttons of his shirt, his dark eyes openly laughing at her. 'But who am I to spoil my mama's enjoyment? She has refused to allow me to speak to you on the telephone, so I have, as a dutiful son, decided to play her game and spend the next few weeks here.'

So that was why it had been so easy to avoid his calls. Anna had made sure of it, and Saffron could not help wondering why even as she responded icily, 'Your mother and

I can enjoy ourselves without you.' If he was staying she was leaving!

She watched as he lowered his long frame on to the soft green grass beside her chair, long legs stretched out before him in lazy ease, his hands clasped behind his head, his face lifted to the sun.

'Hardly the welcome I was hoping for. Alone at last!' he drawled mockingly. 'Isn't this where you tell me you missed me?'

'Missed you!' she exclaimed parrot fashion. 'Like a hole in the head.' The man must be mad.

'I can see my dear mama has not revealed her little game yet.' His eyes were closed, thick dark lashes curving on his bronzed skin; he looked vulnerable but Saffron knew better.

'What game?' she demanded coldly.

'You, my dear Saffron, are one in a long line of supposedly *good* women my mother parades before me every summer under the guise of a companion, whatever, in a vain attempt to get me married off.' He looked up at her, a cynical smile slashing his hard face. 'You should be flattered; you have done better than most; usually I have them out of my life in days.'

Saffron slid her hands under her thighs, fighting down the urge to claw his eyes out. The conceited jerk! He moved to lie on his side, one elbow on the ground, his hand propping his head, so that he could watch her easily, his long body at ease. Even as she hated him she recognised that he was devilishly attractive, all virile male, but superimposed on his face she saw the image of Eve's coffin. She blinked, blotting out the picture.

'My dear mama could put Machiavelli to shame; surely you have realised that by now, Saffron?' he opined lightly, shooting her a questioning glance.

Despite herself Saffron was intrigued as Alex continued.

'Mind you, I have to admit she has surpassed herself this time. I got the report on you yesterday in Athens, and you check out perfectly. There's no doubt that Mama's cover stories are certainly improving,' he drawled with fond amusement.

Saffron was so furious that she did not trust herself to speak. He actually thought her job with Anna was simply a ploy to spike his interest. He had the nerve to have her investigated, when he operated on the very edge of the law himself. What an ego the swine had...

'Last year Mother hired a Greek teacher who couldn't speak more than three sentences, the year before a librarian to catalogue her books, all fifty of them,' he reminisced, a wide smile softening his harsh features, his deep brown eyes laughing up at her, inviting her to share the joke. 'You are her latest marriage bait, and if I were the marrying kind I might just be tempted,' he suggested with a cynical sensuality that made her shudder.

Saffron turned her head away and looked around the garden, anywhere but at the man lying at her feet. She remembered how she had almost succumbed to Alex's easy charm, his kiss, his caress. God! What might have happened if she had not finally recognised him? The very idea made her sick to the stomach. She drew in a painful breath and got to her feet, giving Alex's sprawled body a contemptuous glance. 'You flatter yourself, Mr Statis. I would not marry you if you were the last man on earth,' she said thickly. 'Excuse me.'

In one lithe movement Alex was at her side, his hand on her naked shoulder.

'Don't touch me!' she cried, knocking his hand away.

Alex's nostrils flared as he sucked in an angry breath. 'I wasn't aware my touch was so abhorrent to you.'

'Well, you are now.'

His eyes narrowed assessingly on her pale face. 'There is something different about you.'

Yes, you evil swine; I know how you make money. She didn't say it but the contempt in her icy green eyes said it for her. 'If Anna confirms what you have just told me I'm leaving. I refuse to provide entertainment for your sort.'

'My sort?' A hint of steel entered his voice. 'Why do I get the impression you have just insulted me?'

'Probably because I did.' She was in no mood to bandy words with a man little better than a pimp. 'Get out of my way; I'm leaving.' Alex was standing barely a foot away, blocking her path back to the house.

'No. You can't leave. I will not have Mama upset. She likes you, and you signed a six-month contract, and I intend to make sure you fulfil it, or I will sue you for every penny you have, or ever will have.'

Saffron's head tilted back; her green eyes, flashing fire, clashed with the black implacability of Alex's, and she knew he meant every word. All trace of amusement gone, he was once more the harsh-faced stranger of her memory. 'Yes, I just bet you would,' she sneered, not bothering to hide her contempt.

His look was every bit as contemptuous as hers. 'You disappoint me, Saffron; challenging a man to gain his interest is the oldest trick in the book. I almost believed you were innocent of any involvement in Mama's plan. I thought you were above such games.' He lifted his hand and caught hold of her chin. Her hands balled into fists at her sides, but she refused to struggle, even though her heart began to pound as he gave her a searching look. 'But if that's the way you want to play it I'll oblige.'

'I have no desire to play, and certainly not with you,' she said flatly.

'But I do, Saffron; you intrigue me.' His voice dropped

to a husky growl 'Along with a host of other feelings I fully intend to explore.'

Before she had a chance to do more than register that he was about to kiss her, his head lowered and his lips claimed hers. Saffron instantly froze. Shocked by the harsh possession of his mouth, she shuddered as his arms enfolded her, and his hand slid to her buttocks, pressing her into his hard thighs. Stunned by the speed of his assault, she almost responded to the fevered urgency of his caress. His hand stroked down her naked thigh, binding her tightly to the hard heat of his body.

It was his guttural, 'I want you,' and the realisation of his aroused state that stopped her. How many women had he said the exact same words to? How many had succumbed to his persuasive charm? As Eve had with Rick, his partner, only to end up working in a massage parlour. The sickening knowledge of how he had made his money turned the blood to ice in her veins.

Sensing her lack of response, Alex lifted his head; his dark eyes, black with frustrated desire, searched her pale face. He sucked in a deep, steadying breath and gently put her away from him. His gaze lingered over her scantily clad form and then he glanced down at his suit.

'You're right, I'm hardly dressed for the part and anyone might interrupt us. When I make love to you for the first time, I want you on your own with no fear of interruptions.' He turned, adding, 'I'll see you later,' with a certainty that incensed Saffron into losing her temper completely.

'Not if I see you first,' she screeched after him, derision twisting her delicate features. A cheeky wave of his hand indicated that he had heard her, and was not the least fazed by her angry outburst.

CHAPTER FIVE

SAFFRON watched his departure, his lithe walk, the proud set of his head and shoulders. Her eyes drifted briefly around the garden, and she thought of his wealth and eminent respectability, then her glance rested once more on his broad back as he entered the house, and she longed to put a knife in it...

No. He wasn't worth going to prison for. But with the hot sun incapable of warming the ice in her veins Saffron silently vowed that if there was any way to make Alex Statis's life hell she would do it. She owed it to Eve. It was the Alexes of this world who, in the avid pursuit of money, flirted with the law and exploited and demeaned women.

Saffron's eyes glittered, her small hands clenched into fists. She would have her revenge on Mr Statis supposing it took her a lifetime to find a way...

But she found a way a lot quicker than she could have hoped...

'I owe you an apology, Saffron.' Alex's dark eyes gleamed golden in the flickering light of the candle in the centre of the table. They were dining in a small, intimate French restaurant, at Alex's insistence.

Earlier, Saffron had picked Anna up from her bridge party and Alex had been waiting when they returned. Saffron had tactfully withdrawn to her room and left mother and son alone. It had been a mistake! On returning to the living-room an hour later Alex was still in evidence, and in a few moments had hustled Saffron into having dinner with him. Anna had been no support at all as Saffron had tried to turn down the invitation. She was forced to the conclusion that Alex was probably right about his mother's machiavellian tendencies.

'An apology—from you?'

'Surprising, I know, but I had a word with Mama this evening. She told me all about her accident; it was silly of her to keep it from me in the first place. I have no intention of having her live with me; it would be much too confining. I have set her mind at rest on that score and she assures me you are innocent of any plan to trap me.'

Bully for him, the condescending swine; was she supposed to be flattered that he was absolving her from any conspiracy? she thought, eyeing him almost clinically. He was wearing a conventional black dinner-suit, white silk shirt and dark bow-tie. He wore his clothes with an elegance that few men possessed, and she knew that beneath the outer garments his body was a perfect example of the masculine form; he could put Michelangelo's David to shame. A few weeks ago she would have been intimidated by such raw masculine perfection, but not now. The inside was rotten to the core.

She glanced at his face. He was smiling complacently.

'So how about we start again from scratch—' his hand reached out and covered hers where it lay on the table '—and develop this chemistry, or whatever it is between us, to its logical conclusion?'

'Why not?' she murmured, the germ of an idea so preposterous that she wondered at her own daring taking root in her head, and, deliberately squeezing his hand, she added a husky, 'Yes.'

His brown eyes flashed with pure masculine triumph. 'Good; let's skip dessert and go to my apartment.' Alex spoke throatily, virtually dragging her to her feet. He flung a bundle of notes on the table and without letting go of her hand steered her out of the restaurant and into his waiting black Jaguar.

Saffron was seething at his arrogant, high-handed treatment, but she forced herself not to let it show. Alex started the car with a crash of gears. He was inpatient, and desire or lust—it did not matter which—made his usual steady hand shake, she noted cynically. Battling down her hatred for the man, she gritted her teeth and deliberately moved closer to rest her head on his broad shoulder, allowing her hand to fall teasingly on to his hard thigh.

Alex hardly spoke as he urged her out of the car in the underground car park, and into the lift. As the doors slid closed he hauled her into his arms. She closed her eyes and fought down her disgust at being held fast against the hard muscles of his body. Her lips parted at the thrusting force of his tongue invading her mouth, and she forced herself not to shove him away as she longed to do, her stomach curling in revulsion. But was it? she wondered, her legs weakening as his hands travelled the length of her body with a hard sureness that made her tremble.

Luckily the lift stopped and the doors slid open. 'Alex,' she said softly, pushing against the hard wall of his chest. 'We've arrived.'

'Thank God!' he groaned, lifting his head and looking down at her with black, passion-filled eyes.

There was only one door in the wide corridor, and Alex slipped the key into the lock with a hand that shook slightly. Then, turning, with a hand in the small of her back, he ushered her inside the apartment.

Saffron looked around with interest, and was surprised to note that the place had a homely air, not at all what she had expected. Pictures of his relatives and friends vied with what were obviously paintings by the masters. What looked like a Monet had pride of place over a large pine-framed fireplace. Big deep buttoned hide chairs and a couple of sofas were strategically placed to get the benefit of the fire and view. The curtains were open and the whole of London seemed to be reflected in the plate-glass windows.

'I can't believe you're here, Saffron.' Alex's deep voice interrupted her musing, and once more she was caught in his arms. 'You have no idea how much I want you. From the moment you felled me in Rhodes, I've ached to get you in my bed.' His lips showered tiny kisses on her eyes her cheek, the tip of her nose, all over her face, and Saffron was shocked by the gentleness in his gaze.

'I told myself it was because I wanted to punish you.' His lips moved caressingly down the slender arch of her throat as she tipped her head back, trying to escape his marauding mouth. But it didn't work; her pulse-rate soared and she was in danger of forgetting why she was here.

'Punish me?' she murmured. It was Alex who needed punishing and she had to remember that.

'I know; stupid macho pride. But after Mykonos I realised I wanted you any way I could have you. I didn't even care if you were part of Mama's scheme. Seeing you in this dress again tonight reminded me.' She was wearing her Ralph Lauren, the only formal dress she possessed, and he put his hand on her covered shoulder. 'That night on the *Lion Lore* I nearly lost it when you walked into the dining-room, you looked so beautiful, but I couldn't do anything about it with all the guests around.'

He was good—very good! Saffron recognised. The sensual spell he was weaving with tender words and caresses was almost believable. But then he'd had plenty of practice, she thought grimly, the mood broken by his glib lie. Guests had not stopped him sharing his bed with Sylvia. She leant sharply back from him, but he did not release her.

'I tried to stay away but the last two weeks without seeing you were hell. I found myself missing your red hair and flashing eyes. I thought of you at the most inopportune times, until today I realised I had to do something about it.'

His mouth nuzzled her neck and his hands found the zip at side of her dress. She was perilously close to forgetting why she was here, and, gathering every ounce of self-control she possessed, she pushed him harder.

'Wait, Alex.' She deliberately lowered her voice, a slight tremor to her tone that wasn't all play-acting, unfortunately. 'You said to follow this chemistry to its logical conclusion. But marriage is a big step—are you sure you're ready for it? You have been a bachelor an awfully long time.'

'Marriage? Who the bloody hell mentioned marriage?' He let go of her and stepped back as if he had been stung, and she had to bite her lip to force back the laughter that bubbled up inside her at the expression of shock and horror on his rugged face.

'I'm sorry if I misunderstood,' she said softly, acting for all she was worth. 'But I'm afraid that's the only way you'll ever get me.'

Alex's dark eyes narrowed dangerously. 'If I thought you really meant that I could prove you wrong in five minutes,' he declared hardly. He reached out and ran one long finger delicately from her jaw to her throat over her one naked shoulder and on to the tip of her breast, lightly covered by the soft fabric of her dress. She forced herself to show no response, but her breast hardened to a taut peak beneath his cool manipulation. His dark look turned to one of indolent satisfaction at her body's reaction. 'Make that two minutes,' he amended mockingly.

'God, what an ego!' she jeered, and, deliberately turning her back on him, she headed for the door.

Alex moved swiftly; hard hands caught hold of her arms and spun her around to face him. 'Nobody turns their back on me, lady.'

'Let me go.'

His dark eyes became cold and assessing on her flushed face. 'Why fight it? You want me. Surely you're not going to pretend you're shy?' he said cynically. 'Massage is a pretty personal profession. Hundreds of men must have felt the gentle caress of your hands, Saffron, and ached for more. Did you demand marriage from all of them before granting their wish? I think not...'

One dark brow arched sardonically. 'Playing the innocent does not fool me for one second. No woman gets to your age without knowing the game. So don't try and make the stakes too high, or I might just decide the game isn't worth the candle.'

Saffron despised him at that moment more than she had thought possible. She had worked hard for her career and did not need this immoral, greedy pig sneering at her. She began to struggle, her small hands trying to prise his from her arms, hating the lazy strength with which he held her, but it was no use...

'You have an overrated belief in your charms, Mr Statis,' she spat. He honestly thought she would fall into his arms like a ripe plum; well, he was in for a very rude awakening. 'Let go of me.'

'You're hardly going to convince me to marry you with the hands-off technique.' His smile was without humour. 'I never buy without sampling first.'

'That I can believe,' she snorted disgustedly; knowing how low he would stoop to make money, she wouldn't put anything past him.

'So why the outrage?'

His gaze slid down the length of her body, lingering on

her breast and thigh; she had to force herself not to flinch under his intense scrutiny, and when his eyes fixed on her flushed and furious face once more, her green eyes spitting hatred, his brows drew together in a thoughtful frown.

'You've changed since the yacht. On board you were flustered, embarrassed by my attentions maybe, but always receptive. Now—'

'Now we are virtually alone, and you're much more dangerous...' Saffron cut in. If she was going to go through with her plan for revenge, she was going to have to be a lot more careful. She couldn't let Alex suspect for an instant just how much she despised him.

He gave her a long, speculative look. 'So you're saying you're frightened of me, or is it of yourself?'

'Maybe a bit of both,' she said lightly. 'You're a fast worker, A—Alex.' She almost choked on his hateful name, but to her amazement he mistook her stammer for feminine emotion.

'Saffron, you sweet fool, I would never hurt you—quite the reverse. I only want to make love to you.' The last came out on a triumphant groan as his arms moved around her, moulding her body to his while his lips covered hers.

Every instinct she possessed begged her to break free from the demand of his mouth moving over hers, his hard body pressed so close that she could feel the rapid pounding of his heart, the strength of his arms as he lifted and carried her across the room to deposit her gently on the sofa, his great size lowering over her. But she closed her eyes and fought the desire to shove him away and run screaming from the apartment.

No. She would suffer his kisses and caresses to a point and no further, and eventually, when he was desperate to possess her, she would reiterate her demand for marriage. If she had read his character right he was a man who never accepted defeat, and when she finally had his ring on her finger she would tell him the truth, and take him for every penny she could get. She didn't want it for herself, but there were plenty of charities in the world, and far too many orphanages, and if anyone deserved to pay it was Alex Statis.

'Saffron, where did you go?' She opened her eyes. Alex was staring down at her, a chagrined look on his harsh features. 'I must be losing my touch,' he said with a husky chuckle.

Saffron didn't believe him for one moment: his male ego was too huge for him to imagine that a woman might not find him irresistible. But not by a flicker of an eyelash did she betray her thoughts. Instead she wound her slender arms around his neck and lifted her head for his mouth. 'You caught me by surprise, knocked the breath from my body,' she offered, her slender fingers tangling through the dark hair at the back of his neck, when what she really wanted to do was strangle the devil…

She'd thought that it would be easy to suffer his kiss, but realised he was far too astute; she had to make some response, and, opening her mouth over his, she flicked her tongue against his lips. She felt his large body jerk at her tentative caress, and was congratulating herself on her act-ing ability when insidiously the kiss changed. She was no longer the instigator; Alex had taken over.

The slow kiss became a blazing statement of intent. His tongue plunged in the deep, moist interior of her mouth as his hand smoothed down between their two bodies. She trembled as heat suddenly ignited in her stomach, and his mouth moved down over her firm breast and began to suckle it through the fabric of her dress. She arched and gasped at the same time, mortified by the force of her re-action.

No! her mind screamed. This could not be happening; his touch revolted her. Unfortunately, however, her body seemed incapable of absorbing the message.

Suddenly Alex's hand was on her thigh, her dress pushed up around her waist and then he was touching her intimately, urging her legs apart, his long fingers sliding beneath the edge of her briefs and stroking her soft feminine folds with devastating effect. Her eyes closed; she could not fight the incredible tide of pleasure that his touch evoked. His teeth found the top of her dress where it left one shoulder bare and pulled it roughly down, exposing her firm, full breast to his hungry eyes.

'Alex, you can't.' She knew she had to stop him, but no man had ever touched her so intimately before, and she wanted to drown in the pleasure she was experiencing.

His hand moved to stroke across her thigh, and slowly up over her hips, leaving her aching. His black eyes burnt with a triumphant masculine passion. 'Let me get you out of this and I'll show you I can,' he said arrogantly, holding her shocked eyes with his own as he stood and stripped speedily down to his briefs, then, finding the zip of her dress, eased it down her body in one swift movement.

Defensively she crossed her arms over her naked breasts. How had he got so far so fast? She didn't know, and fought to sit up, but Alex was too quick for her. He caught her hands and spread them out from her sides while he lowered his hard, near-naked body back over her.

'You're beautiful, more beautiful than I remembered,' Alex husked, glancing down at her bare breasts.

'Stop,' she demanded harshly. This had gone far enough.

'No. I want to look at you,' he said, his dark gaze, hard and hot, flashing to her face and colliding with her glittering green eyes. He moved slightly and she felt him swell against her. She looked down between their two bodies, a soft gasp escaping her, then her frantic gaze swept back to his face. His jaw tautened and she felt his body surge even more against the cradle of her womanhood. She trembled, her whole body flushing scarlet.

His hands lifted and covered the soft, creamy mounds of her breasts. 'So soft, so perfect.' He rolled his palms over the rosy peaks, bringing them to aching tips of taut arousal, and then gently he trailed his fingers around each dark aureole. 'You are so beautiful; your skin is like sun-brushed magnolia.' He took each burgeoning nipple between a finger and thumb and plucked gently, teasingly.

A line of fire shot from Saffron's breast to her groin and her body arched helplessly beneath his teasing caress. Then he leant forward, his hands curving her shoulders, and brought her up towards him, her hair flowing down her back in a riot of shimmering curls. Mindless, she lifted her face for his kiss. His night-black eyes held hers as, instead of kissing her, as she had expected, he slowly, delicately brushed his hair-roughened chest over the hard tips of her breasts and smiled a devilish, sensuous smile at her shuddering reaction.

Dear heaven! she groaned inwardly as her body instinctively curved against his chest, her lips parted softly, invitingly. She had to get away. Stop him. But his hand tracing her spine and the soft trail of his lips down her throat and around to her ear, his tongue licking around the soft whorls, sent shimmering arrows of delight through every nerve in her body.

'You and I don't need anything so antiquated as marriage, little one, or the romantic lies of undying love. Your body needs mine now.' He eased back. 'Look at your breasts, full and aching.' She glanced down as he rasped, 'The same as I am full and aching.' He hugged her to him. 'Here? Or the bedroom?' he whispered throatily against her ear. 'I'm easy, but I can't wait much longer.' His body surged against hers once more.

He was easy! he had said. God, what did that make her? Saffron thought in horror, struggling to regain her senses. She hated him and yet she had responded like a sex-starved fool.

She shoved him hard in the chest, not caring what he thought, too horrified by her turbulent emotions to hide the disgust she felt. Catching him off guard, he fell back, lost his balance and ended up on the floor.

Saffron might have found the stunned look on his face amusing at any other time, but right now she was too frustrated and furious. She scrambled to her feet, hauling her dress back on, and snarled, 'You might be easy but I'm not, Mr Statis. Hell will freeze over before I share your bed.' And, with a last contemptuous glance at his sprawled body, she took off at a run for the door.

'What the hell…? Wait, Saffron!'

He must be out of his tiny mind if he thought she was going to wait for him, Saffron thought, ignoring his shout, but suddenly she was grabbed from behind and swung round. Without giving her time to catch her breath, a bristling, angry, near-naked Alex was dragging her back to the sofa and flinging her down.

'Don't you manhandle me,' she cried, green eyes leaping with rage.

'Manhandle? I could bloody murder you, you little tease! What was that exhibition all about?' Alex demanded harshly, his eyes narrowed on her red face.

'I—' She almost told him how she really felt. Wild, irrational anger at Alex and, if she was honest, at herself almost made her tell the truth. How much she hated him… But she stopped herself just in time. Alex was clever. If she told him she would be out of a job, minus her salary, with any hope of getting revenge on the swine out of the window for good. Thinking fast, she said the one thing she thought might just work. 'I've never...' She lowered her lashes over her glittering green eyes, hoping she looked demure. 'I'm still a virgin.'

'You're what?'

'You heard,' she murmured, still not looking at him. She sensed him move towards where she sat, and felt the depression of the sofa as he sat down beside her.

'That's unbelievable; you're twenty-five... How on earth has a beautiful woman like you not been caught before now?' The incredulity in his voice was unmistakable.

'I'm not caught now,' she snapped back, and could have bitten her tongue at her hasty response.

'No?' Alex prompted softly, watching her with narrowed eyes.

'No,' she said with a shake of her head, her stormy gaze meeting him.

'Then I imagined your complete capitulation just now?' Alex's mouth assumed a cynical twist. 'Give me some credit, Saffron; I'm thirty-nine years old, not a young boy, and I have great difficulty in believing in your innocence, however bashfully you proclaim your virginity.'

The steadiness of her gaze told him exactly what she thought of his cynical tone. 'That's your problem, not mine.' She got to her feet. 'Anna will be needing me; I have to go.'

'What about my needs?' he drawled, his dark eyes gleaming with amusement. 'We are here alone; why not finish what we started?'

'No way.' Her eyes brushed over his near-nude, lounging form and she despised herself because, for a moment, she was tempted.

'Oh, there is a way,' Alex said silkily as he stepped into

his trousers and pulled on his shirt. Draping his jacket over one shoulder, he added, 'Your way—marriage. But I'm not such a fool.'

'Shame, but that's my only offer,' she snapped.

'Jewels, furs, a villa in Greece. You would find me a very generous lover, Saffron. Think about it. I'll give you twenty-four hours to reconsider.'

Saffron should have been delighted that she was getting to him, but instead all she felt was fear. 'You don't believe in love and marriage,' she reminded him curtly. 'I do.'

Five minutes later, sitting in the passenger seat of Alex's elegant car, his dark, brooding presence intimidating as they sped through the streets of London, she had a horrible conviction that it was an enormous mistake to try and seek revenge from a man like Alex Statis.

'Anna, I need to ask you something and I want an honest answer,' Saffron said. Her employer was lying face down on the bed, and could not see the grim expression on her face, for which Saffron was grateful. After the fiasco of her dinner date with Alex, she had lain awake for hours, going over in her head everything he had said since arriving in London, and she recalled Alex's comment about his mother always trawling for a wife for him.

'Yes, what is it?' Anna asked lethargically.

'Your son told me yesterday that you had a habit of...' There was no other way of asking except directly. 'Well, he said you turn up with a companion every summer on the flimsiest of pretexts, trying to get him married off.'

Anna chuckled. 'I may have done once or twice. Surely you can't blame me for trying? God knows I would like some grandchildren before I die, and I'm not getting any younger; neither is Alex, come to that. He is very shortly going to be past his sell-by date, as I have told him frequently.'

'So Alex was right. That is why you employed me.' The disappointment was acute; she had honestly thought of Anna as a friend.

'No.' Anna turned over. 'Not you, Saffy. I wouldn't trick you like that. I needed you. Dr Jenkins told you.' She frowned, but her blue eyes avoided contact with Saffron. 'I still need you, and if Alex has told you anything different ignore him.'

If only she could, Saffron thought grimly, and Anna's denial was not the most convincing in the world. She wouldn't put it past the wily old woman to have set her up. Saffron was proud of her abilities and a professional to her fingertips. It hurt her pride to think that she had been tricked into working with Anna.

'He's rather too large to ignore,' she muttered drily, realising that Anna was expecting some response, and, with a quick flick of the sheet over the older woman's recumbent form, she added, 'All finished. I'll just go and wash my hands and you'd better drink some water; you know the aromatic oils can give you a headache.'

Swiftly she put the bottles of oil back in their slots in her workbag and, taking the mixing bowl, headed for Anna's bathroom. Turning on the tap of the vanity basin, she picked up the soap and began lathering her hands.

She had never thought of herself as a vengeful person, but since she'd realised that Alex part-owned the massage parlour that was really responsible for Eve's tragic death the desire for revenge had become a cancer eating at her mind every minute of the day.

She had dreamt of him last night—a dark, evil figure chasing her along a wild, wind-swept moor to the rim of a huge pit. He'd been almost upon her when the vision of

Eve had lifted her to the sky, and the wild, agonised scream of the man as he'd tumbled into the black hole had echoed in her mind long after she had awakened sweating and crying. She recognised the dream as some kind of wish-fulfilment. But the crying she couldn't understand.

Turning off the tap and drying her hands, she sighed dejectedly. In theory revenge was all very well, but in practice it was nowhere near as easy. Saffron wasn't a fool; she knew that Alex desired her, wanted her—he made no secret of the fact—but how to turn his want into hurt was not so easy. She could hurt him through his mother, tell Anna how he added to the family fortune, but it did not seem fair to involve her. That left her original plan of persuading him to marry her and then leaving him on the wedding night still wanting—a massive blow to his pride and, more importantly, his pocket...

She looked at her reflection in the mirror above the basin. Was she a *femme fatale*? Cool green eyes fringed with thick brown lashes looked back at her. She had been told she was beautiful but she didn't see it herself. Her eyes were slightly slanted, and her mouth a little wide and full-lipped. Then there was the mass of ginger hair. Had there ever been a carrot-topped courtesan? She doubted it...

She slipped off her overall. Underneath she was wearing a simple cream cotton jersey sundress, shoe-string straps supporting the narrow, figure-hugging tube. Her one good point was that she had a good figure—long legs, slim hips, a tiny waist and a good bust—maybe a bit too much bust.

A vivid image of Alex nuzzling her breast last night flashed in her mind, and a shiver of fear snaked down her spine. With it came the realisation that her foolhardy plot to seduce him into marriage was just that—foolish! However Alex made his money was of no account. He was perceived by the world at large as a respectable, wealthy entrepreneur. Sophisticated, dynamic, an expert lover, he could have any woman he wanted and he knew it...

Saffron shook her head at her reflection, her carrot curls swinging loose around her shoulders, a self-derisory smile revealing gleaming white teeth, and she chuckled. How could she have been so stupid as to imagine that she could hurt Alex by tricking him into marriage and parting with a fortune? She could no more play a *femme fatale* as fly to the moon, and the only person to get hurt would be herself. Grief at the death of her friend and the shock of recognising Alex Statis had made her act completely out of character. Thank God she had come to her senses in time!

She then felt a pang of sadness. Tilting her head back, she mouthed a silent prayer. Sorry, Eve; if there is any justice in the world Statis will get his come-uppance, but I'm not the sort to do this. Forgive me. And she imagined she heard Eve's hearty laughter echoing in her head. Suddenly she felt as if a ton weight had been lifted from her shoulders, and for the first time in weeks her usual light-hearted optimism lent a glow to her eyes and a smile to her mouth.

She was a mature adult woman, a professional with a business plan to fulfil. She would complete her contract with Anna, and avoid her son like the plague, and by the end of the year she would achieve her ambition and be the proud owner of a small beauty clinic. Her sense of proportion restored, she swung on her heel and went back into the bedroom.

Saffron froze. Alex, wearing well-washed denim jeans and a blue sweatshirt, was leaning against the bedroom door.

Anna turned moisture-filled eyes on her. 'I can't believe it, Saffy, dear.'

What was Alex doing here? And what had he said to

upset his mother? 'Don't upset yourself, Anna.' She crossed to her charge and put a consoling arm around her slender shoulders, shooting Alex a vitriolic glance over his mother's head.

'I'm not upset, you silly girl; these are tears of joy. I'm delighted. You and Alex—to marry…'

'Marry.' Saffron's arm fell from Anna. She turned slightly, her eyes flying open to their widest extent as Alex crossed the room in long, lithe strides even as she spoke. 'Him,' she muttered, her mouth hanging open in amazement.

'Saffron, darling, I thought over what you said and you were right.' His arms came around her and his lips lowered towards hers.

Hoist with her own petard! immediately came to mind. But she had no more time to think, as he kissed her long and deep…

CHAPTER SIX

NUMB, paralysed, frozen in shock. No single word could describe Saffron's state of mind. She looked up into Alex's bland face, her eyes searching his for some hint as to what exactly he was playing at.

'A bit more enthusiasm would be appreciated.' His dark glance pierced hers, and it took considerable will-power to hold back an angry retort.

'You said an affair and gave me twenty-four hours,' she hissed angrily.

'So I changed my mind. Mama's watching—look happy.'

'You caught me by surprise,' she managed lightly, her mind spinning with the knowledge of the chance his proposal presented her with. She eased out of his arms only to be clasped by Anna in a motherly embrace.

'I'm so happy for you both, Saffy. Now don't worry about me; get your bag and run along with Alex to choose the ring.' She kissed Saffron's cheek and stepped back, clasping her hands in front of her, as she added, 'Oh, my! Only three days to prepare a wedding. I must dash.'

Saffron followed Alex out of the door and down the stairs still reeling. She wanted to laugh at the irony. She had just decided to forget all thoughts of revenge and avoid the man like the plague, while Alex, in a complete about-face from last night and his declaration that he did not believe in marriage, had decided to do the exact opposite.

Ten minutes later they were seated in his car moving slowly through the London traffic on their way to the jeweller's, Anna's last comment echoing in Saffron's head like a death-knell.

'Why?' she finally asked baldly, all too conscious of the tension building in the interior of the car.

He did not pretend not to know what she meant. 'I never expected to marry, and I don't usually give in to sexual teasing.' He shot her an angry, accusing glance, and she knew he was remembering last night. 'In my experience so-called decent women are out for one thing from a man— a meal-ticket for life, the wealthier the better. I have a grudging respect for whores; at least they state the price up front.'

'And of course you're an expert on the subject,' Saffron snapped scathingly, disgust and hatred making her green eyes glitter angrily.

Alex flashed a sidelong glance at her flushed face, his eyes narrowing dangerously at her heated reaction. 'No, I have never paid for a woman in my life. I have never needed to.'

Her hair-triggered temper threatened to boil over. Of course he did not pay women; instead he let them make money for him. In that second Saffron decided that revenge would be hers...

'But as for my change of heart about marriage, it is really quite simple. I never lost a night's sleep over a woman until you appeared. Last night I didn't sleep at all, and cold showers are not my scene. It has to stop.' He returned his attention to the road ahead. 'You demanded marriage, I'm giving it to you.'

'Just like that,' she said lightly. 'It would be simpler and cheaper to take a sleeping-pill.' She saw Alex's lips twitch in the hint of a smile.

'So practical, Saffron. But think of the fun I'd be missing,' he drawled suggestively.

'But you can't marry me…' she protested; she couldn't afford to seem too keen. She had to make him sweat…

'I can and I will,' He took one hand off the wheel again, picked up Saffron's and placed it cosily on his hard thigh. 'And there are other compensations. Mama will stop throwing women at me, for one. And I'll be forty next birthday; it's time I thought of an heir. A son to carry on after me,' he clarified firmly, then added with the hard cynicism that Saffron detested, 'If you were honest with yourself, though I know the concept is difficult for women to accept, you'd admit that I am giving you precisely what you have wanted from the first day you set eyes on me and grabbed me so dramatically before blushing coyly and batting those big green eyes of yours, sweetheart.'

'But I don't want to marry you simply to assuage your lust and provide an heir,' she said coolly, feeling anything but cool… Events were sweeping her along at an alarming pace, just when she had thought she had got her life in order again. Alex's unprecedented announcement and, worse, his arrogant assumption that she should fall at his feet in gratitude had made her change her mind, and his last comment only reinforced her determination to seek revenge. To suggest that she had been chasing him from the first day they met was so typically arrogant of him that she had to clench her hand into a fist to prevent herself thumping him.

'Would you rather I declared undying love?' He waited for her answer.

The silence lengthened as she searched for some frivolous response, but words failed her. 'Well…' For a man like Alex to fall in love was an impossibility, so why did the thought hurt, and why did her own reason for marrying him suddenly seem so revolting?

'Too late; you can't back out now. I fixed the special licence on the way to collect you this morning.'

'But surely I have to complete a form, birth date, that sort of thing?' she gabbled. It could not be that simple. Alex had proposed to her and she had accepted more or less by default. Her temper cooled and the doubts rushed in, setting her mind awhirl with a conflict of emotions, none very enviable.

'I had you investigated, remember.'

Saffron had forgotten about that and his reminder only served to fuel her desire for revenge.

'Out you get; we can walk the rest of the way.' He had parked the car in Hatton Garden, and before Saffron could gather her scattered wits she was being ushered into a diamond merchant's.

'Desmond is a partner and friend of mine. He deals in diamonds and precious stones, and keeps a small exclusive selection of special jewellery by a little-known Russian designer. I think you'll like what you see.'

She simply nodded, trying to disguise her wide-eyed wonder at her surroundings, fighting to appear the cool sophisticate. She sat on a comfortable settee with Alex beside her in what appeared to be a rather luxurious lounge; on a low table in front of them were displayed some of the most exquisite rings Saffron had ever seen in her life. In the chair opposite sat a man of about fifty—Desmond.

'I never thought Alex would marry, but, having met you, Saffron, I can see why he's taking the plunge.'

Before she could respond to the compliment Alex interrupted. 'She's mine, Desmond, so keep your flattery to yourself and show us the rings.'

'Mine'. Saffron heard the possessive tone in his voice and felt the sudden stiffening in his large body next to her own. She glanced up at him just as he looked down at her.

Desmond said something neither of them heard as tension ignited the air between them. Saffron could not escape the burning intensity of Alex's gaze. Her lips parted in a small O of shock as she recognised the flare of desire in his dark eyes, and something more sinister—an assumption of ownership, ruthless and total.

What on earth was she doing here? Had she taken leave of her senses completely? She did not want a ring. She did not want to be within a thousand miles of Alex Statis. Her half-baked idea of revenge was futile. She had seen it in Alex's eyes, felt it in his touch. He would possess her completely. Eat her up and spit her out as so much garbage if she let him.

'Do you like this one?'

She looked down at where her hand lay in Alex's, wondering how it had got there. Then she gasped. Two white gold bands were held together every few millimetres with perfectly inset emeralds, the two bands twisting in the centre to form the mount for an exquisite blue-white diamond. It was unusual and intriguing and must cost a fortune. 'It's beautiful, but something smaller...' For a second she completely forgot that she was supposed to be taking the man for every penny she could get. She sucked in her breath as Alex tightened his grip on her hand.

'We will take it.' And, leaning over her, he covered her mouth with his own. She tried to freeze him out but he was not so easily discouraged; his teeth bit her bottom lip and her mouth opened to allow him access. She told herself she hated him, but as the kiss went on and on her resistance crumbled. When he finally lifted his head, she stared up at him, her green eyes dazed, her lips softly swollen. 'To a short but sweet engagement, my little witch,' he drawled throatily.

Saffron thought she smiled and agreed though she was

past caring. She only wanted to get away somewhere on her own, anywhere, and try to make sense of her wildly fluctuating emotions. But she knew it would not be easy...

Later Saffron was to agonise over how on earth she had allowed it to happen. But for the next two days she went around in a daze, one moment determined to back out of the marriage, the next, with one arrogant or possessive comment from Alex, equally determined to go ahead with the wedding simply to teach the swine a lesson...

Anna didn't help Saffron's confused emotional state by suddenly turning into a model of bustling efficiency. The older woman insisted on taking Saffron shopping and to Saffron's horror she ended up with a white wedding gown. A slinky pleated skirt almost to her ankles with a shoe-string overdress in the finest chiffon, the style was slightly 1920s, but the price designer original. The head-dress was little more than a shaped swath of chiffon that bound her topknot of curls and floated down over her shoulder. She looked at her reflection and what she saw was a sophisti-cated bride with the eyes of a child. She had no argument against Anna's declaration that it was perfect for a summer wedding, though she hated the way it made her feel: a complete hypocrite.

Three days later at a simple civil ceremony, Alex stand-ing tall and elegant at her side, her hand firmly clasped in his as the dignitary read the marriage service, Saffron heard Alex's deep, resonant, 'I will,' and wanted to run.

This had gone far enough. She opened her mouth to say no, but Alex, sensing her hesitation, tilted her chin with one finger. Her eyes widened in alarm at the blaze of emo-tion in his, and just for a second she thought she saw his eyes flash—a trace of pleading that was at once suppressed. How powerful, how proud he was, she thought, and in that instant her wildly vacillating emotions of the past few weeks vanished. Like a shutter lifting in her mind she suddenly recognised what she had feared and fought so long to deny. It hit her with the force of a nova star, shattering all her preconceived ideas of love and marriage...

She loved Alex. She hated what he was, but somehow she had fallen in love with him.

'Saffron,' he murmured, his eyes burning into hers, hypnotising her into submission.

'I will,' she said, the words trembling on her lips. Alex lifted her hand and slid a plain gold band on her finger.

'You belong to me now.' And his lips met hers in a devastating kiss, stamping on her his possession in front of the world.

The penthouse and pavilion suite of a top London hotel had been reserved for the reception. Cameras flashed as they arrived. The wedding announcement three days previously in *The Times* had caused a stir among the world's journalists. Alex Statis, the multimillionaire, wedding an unknown. It was yet another reason why Saffron had continued with the charade of preparing for the wedding. Alex had called the papers before he had even told her, and his bullying tactics of the past few days had served to heighten her anger, while his passionate kisses and constant sensual touches had left her floundering in a sea of conflicting emotions she could not begin to decipher.

Talk and laughter echoed around the extravagantly mirrored walls of the elegant pavilion room that led out on to a wide balcony complete with fountain and waterfall and a stunning view over London. Later, in the sumptuously elegant dining-room, they ate excellent food and the champagne flowed freely. Desmond, as best man, made a humorous speech and Alex's acceptance was a masterpiece of wit.

Then Saffron was being congratulated by Anna and Aunt Katherina. She frowned thoughtfully as Maria murmured her congratulations, her green-eyed gaze resting on Anna and Katherina. Given Anna's story on the boat, it was surprising to see how well the sisters-in-law appeared to get along.

'Why the frown, darling? Tired?' Alex's husky voice whispered in her ear.

'No, no. I'm fine.'

'Pity; I want to take you to bed.' She forced herself to look up at him. He was devastatingly attractive in a pearl-grey suit, his dark eyes sparkling with laughter and something else she did not recognise. Just then Desmond made a great production of kissing the bride, although unfortunately he was hampered somewhat by the fact that Alex refused to remove his arm from around his bride's waist.

Saffron stood in the curve of her husband's arm and looked around the glittering throng. Alex was deep in conversation with Sylvia. The other woman had given Saffron one hate-filled glance and gritted congratulations before turning all her feminine charms on Alex. Saffron couldn't care less. She felt as if she was walking through a nightmare. How had she let it come to this? Her grief at Eve's death, her instant attraction to Alex and the discovery of who he really was had thrown her into an emotional minefield; torn between her attraction for Alex and her debt to her friend, her quick temper had done the rest.

A small sad smile twisted her lips as she acknowledged once more what she had been fighting for weeks. She loved Alex, and when she had made her vows it had not been because he had forced or intimidated her but because in her heart of hearts it was what she wanted. Hate and love walked a thin line, and in the throes of what was her first real sexual experience Saffron had managed to tangle the two completely, with devastating results.

She was married to a man she loved but should hate. She glanced at the crowd of smartly dressed guests. Not one of them was hers. She had tried to contact Tom and Vera, the couple she had lived with for the past few years, at Anna's instigation, but they had been away on holiday.

And how Eve would have loved to see this: a top hotel and the top people, and little Saffron Martin married to the catch of the year. She was completely out of her depth and going down for the third time.

She looked up at Alex, her stomach curling in nervous anticipation of the night ahead. Yet the warmth of his large strong hand at her waist was oddly comforting; she felt safe, something she had never experienced since the death of her parents.

Later, having changed into a smart buttercup-yellow suit, with a dramatic black camisole peeking through the jacket lapels, ridiculously high-heeled black court shoes and a black bag, Saffron left with Alex to journey to Paris.

Covered in rice and confetti, she slid into the Jaguar. Alex slipped in beside her, chuckling as he brushed a handful of rice from his thick black hair.

'Enough to feed a child in the Third World,' he remarked with a rueful smile.

'I doubt you worry much about the Third World,' Saffron snapped before she realised what she had done.

Alex started the car; they were driving to Heathrow where the Statis jet was waiting. Then he shot her a curious glance. 'You don't really know me very well, do you, Saffron?' he said softly.

She glanced at him and for an instant she thought she saw something in his brown eyes—a hint of vulnerability?—that made her heart inexplicably lurch in her chest, but quickly she dismissed the notion. She knew him far too well; that was the trouble…

'Not to worry, darling; we're almost there, and very shortly you will know me as intimately as it's possible to know another person. No more delaying tactics. Soon you will be mine utterly and completely,' Alex drawled hardly, his glance flicking over her slim form with a possessive male sensuality that brought a blush to her cheeks.

With hindsight she realised morosely that that was another reason why she had continued with her plan of revenge. On the day he had presented her with the engagement ring, they had shared a celebratory dinner at his apartment and Alex had deliberately set out to seduce her with a sensual sophistication that had had her blushing scarlet and her head spinning. It had taken all her self-control to prevent him bedding her there and then, until he had lost his cool and said, 'For God's sake, woman, we're engaged; I've bought you the obligatory rock to prove it. I've waited long enough. I want you now, damn it!'

His cynical mention of the engagement ring had been enough to have her stiffening in anger, remembering how many poor girls had been destroyed to satisfy his greed, and she had sworn again to have her revenge.

He had taken her home in a cold fury. She had hardly slept for the next few nights, and when she had finally got to sleep her dreams had been full of a naked, erotic Alex inexplicably entwined with Eve…

Saffron closed her eyes briefly as the aircraft took off, and cursed the circumstances and her own quick temper that had led her to this point. She turned her head slightly. Alex was pulling his tie from his strong throat and deftly unfastening the first couple of buttons of his white shirt. Feeling her eyes on him, he cast her a lazy glance.

'Formalities over; now for the best part.' His deep, sexy voice and easy smile sent warning signals through every nerve in her body. He leant closer, at the same time slipping off his jacket. 'Want to join the mile-high club, Mrs Statis?'

The sun's rays slanting through the window caught his profile, accentuating his rugged features and highlighting a few silver strands in his thick dark hair. He gave the impression of power and authority, and a raw male virility that held her gaze even against her will. Then he jiggled his eyebrows suggestively, and Saffron couldn't prevent a smile and a soft chuckle escaping her at his antics.

'Well?' he prompted, one long finger reaching to trace gently the outline of her mouth. He placed his other arm about her shoulder, urging her towards him. 'Tempted, wife?' he prompted again teasingly.

She was... Saffron wanted nothing more than to sink into his arms where she belonged. 'Wife', he had said, and with that one word Alex had opened her eyes to exactly what she had done. She had married the man she loved but could not respect. What hope was there for their future in such circumstances?

'There's no need to look so stricken, darling,' Alex said, the laughter dying from his eyes. 'I was only teasing.' His finger fell from her mouth to settle in the V of her jacket lapels, while his mouth gently grazed hers.

'The flight is barely an hour and the first time I get you in a bed I intend to keep you there for a week—probably longer!' he murmured against her lips. Then, straightening, he added, 'I have a suspicion that this ferocious physical need will not be assuaged so easily,' and grimaced as though he resented his desire for her.

Saffron knew exactly how he felt...his finger on her throat, the touch of his lips and she wanted him. 'I think

I'll rest for a while,' she mumbled as Alex settled back in his seat although his arm remained around her shoulders.

'Do that—I don't want you tired later,' he drawled huskily.

Cowardly she closed her eyes, her thoughts too hard to face. She realised with blinding clarity that she had probably loved Alex from the first time they had been alone together on Mykonos, when she had accepted, to the lush strains of a Rossini overture, her own sensual nature while not realising that it was only Alex who had the power to make her feel that way. She had fallen into a trap of her own making, by denying him her body even after he had given her the engagement ring; he had charged ahead with the wedding simply to slake his physical lust.

She could not settle for that kind of marriage, even if she was foolish enough to try. It was doomed from the start because he was still the man who had shared ownership of Studio 96. Maybe he just owned the building and didn't know what was going on. But common sense told her she was simply searching for excuses for Alex. In her heart she knew she could never forget his past, so her love for him would have to end before it had even begun.

Looking back, she could see what a naïve idiot she had been. Alex had alternately teased and beguiled her on board the yacht, until she had admitted to herself her growing fascination for the man, only to have it destroyed first by her jealousy of the sophisticated Sylvia, and completely by her recognition of where she had seen Alex before.

Her growing love had turned to instant hate, and her red-headed temper had fuelled her asinine plan of revenge. Who was it who said 'Be careful of what you wish for in case you get it'? How true! But what was she going to do now? Unconsciously a deep, quavering sigh escaped her.

'Why the sigh?'

Saffron opened her eyes to find Alex gazing at her with tender intensity and she looked at him for a long moment, a tide of colour washing slowly up her cheeks at his obvious concern. 'I...'

She was saved by the arrival of a stunning blonde stewardess.

'Congratulations, Mr Statis. I never thought I'd see the day.'

Alex's attention was immediately on the tall blonde. 'Thank you, Eve; I didn't know you were back.'

Saffron watched his easy, familiar smile and the blonde's response, her heart freezing at the coincidence. Another Eve, but this one alive and well and obviously very well acquainted with Alex. It highlighted so poignantly her worst fear. She could not go ahead with the marriage and forget about her friend, burying her head in the sand like an ostrich, because there would always be something or someone, perhaps simply a name, to remind her of Alex's involvement in her friend's destruction. She could not live her life on a lie. She sipped the champagne provided and if she was quiet Alex did not seem to notice.

The light was fading when they arrived at the small exclusive hotel in Paris. 'I hope you don't mind, Saffron, but I've spent so much time away from work chasing you that I can only afford three days before I have to be back in the office. But don't worry, I'll make it up to you later.' Alex gave her hand a squeeze as they were shown to their suite. 'In a few months we'll take a long honeymoon cruising the Med or the West Indies, whatever you like.'

What she would have liked was to be anywhere in the world but here, she thought sadly, her gaze flickering around the room, barely taking in the opulent surroundings but studiously avoiding looking at Alex. She had not the slightest idea what she was going to do. In the taxi she had run through a dozen scenarios from going ahead with the marriage, telling Alex the truth, to faking a serious illness.

Her eyes alighted on a table set beside the lusciously draped window. A massive arrangement of red roses was the centrepiece, and there were two place-settings, the finest crystal glasses and champagne in a free-standing bucket at one side. 'We're dining here?' she burst out. Somehow she had thought they would go out to dinner, which would have given her more time, but obviously Alex had other ideas.

'Where else on our honeymoon?' he husked, his arms closing around her from behind, holding her tight against his tall body, his lips nuzzling her neck. 'Alone at last.' His breath singed her skin.

'What a cliché.' She tried to laugh and pulled herself out of his arms. 'You order the food; I need to freshen up.'

She dashed for the door she imagined was the bathroom, and for the first time that day got something right. She closed the door and bolted it, her heart pounding, her mouth dry. In ordinary circumstances tonight could have been a dream come true: she was married to the man she loved and on her honeymoon. But she could not fool herself; it was hopeless…

God help her! She swallowed hard. What a mess! She should have remembered; she had heard somewhere that revenge was best taken cold, and given that she was always hot around Alex her scheme would never have worked anyway, never mind the fact that she had fallen in love with him… She was only putting off the inevitable by hiding in the bathroom. She would have to go for the truth and pray that Alex would understand. That was if he didn't kill her first…

They did not linger over the meal. Saffron had no appetite, and quaffed the champagne as if it were going out of style, while she would have sworn, if she had not known better, that Alex was nervous. They drank a toast to their marriage and Saffron invented a few others simply to delay the hour of reckoning, and amazingly he allowed her to get away with it. Finally however, he drained his glass, placed it quite deliberately on the table and stood up.

'I think we'll forgo coffee; you may use the bathroom first.' And, catching her hand, he pulled her to her feet and led her into the large bedroom.

Her green eyes widened at the sight of the huge bed that dominated the room. Tell him...tell him now...her mind screamed, but she had trouble tearing her gaze away. A frothy white négligé—a present from Anna—lay draped across the white lace cover, beside it a pair of black silk pyjamas. The intimacy of the nightwear brought home to her as nothing else exactly what she had done, and what she was inviting. For the first time in days fear cleared her head with remarkable alacrity.

'Alex, I've made a mistake.' The words were out before she could stop them. She straightened her shoulders and turned to face him. Truth was the only way. She tilted her head back to look up into his handsome face. 'I should never have married you.'

'Say that again.' He shook his head in disbelief, one lock of black hair falling over his broad forehead.

'I want to go back to England. We can get the marriage annulled and forget it ever happened,' she said in a tight, nervous voice. She turned and walked towards the door, but Alex's arm around her waist halted her, hauling her back against his hard body.

'You're nervous,' he said softly. His dark head bent and he nuzzled the soft line of her neck, but she pulled free, stepping away from him.

'No, I mean it.' She reached for the door-handle and was suddenly swept off her feet and into Alex's arms.

'Foolish girl. It's just natural bridal nerves. Hell, surprisingly enough, I'm nervous myself!'

If his words had been meant to reassure her they didn't. She struggled in his arms, crying out, 'I am not nervous, damn you! Put me down.' And he did, dropping her on the bed. She lay flat on her back staring up at him, trying to find the words to extricate herself from the mess she had made of everything.

'Sorry.' Inadequate, she knew. 'I really am sorry, Alex; I thought…' She paused then began to talk and could not stop. 'I thought I could marry you and hurt you the way you have hurt so many people by your determination to make money legally or otherwise. I wanted to make you suffer like my friend Eve. To take you for every penny I could get.'

But I realised I loved you, was what she wanted to say but couldn't, because the one thing she had recognised while she had been agonising over her marriage the last few hours was that Alex did not love her. His reasons for marrying her were not much better than Saffron's had been originally. Instead she added in a flat voice, 'You see, I know all about Studio 96.'

His dark head jerked back. 'You know Studio 96?' he rasped, his eyes narrowed on her pale face.

At least he had not attempted to deny it, Saffron thought dully, sitting up and swinging her legs over the side of the bed, her feet finding the floor. 'Yes, I know it.' She ran her small hands through her hair, brushing it back from her face, and glanced up at Alex, He was standing perfectly still as if carved in stone, his rugged face expressionless. 'I know you owned that disgusting massage parlour.' There; she had finally said it.

'I see, and were you an employee?' he ground out scathingly.

Saffron stared at him. 'I lasted exactly fifteen minutes, the length of time it took me to realise what kind of health club it was, and you, Alex, showed me the door. Unfortunately my best friend Eve was not so lucky. I lost touch with her and then a few months ago a policeman arrived at my door to tell me Eve had died of an overdose and left a letter for me. Working in that supposedly high-class health club had destroyed her, while men like you get rich on the proceeds.'

Her green eyes searched his face in puzzled frustration. 'Why, Alex? You have so many other business interests, why a sordid massage parlour?' She shook her head; it didn't make sense. 'Greed?' she queried, but did not really want to hear his response.

Confession was supposed to be good for the soul, but Saffron was having serious doubts. She stood up, and would have walked past Alex but he reached for her, his fingers digging cruelly into her arm. He spun her round, his other hand curved around her neck, and she raised her eyes to his, and what she saw made the blood freeze in her veins.

'Of course; the young platinum—' He stopped. He had finally recognised her from the past. Shaking his head as if to dispel some image, he carried on coldly, clinically, 'Am I to understand you married me today as some kind of revenge for the death of your friend, and now you want out? So what has changed your mind, Saffron, dearest?' he demanded with chilling cynicism. 'The thought of sleeping with me too much for you to stomach?' he ended in a snarl.

'I… No…' She didn't know what to say; his hand was curved around her throat, his black eyes glittered with an unholy light, and for a second she feared for her life.

'My sweet Saffron, the epitome of all innocence, and more Greek than I when it comes to revenge.' A harsh laugh escaped him as his hand moved under her chin, forcing her head back. His glittering gaze clashed with hers. 'Tell me, you bitch, when did you decide on this plan of yours—the minute we met or before? Is that why you worked for my mother?'

'No—no—I...' Saffron was petrified. Alex's hand slid from her arm to curve around her waist, holding her manacled to the hard, muscular length of his body. His hand at her chin was hurting her jawbone, and the icy fury in his eyes, the harshly forbidding expression on his ruthless face made her want to cry out in terror.

'Answer me,' he grated.

'I—I didn't recognise you until we left the yacht. The business suit, navy... Before, I thought I knew you but the suit and briefcase... I realised who you were and ha—' She almost said 'hated you' but stopped herself in time. She was alone in the bedroom with a furiously angry male. This was not going at all as she had hoped. How idiotic of her to expect that a man like Alex would let her just walk away. She must have been out of her tiny mind... But then it felt as if she had been in that state ever since she'd clapped eyes on the damn man! she thought helplessly.

'Hated me? Then I think I should give you reason.' His pitiless intention was obvious, and even as Saffron tried to struggle she was once more on the bed, but this time Alex was beside her.

CHAPTER SEVEN

'NO, ALEX, you don't understand. I changed my mind. I should…' Her words were stilled by his mouth covering hers in a bitter parody of a lover's kiss. When it was over she lay panting on the bed, his strong body half covering hers as he swiftly removed her jacket and dispensed with her skirt with ruthless efficiency.

'Understand? I understand too damn well, you little cheat. ''I changed my mind''?' he mimicked scathingly, and all the time his gaze never left her face, until she was half demented by the probing black eyes which seemed intent on devouring her. 'I hate to tell you, darling, but you don't have that choice,' he grated with seething sarcasm, the straps of her camisole snapping like matchsticks as he tore the garment from her body, exposing her naked breasts to the brightly lit room. 'Yes, Alex, please, Alex,' he sneered. 'I'll have you begging for it, you little bitch.'

But the cold fury in his voice, his tight mouth, the dull flush on his high cheekbones revealed the massive effort he was exerting to gain self-control and not to take her there and then.

Perspiration broke out on her temples. 'No, please…' But her plea fell on deaf ears as she tried to struggle, lashing out at him with feet and hands, her efforts fruitless because he was so much larger and rage lent him added purpose.

'You're sorry?' he snarled. 'You want to leave?' He slid off the bed but kept her pinned to the mattress with one large hand in the middle of her chest; with the other he removed the rest of his clothes, carelessly throwing them to the floor. 'I'll show you sorry, Saffron,' he vowed ruthlessly, his black eyes roaming over her face and almost naked, trembling form with lascivious intent.

'You can't be serious,' she cried inanely. He towered over her, his nude body gleaming golden in the artificial light, and to her horror a blush ran from her head to her toes. He was so beautifully male that even in her terror she still reacted to him.

'I have never been more serious in my life.' He joined her on the bed and she kicked out at him, but one hard thigh quickly trapped her flailing limbs.

'Did you really think you could get revenge on a Greek? We are past masters at the art. You should have remembered that, Saffron.' He rolled over on top of her and, catching her hands, held them pinned to the pillow above her head in one of his, his full weight pressing the breath from her body, but still she shivered at the intimate brush of his mat of chest hair against her naked flesh.

She bucked against him in a vain attempt to dislodge him. 'Get off me, you great hulking brute. I hate you!' Her quick temper and sheer terror made her strike at him with anything she could think of. 'My God, you and your Greek heritage! Family! What a laugh! Even your own mother is afraid of you; for years you've made her suffer with relatives she can't abide.'

If she'd thought he was angry before, that was nothing compared to his reaction now…

Alex's head jerked back and he stared down at her in violent black fury, his eyes flaming with rage. His grip tightened on her wrists, forcing a low cry from her. 'Wrong move, Saffron,' he grated between his teeth, his dark head bending lower, and Saffron felt herself begin to tremble. 'You will not distract me with wild accusations. I intend having you, and you must have realised by now that I usually get what I want in the end.'

'However low you have to stoop to do it?' she cried unwisely, but fear and anger mingled with sheer panic made her forget all caution. 'About what I would have expected from a man no better than a pimp,' she added, dredging up a last few grains of defiance.

He did not notice her panic, only the derision in her words. 'Don't ever, *ever* call me that again if you value your life!' he snarled, and his hand reached out to tangle in her hair, jerking her head up towards him, his face only inches from her own. For a long moment he stared into her glittering angry eyes, a muscle jerking in his cheek.

'The truth hurts,' she managed to fight back.

'You are either a fool or a very brave woman,' he snarled, like a tiger about to pounce.

She looked at him with bitter resentment. As far as Alex was concerned she was a fool; she had known she was beaten from that day on Mykonos only she'd had too much pride and been too afraid to admit it.

His mouth fastened on hers brutally, kissing her with savage fury, and she moaned in pain and, more humiliatingly, aching longing. Sensing her reluctant response, his lips gentled, his mouth searched hers and his long fingers tightened their hold on her.

His breath seared her mouth and down the vulnerable curve of her throat. 'You are going to give me what I have paid for, my sweet wife.' He looked at her, his lips curved in a deadly smile, then his head lowered to her breast.

'I'm not...' she choked almost incoherently as his teeth bit lightly at her breast; he blatantly watched the nipple swell and tighten and then glanced knowingly up at her flushed face.

'You will, but don't worry—I won't take anything you

aren't prepared to give.' His breathing had deepened but he spoke with a deadly calm that was more terrifying than his earlier rage. 'You have led me a merry dance. No woman has ever succeeded in doing that to me, and neither will you.'

Her heart racing, Saffron realised it was the devil in him talking, the powerful, cynical businessman against whom she had never stood a chance and whom she had been the biggest fool in Christendom even to try to outwit. Already she could feel a sweet tide of pleasure she couldn't resist flowing through her veins, and as his head lowered again, his tongue flicking lightly over the tip of her breast, she gasped and felt her body yielding itself to him in trembling anticipation, his to do with as he wanted, even as her mind tried to deny the ease with which he aroused her. She flinched as he raised his head to watch her.

'I did not mean to bite. There; I've kissed you better,' he said silkily, his free hand covering her other breast and squeezing gently. Saffron arched beneath him in helpless response, and his black eyes held hers, a glint of mockery in their fiery depths.

'It is time to pay the piper,' he rasped as his mouth claimed hers once more. For a second she offered a token resistance, clenching her teeth, but it did not last. His long, supple fingers played with the hard tip of her breast and her lips parted on a low moan, giving him the access he sought.

His kiss hardened, his tongue dancing in and out of every moist, secret corner of her mouth, while his hand taunted and teased, stroking down over her belly and beneath her briefs and garter belt, her only remaining clothes, to the soft red hair at the juncture of her thighs.

'Stockings. My favourite,' Alex said, kissing her navel. 'Hardly virginal,' he mocked, glancing up at her glazed eyes. 'Another little ruse, no doubt,' he grated as with slow deliberation he peeled her panties and stockings from her legs, kissing his way down and back up their shapely length, then once more finding her mouth.

Saffron knew she should fight, but had no will left; the blood pounded thick and hot through her veins, every nerve pulled taut with passion. Alex was an expert lover and his touch, the scent of him, the brush of skin on skin, the subtle play of his long fingers over her quivering, aching flesh melted her bones. He was so large, so powerful; the scent of him filled her nostrils and his touch filled her mind and heart to the exclusion of all else.

She was not aware that he had freed her hands until she felt the strength of his broad shoulders beneath her finger-tips. She began caressing him in urgent need. Her lips parted and she whimpered as she felt the steel-hard weight of him against her thigh, while with mouth and tongue he teased and tormented her, kissing every inch of her soft flesh.

'Saffron, my spicy Saffron,' he growled as he showered kisses back down her stomach, trailing his hands over her burgeoning breasts and down. He nudged her legs apart with one hard-muscled thigh then trailed kisses along her hipbone, and she cried out as his wicked fingers delved in the heart of her womanhood and his kiss became too inti-mate to endure.

Soon she was twisting and gasping, her hands clenching the sheet as her body arched in a bow, seeking, needing only the fulfilment that Alex could give her.

Suddenly he was over her again, his broad chest hard against her breast. His mouth moved insistently over hers with renewed passion, ravaging in its ruthless possession. She felt a brief flare of panic as he swiftly urged her legs wider apart and slid between them. She stiffened slightly but he was having none of it. His large hands curved under her buttocks and lifted her from the bed as he came down, letting her take his whole weight as he moved fiercely into her in one driving thrust…

She cried out with the pain and Alex reared back. She looked straight into his eyes, and for a second she thought she registered regret, then his head lowered, his lips took hers in a strangely soothing, achingly tender kiss and amazingly she was no longer hurting, her slender sheath clenching around his rigid, pulsing length.

'Yes, yes!' he encouraged hoarsely. 'I won't hurt you again. Relax,' he breathed into her open mouth. One strong hand supporting his weight, he curved the other up her back and around her shoulder, still joined but rocking her in his embrace. 'That's it, my little witch; go with it.' As he spoke he eased her back down and moved slowly inside her, his head bent to kiss her in a long, hot, open-mouthed kiss, his tongue following the rhythm of their bodies.

Saffron gasped as she felt her body absorbing and adjusting to Alex's, then cried out as the slow, lazy rhythm picked up speed, his hardness filling her until she cried out again, frightened by her own fervent response. Her small hands curved around and up his back, her fingers digging into his satin-smooth skin, her legs instinctively lifting, clamping high around his waist. She closed her eyes tight, her body clenching in what seemed like anguished pain as Alex, dark and all-powerful, swept her into a maelstrom of feelings and sensations she had never imagined possible. Her body finally convulsed in a shattering climax that went on and on, in wave after wave of storming ecstasy.

Then Alex, with a 'God!' groaned out in a hoarse, breathless sigh, shuddered, his huge body going rigid, before he collapsed on top of her, his heartbeat racing with hers, and he trembled, as Saffron did, for long moments afterwards.

Eventually Saffron, the fires which had consumed her slowly dying down, felt a curious exhaustion, and an emptiness in her heart that brought moisture to her eyes. Alex rolled off her and lay flat on his back, an arm thrown over his eyes, his mighty chest still heaving. The rasping sound of his breathing was the only noise in the brightly lit room. She glanced sideways at him and quickly away, the lengthening silence a testimony to the chasm that lay between them even when they had been as intimate as it was possible for two people to be.

With a choked sob, she slid off the bed and stumbled towards the bathroom. She was surprised but strangely unconcerned when Alex followed her, curving his arm around her waist.

'Allow me.' She stood motionless in his hold as he turned on the taps and they both watched the large bath slowly fill. 'Are you all right?' he asked tersely, lifting her in his arms and depositing her gently in the warm water.

'Of course,' she murmured. They were talking like two strangers, stilted and polite. But Alex was a stranger to her, she thought with sad irony. Now she knew his body, but the man…villain or virtuous?…she would never know, and—please, God!—that fact alone would some day kill this hopeless love she felt for him, and set her free.

Closing her eyes, she lay back; she was so tired and heartsore, she didn't want to think. She felt the gentle touch of the sponge as Alex carefully bathed her but was too exhausted to object.

Later he lifted her out, dried her tender flesh with a large white towel and then, with a rare gentleness, carried her back to the bed again. Reaction setting in, she lay like a rag doll as he covered her with the white sheet. For a second she felt his hand tremble against her cheek, but she must have imagined it as she opened her eyes to stare up into a dark face blank of all expression.

'Go to sleep; we will talk in the morning.'

Her eyelids suddenly seemed too heavy to keep open and, with a shuddering sigh, she fell asleep.

Saffron sighed, and snuggled closer into the enveloping warmth of the hard male body; the steady, rhythmic beat beneath her ear filled her with a deep sense of security and, drifting in the no man's land between sleep and wakefulness, she luxuriated in the rare feeling of utter contentment.

Her lashes flickered against the soft curve of her cheek and she stirred restlessly, reluctant to leave her safe cocoon of peace. Then memory returned and her eyes flashed open. She blinked once, twice. The room was lit with the early morning rays of the sun, the curtains open, the sound of traffic bringing her to full consciousness.

A heavy weight pinned her to the bed, and she carefully looked down at the arm that lay across her waist, and lower to the thigh that anchored her legs. Alex! Slowly her eyes trailed up over a male hip, waist and shoulder until she met the dark, inscrutable gaze of her husband.

'Awake at last,' he murmured softly. He was lying on his side, his elbow on the pillow to prop his head, and his eyes gleamed mockingly down at her as she tried to wriggle free from beneath his arm and leg. 'Why the hurry, Saffron? You aren't going anywhere.'

'I want to get up.'

'So do I—oh, so do I,' he chuckled.

Saffron felt the stirring of his arousal against her hip and blushed scarlet, but could not repress a shiver of reaction as he slowly and deliberately slid his hand from her waist up over her breast, throat, and to her face. He smoothed her tangled mass of red hair from her brow and, sliding his fingers through the glittering strands, spread them across the pillow.

'What time is it?' she croaked.

'Six. Plenty of time.' Alex's hand slid back down over her throat, his fingers lingering on the soft hollows. 'Last night I wanted to kill you.' His hand tightened for a second on her neck.

'No need—I'm leaving,' Saffron said, tension making her words sound harsh. Alex was too close, too overpowering and she had to get away.

As if she had never spoken he continued, 'But this morning I have a much better plan.' His hand resumed its downward journey and brushed the rosy peak of one breast then, with clever fingers, manipulated the tip to pebble-hardness.

'No.' She was protesting against both his plan and the sensual intent she saw in his dark, slumberous eyes.

'But you have not heard my plan, Saffron, my sweet,' he mocked softly, his fingers teasingly walking across to her other breast. 'I will not allow you to leave me; you can forget it. But you wanted revenge. I am half Greek; I can understand that and so you shall have it. You can spend my money how you like.' His thumb brushed back and forward over her pouting nipple, and she bit her lip to keep down the low moan of pleasure.

'I'm a reasonable man; last night I lost my temper a little, but after careful consideration nothing has changed. We both had our own reasons for this marriage. I thought yours was money, and all you have really done is prove me right.'

He sounded so cool, so sensible, and there was a horrible kind of truth in Alex's words that made Saffron cringe even as her pulse-rate leapt at his wandering hands.

'And I shall have my heir and you to play with, sweet Saffron. Whenever, however, wherever I feel like!'

She looked at him nervously, her body already responding to the promise of his, and as she loved him so she hated him for rendering her so helpless. She had not missed the threat in his words. She felt his hard thigh press down on her slender legs and, with one arm trapped under Alex's body, she was at a hopeless disadvantage, but with her free hand she clasped his wrist, trying to stop the torment he was inflicting on her swollen breasts. 'Stop.' But he simply dragged her hand with his.

'I might stop some day.' His dark eyes gleamed with sardonic amusement. 'But certainly not today, and if you were honest you would admit you don't want me to.'

Saffron glared at him bitterly; the fiend was right and he knew it. She dug her nails into the underside of his wrist, hoping to hurt him and get him to stop.

Instead one dark eyebrow rose and his lips thinned as he unhurriedly used the hand that was propping his head to catch hers and force it over the top of her head. 'Now what, Saffron?' he mocked silkily.

She shivered as his free hand returned to tormenting her swollen breasts and her green eyes, sparkling with a mixture of anger and arousal, clashed with his. 'Don't do that.' She tried to twist away from him but it was a futile gesture. Alex, stretched out beside her, his rugged face looming over her, the early morning stubble casting a shadow over his square jaw, was obviously enjoying her discomfort; it was there in the cynically smiling mouth and his cool, assessing brown eyes fixed firmly on her flushed face.

'I said anytime anywhere—my choice,' he reiterated with deadly determination. 'My money, my plaything,' he murmured as he bent his head.

She was trapped, spread out before him, one hand still under his body, the other forced over her head and pinned to the pillow, while he moved his heavy thigh lightly up and down her lower body, and his free hand took impossible liberties with her tender flesh as his mouth sought hers in a slow burning kiss that built into a ravishment of her senses. She trembled as heat gathered in her loins, and his mouth suddenly dropped to her breast and began to suckle on the rigid tip.

Saffron gasped and arched at the same time as Alex's leg forced hers apart and his long, tactile fingers slid between the secret soft folds of her feminine flesh, finding the pulsing sweet centre of her desire. 'Please—you can't,' she murmured in anguish, torn between the delicious delight of his mouth and hands and the humiliation at her weakness.

But Alex simply moved from one breast, his black eyes flashing triumphantly to her face, and resumed suckling its partner, while his hand kept up an insistent teasing, tantalising rhythm. She felt her muscles clench, her body lifting, yielding to the demands of her own sexuality and Alex's sensual mastery. She closed her eyes, her face taut with pleasure, as Alex increased his rhythmic caress and the pressure of his mouth on her breasts.

'Please—oh, please!' she cried as her body trembled on the pinnacle of relief, and then clenched in a convulsive surrender.

The shuddering tremors stopped and Saffron finally opened her eyes. Alex had slipped an arm around her shoulder and his other hand rested lightly on the soft nest of red curls at the juncture of her thighs. She flushed scarlet as she met his dark, enigmatic gaze, shocked at his manipulation of her body, but more confused than anything. 'Why did…?' She couldn't continue.

He kissed her damp forehead, and smiled, a long, slow, completely masculine grin. 'Proving a point, maybe. You're mine to do what I like with.'

Tears of utter humiliation hazed her green eyes, but she refused to give in to them. She glanced down his long, naked body. 'Humiliating me doesn't do much for you, though, does it?' she retaliated, aware of his aroused state.

Reaching out his hand, he tilted her chin, his eyes dark and oddly intent. 'Maybe pleasuring you was all I intended.'

Saffron's eyes widened in surprise and puzzlement. 'Degrading me, you mean.'

'Don't look so shocked, Saffron; it's very flattering for a man to know he can please his woman in many ways, and nothing that brings pleasure between a husband and wife is degrading, you little innocent.'

His husky chuckle only fuelled Saffron's bitter humiliation. She tried to twist out of his arms, but he held her fast.

'Surprisingly, last night you were a virgin, and maybe I was less than gentle,' he admitted. His dark eyes caught and held hers as his hand, at the nape of her neck, kept her face towards his. 'You must be sore after last night; maybe this morning I was simply being considerate.'

Alex, considerate? The mind boggled, Saffron thought sadly, and closed her eyes, wishing she could shut out Alex and her love for him as easily.

'Come on, Saffron, get up,' he commanded softly. She opened her eyes, and he was standing leaning over her, a slight smile quirking the edges of his finely chiselled mouth. 'I need a cold shower and you need to pack; we're leaving in a couple of hours.'

'What?' she queried, momentarily fascinated by the length of his thick dark lashes curving over his half-closed eyes, successfully masking his expression. No man should have eyelashes like that; it was sinful.

'Pack—Saffron—we—are—leaving...' Alex said each

word deliberately as though speaking to a child, his dark eyes gleaming with amusement as hers widened in shock.

'Why? Where are we going?' she asked, gathering her scattered wits. She had not given up hope of running back to England and forgetting the last disastrous and traumatic twenty-four hours, but that hope vanished as Alex straightened, all trace of amusement gone from his expression.

He stood, tall and naked but completely at ease with his nudity, as he levelled her with a hard glance. 'I am not such a fool as to give you a chance to run away, Saffron. I told you my terms; you work for your money with me,' he said starkly, his eyes hardening. 'We are going to Serendipidos where I can be assured of your safety.' One eyebrow slanted as he added silkily, 'And make sure you keep to our bargain, at least until I decide otherwise.'

She had no choice. Her heart-searching of yesterday, her conclusion that honesty was the best policy and all that, her reliance on the truth, had led her to this, she realised bitterly. If she had kept her mouth shut about the health club, if she had simply accepted what Alex had offered, and been prepared to forget his ignoble past, perhaps their marriage would have stood a chance. But now she was stuck with a husband who did not trust her, actively disliked her, and intended to keep her a virtual prisoner. A plaything to assuage his lust, and present him with an heir, his until he tired of her… 'Damn, damn, damn,' she swore.

Alex shot her a wry glance. 'Damning me won't help you, sweetheart.' And, turning, he strode off to the adjoining bathroom.

Saffron picked up the pillow and threw it after him, but it was wasted effort as it fell unnoticed and harmlessly against the closed door.

At the airport, Alex led her towards the private jet, parked some way away from the commercial flights, his strong fingers curved around her elbow, denying her any chance of a last-minute dash for freedom. He had never let her out of his sight for the past three hours, and she hoped it was not a foretaste of what was to follow.

The trouble was, she realised hopelessly, Alex had it all. The jet was simply a symbol of his success. She had heard a lot about him from his mother in the past few days; as a businessman and financier his success and wealth were apparently legendary, and Saffron, poor fool that she was, had had to go and fall in love with him.

If she had been thinking straight she might have realised the incongruity of Alex profiting from a massage parlour, but it did not occur to her until much later...

She allowed herself to be seated and barely noticed as Alex fastened her seatbelt. He must never know she loved him! That much she sadly recognised. He had married her for basically sensible reasons: lust and an heir. He did not believe in love and it would be the ultimate humiliation if he ever discovered how she really felt about him.

'Comfortable?' Alex's voice intruded on her worrying thoughts. She turned slightly, her glance skating over the proud head and hard features to rest on where his hands were deftly opening the briefcase on his lap.

'Yes, thank you,' she said politely.

'Good. I have work to do.' He wasn't even looking at her; she was already dismissed, his whole attention on the file he had taken from the briefcase.

'Plaything', he had said, and obviously meant, Saffron thought bitterly, and wondered how long she could stand the situation.

They left the plane at Athens and transferred to the helicopter, and twenty minutes later Saffron had her first view of Serendipidos.

'Your new home, Saffron; what do you think?' Alex queried, his deep voice sounding strangely remote through the headphones they were both wearing to cut out the noise of the helicopter.

She gazed out of the window at the panoramic view beneath. The blue-green sea, clear as crystal, broke into white horses around a tiny crescent-shaped island that rose steeply in the middle. It was no more than a mile square, if that; a wooden jetty stuck out like a black finger into the bay, and there were a few houses, hardly enough to call a village, and a winding white road that meandered in ever decreasing loops to the top of the hill above the bay.

'Beautiful,' she murmured appreciatively, then gasped as the helicopter circled a magnificent, long, low white villa overlooking the sea and surrounded on three sides by a high wall. In the enclosure she had a fleeting impression of gardens and terraces a riot of colour, saw the sun glinting off an oval swimming-pool, and then they were landing on the concrete pad at the rear of the house.

'I like to think so,' Alex responded to her comment, his smile one of sardonic amusement as, helping her to the ground, he added, 'And it is very private; the only way in or out is by helicopter or boat. Everything we need I have flown in. The relatives stay every year for a month or so, but most of the time we will be alone.'

'How long are we staying?' Saffron asked nervously, her agile mind very quickly digesting the fact that the island would not be easy to escape from.

'As long as it takes,' Alex murmured enigmatically, then strode towards the small dark woman rushing to meet him from the rear of the house.

As long as what takes? Saffron thought, trudging along behind him, the heat of the midday sun hitting her like a blowtorch. She was not in the least surprised that Alex no longer felt it necessary to lead her around by the arm; the arrogant oaf knew very well there was nowhere she could run to.

She stopped and watched him greet the elderly lady with a bear hug, and then shake hands with a surprisingly wizened old man whose currant-black eyes looked past Alex to where Saffron stood. His face split in an ear-to-ear grin then he said something in Greek that made Alex fling his head back and burst out laughing.

For a second Saffron was stunned by the sight of Alex, tall and casually dressed in cream trousers and a soft blue shirt, his darkly attractive face lit with laughter, the sun glinting off his night-black hair. He looked so handsome and carefree, and she felt her heart squeeze with longing for what might have been.

Introductions were over in a trice. The housekeeper and her husband, Despina and Georgos were all smiles as they led the way into the welcoming coolness of the house.

'What did Georgos say to make you laugh?' she asked as Alex ushered her into the main living-room with a hand on her back.

'Male joke; I doubt you would appreciate it.' And to her amazement he leaned towards her and kissed her slightly parted lips with a thoroughness that made her go weak at the knees. 'Come on, I'll show you around my home.'

'And my prison,' she shot back, more angry with herself because of her helpless reaction to his kiss than with him.

'It will be a prison of your own making, if you insist on being childish,' he said drily.

The house was lovely; Saffron could not pretend otherwise. The living-room and dining-room, family-room, study and kitchen all opened on to the garden and the sea but were connected by a long, wide, curving hall at the end of which an elegant marble staircase led to the upper floor.

'The hall was designed to be used as a reception area when I hold parties, or there are a lot of guests. It allows the rest of the family-rooms to be a more manageable size,' Alex informed her. 'More cosy.'

'You're hardly the cosy type,' Saffron snapped back.

He reached out and took hold of her chin, lifting it so that she had no option but to look at him. 'You will find out just what type I can be, if I have to put up with any more of your backchat, and I can promise you you will not like it.'

Her gaze was trapped by his, and she fought back the angry retort that hovered on her lips. His only visible sign of anger was the darkening glitter in his deep brown eyes, but she sensed the tension, the leashed strength, in his large body, and fear made her swallow her words.

'That's better, Saffron. You're learning,' he mocked, aware of her battle for control. Pulling her into his arms, he continued, 'Neither of us has got exactly what we expected from this union, but there's no reason why we can't behave like civilised adults.'

His knowing smile held no humour, and sent shivers of apprehension down her spine. 'No.' She drew a deep breath; held in his embrace she was much too vulnerable. The musky male scent of him, the warmth of his body undermined her self-control.

His eyes narrowed faintly as they travelled over her flushed, mutinous face. 'You are my wife and I am master in my own home. You will do as I say, and show respect to the staff, and that way we will get along just fine. Agreed?'

His grip tightened around her waist, his head bent and deliberately his breath feathered her cheek. 'Agreed?' he repeated hardly.

'Yes, yes,' she answered quickly, seconds before he kissed her thoroughly, declaring her his possession.

CHAPTER EIGHT

SUBDUED, Saffron followed Alex upstairs and into the master bedroom. She gazed around, her eyes widening in awe at the splendour before her. A huge bed on a raised dais dominated the room, the coverlet a work of art in white handmade lace, the headboard a swan with wings unfurled and incorporating side-tables, lights and what looked like a computer console. The floor was finely polished marble in a stunning white streaked with pink.

A door was standing half-open to one side and she had a brief glimpse of an equally extravagant bathroom. On the other side was another door which she imagined must lead to a dressing-room as there were no wardrobes in the bedroom, only an exquisite dressing-table, a casual arrangement of two long satin-covered sofas and an oval crystal and gold low table—minimal furniture but effective.

She turned and walked towards the large expanse of glass at the far end of the room and the balcony beckoning beyond. She slid open the door and stepped out; the heat hit her once again but she barely noticed as her green eyes filled with wonder at the view before her.

The gardens stretched out, gently sloping for about two hundred yards, and then fell away in a riot of colour, terrace upon terrace, to end on a beach of silver sand, washed by an azure sea. To the left she could just see the end of the jetty and the roofs of a few houses; to the right was simply more sand and sea, and then a sharp black cliff-face.

'It looks absolutely beautiful, and so quiet, so peaceful,' she murmured, almost to herself.

Alex had come up behind her and his arms slid around her waist, drawing her back against him, one hand holding her firm while his other slid up to cover her breast through the soft silk of the blouse she had teamed with matching cream silk trousers for travelling.

A quivering awareness darted through her as he nudged aside her long hair, his mouth sucking gently on the soft curve of her neck and then tracing up to her small ear.

'Beautiful! So are you, my sweet Saffron; pity the peace and quiet does not also apply to you.' He chuckled as his fingers found the waistband of her trousers and deftly unfastened the button, slipping down the zip, splaying out over her flat stomach. 'Come to bed,' he prompted throatily, his tongue licking gently around her ear as his other hand gently palmed her breast. 'Siesta, hmm?'

Saffron closed her eyes and bit down hard on her lip, trying to fight down the rising tide of desire that his touch evoked.

'You know you want to; why deny yourself?' Alex turned her in his arms. 'And me.' She felt his need against her belly, and hated the conflicting emotions that assailed her.

He was right, as usual, and with a low moan, half need and half despair, she curved her slender arms around his neck, urging his head down to her waiting lips.

That afternoon set the pattern for the weeks to come, though if Saffron had guessed what was to follow she would have fought harder to resist...

Saffron walked out of the sea, brushing her hair from her eyes, and ran across the beach to the shade of a large overhanging rock where she had left her towel. It was September now and the temperature was still in the hundreds, unseasonably hot; the only sensible place to be was in an air-conditioned room, but she could stand the silence of the villa no longer and, donning a brief black bikini, had ventured out in the afternoon sun.

Collapsing on the towel, her breathing heavy—she had swum longer and further than she should have—she rolled over on to her stomach and laid her head on her arms. She glanced along the deserted beach to the small huddle of houses and jetty and wondered for the millionth time how she was going to get away, or if she even wanted to...

From the first day on the island, when, in the middle of the afternoon, she had found herself on the large raised bed with Alex, who had conducted a relentless assault on her senses with a devilish expertise that had her crying out in ecstatic fulfilment, and then sunk in the depths of despair at her own degrading surrender, she had alternated between heaven and hell.

Over the weeks that had followed, she had begun to realise that the satiation which she had thought would follow quickly, and then she would be immune to him, was not about to happen. Instead, every night in the big bed she fell deeper and deeper under Alex's spell. He led her through the paths of the perfumed garden of eroticism with a hungry delight that encouraged her own surprisingly sensual nature to respond in kind. Together they found new and wondrous ways of pleasing each other until quite often the light of dawn threaded the sky before they fell into exhausted sleep.

It should have brought them closer together, but the reverse was true. In the first couple of weeks Alex had taken her shopping and to dinner in Athens a few times. She now had a wardrobe a film star would be proud of, and a diamond bracelet, and earrings to match her stunning engagement ring. Alex was lavish with money, and would not allow her to refuse whatever he offered, simply reminding her that she had married him for money, which in a way she had.

It was her own stupid fault that she had recognised that she loved him on her wedding-day and even more foolishly told him her ulterior motive for marrying him. Now she dared not tell him the truth. Instead she fought with him almost constantly. Thank God the house was isolated, otherwise everyone for miles around could hear their verbal sparring matches. As it was, Despina let her disapproval be known, even though she barely spoke English.

They had had one good day out, Saffron mused. The day he had taken her to explore the sights of Athens—the Acropolis, the Parthenon, and the ruins of the ancient theatre of Dionysus, which she had marvelled at. Then, later in the evening, when the sky was black, they had sat in the open-air theatre high above the Acropolis and watched in awe the sound and light show which illuminated the mighty Acropolis while the history of the city was told on tape by actors such as Richard Burton.

But over the past few weeks they had grown further and further apart. Saffron had not been off the island for six weeks. Alex, on the other hand, was rarely around. Every morning at eight the helicopter whisked him into his office in Athens, returning later and later at night as the weeks passed by. Last weekend he had not returned to the island at all; leaving a brief message with Despina, he had not spoken to Saffron, and had returned last night with no explanation.

Saffron had thought she was lonely before. An orphan, always on the outside looking in. But at least she had had her work her plans and ambition to comfort her. Now she was beginning to realise what true loneliness was.

She rubbed her hand idly across the moisture hazing her lovely eyes, The fact that Despina and Georgos spoke very little English did not help; she had tried walking to the jetty, but one bar, strictly for men, and a couple of houses did not make for a lively social life. A few smiles and a courteous Greek greeting and that was it. In desperation she had tried to offer Despina a make-up session and massage but had been greeted with a giggle and a no. Saffron honestly did not know how much more of this enforced idleness and brief, superficial conversations, or blazing rows with Alex, she could stand without going crazy.

Alex had arrived home after dinner last night and said curtly, 'I had a call from Mama today. She will be arriving on Friday, as will Aunt Katherina and Maria; arrange it with Despina, will you?'

Saffron, relaxing on the sofa, her legs curled under her, had looked up at Alex's entrance, and realised she had missed him. 'How?' she'd sneered mockingly. 'Sign language?' He strolled in at eleven at night without so much as an explanation and immediately began issuing orders. He was a pig...

'Cut out the sarcasm, Saffron; I'm not in the mood. I've had a hard few days.'

She had not seen him for three days, and he did looked tired; his tanned face had a greyish tinge, emphasising his rugged features. 'Have you had dinner? I could make you something.'

'I'm tired, not hungry.'

'Then go to bed.'

A grim smile tugged the corners of his hard mouth. 'Is that an invitation?' he demanded with a short, mocking laugh. 'My, we are getting bold.' And he bent over her to kiss her long and hard.

'No—no, it wasn't,' she spluttered, jumping to her feet.

'Sit down. I need a drink.' Alex walked to the array of bottles displayed on a long sideboard and poured a hefty shot of whisky into a crystal glass. He looked back over his shoulder, his dark eyes meeting hers. 'Join me in a nightcap?'

Saffron sank back down on the sofa. 'Yes, please—a small brandy and soda.'

Alex fixed the drink and handed it to her, the brush of his fingers against her own sending a too familiar tingle through her flesh. 'Thank you,' she said stiltedly, and took a swift swallow of her drink. Alex sat down beside her on the sofa, stretching the muscled length of his legs elegantly out in front of him, his head dropping back against the soft cushions, and drained his glass in one long swallow.

'I needed that. And now we need to talk.' His dark head turned slightly to the side so that he could study Saffron's delicate profile.

'What about?' she queried, shooting him a bitter glance. 'We said it all on our wedding night, I would have thought.'

'Not about us; that's not important,' he dismissed lazily, almost insolently. 'About the weekend. I do not want my mother or aunt or any other guests that may arrive upset in any way.' His hand reached out along the back of the sofa and tangled in Saffron's hair, turning her head towards him. 'In other words, Saffron, my sweet, I expect—no, demand that you keep control of that fiery temper of yours, and try to think before you open that delectable mouth in front of anyone else.'

His hand at her neck was sending shivers down her spine,

and she stiffened involuntarily. 'I do not have a bad temper,' she flared.

He laughed and took her glass and put it down, then drew her into his arms. 'Whatever. Any uncontrolled outburst and this is how I will deal with it.'

His mouth covered hers, and he began an assault on her senses that left her meekly agreeing to his demands as he carried her up to bed.

Saffron squirmed restlessly on the towel and turned over on to her back. Even thinking about it now still had the power to make her blood run hotter in her veins. Last night Alex had made love to her with a slow, aching tenderness that had left her sensually replete but with a pain in her heart that had brought tears to her eyes. They had curled up to sleep in each other's arms like two halves of a whole, and oddly enough this morning Alex had delayed his departure for Athens until nine-thirty, long enough to bring her a cup of tea in bed and share breakfast with her.

Saffron did not understand the man at all. The villain she thought him to be did not equate with the Alex of this morning. He was a complete enigma to her, and she had a growing, disturbing conviction that she would never be free of the sexual hunger, her unrestrained longing for him.

It made no sense. For twenty-five years she had managed to retain a cool outward control over her temper and her body, but in no time at all Alex had turned her into a wild, sexy woman with a lightning-quick temper. It was almost unbelievable. Except that she loved him, a little voice inside her whispered, reminding her of what she was trying so hard to forget. She loved him…

The sound of a helicopter broke the silence, and she jumped to her feet, swiftly gathering up her things. She picked up her watch and slipped it on her wrist. Only four!

She looked up and watched as the machine disappeared behind the house. Could it possibly be Alex back so early…? What was he playing at?

She walked across the sand to where the gate opened on to the first terrace and began the long climb back up to the house.

Alex met her on the lawn. 'I thought I'd join you for a swim; the heat in Athens is unbearable.'

He was stripped down to black swimming-trunks, a towel swung carelessly over one broad shoulder, his hard-muscled body gleaming golden in the sunlight, his eyes hidden from her by dark sunglasses.

'I've had a swim,' she said; she could not read his expression and it made her nervous.

'So indulge me, hmm?' And, catching her hand in his, he swept her around. 'I feel the need of some R and R, and preferably with you.' And once more Saffron descended to the beach with a heart that for some inexplicable reason suddenly felt much lighter.

They swam and frolicked in the clear blue water, and to Saffron's secret delight Alex made no effort to swim off for miles on his own as he usually did; instead they played a ridiculous game of tag and dunk, their mingled laughter and shouts of triumph at each tag echoing in the clear air, until they were both breathless and in Saffron's case almost half drowned.

Later, over a superb dinner served outside on the terrace, the house and garden aglow with hidden lights among the shrubs and trees, Saffron sighed as she drained her coffee-cup.

'Why the sigh, Saffron?' Alex queried softly.

'I was just thinking how perfect this setting is—the house, the lights, the weather—but…'

'But the company is not… Is that what you're trying to say?' he demanded hardly, the flash of anger in his dark eyes searing her to the bone.

'No, I was going to say, but I miss my work, that's all.' She did not want to spoil what had been a lovely day. She saw him visibly relax, and his dark eyes suddenly glinted with devilment.

'That's no problem.' Rising to his feet, he caught her hand and dragged Saffron to hers. 'Never let it be said that I deprive my wife of her work.' And, leading her into the house, he added, 'You can massage me any time.'

'I'd rather make you up,' she teased, not at all sure that she could massage Alex without jumping his bones.

'No way!' he exclaimed, horrified.

'Men should at the very least use a moisturiser. The old-fashioned colognes simply dry the masculine skin—no good at all,' Saffron blustered on, her pulse racing, and not with the effort of walking upstairs.

'Go bury yourself in the study, Alex. We ladies are going to have a hen party,' Anna instructed her son with the wave of a beringed hand.

Saffron could not repress a smile as she saw Alex's look of puzzlement and then his cautioning glance at herself, before he reluctantly walked off to his study. His mother, aunt and cousin had arrived for lunch, and over coffee it had been decided that Saffron would make all three of them up for tonight's dinner party. Anna had declared, 'What's the point of a beauty therapist in the family if we can't make use of her?' and Saffron had laughingly agreed.

In fact, as she carefully set out all her materials in Anna's bedroom, she could not help concluding that Anna, far from being the poor, put-upon lady she had described when telling Saffron the sad story of her husband and Katherina, was in fact a very strong-willed woman. Look at the way the two older women had arrived together today, laughing and joking and obviously intent on enjoying their holiday. It didn't make sense.

But then nothing in her life for the past few months had made much sense. If she could only turn the clock back to May and the fateful day she had agreed to leave the agency and work solely for Anna Statis—safe and secure in London, no one to worry about but herself, no one to care about but herself—would she do it? Was that really what she wanted? To live out her life alone with only her work for company, never to have felt the touch of Alex's hands, the warmth of his embrace…? Saffron shuddered.

'Are you all right, Saffy, dear?'

Saffron swung round to face the door; only Anna ever called her Saffy. 'Yes, a ghost walked over my grave. It was nothing.' She could not let the older woman discover the truth about her marriage; Alex was her son and she loved him. Pinning a smile on her face, she asked, 'Right, who's first?'

For the next hour Saffron carefully applied her skills to making first Maria look stunning then Aunt Katherina and finally Anna. The conversation was pure woman talk— clothes, make-up and of course men…

Then Katherina began recounting a tale from when her first husband was alive.

'Remember, Anna, that time all of us were in London and you and Nikos were looking for a house to buy for Alex starting college? I had met my brother for lunch—he was living in London at the time—and afterwards I met up with you there again. Don't you remember? We were walking around Trafalgar Square.'

'Vaguely,' Anna replied.

'Well, my husband was so old-fashioned.' Katherina turned laughing brown eyes on Saffron. 'Rather like your Alex about family. Anyway, to get back to the story, when I told my husband my brother's new business venture was a partnership in a health club—Studio 96—he was furious, insisting the place was a massage parlour only one step removed from a brothel. We argued, and I chased him around Trafalgar Square, and finally I shoved him into the fountain.'

'Yes, I remember now.' Anna burst out laughing. 'You were screeching, "Anyway, how the hell do you know unless you've been there?"'

'That's right.' Katherina chuckled. 'He gave me some fairy-tale about a well-known aristocrat recommending the place. Then my poor husband died a few weeks later.'

'Saffy, that was my eye.' Anna's head moved to one side as Saffron's hand jerked with the mascara brush.

'What? Yes, sorry.' Saffron was shocked. How could these respectable old ladies be so casual about something so sordid? 'But weren't you horrified?' she could not help asking Katherina.

'Horrified, yes, but I didn't believe it.'

'Oh…' was all Saffron could muster, but her facial expression must have given her away because suddenly Katherina was very serious.

'Alex will probably kill me for telling you, but every family has its black sheep and unfortunately my brother Akis was ours; he believed in sailing close to the wind, but never anything out-and-out illegal. When he died seven years ago Alex had to go to London to arrange the transportation of his body to Greece for the funeral and sort out his business affairs. I doubt if he would have told me the truth, but I had seen the accounts for the health club—very profitable—and I could not see why it had to be sold. Finally Alex confessed the place was a very expensive massage parlour on the edge of the law.'

'It never belonged to Alex,' Saffron said hoarsely, the full enormity of what she had done finally sinking into her horrified mind.

The laughter of the other three sounded like the witches in *Macbeth* to Saffron's stunned brain.

'Good God, no!' Katherina exclaimed. 'Apparently he walked in one morning, cleared the place within half an hour, then signed over my brother's share to Akis's junior partner—an Italian, I think—for next to nothing simply to get rid of it before any, however tenuous, connection could get out and affect the Statis name and Alex's impeccable reputation. Goodness knows what went on there after that.'

'Cousin Alex, owning a massage parlour?' Maria hooted. 'The mind boggles! He is so strait-laced, he once stopped my allowance for a month simply because at eighteen I shared a holiday apartment in Paris with another girl and a *boy*!'

Saffron tried to smile, to join in the obvious amusement of the other three, as she finally, with a none too steady hand put the finishing touches to Anna's make-up. Then she quickly gathered up her kit and, with a deep-felt sigh of relief, made her excuses and left Anna's room to return to the comparative safety of the master bedroom.

She dropped her make-up case on the bed and, like an automaton, slipped off her simple cotton skirt and blouse. On leaden feet she walked into the bathroom, stepped out of her briefs and unfastened her bra, letting it fall to the marble floor. She walked into the huge double shower and turned on the overhead spray, her mind in chaos. Lifting her face to the warm water, she let it wash over her, wishing it would wash her mind clear as easily.

How could she have been so dumb? He own common sense should have told her that Alex, with all his wealth, would not be bothered about a part-share in some seedy massage parlour.

'My God, what have I done?' she cried, unaware that she had said the words out loud.

The folding glass door was pushed open and a naked Alex joined her. 'What have you done?' he queried mockingly, his hands reaching out for her shoulders, holding her steady. 'Let me guess—slipped and shaved their eyebrows off.' He raised his dark brows teasingly. 'Or hopefully glued their mouths shut?' he prompted with a wry grin.

Saffron, her green eyes wide on his roughly handsome face, was suddenly struck by the realisation of how little she knew her husband. They were as intimate as it was possible for two people to be in the physical sense, and yet on a mental level she had never even tried to find out what made him tick. She had clung to her own opinion and prejudice unquestioningly. It had not occurred to her to try and delve beneath the macho, arrogant mask he presented to the world, even to consider that there might be a more sensitive soul beneath.

Her gaze slid lovingly over his broad shoulders, the massive hairy chest, his slim waist, narrow hips and long, long legs. The water cascaded over his bronzed flesh like a lover's caress, flowing over hard-packed muscle and sinew. She reached up her hand and gently outlined his firm mouth, down his chin, then trailed her fingers down into the damp forest of hair surrounding the small male nipple. He was her husband, and she...she had... She could not bear to think of what a fool she had been...

'Saffron,' Alex murmured huskily. But even as her touch aroused him, 'What is it?' he asked, recognising the change in her.

Trust, that was what she had lacked; she should have trusted him. And yet it was not entirely her fault—her upbringing had taught her to trust no one. In that second she took a great leap of faith, and, tilting back her head, looked straight up into his concerned dark eyes.

'You never owned Studio 96; that day I saw you there was the first and only time you'd been there, wasn't it?'

Alex stiffened, his fingers tightening on her shoulders, his expression suddenly bland. 'So?'

'Why did you let me believe it was yours? Why? Why did you not tell me the truth, deny my accusation?'

'Why should I? It changes nothing.'

'But it does, don't you see?' Saffron was getting desperate. 'If I had known I would never have even contemplated revenge. I would never have told you about Eve. We would have married and everything would have been fine.' How could he not understand? Her puzzled eyes searched his face.

'Everything *is* fine, my sweet Saffron,' he drawled softly, pulling her closer to him; her naked breasts snuggled into his damp body hair and hard flesh as his strong hands stroked down her back and curved over her bottom, hauling her against the taut heat of his arousal. 'Couldn't be better,' he husked against her mouth as his lips found hers.

'Wait, Alex,' Saffron murmured a long moment later. 'I want to explain.' It seemed imperative to her that she confess her foolishness in believing Alex capable of such despicable behaviour. She would get on her knees and beg his forgiveness if she had to.

He held her away from him, his darkening eyes raking

her from head to toe in a long, lingering scrutiny. The water had plastered her wild curls flat to her head, the rest straggling like rats' tails down her back. She had no idea of how desirable she looked, her small face flushed, her gorgeous green eyes pleading, her full breasts hard-tipped, pouting, and his gaze moved lower to the tiny waist, the soft flare of her feminine hips, and smooth, shapely legs. 'There is nothing to explain, Saffron,' Alex declared throatily.

'But there is,' she wailed, amazed at his denseness. 'Katherina told me all about her brother—the black sheep of the family—and the health club. If only…'

'"If only…" Really, Saffron, have we come to that—the tritest phrase in the English language?' With a snort of disgust, he stepped out of the shower stall and, collecting two towels, threw one to her. His expression grim, he hitched the other towel strategically around his hips.

'You want to talk? OK, we'll talk. Dry yourself; if I touch you again, conversation will definitely be out.' And, turning, he strode out of the bathroom.

Saffron rubbed herself dry, swiftly wrapped the fluffy towel under her arms and over her breasts sarong style, and dashed after him.

He was sitting on the edge of the bed and his dark, assessing eyes lifted to her flushed face. She walked towards him and stopped a foot away; it was strange to be looking down on Alex for a change, and somehow it gave her confidence to ask, 'Why did you not tell me on our wedding night when I accused you of…? Well, you know what.'

'Because, Saffron, I did not think it that important. I know who and what I am; the misguided opinions of other people hold no interest for me.'

'But we were married.'

'Yes, but a marriage licence did not give me licence to blacken my aunt Katherina's name.'

Saffron had never felt so small in her life; while she had ranted about Eve, her dead friend, Alex, however misguided his reasons, had remained silent to protect a female member of his family. For once, her mind clear of the guilt and chaotic emotions that had beleaguered her from first meeting Alex, she saw the man beneath the hard, sophisticated surface. How could she have been so blind? Alex was half Greek and all male; it was an integral part of his nature to protect the family, especially the female members.

She stepped forward between his knees and, reaching down, placed her hands either side of his head, her fingers tangling in the damp black hair. Tilting back his head, she bent and, for the first time in their relationship, kissed him full on his sensual lips. She put her heart and soul into it, and when she finally lifted her head Alex's hands were firmly clasped around her thighs.

'What was that for?' His eyes, holding a gleam of amusement, slanted upwards. 'Not that I'm complaining,' he drawled, and fell back on the bed, taking Saffron with him.

'Because I love you, you fool.' Saffron laughed out loud; her legs trapped between his powerful thighs, she lay sprawled across his broad chest. 'And you're too damn macho, too noble for your own good,' she teased, biting lightly down on a very tempting male nipple.

'Noble, eh?' Alex repeated with obvious pleasure. 'A vast improvement on being a crook, pimp et cetera. Noble I can live with.' And, in a lightning move, Saffron was flat on her back, her feet on the floor, and Alex was between her thighs, leaning over her.

Her slender arms looped around his neck, her heart full of love and laughter. She felt light-headed with joy. The sense of betrayal she had felt towards Eve at the pleasure she found in Alex's arms no longer existed. The man indirectly responsible for Eve's death had nothing to do with her husband. She was free, free, free...

Pulling his head down until his mouth was a breath away from hers, she whispered, 'And I can live with you, my noble Alex, my love...'

He looked at her for a moment, his face grave, questioning, as if he doubted her words. Then his mouth came down on hers, crushing her lips against her teeth in a sudden savage assault. She opened her mouth, welcoming his passion as her body arched up to him, urging the more powerful, steely invasion of his masculine form.

There was no need for preliminaries; her body was hot and waiting for him. His large hands slid down around her waist and hauled her on to him and she clung to him, buffeted by wave after wave of passion, until a tumultuous release shook her to the depths of her soul and Alex, with a shuddering cry, spilled his life force into her. For a moment his hands tightened around her waist and his lips brushed hers in a tender kiss.

Then abruptly he straightened up. 'That was not so noble of me,' he said at last, his voice low, his dark eyes intense.

Saffron smiled up at him. 'I enjoyed it; I always enjoy you,' she confessed freely, happily.

Their eyes met and clung, and then Alex's lips quirked in the beginnings of a smile. 'My spicy Saffron,' he drawled endearingly, 'I'm beginning to think I will never get enough of you as long as I live, but right now three beautifully made-up women are waiting downstairs to greet the rest of our guests—the yacht is due to dock any minute with about a dozen friends and business associates.'

'A dozen more...' She gasped her dismay.

'Not to worry, Saffron. Despina has it all under control.'

She felt a brief twinge of resentment. Obviously Alex had not thought her capable of arranging a large party, and that hurt. Did he still see her as simply a plaything? Surely not after the afternoon they had just spent together?

'Come on, we will share the shower.' He held out his hand and she trustingly took it and allowed him to pull her to her feet. 'But this time let's try and get washed, hmm?'

Half an hour later Saffron walked down the stairs on Alex's arm, her earlier doubts forgotten. She felt as though she was floating on air. Alex was magnificent in a white dinner-jacket and she knew she looked good too. She had swept her red hair up in a bunch of curls on her crown, leaving a few stray curls to hang tantalisingly on her bare shoulders. Her dress was a strapless cream wisp of silk that contrasted beautifully with her golden skin. The skirt was straight, ending just above her knees, revealing her long, tanned legs, and on her feet she wore high-heeled gold sandals. Around her slender throat hung a brilliant diamond and emerald necklace—a gift from Alex only five minutes earlier.

It was the best party Saffron had ever attended, though, as the hostess, she knew it was conceited of her to think so. Sixteen sat down at the elegant dining-table for the formal meal. The food was superb, the conversation scintillating, and everyone appeared to be having a marvellous time. Alex was at the head of the table and Saffron at the opposite end, but it did not seem to matter; she felt closer to him tonight than ever before. Occasionally their eyes would meet and a swift secret smile pass between them. He gave her confidence with just a glance.

Luckily she had Katherina and Spiros, Maria and James nearest to her, so it was not as if she was among total strangers. The rest of the guests were fashionable and wealthy and regarded Saffron with avid interest, trying to decide just what there was about her that had captured the mighty Alex. She could not suppress a smile at some of the more blatant questions, but with Alex's help managed to field them expertly.

Coffee was served out on the terrace, and the party became informal. Soft music played from strategically placed speakers and a few people elected to dance, but most settled into comfortable groups, chatting about friends and relatives, and, as with most Greek parties, the alcohol flowed as freely as the conversation.

Saffron stepped back out of the circle of light and leant against the balustrade, surveying the laughing faces of her guests—a moment's breather, she thought. Then James approached her.

'Congratulations, Saffron, on your marriage and on your first house party. You're a natural.'

'House party?' she queried. 'Dinner party surely?'

'No, Saffron, most of us are staying on the yacht, the rest here, for the next two days. Surely Alex told you?'

'Yes—yes, of course.' But he hadn't! Though she refused to let James see her embarrassment, was it pity she saw in his pale eyes?

'Don't worry, I'm a push-over for a beautiful lady. If you need any help, give me a call.'

'That's highly unlikely,' she said with a slightly forced smile. 'But thanks for the offer.'

'James, Maria needs a drink; see to it.' Alex's curt command put an end to what for Saffron was a disturbing conversation. 'OK, Saffron?' he queried, reaching her side and putting a possessive arm around her waist.

She shot him an angry glance. 'Yes, of course. Why?

Were you worried that I would be incapable of looking
after your friends for *two* days? Frightened I might disgrace
you?' she snapped, James's words lingering in her mind.

Alex muttered a curse under his breath and in full view
of everyone turned her in his arms, his hard mouth hovering
inches from hers. 'Foolish girl, you're far too sensitive, and
for what it's worth I don't think you could disgrace yourself
if you tried. You're too much a lady—my very lovely lady.'

Their breath met and mingled, and his lips, firm and
tender, moved against hers. Saffron vaguely heard the
cheers of encouragement, and not so proper comments, but,
locked in his arms, she forgot her anger and her doubt; she
knew no shame, no embarrassment, only a deep, abiding
love for the man who held her so close to his heart.

CHAPTER NINE

Two days later Anna and Saffron stood in the garden and watched the yacht carrying the guests depart for Athens.

'That was without a doubt the best house party ever, Saffy, dear,' Anna remarked complacently. 'You're a natural when it comes to putting people at their ease. Maybe it has something to do with your training. But I want you to know I couldn't have wished for a better daughter-in-law. You make Alex the perfect wife and it was obvious to everyone he loves you dearly.'

'That was your son's fault.' Saffron raised one finely arched eyebrow at Anna. 'He saw me talking to James and decided to take action.'

Anna laughed. 'Yes, a good dose of jealousy was just what my arrogant son needed to appreciate you fully. I've watched him and he has never been more than an arm's length away all weekend.'

A secret smile curved Saffron's lips. And at night he had been a whole lot closer, she thought dreamily. It was going to work; her marriage was going to be a great success, and she was slowly beginning to believe that there was such a thing as happy ever after.

Life took on a new zest. Anna was a marvellous companion, and a great raconteuse, and as October and most of November slipped by Saffron had never been so happy. The discovery that Alex had never intended to keep her a prisoner on the island only added to her respect for him. The first week of her mother-in-law's visit Saffron had been stunned when Anna had said one morning, 'Come on, let's go to Athens.'

When Saffron had said there was no transport, Anna had laughed out loud. Apparently, the male bar Saffron had not dared enter was also the local ferry. She could have walked in any time and asked the proprietor, and his son would have taken her to the mainland in his speedboat for one thousand drachma—next to nothing!

'Well, what do you think?' Saffron walked the length of the bedroom and back, an exaggerated sway to her slim hips. 'Your mother loved it.'

She had been shopping in Athens with Anna; the older woman was leaving for England the next day and had insisted on one last shopping trip, then had quite shamelessly encouraged Saffron to use her husband's credit card like a woman with ten hands, saying that Saffy needed a winter wardrobe.

With dinner over, and in the privacy of their own bedroom, she was putting on a fashion show for Alex. Fresh from the shower, he lay sprawled on the bed, a towel covering the essentials, his dark eyes following her around the room.

She glanced back over her shoulder at him. 'So…?' she prompted, slowly turning and running her hands lightly over her hips, smoothing the already figure-hugging fabric of the electric-blue jumpsuit even tighter to her body. She watched Alex's eyes darken as he followed the trail of her hands, and then lazily he allowed his glance to meander up her body, stopping at the proud thrust of her breasts, the nipples clearly outlined by the clinging wool jersey, the deep cleavage where she had left the zip only partly fastened. She was tempting him and loving it…

'So, my sweet, sexy wife,' he drawled finally, raising his gaze to hers. 'Two questions. Do you expect me to take you skiing? And as a man I'm no expert on these all-in-one things, but isn't it an effort to go to the lavatory?'

'Oh, Alex, how prosaic,' she groaned. 'Here I am trying to seduce you and you come out with a question like that.'

'I hate to disillusion you, Saffron, but most men prefer to be seduced by women in floaty bits of silk and lace underwear, not a wool suit reminiscent of a battle dress that will take some time to remove.'

'We could put it to the test,' she murmured throatily, approaching the bed and lowering the zip still further. Alex looked so good lying there, tanned and relaxed, and it had been almost twenty-four hours since the last time they had made love.

'Is this a none too subtle way of getting out of telling me how much money you've spent today?' Alex queried cynically, his dark eyes mocking her. 'Because if it is it is quite unnecessary. As I've told you before, I have money enough to last a hundred lifetimes; you don't have to pay for each item you buy with sex.'

Saffron stopped; she felt as if she had been punched in the stomach. Her green eyes sought Alex's; he had pulled himself up and was sitting propped up on the bed, the pillow at his back, and his expression was one of cool disdain. Was that what he truly thought?

All the colour drained from her face and she stared at him, unable to believe that he had said that, and some tiny devil inside her whispered, Is he right? Did I set out to seduce him tonight because of all the money I've spent? No! her heart cried in denial. It was not like that. She loved Alex with every fibre of her being.

She stepped forward, and stopped again. But all these

weeks when she had thought they were making love Alex
had never mentioned *love*. Did he see it as just sex?

'The thought never entered my head,' she managed to
say lightly, but it was beyond her capabilities to carry on
with the seduction she had planned. 'So you don't like the
blue. I must remember that,' she murmured, pulling the zip
right up to the neck before turning away from his lounging
figure, adding, 'I'll show you the rest some other time. I
need a shower.' And she escaped into the bathroom.

Two hours later she was lying in the big bed, the sound
of Alex's even breathing the only noise in the quiet room,
but sleep was elusive. In her euphoria at realising that Alex
was not the swine she had thought, she had rashly declared
her love, and somehow assumed he felt the same, but his
words this evening had burst her bright balloon of happiness.

She turned over restlessly and slid her arm around his
waist to hug him. They had made love, and it had been as
good as always—she was worrying unnecessarily, she tried
to tell herself, but sleep when it finally came was shallow
and broken.

In the morning Anna departed with Alex for Athens and
Saffron was once again virtually alone and very aware of
the isolation of her island home. She told herself she would
soon settle down, but when Alex called a couple of hours
later and told her he would not be home that night—a vital
meeting—doubts about herself and him plagued her mind.

Was she really cut out for the life of a lady of leisure,
waiting on a paradise island until her husband needed her,
her dream of her own beauty salon just that—a dream?
Strangely restless, she strolled along the beach. The summer had gone and a cold wind blew in off the sea. In a few
more weeks it would be Christmas.

Then it came to her. Why stay on the island? Alex commuted to Athens, so why couldn't she? Perhaps she could open a salon, or work in a city hospital as a clinical beautician; there were dozens of opportunities if she really sought them.

Fired up with enthusiasm and eager to discuss the idea with Alex, she returned to the house, packed an overnight bag and called the local bar to book the ferry for the mainland. She would surprise Alex, cook him dinner in his small *pied-à-terre* in Athens, and maybe tomorrow look for suitable premises. Always supposing Alex was agreeable… And always supposing he loved her…the voice of reality rang in her mind. But she refused to listen; she didn't dare because she was almost certain she had already fulfilled one part of their bargain: she needed to buy a pregnancy-test kit. But she could be a mother *and* a businesswoman!

Saffron walked into the glass and steel structure that was Alex's corporate headquarters, and went straight to the directors' lift. She walked out at the top floor and into the reception area. She had visited the office a couple of times with Alex and the secretary recognised her.

'Mrs Statis. This is a surprise. I'm not sure your husband is here.'

'It's not that important; I only wanted to collect the spare key for his apartment—I know he leaves one here.'

The young girl opened the top door of her desk and handed over the key. 'Well, you are his wife so it must be all right,' she said with a smile.

At that moment a door opened at the rear of the office and James strolled out. He stopped, his blond head going back as he saw Saffron. Did he hesitate before dashing across to take her hand, or was it her imagination?

'Saffron, lovely to see you, but what brings you here? I don't think Alex is expecting you.'

'No, I want to surprise him; I've had a great idea and I can't wait to tell him.'

'Well, he isn't here.'

'No, that's a shame; still, he did say he was busy and was going to be working late, but when he gets in touch can you tell him I'll be waiting at the apartment?'

'Apartment! Do you think that's a good idea?' James questioned, his blue eyes oddly intent on her smiling face. 'Why not allow me to take you for an early dinner and arrange for the helicopter to fly you home? I'm sure Alex really will be very late.'

Saffron's eager optimism was trickling away. Perhaps she had been a bit rash, but still it could do no harm to wait for Alex, even if it was midnight when he got back. 'No, James, really; it's nice of you to offer, but I'll be perfectly all right on my own until Alex arrives.'

'But I'm not sure I can get in touch with him. It is a very important meeting,' James responded with a strange urgency, and was it sympathy she saw in his blue eyes? Surely not...

'Look, James, don't worry,' she said over-brightly. 'I'm going to hit the shops for an hour or two. I'll be fine.'

'Here, take my card; if you need...' He stumbled over the words, most unlike his usual suave, very English self. 'If you change your mind call me at home.'

'Yes, OK.' She took the card from his outstretched hand and beat a hasty retreat. Somehow James's attitude worried her, and why, as Alex's PA, wasn't he with him, if it was such a vital meeting?

The apartment was small, with a kitchen, living-room, bathroom, bedroom and balcony. Saffron had visited it with

Alex when she had been in Athens, but only for a few minutes while he dropped off his briefcase. He had told her that Athens, although home of the Acropolis and some of the most marvellous ancient ruins in the world, was also the second most polluted city in the world. The traffic was horrendous and the smell of carbon monoxide hung in the air twenty-four hours a day. No one made it their permanent home if they could avoid it. She'd forgotten that in her rush to make plans, but it wasn't important, she told herself firmly.

With her shopping lying on the floor, a cup of coffee in front of her, Saffron settled on the sofa and, curling her feet up beneath her, felt quite at home. She heard a key turn in the lock and turned her head towards the door, a broad smile lighting her lovely face. Alex was back, and not that late after all. But when the door opened her smile vanished and her eyes widened in shock as Sylvia walked in as if she owned the place.

'Well, a visitor. What are you doing here?' the dark-headed woman asked casually, dumping a briefcase on the table in front of Saffron.

'I could ask you the same question,' Saffron shot back. She had not seen the other woman since the wedding, and she had deliberately refused to think about Sylvia's relationship with Alex, convincing herself that it was all in the past—another ostrich act, some simple explanation for Sylvia's being here, having a key… Perhaps she was delivering something for Alex. Yes, that must be it.

'I live here.'

Saffron stared, struck dumb. Sylvia lived here…in Alex's apartment. It wasn't possible. Slowly she uncurled herself and stood up; she was not going to let this woman intimidate her. She was Alex's wife.

'I don't believe you.'

The other woman, her dark eyes glittering malevolently, said, 'Follow me, if you dare,' and headed towards the bedroom door.

On trembling legs Saffron followed her, and watched as she slid back a mirrored wardrobe door to reveal a row of feminine clothes, and then quite deliberately slid back the next door, revealing more clothes, but this time Saffron could not fail to recognise a couple of masculine suits, shoes and shirts. Alex's!

'You're a fool, Saffron; you didn't really think Alex was the type to settle for one woman, did you? He only married you to please his mother. I did warn you on the yacht— you should have listened.'

'Yes—yes, I should…' Saffron whispered, and, turning on her heel, she walked back to the living-room. Her gaze grazed over the shopping she had left on the floor; the name of a pharmacy on one package brought a bitter twist to her lips. Now was not the time to discover if she was pregnant.

Picking up the parcels and her jacket, she walked out into the cold, dark night. Some time later a screech of brakes shocked her back to reality and prevented her being mown down by a huge truck.

She jumped back on the pavement and stared about her. She had no idea where she was or how far she had walked. The rain was beating down, a storm brewing, and her skirt and blouse were soaked. She put her hand in her jacket pocket, her fingers curling around the card James had given her earlier. Now his offer of assistance, the sympathy she had seen in his eyes made sense. As Alex's PA James must have known about Sylvia all along; probably all Alex's business acquaintances did—the people at the house party! Tears blurred her vision; her shame and humiliation were complete.

The little wife, his mother's choice, tucked away on the island, living in cloud-cuckoo land, imagining herself loved. What a naïve fool she had been, and she had only herself to blame.

But no more, she vowed silently, brushing the tears from her eyes. Straightening her shoulders, she glanced once again at the card in her hand. Why not? she thought. At least James could help her get back to England.

'Saffron!' James exclaimed, taking in at a glance the distraught state of the woman at his door. 'Come in. You're drenched; what happened?'

Saffron forced a brief attempt at a smile, but her lips quivered, her eyes filling with tears, and she gave up trying. 'Nothing much, James,' she said sadly. 'Nothing that can't be cured with a ticket to England on the first available flight. That's why I'm here; could you fix it for me, please?' And, walking past him, she collapsed on the first seat she reached in his comfortable living-room.

James, bless him, did not ask questions; he simply poured her a large brandy, watched while she drank it, and then directed her to the bathroom, handing her his bathrobe and instructing her to get out of her wet clothes; they could talk later. Saffron was glad of his restraint; she had the horrible conviction that if she once began talking about her marriage she would fall apart completely and irreversibly.

She had to concentrate single-mindedly on getting back to England. Standing naked under the warm spray of the shower, she chanted under her breath, 'Flight, hotel, work,' over and over again. She had been alone most of her life, except for Eve! The tears threatened again, but she clenched her teeth and refused to give in to them. Eve's last message, urging her not to let any man get to her, but to pursue her dream of starting her own business, whirled around in her mind.

She had been side-tracked from her ambition, but not any more. On the island of Mykonos she had fallen in love, flustered and flattered when Alex had likened her to a Rossini overture, but now his softly murmured comment at the time, which she had conveniently ignored, came back to haunt her. He had said that he hoped the title did not accurately reflect her as well: *The Thieving Magpie*.

He had never seen her as anything other than a greedy woman in cahoots with his mother to trap him into marriage. He had gone along with the plan because it suited him to do so. He lusted after her body. Nothing more. In fairness to him, she was forced to admit that he had never pretended it was anything else. She had fooled herself. In love for the first time in her life, and with the matter of Alex's involvement with the health club resolved, she had naïvely assumed that because she loved Alex he must love her. Talk about rose-coloured spectacles…

The last few months were a nightmare she had to forget, pretend had never happened. Deep in her inner being she had known from the start that her relationship with Alex was doomed to failure. Eve apart, she quite simply was not in Alex's sophisticated league and did not really want to be. She had been a fool to believe otherwise. The pain in her chest would fade. Hearts did not break, she told herself firmly, ignoring the ache in her own; they simply atrophied.

She stepped out of the shower, turned off the water and picked up a couple of towels from the rail. She wrapped one around her wet hair and rubbed herself dry with the other until her soft skin was red with the effort, then pulled on the robe James had given her, grimacing wryly at the colour. Black! How fitting! she thought bitterly. The death of love! The death of a marriage! The death of foolish dreams!

She must stop thinking like that, she remonstrated with herself, and, moving to the vanity basin with the mirror and wall-mounted hairdrier above, she unwrapped the towel from her head. For a second she thought she heard a ringing in her ears; probably lack of food, she told herself staunchly, and, turning on the drier, began to run her fingers methodically through her long red locks. She didn't see her reflection in the mirror; she didn't want to; instead she succumbed to the mindless task of drying her hair, oddly soothing to her shattered emotions.

Finally, her toilet complete, she stared at her reflection, sure that the traumatic events of the evening must have marked her for life. But she saw the same ginger-headed, solitary girl she had always been. Reassured, she turned to leave the room, and only someone who knew her well could have recognised the change... The green eyes, once sparkling with life, quick to flash in humour or anger, were oddly opaque; the light had died from them, and with it an intrinsic part of Saffron was lost...

She tightened the belt around her waist, rolled the overlong sleeves of the robe halfway up her arms and silently, barefoot, moved down the short corridor. She pushed open the door of the living-room. Time to face James, get his help and get on with her life...

James was sitting on a wing-chair; his blond head turned as she entered, his blue eyes flashing a negative message she didn't understand.

Slowly her gaze slid to the opposite side of the fireplace

and a long sofa. Alex! Alex was here, his black hair damp and plastered to his broad brow, his dark eyes narrowed to mere slits in the bronzed sculpture of his face, his sensuous mouth a thin slash of barely controlled fury. For a second, in the tense silence, Saffron thought she heard his teeth grinding together.

His piercing eyes raked her from head to toe, taking in the wild, freshly washed hair, the low V of the man's robe skimming her breasts, the cinched waist and the bare feet. His gaze returned to her face, and the implacable rage, the contempt glittering in his eyes would have intimidated her at any other time, but not tonight. Tonight her heart had died; she was numb, her emotions buried, as frozen as an Arctic ice-cap.

Silently Alex rose to his feet, his large hands curled into fists at his side. Idly Saffron noted that his knuckles gleamed white, and watched as his proud head turned to pin James with a lethal look.

'So this was why you told me you hadn't time to discuss the new business, James. You were entertaining my wife.'

'Entertaining, no. Saffron came for my help, nothing more.'

'And I can see what kind of help you gave her. The bitch is standing there naked beneath your robe.' Alex's hand gestured wildly to where Saffron was standing immobile as he lunged forward, towering over James. 'Stand up, you bastard, so I can knock you flat,' he roared like an enraged lion.

Saffron cried out, 'No—no, you're wrong,' shocked by the murderous look on Alex's face.

Ignoring her, Alex grabbed James by his shirt-front and hauled him to his feet; his fist shot out and knocked James straight back into the chair with a crunching blow to his face.

'Stop it! Stop it!' Saffron dashed across the room and grabbed Alex's raised fist as he prepared to repeat his action.

'Listen to your wife,' James drawled with remarkable English restraint considering his nose was pouring blood. 'One punch I'll take—the situation could be misconstrued, I'll grant you. But two and I'll retaliate,' he offered phlegmatically.

'Please, Alex,' Saffron pleaded, hanging on to his arm. 'Leave James alone.' He shook her off as he would dispense with a fly and she fell heavily to the floor, a cry of shocked pain escaping her.

Alex turned his furious gaze on her dishevelled form; her robe had fallen open to reveal a long, shapely leg. 'You conniving, enticing bitch, I should kill you,' he snarled.

For a second the breath was knocked out of her, and she gazed helplessly up at him, convinced that he would carry out his threat. It was in his voice and the wild, primitive savagery in his black eyes.

He looked at her for a long, tense moment, then, like a mask falling, his expression changed; his dark eyes went blank and only a small muscle jerking beneath the skin of his cheek revealed his inner turmoil as he added scathingly, 'But you're not worth swinging for.' With a last contemptuous glance at her sprawled body, he spun back to James. 'As for you, clear your desk tomorrow; I never want to see you again.' Then, turning to where Saffron had struggled to her feet, he snarled, 'Get dressed; we're leaving.'

She did not argue, simply stalked past him to the bathroom and hauled her damp clothes back on. Head high, she marched back into the room, and before she had a chance to open her mouth she was swung over Alex's shoulder in a fireman's lift. But by the time she realised what had happened he was out of the door and marching towards the car.

'Put me down!' she screamed, her temper flaring white-hot; she thumped his broad back with her curled fists, but it was like trying to dent steel.

'Shut up, just shut up,' Alex growled, flinging her into the front seat of the car and slamming the door. She made to get out again, but he was too fast; in seconds he was in the driving seat and hurtling the car through the city traffic like a man possessed.

She fastened her seatbelt then glanced at him with cold, furious eyes. How dared he suggest for one minute that she and James…? Deceitful, debauched son of Satan! she cursed silently. 'Bloody Neanderthal brute,' she swore out loud. She shot forward as the car screeched to a halt, only her seatbelt saving her from hitting the windscreen.

Alex's hard hand caught her chin and turned her face towards his. 'Don't you ever swear at me again. I won't tolerate any more from you,' he grated, his hand on her face shaking with the force of his rage.

'That's rich coming from you,' she shot back. 'At least my meeting with James was perfectly innocent.' Not like his permanent arrangement with Sylvia, and as she remembered her reason for going to James in the first place the anger that had consumed her for the past half-hour vanished. What was the point?

'*Innocent*?' he sneered with cynical disbelief. 'Wearing only the man's robe? What do you take me for—an idiot…?'

She opened her mouth to respond, but Alex locked the words in her throat as he covered her mouth with his own;

his fingers dug into the flesh of her jaw while his mouth ground against hers in a raging travesty of a kiss, forcing her lips against her teeth, stealing the breath from her body until she thought she would choke.

For once her body did not respond in its usual wanton way. She felt nothing but horror and disgust as his other hand closed over the damp material of her blouse and roughly kneaded her breast until finally, as he sensed her lack of response, with a muffled curse, his hands dropped from her face and breast and she fell back against the seat, gasping for breath, her green eyes stormy with suppressed fury.

'Sated by James... But not for long. I know your wanton ways too well,' he opined with sneering sarcasm, and, swinging back to the steering-wheel, he started the car again.

Saffron curbed the angry impulse that made her want to scream her hurt and rage at his hateful face; instead she closed her eyes, blocking him from her view as she blocked him from her heart. Where he was taking her she didn't know and didn't much care. The marriage was over; he could keep his Sylvia and good luck to them. The side of himself Alex had displayed tonight had horrified her and only confirmed what she had already decided, what she had always known... She was better off on her own...

CHAPTER TEN

TEN minutes later Saffron was strapped into the helicopter and Alex was at the controls. The rain lashed the reinforced glass and the wind buffeted the fragile fuselage. 'Isn't it rather stormy for flying?' she asked icily, pulling her soaking clothes around her shivering flesh.

'If we go, we go together. Till death us do part and all that—something you have obviously forgotten,' Alex responded with mocking cynicism.

Saffron shot him a furious glance and pressed her lips together. Let him play his two-faced game, she thought. She knew he had kept Sylvia as his mistress, and to try and tar her—Saffron—with the same brush was simply despicable and not worth denying.

She felt some sympathy for James. He did not deserve to lose his job because of her, and on the short, stormy flight to Serendipidos she resolved that when she had finally left the island for good, which she fully intended doing at the first opportunity, a letter exonerating James must be one of her first priorities.

By the time she was standing once more in the reception hall of the villa, Saffron was frozen to the bone and shivering from head to foot.

'For God's sake, woman, do you want to get pneumonia?' Alex exclaimed, and, picking her up yet again, he carried her upstairs and into the bathroom. Ruthlessly he stripped her naked, his face like thunder as he turned on the shower tap and pushed her beneath the hot, reviving jets. 'Can you manage or shall I help?'

She tossed her head back, her green eyes burning with bitter resentment. 'No way,' she snapped back, but her chattering teeth rather spoiled her defiant attitude.

Alex stared at her naked, shivering form for a tense, angry moment, then spun on his heel and strode out of the bathroom, the violent crashing of the door making even the shower spray quiver.

The next day, Saffron awoke from a deep sleep to the sound of the helicopter departing. She stretched out a hand to where Alex had lain, as she did every morning, seeking the security and comfort of his lingering warmth, when it hit her! It was finished, over. She hauled herself up into a sitting position and glanced across the wide bed to the other pillow; it was smooth, unused.

She should be grateful, she told herself; at least Alex had had the decency to sleep somewhere else last night. After her shower, exhausted by the day's events, she had crawled into bed, her body warm, her heart a frozen lump in her chest.

A cross between a yawn and a sigh escaped her as, swinging her feet to the floor, she slipped out of bed and moved to the window. The sky was a uniform grey; it fitted her mood exactly. She glanced down at the garden; the ravages of the storm were very evident—broken branches scattered the lawn and the flowers still blooming in November were now flattened to the earth. A bit like herself, she thought sadly.

She glanced at the sea; it was cold and black, but calm. She could leave today; there was nothing to keep her here any more. Alex had never cared for her. Oh, he had raved when he'd found her with James, but it had not been out of jealousy or any real emotion. It had simply been a male reaction to an apparent blow to his ego.

Saffron turned and walked across to the dressing-room, the set of her shoulders taut and somehow lonely. Slowly she packed her case with her own clothes, barely glancing at the things Alex had bought her, pushing them to one side without a thought. She felt nothing. Zombie-like, she washed and dressed in blue jeans and a wool shirt—ideal for travelling. She carried her case and holdall into the bedroom, placed her navy reefer jacket over the top, and then picked up the telephone.

She rang the airport, and within minutes was booked on a flight from Athens to London leaving that afternoon. She glanced at her wristwatch; it was nine-thirty, so she had plenty of time.

Despina gave her a funny look as she walked down the stairs carrying her bags. 'You go?' she said in fractured English.

Saffron simply smiled, a twist of her lips that did not reach her eyes, and strode into the kitchen. She helped herself to coffee and sipped it slowly, staring blankly out of the window. Her stomach rumbled loudly. I must eat something, she thought, trying to remember the last time she had eaten. Yesterday morning.

She eyed the loaf of bread that had been left on the table, strode over and cut off a chunk. She chewed the tasteless fare, her small face pale, her green eyes remote as she did so.

Five minutes later she walked out of the house with her belongings and never looked back.

The bar was almost empty, except for the proprietor. Saffron calmly requested a ride to the mainland. He gave her a puzzled look, but instructed his son to get the boat ready.

With a soft, 'Thank you,' Saffron sat down on a hard-wood chair at a precariously balanced plastic table. She stacked her bags next to each other and then checked her purse. She had money and her passport; everything was in order. Soon, very soon, it would all be over…

The bar door swung open; the boat had arrived. She half rose, glancing sideways at the open door, and sank back down on the seat as Alex walked in.

His dark gaze flicked over her still form, and on down to where her cases stood. 'Going somewhere?' he asked flatly.

'I didn't hear the helicopter,' she murmured, her eyes going to his hard face. He looked dreadful—unshaven, his eyes sunken in their sockets, his mouth a grim narrow line, like a man who had not slept for a week.

Alex stared at her. 'I came across on the yacht.'

'The yacht?' she parroted, unable to think clearly. She had her departure planned, and it did not include seeing Alex again.

Alex stepped closer and stopped, thrusting his hands into the pockets of his faded jeans, pulling the fabric taut across his muscular thighs.

Saffron's eyes followed his actions and incredibly her frozen heart jerked painfully inside her. 'I'm just leaving,' she said quickly.

'Yes, I know.' Alex moved and, bending, picked up her case and bag. 'Let me help you.' And before she could object he was striding out of the door.

She leapt to her feet and dashed after him. 'No, wait. I can manage…' Her voice petered out as she saw the yacht moored alongside the jetty and Alex standing on the gang-way leading to the *Lion Lore*.

He turned; his burning dark eyes raked over her. 'I can't,' he said in a gruff voice. 'Get on board or I'll carry you.'

She closed her eyes briefly. This cannot be happening, she told herself, but when she opened them again Alex was still waiting. She glanced at the silent men standing around. Obviously they had been awaiting the arrival of the yacht to assist in the mooring. She had never looked out to sea. What an idiot! There was a long, intense silence; only the lapping of the water against the jetty broke the quiet. It was as if everyone was watching to see what would happen next.

'Saffron…' Alex's voice cracked like a whip.

She looked at him. 'A lift to the mainland,' she prompted, in an attempt to preserve some pride, and forced herself to move. She flinched as he placed a large hand under her elbow and urged her on board. He glanced at her and withdrew the hand as soon as they reached the deck.

'Go below; there isn't a full crew and another storm is brewing. I have to help.'

Her arm stung from his touch. No, please, God, no! she prayed; she did not want to feel again. Not ever… On leaden feet she walked along the deck and into the main cabin; collapsing on a softly upholstered sofa, she folded her arms defensively across her chest, and was not aware that she was rubbing the elbow he had touched with her hand.

She heard the heavy throb of the engine. She felt the motion of the boat. Not long now and she would be on a flight back to England, she told herself optimistically; then the hair on the back of her neck prickled. She turned her head.

Alex was standing blocking the door, his raw physical presence somehow filling the room. He was watching her with narrowed eyes, his expression unreadable, yet the menace, the iron will behind the impassive face warned that this man was not used to being thwarted by anyone, and certainly not by a woman—especially his wife!

Saffron swallowed nervously. 'What time do we arrive?' she asked—anything to break the fraught silence.

'We already have.' And in a voice as cold and calm as the Arctic he continued, 'We have a deal, you and I—my money for your body and a child; nothing has changed except that I intend to keep you on the yacht until you have fulfilled your part of the bargain.'

She had once compared him to a pirate, and looking at him now, standing barring the door, rock-solid and indomitable, she knew she had been right. 'I don't believe this!' she murmured softly, shaking her head.

'Believe it; you have no choice.'

'Do you honestly expect me to stay with you after last night?' He kept a mistress in Athens and he actually thought he could wield his power and money to pressure her into accepting his infidelity and carrying on as his wife. He was insane!

'You should be grateful it was your lover I punched out. I've never hit a woman in my life, but last night I came pretty close.' His lips twisted in a cynical parody of a smile. 'I blame myself; usually when I make a contract I'm meticulously thorough. In our deal I forgot to stipulate fidelity—an oversight on my part, but one you will never get another chance to exploit.'

Saffron stared at him white-faced, but deep inside the numbness that had encased her for the past few hours was melting and fury was growing, a smouldering anger fed by pain at his betrayal, a pain so sharp that she struggled to breathe. The two-faced, arrogant swine! she thought.

Suddenly her temper snapped. In a blue fury she got to her feet and covered the space between them in a flash, her small hand curved in a fist aimed straight at his jaw.

His hand fastened on her wrist, and her knuckles harmlessly brushed his cheek as he forced her arm behind her back, hauling her tightly against his hard body. 'You little hellion,' he grated between his teeth. 'I'll show you.'

But Saffron was past caring what he said or did. 'You forgot fidelity!' she screeched. 'Don't make me laugh! I know! Do you hear me? I know, you two-timing, sanctimonious pig! James was never my lover, never; I went to him for help after finding your bloody mistress living in your apartment.'

She was free so suddenly that she stumbled back. His hands caught her shoulders to steady her, and his black eyes fastened on her flushed and furious face with a puzzling intensity. 'You went to the apartment last night? What for?' he demanded.

'Not to find Sylvia, that's for sure,' she shot back scathingly.

His grip tightened for a second then relaxed. 'You were looking for me.' An intensely speculative look gleamed in his dark eyes. 'And you found Sylvia.' His hands kneaded her slender shoulders. 'You were jealous.' A hint of a smile curled his lips. 'You were jealous and furious and ran out into the rain, and that's when you sought out James,' he surmised triumphantly, his eyes never leaving her face. 'Have I got it right?'

He was far too astute; he saw far too much, Saffron thought bitterly. 'Bully for you—a regular Sherlock

Holmes, no less.' She shrugged. 'So what? It doesn't matter any more.'

'No?' he queried softly. 'I think it does. I think you and I need to talk.'

'We have nothing to talk about. It's over,' she snapped back, and at that moment the yacht hit a large wave and Saffron fell forward hard against him; she felt his body tense to keep their balance, and suddenly she was swept up in his arms and he was striding purposefully across the room and up the gangway to his stateroom.

'Put me down,' she commanded, but she instinctively curved her arm around his neck to prevent herself falling and the numbness that had cushioned her for the past few hours melted completely, an electric awareness jolting through her body. His face so near to hers, the subtle male scent of him, the steady rhythm of his heartbeat were so achingly familiar; she loved the man, and the hurt he had caused her was like a knife shredding her heart.

Alex opened the door and backed into his cabin still holding her. 'Please let me go,' she pleaded, and she meant for good. She could stand no more pain; her emotions were raw, her pride in tatters.

'Never, Saffron,' Alex murmured, and he lowered her slowly down his long body, but kept his arms firmly around her.

She was trapped. She tried to wriggle free, and gasped as she felt the telling stirring of his arousal against her belly. With one hand he stroked up her back and tangled his fingers in her hair, forcing her to look up into his dark, brooding face.

'Sex is no solution,' she said, recognising the deepening gleam in his brown eyes and determined not to give in to his potent masculine appeal, even as her body ached to do so.

'No, but love is!'

'What would you know about love? You've had more women than hot dinners—a mistress, a wife—even your own mother is frightened of you!' Saffron lashed back, staring up at him with unconcealed belligerence. He had the nerve to mention love to her! He didn't know the meaning of the word. His wealth and looks, his confidence and power assured that he always had a willing woman in his bed. He didn't need love, didn't understand the concept. And she had been an idiot to imagine for a moment that she could change him.

'I love you.' He smiled without humour. 'Though I don't expect you to believe me.'

Saffron blinked. Had she heard right? Her eyes flashed up, wide and wondering. He avoided her gaze, his long lashes shielding his eyes but not quite masking the unfamiliar vulnerability in their black depths.

'I know I've treated you badly, but you must listen. Allow me to speak in my own defence.' And with a quick return to his usual self he pinned her with a look of arrogant authority. 'You're my wife—you owe me that much.'

Intrigued, and with a glimmer of hope in her shattered heart, Saffron said, 'So talk.'

'Can we sit down first?' he asked, and she allowed him to lead her to the bed. They sat side by side, not touching.

'When I first met you, you attacked me, infuriated me and entranced me all at the same time. I thought I was too old for love, didn't really believe in it. I told myself it was simply sex, a fierce chemical reaction whenever I was near you. I was determined to have you in my bed.'

'I remember.' Saffron smiled slightly as the image of a

near-naked Alex the first morning on the yacht rose up to tempt her.

'Yes. Well.' Alex turned slightly and, lifting his hand, brushed a few golden curls from her brow. 'A red headed vision of loveliness, you fascinated me so much that I didn't care if you were another of my mother's traps. In my conceit I thought it was only a matter of time before you fell into my arms. But you proved me wrong.'

If only he knew, she thought, that from the first day she'd been aching for him. She lowered her eyes, her gaze fixed on her hands clasped in her lap. 'A first for you, no doubt,' she said with a tinge of sarcasm. She wanted to believe him, but…

'Damn it, look at me, Saffron!' The forceful command surprised her, and her eyes flashed to his as he grasped both her hands in his much larger ones. 'Cut the sarcasm and give me a chance. Give us a chance.'

'Us'. His voice was persuasive, deep and soft as velvet. She looked at him and oh, how she wanted to trust him!

'You were a first for me, a woman who wasn't mine for the taking. I had never had that trouble before. I'm a wealthy man; women fall over themselves for my money, and I thought you would be the same.'

'You believe I am the same,' Saffron could not help inserting. 'Your deal said as much.'

Alex turned her hands over in his, his thumbs rubbing her palms, sending tremors of delight through her. 'I said a lot of things I didn't mean.' He raised his dark eyes to her face. 'But you drove me to it, Saffron. When you left Greece for London, I told myself it didn't matter, I would see you again, but the very next day I was telephoning you. I missed you. But I was still not prepared to admit it was anything more than sex, even when I followed you to

London and took you out to dinner and back to my apartment. It was only when you walked out that night after demanding marriage that I began to worry.'

'You, worry?' Saffron could not imagine anything bothering the indomitable Alex.

'Yes; I'm as human as the next man. Very human,' he husked, and, lifting her hands, he pressed a kiss on each palm.

'No. You said talk; the truth.' Saffron knew they had to get everything out in the open; there could be no secrets between them if their marriage was to have any chance at all.

'Yes.' He smiled grimly. 'The truth. I spent a sleepless night, and convinced myself marriage was a good idea. A good deal. I was nearly forty, it was time I thought of an heir, it would make my mother happy, and I got you in my bed. I refused to admit to myself it was anything more. Even when I proposed the next day I was still deluding myself.'

Saffron knew all about delusions; hadn't she suffered from the same virus, with her stupid plot for revenge? 'Alex…'

'Let me finish, Saffron—now, while I have the nerve. I spent all last night preparing this speech and I have to do it.'

This was an Alex she had never seen before—her all-powerful husband was uncertain, nervous, even contrite! 'Go on,' she prompted softly.

'On our wedding-day, putting the ring on your finger, I was exultant. Arrogantly I congratulated myself on having got the girl I wanted, desired above all others, without having to admit I was in love. I couldn't wait to get you alone in Paris. But my devious desire backfired spectacularly on our wedding night when you told me the reason behind your demand for marriage.'

She gazed up at his sombre face and saw the lingering trace of remembered pain in the depths of his dark eyes. How could they have got it so wrong? she asked herself, moisture glazing her eyes. 'I accused you of being little better than a pimp,' she said with a regretful shake of her head.

'I could have killed you then.' Alex's eyes flashed briefly with remembered anger. 'That the woman I was finally beginning to realise I loved could think so badly of me, that I could be so easily deceived only proved what I had always known: love made one vulnerable and was to be avoided at all costs. But I couldn't let you go, I wanted you too much, so I suggested our bargain.'

'Suggested? Ordered more like,' Saffron corrected him, then lifted her hand from his and reached up to stroke her slender fingers down his hard cheek. He had said he loved her again. Perhaps it was her turn to be brave and take a chance, try to explain.

'I confessed the truth on our wedding night not because I wanted revenge, but simply because I knew I loved you, and I couldn't go through with a marriage made for all the wrong reasons. I think I secretly hoped that if I could forgive the fact that you owned the club that destroyed Eve and you could forgive my stupid bid for revenge then maybe we could start again.'

'You loved me then?' Alex queried in amazement. 'Enough to think that badly of me and still forgive me?' His voice was hoarse and, slipping an arm around her narrow shoulders, his free hand covering hers where it rested on his cheek, he continued, 'You humble me with your love and compassion, Saffron, and to think I repaid you by making love to you on our wedding night in anger. Hurting you, destroying your love. I'm sorry.'

'Don't be.' Safe in his arms with his avowal of love echoing in her heart, she freely confessed, 'You didn't hurt me; it was the most wonderful experience of my life. I enjoyed it.'

'That has been part of my trouble,' Alex said ruefully. 'I enjoy you too much. I've never known or imagined a woman like you. In my arms, in our bed, you're so beautiful, so passionately responsive, you make me lose all control. It frightens me.'

'It's the same for me,' Saffron murmured.

'But don't you see?' he swept on. 'Because sex between us was so fantastic, when I got you on Serendipidos, in my conceit, I smugly concluded that our deal was perfect and much better than mushy avowals of love. You were great friends with my mother and I was your first and only lover; there was no way you would leave me.'

'Modesty becomes you,' she said drily.

His smile was wry as he lowered his head and kissed her softly. 'Jackass springs to mind,' he derided himself, before adding in a much more serious tone, 'But last night, seeing you in James's apartment, I was knocked right off my axis, my supreme arrogance destroyed. By sheer chance I had called there, and to find my half-naked wife coming out of the bathroom...' He shook his head as if to banish the image.

Quick to reassure him, Saffron said, 'Nothing happened, Alex; I arrived half an hour before you, soaked to the skin and in tears. I asked James to arrange for me to return to England immediately. Instead he gave me a stiff drink and told me to get out of my wet clothes and then we could talk. You know the rest.'

'God, yes! I saw red and hit him, but even in my rage the worst part, the thing that ripped my pride to shreds, was the fact that I never for a second considered letting you go. I didn't care if he was your lover.' His dark gaze burned into hers as he amended quickly, 'No, I did care, I was absolutely gutted, but there was no way in the world I could live without you. Never to have you in my arms again, to bury myself deep in your feminine softness... Ego, pride, you could trample on the lot and I still couldn't let you go. I love you...'

Saffron's eyes widened. She had longed for his love for so long and had tried to believe that it was possible. But she hadn't dared hope for anything like this. Her dynamic, powerful husband was laying his heart at her feet. She leant towards him. 'I lo—' But she stopped as the reason for her distress the previous evening came back to taunt her.

Alex, sensing her hesitation, pulled her up and on to his lap, his arms tightening fiercely around her. 'You don't have to say you love me. Not now. I simply want the chance to win your love.' His dark eyes searched her beautiful but wary face. 'I will in the end; I'm a determined man and I'll never give up, supposing it takes a lifetime.' His hand slipped beneath her shirt and stroked up her back while his other hand caught her chin and turned her face to his. 'How can I persuade you to take a chance on me?'

'I went to Athens yesterday to surprise you, and hopefully talk you into letting me go back to work.' Saffron burst into speech, refusing to give in to the seductive trail of his hand on her bare back. 'The island is quiet in the winter; I was feeling lonely and it seemed a good idea at the time—until I went to the apartment and discovered you shared it with Sylvia.'

All his protestations of love faded against the incontrovertible truth, Saffron realised sadly. Sylvia was his mistress. She had seen it with her own eyes on this very yacht, outside this very cabin, never mind last night.

She attempted to slide off his lap but with easy strength Alex held her close and, falling back on the bed within seconds, she was flat on her back, Alex leaning over her, his lower body imprisoning hers while his hands rested either side of her head.

'It's no good denying it, Alex. I saw your clothes next to hers in the wardrobe.'

'Saffron, darling, I'm flattered by your jealousy but I swear I have never, ever made love to Sylvia. In fact I have never so much as looked at another woman since the moment I saw you. A few of my clothes may still be in the wardrobe, but I have never stayed there with Sylvia or any other woman. I offered Sylvia the use of the apartment for the rest of her stay in Greece simply because she told me she was tired of living in a hotel, and as it was my fault she had to stay here to oversee the selling of the health club chain I thought it was the least I could do. I moved out to a hotel.

'In a way it was your fault. I'm off-loading the health clubs so you can't possibly think, even for a second, I would be involved in anything so seedy as a massage parlour.' He grinned cheekily. 'Anyway, I hope to keep my own personal masseuse.'

Saffron was stunned by his action but still found it hard to forget Sylvia so easily.

Seeing the uncertainty in her eyes, Alex lowered his head, his hard mouth brushing gently over her brow, down her nose and finally touching her lips. 'Think, Saffron. We have never spent a night apart since Aunt Katherina revealed I was not the villain you thought.'

He was right but she still wasn't convinced. 'Alex, I know you and Sylvia were once lovers.'

'Rubbish.' He bit the tip of her chin gently. 'Forget Sylvia; I love you and right now I want you quite desperately.'

Saffron sighed softly, her pulse speeding as Alex moved his long legs either side of hers, allowing her to feel his urgency. 'When we were cruising I saw Sylvia leaving your cabin early one morning,' she got out breathlessly.

Alex reared back. 'Never.'

'Don't lie to me, Alex. I walked into the hall one morning and Sylvia was leaving your cabin.'

'Saffron, I swear to you she had not spent the night with me. For God's sake, you know I spent the whole of the cruise trying to get you into bed; how could I look at another woman?'

That much was true, Saffron allowed.

'I don't know why the damned woman was at my door, but I'm telling you the truth.' His dark eyes bored down into hers, his expression grim. 'Sylvia's leaving my employ next week, she's going to work for the new owners, but before she does I'm damn well going to get to the bottom of this.' He rolled on to his side and sat up, shoving his hand distractedly through his black hair. 'I don't know how to convince you, but I will,' he said adamantly, with a swift return to his usual masculine arrogance.

Saffron tried to sit up, but he shoved her back among the pillows. She saw his shoulders coming near, the determined light in his black eyes, and she lifted her hands to his chest in an effort to restrain him. She refused to let him convince her with sex. It was too important.

'Saffron?' he rasped in query.

She looked at him, his jutting chin, the firm line of his jaw, and she almost believed him, wanted to give in to the promise in his eyes. But she remembered just how hard and insensitive he could be, even resorting to violence with James.

'Your own mother told me you always took one or more of your women on the family cruise.' And, determined to air all her grievances, Saffron added, 'And she didn't dare tell you that your father loved Aunt Katherina.'

She stopped. She should not have said that; she knew Anna had a great ability to be economical with the truth. She waited, holding her breath, expecting Alex to explode, but instead, to her absolute amazement, he threw his head back and laughed out loud.

'My God, I should have guessed; dear, demented Mother.' And, gathering her in his arms, he rolled across the bed, swinging her on top of him.

Sprawled across his hot, hard body, his arms tightening around her, she could only gasp, 'Demented?' Alex was the only demented person around here, she thought as he continued to laugh.

'Saffron, my sweet, naïve Saffron,' he teased, and she glared down at him, only to be rewarded with a swift kiss on her full lips. 'Surely you've realised by now that my mother is the original drama queen?'

'Drama queen?' she murmured. Alex's amusement and the surge of desire that went through her at his kiss, and his hand stroking up and down her back as she lay against him, were hazing her brain.

'My mother, much as I love her, can't help herself,' Alex said, and, finally controlling his amusement, he continued, 'She was a dancer when she met my father, but her ambition was to be an actress. My father worshipped the ground she walked on, and if anything was far too indulgent. He listened to her dramatic stories, put up with her trips to London for the theatre, the opera, the art.

'She probably told you the old story of Aunt Katherina and my father; it was nothing. Katherina dated my father twice, met his brother and that was it, but Mama likes to embroider the truth; she can't help herself. I should have stopped her years ago, but, like my father, I tend to indulge her. I was eighteen when I had to take over the running of the family, and I can tell you that looking after three women—my mother, aunt and cousin—is no joke; I would rather run a multinational business any day.'

Saffron believed him. Hadn't she been puzzled by the easy friendship of the two women on Serendipidos? 'The chopstick poet,' she murmured.

'Exactly; that sounds like Mama.' An affectionate smile curved Alex's mouth. 'You can't believe half she tells you, and the rest is usually a vast exaggeration. But I love her.' His voice thickened as his hand slipped under the waistband of her jeans, curving her bare bottom. 'And I love you, quite desperately, Saffron. Believe me.'

She did... It was in character, Saffron realised, for Alex to allow Sylvia the use of the apartment. He had been taking care of women all his life, and, thinking back to the morning on the yacht, she had not actually seen Sylvia leave his cabin; she had been standing with her hand on the door. In that moment Saffron acknowledged that there were some things she would have to take on trust. The decision made, she smiled, a wide, beauteous curve of her full lips.

'I do believe you, Alex, and I do love you,' she said simply, her green eyes, soft and full of emotion, gazing down on his darkly handsome face. Tomorrow, she would use that test and, God willing, she would be able to give him the greatest gift of love—a child.

'Saffron, my darling,' Alex husked, pulling her head down to his and kissing her with all the urgency and pent-up emotion of a man starved of love for years, instead of only one night.

Clothes were discarded in frantic haste as they rolled around the wide bed in a tangle of arms and legs, mouth seeking mouth, hands touching, caressing, teasing, tormenting, until finally Saffron lay beneath her husband's taut, poised body, shaking on the brink of completion. 'Please, Alex,' she pleaded. 'Now.'

Alex raised his head, his eyes glowing with an incredible warmth and passion as his broad chest rubbed over the throbbing fullness of her breasts. 'Now—' He joined with her. 'Now and forever I will love you, in this world and through all eternity,' he declared thickly as finally he moved slowly and deeply, his great body claiming her, fulfilling her wildest dreams.

Sara Craven was born in South Devon, and grew up surrounded by books in a house by the sea. After leaving grammar school she worked as a local journalist, covering everything from flower shows to murders. She started writing for Mills & Boon® in 1975. Apart from writing, her passions include films, music, cooking and eating in good restaurants. She now lives in Somerset. Sara Craven has appeared as a contestant on the Channel Four game show *Fifteen to One* and is also the latest (and last ever) winner of the Mastermind of Great Britain championship.

Look out for Sara Craven's next passionate read:
MISTRESS AT A PRICE
Coming in June 2004, in Modern Romance™!

THUNDER ON
THE REEF
by
Sara Craven

CHAPTER ONE

SHE knew, of course, that she was being watched.

In normal circumstances, it wouldn't have bothered her too much. She was accustomed, even hardened, to the effect her spectacular looks had on people. She'd even learned to live with the flash of cameras when she appeared in public, and the resulting pictures in glossy magazines. 'Sir Edwin Gilmour's lovely daughter.'

Macy's mouth curled in self-derision. At one time that had seemed the only identity she possessed. But not any more. She was someone in her own right now, with a life—a career that had been almost a salvation.

And that was why she was here on Fortuna—to prove to Cameron and her father and the rest of the board at Gilmour-Denys that the nursery slopes of property negotiation were behind her, and she could handle deals even as tricky as the purchase of Thunder Cay promised to be.

And the last thing she needed was to be recognised at this stage in the game, she thought with irritation as she sipped her iced tea, and tried to ignore the prolonged and intense scrutiny she could feel being directed at her from the other side of Fortuna Town's bustling Main Street.

Because any negotiations for Thunder Cay were to be strictly confidential. The unexpected tip-off Sir Edwin had received had made that clear. Any hint that the island might be on the market would bring other types of shark to those normally inhabiting Bahamian waters thronging around.

'And we have to be first,' he'd said with intensity. 'Our syndicate wants that land, and I—I need this deal, Macy.' For a moment there was a note of something like desperation in his voice. She'd stiffened in alarm, her eyes searching his face, questions teeming in her brain, but, after a moment, he'd continued more calmly, 'I'd go myself, of course, but if I was spotted it would give the game away immediately. So it's all down to you, my dear.'

She'd said, 'No problem,' with more confidence than she actually possessed.

The elaborate model for the hotel and leisure complex which would turn Thunder Cay into the Bahamas' latest and most expensive resort had graced the penthouse office at Gilmour-Denys for a long time now.

Privately, Macy had termed it the Impossible Dream, because Boniface Hilliard, the reclusive millionaire who owned Thunder Cay, had always adamantly refused to sell. She'd been convinced he never would.

Yet in the last week, a whisper had reached Edwin Gilmour's ears from some grapevine that the old man, a childless widower, was said to be ill, and prepared to discuss the disposal of some of his assets.

Thunder Cay wouldn't be the only item up for grabs, Macy thought. There was the fortune he'd made from investment worldwide, and the mansion Trade Winds, overlooking the best beach on the south side of Fortuna itself.

But the bulk of his massive estate wasn't her concern. All she had to do was convince his lawyer, Mr Ambrose Delancey, to recommend Gilmour-Denys's bid for Thunder Cay to his client. For someone apparently prepared to negotiate, Mr Delancey had proved annoyingly elusive. She'd spent three fruitless days so far, trying to make an appointment with him.

Ostensibly, of course, she was a tourist, booked into Fortuna's main hotel, using her mother's maiden name Landin as an added precaution. She'd thought she'd be safe enough. Fortuna, after all, wasn't one of the most fashionable islands of the Bahamas. It didn't appeal to the jet-setters and generally well-heeled who thronged to New Providence and Paradise Islands, and there were no *paparazzi* eagerly face-spotting around the bars and cafes on Main Street, or the bustling harbour area.

On the whole, it was a man's resort, a haven for the big-game fishermen who came to chase the blue-

fin tuna, the sailfish aṉ 1 the blue marlin by day, and
enjoy a nightlife more lively than sophisticated when
darkness fell.

Accordingly, Macy had deliberately played down
her appearance, choosing a plain navy shift dress,
with matching low-heeled leather sandals, as well as
concealing her cloud of mahogany-coloured hair under a bandanna, and masking her slanting green eyes
behind an oversized pair of sunglasses.

And yet, incredibly, it seemed she'd still been recognised. Damn and blast it, she thought with exas-
peration.

She ventured a swift, sideways glance across the
busy road, searching between the slow-moving hurly
burly of carts, street-vendors' bicycles, and luridly
hued taxis.

She saw him at once, lounging against an ancient
pick-up, its rust spots held together by a virulent yellow paint-job. He was tall, with a shaggy mane of
curling dark hair, the upper part of his face concealed
behind sunglasses as unrevealing as her own, the
lower hidden by designer stubble. But even from a
distance she could see his teeth gleam in a smile of
totally cynical appraisal.

The rest of him, Macy noted, bristling at the implications of that unashamed grin, was bronze skin
interrupted by a sleeveless denim waist-coat, and
matching trousers raggedly cut off at mid-thigh.

He was as disreputable as his tatty vehicle, she

thought with contempt, averting her gaze. A later-day Bahamian pirate turned beach-bum. She supposed that, as a woman sitting alone at a pavement table, she was obvious prey for his kind. Nevertheless that prolonged, oddly intense observation made her feel uneasy—restless, almost unnerved.

Idiot, she thought, glancing at her watch, then signalling to the waiter, as she finished her tea. She was out of here anyway. It was time to find her way to the office of Ambrose Delancey, attorney-at-law.

As the bill was placed in front of her, a shadow fell across the table. A tanned hand dropped a scatter of loose change on to the folded slip in the saucer.

And a voice she'd never thought to hear again said laconically, 'Have this on me, Macy.'

Shock mingled with disbelief paralysed her. Turned her dumb. The traffic noises, and the buzz of laughter and chatter around her faded into dizzying silence. All she could hear, echoing and re-echoing in her brain, were those few drawled words.

Turning her ordered world to sudden reeling chaos.

Her nails became claws, curling into the palms of her hands, scoring the soft flesh. But, as they did so, bringing her back to stark reality.

No wonder, she thought, swallowing back sudden nausea. No wonder she'd felt uneasy. Some undreamed of sixth sense must have been warning her.

She turned her head slowly. Looked up, with an assumption of calm enquiry.

He was standing over her, close enough to touch. She had to force herself not to shrink away. But it was imperative not to allow him any kind of ascendancy.

She said coolly, 'Ross. What a surprise.'

'You could say that.' He sounded faintly amused, as he hitched a chair forward. 'Mind if I join you?'

His presumption galled her. She said between her teeth, 'Yes, I bloody well do mind,' and he laughed.

'Now that's far more in character.' He looked her over, a tingling top to toe assessment that missed nothing on the way, and made her cringe inside with anger, and a kind of unwilling excitement. 'You're looking good.'

'I wish I could say the same for you,' she said tersely. 'I didn't recognise you.'

'Now I,' he said softly, 'would have known you anywhere. The beautiful Macy Gilmour. I hope I've got the label right.'

'Absolutely.' She pushed the coins back at him. 'Save these for your next meal.'

'Always the soul of generosity.'

'A family trait,' she said. 'But maybe you don't remember.'

'By no means. I recall all the details of every transaction between us, Macy, my sweet, sexual as well as financial.' His voice lingered on the words, deliberately creating all kinds of intimate images. Deliberately winding her up, she realised with vexation, feeling swift blood rise unbidden in her face,

'Fortunately, I don't,' she said crisply, trying to take control of herself, and the situation. She couldn't believe what was happening to her. For four years, she'd striven to dismiss Ross Bannister from her mind as completely as he'd disappeared from her life. Of all the people in the world, she thought despairingly. Of all the places in the world. And of all the lousy, stinking, rotten luck.

'So, what brings you to Fortuna?' Ross asked lazily, sitting down in spite of her denial.

'I'm on holiday,' she returned shortly. To her annoyance, the waiter whisked away the bill and the money before she could stop him, lifting a hand to Ross in obvious camaraderie as he did so.

Above the enigmatic shades, his brows lifted sardonically. 'Are all the usual flesh pots fully booked? I wouldn't have thought this was your scene, although there are some good beaches.' He paused. 'I won't tell you to watch out for sharks. You've been mixing with them all your life.'

'You,' she said, 'were the first.' She reached for her bag, and got to her feet.

'Going so soon?' Ross rose too, with a courtesy so exaggerated it bordered on insolence. 'But our reunion has hardly begun.'

'Wrong,' she said. Her mouth was dry, her heart was hammering. 'It never started.'

He stroked his chin meditatively. 'I hope the beard hasn't put you off.'

'By no means,' she returned. 'It looks wholly appropriate. Wasn't there a pirate called Blackbeard?'

'Indeed there was,' he said. 'He used to operate round Nassau way.'

'What a pity you don't do the same.'

'I prefer to work on a smaller scale.' She'd forgotten his smile. Forgotten too how heart-stoppingly handsome he was, in spite of the scruffy hair and stubble. In fact, there was a lot about Ross Bannister she'd have preferred to dismiss permanently from her mind.

'You're not very relaxed for a holidaymaker,' he commented. 'You seem constantly on edge.'

'Do you wonder?' She paused. 'May I be frank?'

'You always were,' he murmured.

'Thank you.' She faced him squarely, chin up. 'The fact is, Ross, I'd hoped you were out of my life forever. Meeting you again is like the worst kind of bad dream.'

'Well, that is being frank. Unfortunately for you, it could also be a recurring dream,' he said. 'This is only a small island. We could bump into each other quite regularly.'

'No.' She said it so loudly and vehemently that

people at neighbouring tables looked at them curiously.

'Alternatively,' Ross went on imperturbably, 'you could always ask your hotel for a transfer to another island.'

If the choice were hers, that was exactly what she'd be doing, Macy thought angrily. Only she couldn't cut and run. Not yet. She had business to attend to. An important deal to get off the ground. Her personal emotions couldn't be allowed to interfere with that.

She said coolly, 'Using the excuse that I'd been frightened by a rat, I suppose. But, no, I don't think so. I like it here.' She paused. 'How much, this time, Ross, to get you out of my life?'

He said softly, 'Forget it, Macy. There wouldn't be room for all the noughts on the cheque.' He slanted a brief smile at her. 'See you around,' he added, and walked away.

Macy walked too, back up the street, oblivious to the jostling of other pedestrians, as she stared unseeingly ahead of her. Her head was whirling, her thoughts going crazy.

It had been four long years since Ross Bannister had walked out on her. Four years in which to heal herself, and rebuild her shattered self-esteem. Find a new identity.

She thought she'd succeeded. But his sudden reappearance, just when she needed it least, had shaken her world to its foundations.

For the first time, she realised just how much her hard-won security and confidence depended on never being reminded of Ross. Certainly of never seeing him again.

Yet, like some evil genius, here he was.

Under the laws of probability, she wondered just what the chances were of them bumping into each other like this. Probably a million to one. It had to be the most appalling coincidence of the decade.

She cursed herself silently for not staying safely in the confines of the hotel until it was time to go to Mr Delancey's office. If she hadn't taken time out to explore, shop-gaze and have a drink at that particular pavement bar, Ross might never have seen her.

She was surprised that he'd recognised her at all. She wasn't the girl he'd left behind four years before. And she was astonished that, after all that had passed between them, he should want to make contact with her again, however fleetingly.

He could have no conscience, she thought bitterly. No sense of shame.

And there was no guarantee this was the only time they'd run into each other.

'This is only a small island…'

Had she imagined the note of warning in his voice? She didn't think so.

She felt sick again. She could always call her father and ask his advice. Except that she knew what he'd say. He'd summon her back instantly, and hand the Thunder Cay negotiations to someone else.

And she didn't want that. She'd fought hard for her place on the Gilmour-Denys team. At first work had been a form of therapy in the wake of Ross's desertion. Lately, she'd become involved for the sake of the job itself.

Among other things, she'd taken over the administration of the charitable trusts left by her wealthy American mother. The bulk of Kathryn Landin's considerable estate, bequeathed to Macy personally, would come to her in four years' time, on her twenty-fifth birthday.

Up to now, her father had acted as her trustee and adviser, while she'd merely been a figurehead, following his direction. She'd gathered, wryly, that that was how he thought matters should continue.

But she had other ideas. She planned to manage the Landin bequest herself, alongside her career at Gilmour-Denys. She had no intention of being treated as a pretty ornament, to be produced at dinner parties and other social events. She had a sharp business acumen like her mother's before her, and no emotional shock, however acute, was going to throw her off balance. She couldn't afford to get hysterical just because an ex-lover had crossed her path.

But not just an ex-lover, said a sly voice in her head. Ross was your first, and only lover. The one you fell so hard for that you gave him your whole life.

Only that wasn't what Ross wanted at all, she thought, inner pain slashing at her. He'd had very different plans for the future.

Don't look back, she adjured herself. Look forward. Concentrate on the job in hand. Make the deal, and get out as fast as you can. The fact that you've seen him doesn't have to affect your plans at all.

As she turned to hail a passing taxi, painted like a mauve and white zebra, she found the image of Ross, tanned and unkempt in his raggy denims, disturbingly entrenched in her mind. Looking, she thought, exactly like the drifter and layabout her father had accused him of being.

She supposed she should be glad her father had been right about him all along. At the same time, she couldn't help wondering exactly what Ross had done with all that money.

The money her father had paid him to get out of her life forever.

Ambrose Delancey's law offices were situated on the first floor of a pleasant white-painted building, in a square of similar buildings.

In the middle of the square was a fountain, surrounded by flower-beds, and surmounted by a statue of a man dressed in the elaborate style of the seventeenth century. A plaque announced that this was Bevis Hilliard, Fortuna's first governor.

As a family, the Hilliards had clearly enjoyed power here from the first. The sale of Thunder Cay was the first chink in the wall of autocracy they'd built around themselves. A tacit acknowledgement, perhaps, that Boniface Hilliard was the last of his name.

There was a certain sadness about that, Macy thought, as she went into the office building.

She found herself in a small reception area, confronted by a girl with a smile as wide as the sky.

'My name's Landin,' she introduced herself. 'And I have an appointment with Mr Delancey.'

'He's expecting you, Miz Landin.' The girl lifted a phone and spoke softly into it. 'Will you take a seat for just one minute. May I get you some coffee, or a cold drink?'

Macy declined politely. She was feeling frankly nervous, and took several deep breaths to restore her equilibrium.

Then a buzzer sounded sharply, and she was shown through a door at the rear of the room into a large office. One wall was mostly window, shielded against the worst of the sun by slatted blinds. Two of the other walls were lined in books, and a display of green plants gave an impression of coolness as well as discreetly masking another door, presumably leading to further offices.

Ambrose Delancey was a tall black man, impeccably clad in a lightweight cream suit. He greeted Macy with reserved friendliness and a firm handshake.

'What can I do for you, Miss Landin?' he asked, offering her a black leather chair in front of his imposing desk.

'I hope you can open negotiations for the sale of Thunder Cay to Gilmour-Denys,' Macy returned coolly and crisply. 'You've seen a copy of our proposal, and had time to consider it. We'd now like to hear your client's response.'

Mr Delancey smiled reluctantly. 'You don't waste any time. But this is Fortuna, Miss Landin, and we take things at a slower pace here.'

'So I've noticed,' Macy said drily.

'I'm not saying my client isn't interested in your offer,' Mr Delancey went on. 'But there are certain— formalities he insists on, before any serious discussion takes place.'

'What kind of formalities?'

He toyed absently with a pen. 'The fact is, Miss Landin, Mr Hilliard wishes to meet you.'

'To meet me?' Macy was taken aback. 'Why should he want that—at this stage?'

He shrugged. 'Maybe he wants to assess the calibre of your company from you as its representative.' He let that sink in, then continued, 'I take it you have no objection?'

'No,' she said. 'If that's what it takes. Will you arrange a further meeting here?'

He shook his head. 'Mr Hilliard's state of health doesn't permit that, so the interview will be at Trade Winds. I'll contact you at your hotel as soon as the appointment's been made. I trust that's convenient.'

'Perfectly,' Macy returned. It seemed to her that Mr Delancey's gaze had strayed a couple of times towards the door in the corner, and that she'd heard vague sounds of movement from behind it. Another client, she surmised, growing restive.

She got to her feet. 'I realise how busy you are,' she said pointedly. 'I'll wait to hear from you.'

Outside, in the baking afternoon heat, she drew a deep, shaky breath. What did they say about the best laid plans?

It seemed that, for good or ill, she was stuck here indefinitely.

She would have to wait with as much patience as she could muster for her summons to Trade Winds. Play the game on Fortuna terms. She wasn't enamoured of the idea of being inspected by Boniface Hilliard, but there was no point in objecting. Softly, softly was the only approach.

Under different circumstances, of course, she could have shrugged off the inconvenience, even enjoyed her enforced break, especially as this was her first time in the Bahamas.

If, that was, it weren't for Ross...

His presence on Fortuna made all the difference, of course. That was why she was so on edge, she thought.

'This is only a small island.' That was what he'd said. And 'See you around.'

Macy tasted blood suddenly, and realised she had sunk her teeth deep into her bottom lip.

'Not,' she said under her breath, staring up at the merciless blue of the sky, 'not if I see him first.'

CHAPTER TWO

MACY still felt restive as she showered and changed for dinner that evening.

She put on white silk trousers and a matching sleeveless, low-necked top, defining her slender waist with a favourite belt of broad silver links. Her hair she pinned up into a loose coil, and she hung silver hoops in her ears.

She looked like the ideal tourist, anticipating an evening of leisure and pleasure, she thought, grimacing at her reflection before turning away.

She'd spent a quiet afternoon in a sheltered corner of the hotel gardens, making herself think coolly and rationally about the best course to follow when she came face to face with Boniface Hilliard. How to make the best impression.

But in spite of everything, her thoughts kept turning compulsively back to Ross, although she knew she was a fool and worse than a fool to let him impinge even marginally on her consciousness.

She didn't mention his presence when she left a message on her father's answering machine about the latest development in the negotiations.

What Sir Edwin didn't know wouldn't hurt him,

she told herself defensively. She could imagine only too well how he'd react if he discovered Ross was within a thousand miles of her again.

But then they'd been oil and water from their first meeting, she recalled with an inward shudder. On almost every issue—personal, professional, and political—they'd been on opposite sides of a steadily widening gulf, with her, trapped between them, suspended over some bitter, bottomless pit of divided loyalties.

But she'd still hoped, with absurd optimism, that they might learn to get along for her sake.

But then I was very naïve in those days, she thought in self-derision. My father, of course, saw through Ross right away—realised he was simply on the make. Why couldn't I have believed him instead of finding out the hard way?

In the thatched roof bar, adjoining the hotel dining-room, she chose a table overlooking the sea, and ordered a Margarita while she studied the menu.

Once again she knew she was the object of scrutiny, but this time no mental alarms were being sounded. She was simply encountering the usual speculative, semi-lustful attention that women on their own tended to be subjected to. And apart from closeting herself in her bungalow, or wearing a bag over her head, there wasn't a great deal she could do except ignore it, and hope the hint would be taken.

The menu was heavily weighted towards seafood.

Macy had noticed the huge conch shell displayed at the dining-room entrance, and conch was being offered cracked, frittered, as a salad or in the ever-popular chowder, along with grouper, snapper, and stewfish.

I wish I were going to be here to sample them all, she thought, wondering at the same time how long she was going to be kept dangling.

After due deliberation, she decided on asparagus tips in chive butter, baked in a pastry case, followed by lobster tails grilled with garlic and lemon juice, and accompanied by a bottle of crisp white wine.

As the waiter left, Macy realised uncomfortably that there'd been no relaxation in the attention she was attracting. In particular, she was being fixedly stared at by an overweight man with thinning red hair and the loudest sports shirt in the Western hemisphere, who was sitting at the bar with three male companions of similar age and build.

Macy delved into her bag and produced a paperback novel, using it as a barrier as she sipped her drink. Usually it worked. But not always, apparently.

An ingratiating voice said, 'All on your own, sweetheart.'

The colours in his shirt were even more dazzling close at hand.

'Yes.' Macy kept her voice cool and level. 'And that's how I prefer it, thanks.'

'Aw, come on, be friendly.' The man put another

Margarita down in front of her, then deposited himself in the opposite chair with his own beer. 'Strangers in a foreign land, and all that.'

Macy's lips tightened. She said quietly, with glacial emphasis, 'Would you rejoin your friends, please? I didn't ask you to join me, and I don't want another drink.'

'I'm under orders to bring you back with me,' her unwanted companion said with a leer. 'We'd like to buy you dinner, a few drinks, a few laughs—know what I mean?'

Only too well, she thought, her heart sinking.

Aloud, she said, 'You're beginning to annoy me. Would you please leave me alone?'

'What's the matter. Think we can't afford you?' He showed her a wallet, stuffed to the gills with Bahamian dollars.

'Very impressive.' Macy lifted her chin. 'Now go away before I call the manager.'

He snorted. 'Call who you like, girlie, and let them draw their own conclusions. Lookers like you don't hang around on their own in bars for no reason.'

'But the lady's not by herself.' Another voice, icily incisive, and all-too-familiar, cut into the confrontation. 'She's with me, and we'd both like you to leave.'

Macy's lips parted in a gasp of astonished outrage as Ross bent, lightly brushing his lips across her cheek.

'I'm sorry I'm late.' His eyes smiled into hers, challenging her to deny him. 'Has it caused problems?'

'Nothing I couldn't handle,' she returned tautly, glaring back at him. This time her warning antennae had let her down badly.

'So I noticed.' He turned to Loud Shirt who was already making himself scarce, apologising volubly for any misunderstanding.

Ross watched him go, hands on hips, then turned back to Macy, who was struggling to regain her self-command. She could still feel the brief touch of his lips on her face as if she'd been branded there.

How dared he take advantage of the situation like that? she thought angrily. But she couldn't tax him with it. The last thing she wanted Ross to know was that he still had the power to disturb her. Play it cool, she adjured herself, her stomach churning.

He was hardly recognisable as the man who'd accosted her that morning, she realised dazedly. The stubble had gone, his hair had been trimmed slightly, and instead of ragged denims he was wearing faultlessly cut grey trousers, fitting closely to his long legs, and a short sleeved, open-necked shirt, striped in charcoal and white. There was a thin platinum watch on his left wrist, too. He looked a combination of toughness and affluence.

Ross turned back to her. 'You shouldn't have any more trouble there,' he said.

'No,' she acknowledged stiffly, adding a reluctant, 'Thank you.'

His grin was sardonic. 'I bet that hurt.'

She ignored that. 'What are you doing here?'

'This is a good restaurant. I like to eat.'

'Oh.' There was no real answer to that, she thought, nonplussed.

'Also,' he went on softly. 'We have some unfinished business to conduct.' He pulled up a chair and sat down, signalling the waiter to bring him a Bourbon and water.

Macy's heart began to thud apprehensively. She said, 'Rather an expensive place to do business, surely.'

'Oh, I've been able to afford something better than hamburger joints for some time.' The cool aquamarine gaze flickered over her, lingering openly and shamelessly on the thrust of her breasts against the white silk top.

Macey felt the breath catch in her throat, and the tremor of an almost forgotten weakness invade her stomach. She struggled to keep her voice level. 'Of course. I was forgetting.'

'No, darling,' he said gently. 'You haven't forgotten a thing, and neither, I promise you, have I.'

Her uneasiness increased, and she was thankful to see the waiter approaching.

'Your table's ready, Miz Landin.' He turned to her

companion. 'How yo' doin', Mister Ross. You dinin' here tonight?'

'Yes, with Miss—er—Landin here.' Ross's oblique glance dared her to object. 'Just a steak, George, please. Medium rare with a side salad.'

When George had gone, Macy said thickly, 'You have one hell of a nerve.'

'Since childhood,' he agreed. 'But as I told your would-be admirer we were together, we can hardly eat in isolation.' He paused. 'Unless you'd prefer to join his party, after all. They look like a fun-loving bunch.'

Macy gave him a fulminating glance, and stalked ahead of him into the restaurant.

Their table, to her annoyance, was in a secluded corner, lit by a small lamp under a pretty glass shade. The centrepiece was orchids, cream edged with flame, swimming in a shallow bowl. Macy sat down, her lips compressed at the overt romanticism of it all, aware, also, of the resentful gaze of Loud Shirt and his friends a few tables away.

At least she'd been spared any further harassment from that quarter, she thought, but at what cost to her own peace of mind? Instead she had to dine with a man who'd rejected her love, and whose mercenary heartlessness was almost beyond belief.

'So, why Miss Landin?' Ross asked, as he took his seat. 'Are you travelling incognito for some reason?'

Macy gave a shrug, trying to sound casual. 'Not particularly. I like to use my mother's name sometimes.'

'I'm sure you do.' There was an odd note in his voice which she found it impossible to decipher. But that was the least of her problems, she thought grimly.

Her appetite seemed to have deserted her, but to cancel dinner would give Ross some kind of psychological advantage, which she couldn't allow. She had to convince him—and herself too—that his presence was a matter of indifference to her.

So, she'd eat this meal if it choked her. As well it might.

'The chef's name is Clyde,' Ross said, watching her push her first course round her plate. 'He's a sensitive soul, and it'll spoil his night if you send one of his specialities back to the kitchen.'

'Oh.' She gave him a hostile look and dug her fork into the puff pastry crust. To her annoyance, it melted in the mouth, and the asparagus tips were ambrosial.

'I'd say this holiday of yours is long overdue,' he went on. 'You have that indoor look—very unhealthy.'

'As a matter of fact,' she offered curtly, 'I've never felt better in my life.'

'Then you should be extremely worried.' Ross

poured the wine. 'For one thing, you're like a cat on hot bricks.'

'Is it really any wonder?' She put down her fork. 'I thought I'd made it clear you're the last person in the world I ever wanted to meet again.'

He lifted his glass in a mock toast. 'I apologise for my inconvenient existence.' He paused, his glance speculative. 'You sound incredibly bitter, Macy. They're not all bad memories, surely.'

'Not for you, perhaps,' she snapped.

'Or for you, my lovely hypocrite. ' A reminiscent smile played about the corners of his mouth. 'We had our moments.' He leaned forward, his eyes holding hers across the table. 'Shall I jog your memory?'

'No,' she said hoarsely. 'I don't…'

'That sexy French film we went to see,' he said softly. 'My God, you were so turned on, you practically dragged me back to the flat. We were undressing each other on the way up the stairs.'

'Stop it,' she hissed desperately.

'And then there was that evening at the bistro round the corner,' he went on relentlessly. 'When the guitarist played all your favourite love songs, and a girl came round, selling roses.'

He touched the edge of one of the orchids with the tip of his finger.

She remembered the rose he'd bought her, crimson and long-stemmed. In bed that night he'd teased her nipples with its dusky velvet petals…

Her throat closed.

'Enjoy your trip down memory lane,' she said harshly. 'It does nothing for me.'

'No?' His smiling gaze shifted again to the revealing outline of her breasts. 'You don't seem entirely unmoved, darling.'

'You disgust me.' She pushed her plate away.

'Then I'll try and control my baser urges for the rest of the meal, at least.'

He paused. 'So—why Fortuna, Macy?'

Her heart jumped. She had not, she thought grimly, been expecting that. She swallowed. 'Why not? I've been working very hard. As you say, I needed a break.'

'Perhaps,' he said. 'But unless you're into big-game fishing, the island hasn't a great deal to offer.'

'Oh, I wouldn't say that.' I'm after a different kind of game, she added silently. Mr Boniface Hilliard himself. She shrugged, allowing herself a negligent smile. 'But maybe I'm just easily pleased.'

'No,' he said gently. 'I don't think so.' He sat back giving her a reflective look over the top of his glass. 'You haven't told me yet what you do to earn this arduous crust of yours.'

Macy hesitated. The last thing she wanted was to mention her connection with Gilmour-Denys.

'I'm involved with the Landin Trust now,' she returned neutrally.

'A heavy responsibility, indeed.' His tone was ironic.

'As you, with your fondness for money, would be the first to appreciate,' she bit back, and saw his mouth tighten.

'You've always found cash the answer to everything yourself, my pet. Let's not forget that.' He paused. 'I hope it hasn't been your only means of fulfilment over the past years.'

'By no means,' she said sharply, and he lifted an eyebrow.

'Why, Macy,' he drawled. 'Are you telling me you've been unfaithful?'

'I'm telling you nothing,' she said.

'You're denying my right to know?'

'You have no rights where I'm concerned,' she said. 'Not any more.'

He looked at her bare hands, clenched in front of her on the table. 'You seem to be overlooking one salient fact, darling,' he said. 'Whether we like it or not, you and I are still legally married.'

'That is a mere formality.' Her voice shook. 'Which I intend to dispense with shortly.'

Ross was silent for a moment, toying with the stem of his wine glass. Then he said mildly, 'Do I take it you're here to ask me for a divorce?'

'I'm not here to ask you for anything,' she said. 'I don't need to. In another year, I can end our so-called marriage, even without your consent.'

'How convenient,' he said. 'I'm only surprised you didn't set the ball rolling long ago.'

She looked down at the table. 'You forget, I didn't know where to find you.'

'Of course not. But I imagine Daddy's tracker dogs would have managed it without too much trouble.'

Macy moved quickly, restively before she could stop herself, and his voice sharpened. 'Unless, of course, you still haven't told him. My God, Macy, is that it?' His laugh held disbelief. 'You've kept our marriage a secret all this time?'

She said tightly, 'Who wants to make public a serious error of judgement?'

'Touché,' he said drily. 'Clearly your next choice will be based on sound common sense and good fiscal principles. I wonder if I can make an educated guess at his identity.'

'There's no one. I simply want my legal freedom.'

His brows lifted sceptically. 'You mean Daddy hasn't been able to persuade you to make Cameron Denys a happy man at last. You amaze me.'

Macy bit her lip angrily, aware of a faint betraying flush. Cameron's unswerving pursuit of her, with her father's encouragement, had been a bone of contention between them particularly in the last year. 'Don't be snide about my father,' she said curtly. 'He managed to see through you without much difficulty.'

'And I found him equally transparent. Not that it matters. I never gave a damn what he thought of me. The only opinion I cared about was yours.'

For a moment, she was very still.

She said, 'That must be one of the most cynical statements I've ever heard. You—walked out of my life with a golden handshake of one hundred and fifty thousand pounds. That's how much my—opinion mattered. That's how much I was worth to you.'

Ross's mouth twisted. 'It seemed a pre-emptive offer,' he said, 'leaving no room for negotiation. You have to want to be rid of someone very badly to put up that kind of money.'

'Or have a fairly accurate assessment of their level of greed.' She waited for an explosion of anger, but none came.

Ross merely shrugged. 'They say everyone has their price,' he countered. 'Why argue?'

For me, she thought in sudden, swift agony. You could have argued for me—fought for me—told my father to go to hell and take his insulting offer with him.

But you didn't, Ross—you didn't...

Aloud, 'Why indeed?' she said calmly. 'As a matter of interest, would you have gone for less?'

'Probably, in the circumstances.' He sounded almost casual, she realised, pain slashing at her. 'I hope you're not expecting a refund, Macy.'

'Certainly not,' she retorted briskly. 'It was money well spent.'

'I'm glad you think so,' he said evenly, signalling to the hovering George to bring their main courses. 'If they ever have to open you up for surgery, darling, they'll find a bank statement where your heart should be—and showing a credit balance.'

Macy digested that, smarting, while they were being served.

'So—what did you do with your own credit balance?' she asked, once they were alone again. 'Waste it—gamble it away?'

He was silent for a moment. 'I made good use of it,' he said at last.

'To further your career as a photographer?' She despised herself for asking.

'No.'

The flat monosyllable was uninviting, but she persisted. 'Do you still take photographs?'

'Yes, but I'm commissioned these days. Thanks to you, I don't need to pursue the precarious freelance existence your father objected to so strenuously.' He drank some wine. 'I'm obliged to you.'

'Don't be.' Her bitten lip felt raw. 'All the same, I'm glad for you.'

'Are you?' He sounded sceptical. 'Why?'

She put down her fork. 'Because you were good,' she said slowly. 'I always thought you'd be in some wilderness, making a record of it before the bulldozers moved in and spoiled it. Just as—you always planned.'

She'd nearly said 'we', she realised with a pang. Because it had been a mutual and cherished dream, or so she'd thought. One of the many, she reminded herself, that had died when he'd walked out on her.

'How flattering,' he said softly, 'that you do remember some things at least.'

'Not really.' The last lobster tail tasted like poisoned leather. 'Someone who hurt me as you did isn't easy to forget—however hard one may try.'

'And I'm sure one has tried,' he said courteously. His voice hardened. 'Just what the hell did you expect, Macy? That I'd turn down the money? God knows it was an offer no one could refuse. Wasn't that the whole point of it?' He paused. 'Or were you just testing me?'

She shook her head. 'No, it was quite genuine. You'd have been a fool to walk away from it.'

A fool for love, as I was. I trusted you, Ross. Even when my father told me you were for sale, I didn't believe him. Even when I saw the evidence with my own eyes...

'That's what I thought,' he said. His smile didn't reach his eyes, as he ran a hand over his chin. 'When you saw me earlier, you thought I was down-and-out, looking for handouts, didn't you, my sweet? Well, I'm sorry to disappoint you, but I'm doing fine, which is why I'm so glad to be able to buy you dinner tonight. As a small thank-you for showing me the way—giving me my start in life.'

He shrugged. 'As they say, I'd never have managed it without you.'

'Think nothing of it.' The night air was warm, but Macy felt deathly cold.

'And now George is on his way to ask if you want dessert,' Ross went on. 'I recommend the Key lime pie.'

Macy shook her head. 'Nothing more for me,' she said. 'I—I seem to have lost my appetite.'

'Oh, don't say that.' There was mock concern in his voice. 'You have to be able to keep up with Daddy, Cameron and the rest of the carnivores.'

'How dare you say that?' Macy, trembling, pushed her chair back. 'You have no right. You're not fit to—to…'

'Lick their boots?' Ross supplied silkily. 'Quite right. There are whole gangs of far better qualified people hanging round Gilmour-Denys to do just that. But I never thought you'd be one of them, Macy. What a disappointment.'

'Damn you.' She got to her feet, her breasts rising and falling swiftly under the force of her tangled emotions. 'Damn you to hell, Ross Bannister.'

'Too late, darling. You already did that—four years ago.' He rose too, and came round the table to where she stood. He took her by the shoulders, pulling her towards him. For one endless moment, she felt his mouth on hers, without gentleness, without mercy. An act of stark possession.

And somewhere, buried in the depths of her being, she felt a sharp, unbidden flicker of totally shameful response.

Then, just as suddenly, she was free, staring dazedly up into his cool, aquamarine eyes.

He said expressionlessly, 'Goodnight, Macy. I'll be seeing you.'

Shaking, totally oblivious to the interested stares from the adjoining tables, Macy watched him cross the restaurant, pause briefly to scribble his signature on the bill, then disappear out into the night.

CHAPTER THREE

MACY got back to the bungalow somehow. She slammed the door behind her, and stood, panting, her hands pressed against the woodwork as if she was somehow drawing strength from its solidity.

Her mouth felt ravaged. She could make no sense of anything that had happened that evening, but Ross's kiss had burned itself into her consciousness forever.

She felt as if she was crumbling inside, the sane, rational core she'd come to depend on disintegrating. Meltdown.

Don't be a fool, she thought, staring into the darkness. Ross sold you out in the worst possible way. Betrayed you totally. When he went, you had to drag yourself back from the abyss, and learn to live again. You were the one in hell, not him. Never forget that.

He'd actually thanked her for giving him his start in life, she recalled with stark incredulity. The sheer cruelty of it flayed her like a whip.

But that was all she'd ever been to Ross—a meal ticket—a step on the ladder.

Yet during those first dizzy months he'd made her believe she was everything in the world that he wanted. That she was necessary—even essential to him, like the air he breathed. And she'd accepted that precious valuation—gloried in it. Letting herself forget that no one was indispensable.

'A freelance photographer?' She could still hear her father's voice, lifted in outraged astonishment. 'Does that mean he's not in any kind of regular employment?'

'Well, in a way,' Macy had returned defensively. 'He earns fees from newspapers and magazines when he sells them picture spreads.'

'And does that provide him with a living?'

'Yes, because he's good,' Macy had said flatly. 'He's not rich by your standards, perhaps, but he will be one day. He wants to travel.' Her eyes shone. 'He wants to bring the forgotten places of the world to life—remind us all what we have to treasure, before we throw it all away...'

'My dear child.' Sir Edwin had looked pained. 'Where did you meet this—er—freelance?'

'At an exhibition.' Her smile had almost hugged itself. 'I stood back to get a better look at some pictures and trod on his foot. I thought I'd done permanent damage.'

She giggled, remembering her conscience stricken apologies.

'Have I hurt you?'

'Mortally.' His face was solemn. 'But if you had

supper with me tonight, it might ease my final hours…'

'Indeed—' Her father's unwontedly grave voice had brought her back to reality. 'I see that I should have insisted on your accompanying me to the States. Then this unfortunate accident might have been prevented.'

Macy had laughed out loud. 'But I didn't want to avoid it,' she'd objected. 'I'm in love with Ross. We're going to be married.'

After a moment, he said, 'Don't be silly, my pet. You only met him—what?—a fortnight ago. You hardly know him.'

Macy bit her lip. 'Daddy, I know him better than I've ever known anyone in my life.' Even you, she thought, but did not say it.

She'd never heard her father's voice so harsh before. 'Are you saying you've been intimate with this man?'

She knew what he meant, of course, but the use of the word in that context puzzled her. Yes, she'd been intimate with Ross, but in so many ways that had nothing to do with the wild, sweet, crazy passion they'd discovered together on the narrow, hard bed in his flat.

Because, to her, intimacy was also cooking meals together in the impossibly cramped kitchenette, sharing a shower, and the small piece of soap that they kept dropping, seeing Ross shave for the first time, or even watching him read, her own book forgotten, as she scanned, with mounting excitement the strongly moulded contours of his face, until he looked up, alerted in turn by her prolonged scrutiny…

'Macy.' Sir Edwin took hold of her by the shoulders, shook her. 'Answer me.'

She pulled free and stepped back, startled by the sudden grey look in his face.

'Yes, he's my lover,' she said quietly. 'And he's going to be my husband.'

'My God,' her father whispered. 'Have you no shame? Is this all your upbringing—your education has taught you? To jump into bed at the first opportunity with some nobody—some ne'er do well?'

'You've no right to say that,' she flared back at him.

'Very well, then. Who are his family? What is his background? These are questions any father is entitled to ask.'

'I don't know.' She shook her head. 'I suggest you ask him yourself.'

'Don't worry,' Sir Edwin said grimly. 'I shall.'

And even after that, I still hoped they might find some common ground for my sake, Macy thought now, pushing herself away from the door, and treading wearily across the living area to her bedroom. Instead, it had been a total disaster from beginning to end.

Because her father had been quite right. Ross was a stranger to her. She'd never really known him at all. And he was still an enigma even now, she thought, shivering, as she put on the lamp beside her bed.

Across the room, reflected in the long mirror, she saw again the image of a girl, dressed in white, pale-faced, her eyes wide with strain, her mouth bruised and swollen from a kiss. A stranger's kiss...

Then, and only then, she burst into tears.

The bed was wide and cool, with the crisp fragrance of fresh linen. It was too warm for a quilt, or other form of covering, so she lay, naked, in the languid night air, staring into the shadows, waiting for him.

He was smiling when he came to her, easing himself on to the mattress beside her with a sigh of contentment and anticipation.

'My love. My sweet love.'

The whispered words, signalling the commencement of their private, erotic ritual.

His hand touched her breast, cupping its scented warmth, while his fingers circled the rosy nipple, making her catch her breath in instant need.

He knew exactly what he was doing. He'd always known—from that first, overwhelming time together—as if his instincts matched hers, making the desires and yearnings of their bodies identical.

She lifted her hands to his face, running her fingers

pleasurably along the faint and familiar roughness of his jawline, drawing his mouth down to hers.

Lips parted, they teased each other with the tips of their tongues, brushing, caressing, retreating, enjoying the excitement of passion deliberately held in abeyance.

She slid her hands to his shoulders, and down the length of his back, relishing the strength of bone, the play of muscle under her fingertips, making him groan softly in pleasure.

Sometimes the delight of touch, the warm liquid exploration of hands and mouths contented them for half an hour or more, but this time it would not be like that, she knew.

She could feel the urgency building in him, like an underground spring, forcing its way to the surface. She moved against him, brushing her nipples with his, kissing the hollow of his throat where the pulse raged, running her fingers through the damp chest hair, then down over his flat belly to the narrow male loins.

They came together, fitted together so harmoniously, that it seemed as if their bodies had been created for no other purpose. As if, indeed, they were each the perfect half of the other.

They rose and sank together in the moist, heated rhythms and patterns of their lovemaking, each movement revealing some new discovery, some uncharted plateau of delight to be explored.

She heard herself say his name, her voice blurred and drowsy with passion, her arms tightening to draw him even nearer, hold him within her, so that he would be absorbed into her very being at the moment of fulfilment.

But her arms closed on nothing, and no one. A scream rose in her throat, and her weighted eyelids flew open as her gaze frantically raked the moonlit room, and the stark emptiness of the bed beside her.

For a moment, she lay still, letting the frantic thud of her heart against her ribcage subside a little. Then she sat up slowly, pushing back her damp cloud of hair from her face, shivering a little as she disentangled the sheet from her sweat-slicked body.

A dream, she thought, swallowing. Another dream. That was all it was. But, oh, God, it was so vivid— so real. But then, they always were.

She drew her knees up to her chin, and sat for a while. Then she left the bed, and went into the shower, adjusting the controls so that tepid water cascaded over her head and down the whole length of her body, drenching her, cleansing her. Washing the demons away.

She wrapped herself in a bath sheet, hitching it up, sarong-style, then padded into the living area. She chose a can of fruit juice from the selection in the tiny refrigerated bar, and carried it out on to the terrace. She snapped the ring pull, and emptied a long, grateful mouthful of the cold juice down her dry throat.

The can was icy, pearled with moisture from the fridge, and she rested it against her forehead for a moment, letting its coolness counteract the aching heat above her eyes.

The moon swung above her like a great benign face. The air was like a warm blanket, carrying the scent of a thousand flowers, and she breathed it deeply, leaning back on the rattan lounger, listening to the distant play of the ocean on the beach.

She knew, of course, that it was impossible to control one's dreams, but for all that she was bitterly ashamed of the sensual labyrinth her subconscious had drawn her into once more.

Particularly so when she'd just cried herself to sleep.

After Ross had left her, she'd been tormented for months with dreams like that—sensuous, arousing dreams, carrying her to the edge of consummation, then abandoning her there, solitary and sterile.

Wasn't it bad enough that, unasked and unwanted, he'd invaded her waking hours once more? Surely, dear God, she could blot him out of the darkness—prevent him creating havoc in her sleep as well.

She didn't need to be reminded of the joy they'd created together. She wanted to forget.

I've got to forget, she thought, with a little dry sob. Got to…

She was realistic enough to know that part of the problem was her self-imposed celibacy of the past four years. Although she had never been seriously tempted to break it, in spite of the attention and admiration that had been heaped on her, especially by her father's business partner, Cameron Denys.

Cameron had asked her to be his wife countless times, she thought, with an inward sigh. He was wealthy, floridly good-looking, and not without charm, but she knew she would never have accepted his proposal, even if the guilty secret of her hidden marriage hadn't stood in the way.

Maybe, one day, she might meet someone she could trust and care about enough to commit herself again. In the meantime, she supposed she could always try hypnotherapy.

She drank down the rest of her juice and sat up, wiping the faint stickiness from her lips with the back of her hand. Her mouth still felt faintly tender, she noticed, frowning.

But that, of course, was why she'd had the dream. It was all the fault of that merciless kiss Ross had inflicted on her. He'd wanted to punish her—and he'd succeeded. But why?

He was the betrayer, who'd vanished from her life with her father's pay-off. Yet he'd spoken almost as if he blamed her for his own greed and weakness. As if meeting her again had resurrected some long-buried feelings of guilt which he was trying to exorcise.

If so, surely he would be as anxious to avoid her from now on as she was to keep away from him?

Yet, 'I'll be seeing you…' His parting words had not been of separation.

It was as if he was out there, somewhere, in the velvet darkness, watching her again.

Macy shivered, and got determinedly to her feet. It was high time she went indoors, and tried to get some rest for what remained of the night. It could be a big day tomorrow. A day when she would need all her wits about her.

She felt the bath sheet slip a little, and as her hand moved to anchor it more firmly she was suddenly, crazily tempted to let it fall away completely. To walk naked down the winding path between the whispering, fragrant shrubs to the crescent of silver beach. To let the fantasy begun in her dream go on to its ultimate conclusion with the man who must surely be waiting for her—there, on the edge of the sea.

She stopped, with a sharp gasp, flinging back her head. That, she berated herself, would be a self-betrayal beyond words.

Because there was no man, no tender, sensuous lover waiting to beguile her into rapture with his words and touch, and she knew it. He'd never really existed at all—always been a figment of her imagination, and she had to remember that.

All the same, she knew she dared not go and see for herself.

She turned and fled back into the shelter of the bungalow, closing the louvred doors against the rustle of the night breeze among the leaves, and the siren call of the sea breaking on the sand.

Moon madness, Macy told herself firmly over breakfast the next day. That was all it had been. An emotional storm in a teacup which had left her drained, but composed, and able to get matters back into perspective.

But it was unpalatable but undeniable that Ross, however mercenary and worthless he might be, was still incredibly attractive with a strong sexual charisma.

The physical chemistry between them had always been a dangerously potent force, blinding her to the flaws in his character that had been clearly apparent to her father.

Although it had not been simply his faults that Sir Edwin had objected to.

Questioned directly over dinner at that first nerve-racking meeting, Ross had admitted, with a shrug, that he was illegitimate, and that his mother, now dead, had brought him up unaided as a single parent.

Macy, with a sinking heart, saw her father sitting back with an expression of almost harsh satisfaction.

'Why didn't you tell me?' she asked as they drove back to the flat.

He smiled at her. 'Because you never asked.'

'But I told you all about my family.'

'Yes.' The glance he gave her was tender. 'How your father saw this beautiful girl in a New York department store, and followed her from shop to shop until he could make an opportunity to speak to her. Which is why you were eventually christened Macy. I could never compete with that.'

'It's not a matter of competition,' she insisted, troubled.

His mouth twisted wryly. 'Isn't it? I think your father might not agree. And I'm sure he wouldn't want me to know anything as human about himself as that story.' He paused. 'Let's call it a matter of pride, and leave it at that.'

But she couldn't. 'Do you—know who your father is?'

'You mean Sir Edwin hasn't been able to find out?' The barb in his words had stung. He saw her flinch, and his voice gentled. 'No, Macy. I don't know my father at all. Now, can we drop the subject—please?'

She agreed, but the thought—the suspicion that he hadn't been completely honest with her rankled.

Looking back, Macy could see that it was a warning, a cloud on the horizon, a faint rumble of thunder on a summer day.

I should have seen then that he couldn't be trusted, she thought bleakly.

Which made it even more frightening to realise that, even after four years of heartbreak and self-regeneration, her sexual awareness of Ross was apparently as strong as ever. Shaming too, she reproached herself. How could she want, even for a moment, a man who'd used her as Ross had done?

Well, the short answer to that was—she didn't. She was going to regain control of her wayward emotions, bury the past where it belonged, and get on with the task in hand. Which was bringing off the Thunder Cay deal without further delay.

Especially as a note had been delivered along with her breakfast telling her that Mr Delancey would be sending a car for her at ten o'clock.

She drew a breath, half excited, half apprehensive. Let battle commence, she thought.

She decided to dress smart-casual, teaming a white knee-length skirt with a silky top in shades of jade and turquoise. Her hair she twisted into a thick plait. She put all the documentation she needed into a big shoulder-bag and set off for Reception.

Loud Shirt and his friends were there before her, checking out. He gave her a sullen look but said nothing, so she supposed she should be grateful to Ross for that, if nothing else.

'Miz Landin?' The clerk smiled at her. 'Your car's out front, waiting.'

She pushed open the heavy glass door and went out into the sunlight.

And stopped dead. The only car waiting was a dark blue American convertible. And leaning against it, totally at his ease in white shorts and a bronze-coloured open necked shirt, was Ross.

'So there you are,' he greeted her lazily. 'The day's half over.'

Macy's fingers tightened round the strap of her bag until her knuckles turned white, as she strove to maintain her composure.

She said icily, 'Just what is the meaning of this?'

'You were expecting a car, I think,' he said. 'Well, this is it, complete with driver. It's your lucky day.'

She shook her head. 'I don't think so. And I'm not in the mood for games.'

'Who is?' He opened the passenger door. 'Jump in, darling. Time's wasting.'

She said, 'Whatever you're up to, Ross—which I really don't want to know—it won't work. I don't require your services, now or ever. I have my own plans for today.'

'Of course.' His voice was matter of fact. 'And while I don't want to seem pressing, it's a fair drive down to Trade Winds, and Mr Hilliard isn't a man who likes to be kept waiting.'

For a moment, she looked at him blankly, as winded as if she'd been kicked in the stomach.

She said, her voice faltering a little. 'I don't know what you mean.'

His firm mouth compressed impatiently. 'Come off it, Macy. Now who's playing games? Either go with me, or stay,' he added flatly. 'The choice is yours.'

For a long moment she stared at him. There was faint amusement in the aquamarine eyes hiding something else less easy to decipher. Something disturbing.

She said slowly, 'I don't really have a choice—do I?'

'No,' he said. 'Not if you want Thunder Cay.' His smile mocked her stunned expression. 'I've told you before, Macy, this is a very small island.' He took her arm, his grasp firm, almost, she thought faintly, implacable. 'Now, let's go.'

CHAPTER FOUR

THEY drove out of the town in silence, and headed southwards.

The ocean was rarely out of sight along their route, its azure glitter glimpsed between the casuarinas which lined the dusty roadway. Apart from small, scattered fruit plantations, much of the landscape seemed to consist of scrub, interspersed with clumps of tall cacti and ferns.

The hood of the car was down, and under ordinary circumstances, Macy would have enjoyed the controlled power of the car on the well-nigh empty road, and the sensation of the cooling breeze from the sea in her face.

But she was too tautly aware of the man next to her to be able to relax. The heated sexuality of her previous night's dream was all too vivid in her mind. She found she was glancing sideways, registering the movement of his lean, strong hands on the wheel. Remembering the soaring excitement he could so easily evoke.

But she had to dismiss that from her mind, she told herself savagely. Her sole concern should be his apparent involvement with Boniface Hilliard, and fa-

miliarity with Gilmour-Denys's plans for Thunder
Cay. It occurred to her that, if he wanted, Ross might
be able to throw a hefty spanner in the works.

She sat staring rigidly through the windscreen, a
thousand bewildered questions teeming unanswered
in her head.

He said at last, 'You're very quiet.'

She offered him an icy smile. 'I have a lot to think
about.'

'And I thought you were simply admiring the
scenery,' Ross said mockingly. 'Talking of which, if
you glance to the left, you'll see one of our main
attractions—Morgan's Point.'

She turned her head unwillingly, to see a rocky
headland crowned by a ruined tower, resembling a
lighthouse stunted at birth.

'History says that Henry Morgan the buccaneer
used it as a lookout to spot likely ships to pillage,'
Ross told her. 'Want to stop and see if you can pick
up any piratical vibrations?'

'I think I already have more than I can handle,'
she said coolly. 'Besides, as you say, I don't want to
keep Mr Hilliard waiting.

'Very understandable,' he said gravely.

They reached the turn-off some thirty minutes
later. It wasn't particularly impressive. Just a single-
track dirt road, barred by an elderly wooden gate,
half hanging off its hinges. Presumably Boniface
Hilliard was loath to spend any of his fabled wealth

on such mundane matters as simple maintenance, Macy thought drily.

There was a faded sign at the side of the track, stating 'Trade Winds'. And, more dauntingly, 'Private. No admittance'.

'Can you manage the gate?' Ross requested.

Macy approached it gingerly. She touched the sagging timbers which immediately collapsed in terror back against their supporting post. She patted them kindly, amused in spite of herself.

'It's all right,' she said under her breath. 'I won't hurt you.'

She watched Ross drive through, then lifted the gate gently back into place.

'Beautifully done,' he said sardonically as she got back into the car.

'I know.' She flashed him a brilliant smile. 'And I help old ladies across the road.'

'I hope you haven't told Daddy,' he said, and she changed the smile to a glare, as the car moved forward.

The track beyond the gate was in poor condition, and led sharply upwards. Ross proceeded carefully, avoiding the worst of the ruts. When he reached the top of the slope, he braked slightly, giving her a chance to look down.

In spite of herself, Macy caught her breath in swift excitement. Beneath them was a small cove, fringed by palm trees, its sand gleaming silver in the sun. A small landing stage h. d been built out into the lagoon, and she could see a boat, sleek and powerful, moored beside it.

Inside the lagoon, the sea was smooth and pale turquoise, but beyond the line of creamy foam which marked the reef, it deepened to indigo and emerald.

Macy shaded her eyes, and looked out to the open sea. Half-hidden in the shimmering haze between the vivid blue of the sky and water, was a darker, almost purple smudge.

'Yes,' Ross laconically confirmed, as if she'd spoke aloud. 'That's Thunder Cay.'

Trade Winds itself lay directly below, dominating the cove. It was a big, sprawling white house without any of the grandeur she'd imagined, and set so close to the beach that the steps of the front veranda, draped in crimson bougainvillaea, descended directly on to the sand. A balcony with a wrought-iron balustrade encircled the house at first floor level, and Macy saw a woman dressed in white emerge from one of the rooms and stand, a hand shading her eyes, looking up at the car.

Ross took the car gently down the slope, and parked at the side of the house.

He glanced at Macy, brows raised. 'Ready?'

'Of course.' She hitched her bag on to her shoulder, and walked ahead of him along the veranda, and into the house.

For all his wealth, Boniface Hilliard favoured simplicity around him, she thought. The floors were of mellow golden wood, the walls painted in clear pale shades that reflected the hues of the sand, sea and sky. Furniture had been kept to a minimum, and was all very old, and undoubtedly valuable. The whole effect was one of air and space, and Macy found it immensely attractive.

Nor was it lost on her that Ross seemed completely at home there.

She ran the tip of her tongue round dry lips. If he was working for Boniface Hilliard, and in a position of trust, he'd certainly fallen on his feet. Although that wouldn't guarantee his loyalty, of course.

It certainly explained the affluence he'd displayed last night, but not the earlier beachcomber guise, she thought frowningly. Surely Mr Hilliard didn't allow his henchmen to look as if they belonged on Skid Row?

She heard a faint sound, and looked up to see a girl walking down the stairs towards them. It was the one she'd seen on the balcony, Macy realised, and much younger at close quarters than she'd originally thought. She had long blonde hair, worn in a neat top-knot, and an attractive kittenish face with wide blue eyes and a full mouth. The white dress which showed off her rounded figure to such advantage was a nurse's uniform.

She was also, Macy realised, frowningly, oddly

familiar, although she could swear they'd never met…

'I was wondering where you were, Judy.' Ross sent her a swift smile. 'Macy, meet Nurse Ryan, our resident angel.'

The expression in the other's long-lashed eyes, as they looked Macy over, was far from angelic, and she shook hands without warmth.

'Miss Gilmour is here to see Mr Hilliard,' Ross went on. 'Can we go up now?'

Judy Ryan pursed her lips. 'I wish he wouldn't take the law into his own hands like this,' she protested. 'I'd have advised against any appointments today. It's so bad for his routine to be interrupted.'

'I think we'll have to relax the rules for once.' Ross spoke pleasantly, but an order had been given, and by the way Nurse Ryan bit her lip she knew it.

She said to Macy, 'Follow me, then, please, but keep your business brief, and try not to tire him.'

She led the way up the wide, curving staircase. She had good legs set off by smart white court shoes. Macy trailed behind her, uncomfortably aware of Ross at her shoulder. Her interview with Boniface Hilliard was not to be a private one, it seemed. But she could hardly protest until she knew what influence he had with his employer. And Ross seemed only too well acquainted with her business there anyway, she thought with a mental shrug of unhappy resignation.

The room she was conducted to was clearly the master bedroom, but the master wasn't in bed. Clad in silk pyjamas and a light Paisley robe, he was lying, propped up by cushions, on a couch by the window, overlooking the sea.

Boniface Hilliard had once been a big man, but illness had diminished him, wrinkling his skin and making it hang on his bones as though he no longer fitted inside it. His hair was white and very thick, and he had the look of an outdoor man, confined against his will.

'Welcome to Trade Winds, Miss Gilmour.' His handshake was firm, but the skin felt papery. 'I was told you were a determined, single-minded young woman. Your presence here today would seem to confirm that.'

He looked past her at Ross. 'Tell Judy to bring that coffee now, boy,' he directed. 'And you, Miss Gilmour, pull up that chair.'

Macy, obeying, found she was being studied closely as she sat down. The pale blue eyes were taking in everything there was to her, but it was not a particularly friendly examination, she realised with a sense of shock. She wondered what reports Ross had made about her? Not the truth, that was for sure.

Judy Ryan appeared, carrying a tray which she set down on a table by the couch.

'Shall I pour, Mr Hilliard?' Her voice was sweetly deferential.

'No, Miss Gilmour can do it, unless such a domestic chore's beneath her.' He turned a faintly caustic eye on her as Judy Ryan left the room with something of a flounce.

'By no means.' Macy refused to be thrown.

He watched broodingly as she manipulated the heavy pot, adding cream and sugar to order, his scrutiny turning the simple task into a minor ordeal.

'You don't wear any jewellery, Miss Gilmour,' he remarked unexpectedly as she handed him his cup.

'Not during working hours, Mr Hilliard,' she returned coolly.

'But this is a social occasion.' He took a sip of the coffee, the pale eyes regarding her over the rim of the cup.

'Yes, but I hope we can combine business with pleasure.' She took a deep breath, sharply aware of Ross, who'd taken up a position by the window, arms folded across his chest. 'I understand that, in the right circumstances, Thunder Cay might be available for sale.'

He nodded, a faint smile curling his mouth. 'That's my understanding too.'

'Then I hope very much you'll allow me to put an offer from Gilmour-Denys for the property before you.'

She was doing it all wrong—playing it like a complete novice. She wouldn't be surprised if he told her to drink her coffee and go.

He was shaking his head. 'It wouldn't be proper for me to let you do that, Miss Gilmour. You see, Thunder Cay doesn't belong to me any more. It's being marketed by the new owner.'

Macy nearly dropped her cup, as shock mingled with mortification assailed her. Oh, God, she thought, shuddering, how could our information have been so inaccurate?

And what made it a hundred times worse was that Ross was there to witness her discomfiture.

She lifted her chin. 'I wasn't aware the property had been disposed of.'

'Nobody was,' Ross said. 'It was a very private transaction.' She could almost hear the smile in his voice.

I've been set up, she thought angrily. But why? She sent the two men a glittering smile. 'Then I'm sorry I've wasted your time.'

'Oh, I wouldn't say that.' Boniface Hilliard fingered his chin. 'It so happens I'm well acquainted with the new owner, and I could furnish you with an introduction.'

Macy looked at him, nonplussed. This offer of help hardly gelled with the hostility she'd felt earlier, or any of the conflicting vibrations in the room. Yet she couldn't afford to turn it down.

She said, slowly, 'That's very kind, but...'

'But you're wondering why I went to the trouble of having you brought here first?' He shook his head again. 'When you get to my age, Miss Gilmour, a visit from a beautiful young woman is a rare and refreshing treat. And you have more than your share of looks, as I'm sure you know.'

Macy's face was burning. She was sincerely glad that Judy Ryan hadn't been around to hear that little speech. It wasn't what she'd expected him to say, nor was she sure, judging by Ross's cynical grin, that he even meant it. 'Mr Hilliard,' she began uncomfortably.

'But I won't embarrass you any more,' he went on. 'You'll want to get over to Thunder Cay.'

'You mean—go there—today?' Macy's head was whirling.

'That's where the current owner lives,' he returned.

'I didn't know it was inhabited.'

'I used to live there myself, in a house I built on the beach,' he said. 'It's basic, but it's a good place to escape to when you're under pressure.'

Macy gave him a level look. 'I can't imagine you ever running away, Mr Hilliard.'

He chuckled. 'Oh, you'd be surprised, Miss Gilmour. You'd be surprised.' He turned his head. 'Ross, you can take Miss Gilmour over to the island in *Sweet Bird*.'

'Of course,' Ross said laconically. 'As soon as she's ready.'

Oh, no, Macy thought, with a sense of dread. She

said hurriedly, 'A simple letter of introduction would do. I can make my own arrangements.'

'We wouldn't hear of it. Strike while the iron's hot. There's never a better time than the present to make a deal.'

She couldn't argue with that, at least.

'We want your visit to Fortuna to be a complete success,' Boniface Hilliard continued. 'Isn't that so, Ross? We don't attract the tourists like Paradise Island, maybe, but those of us who live here feel it has its own charm.'

'Perhaps Miss Gilmour hasn't had sufficient time to appreciate it,' Ross put in silkily.

'I've had plenty, thanks.' She didn't look at him. 'Far more than I anticipated. Anyway Fortuna's tourist industry could stand to benefit from Gilmour-Denys's plans for Thunder Cay. The kind of leisure facility we envisage is bound to have spin-offs for the adjoining islands.'

'Like a big, fat spider in a web,' Ross said softly. 'What makes you think that Thunder Cay should be exploited in this way, Macy?'

She said, 'That's something I prefer to discuss with the present owner.'

'I hope there won't be too many changes.' Boniface Hilliard leaned back against his pillows. 'My family has been connected with this island since the seventeenth century, when Old Bevis made himself governor here—or that's what he called himself.

He had no lawful authority from the king or anyone else. I guess really he was just a goddamn pirate—a freebooter. Some people say that's what I am too— just a twentieth-century version of Old Bevis.' He gave a hoarse chuckle. 'Although I've built up my fortune from the world stock markets rather than Spanish gold.'

Macy was interested despite herself. 'I saw the statue of him in town,' she said. 'Near your lawyer's office. I realised he must be a relation of yours.'

'Careful, Macy,' Ross cut in silkily. 'You're interested in real estate, remember, not human beings.'

She said curtly, 'I didn't know the two were incompatible,' and replaced her cup on the tray.

Judy Ryan's arrival was almost a relief. 'It's time for your medication, Mr Hilliard.'

'And a hint that we should leave you in peace,' Ross said. He put a hand on the older man's shoulder, and pressed it quietly, then looked at Macy. 'Are you ready?'

She hesitated. She didn't feel ready at all, especially to go with him. The new turn of events had thrown her off balance. Besides, there were strange undercurrents—tensions in the room that she didn't understand.

But if she had to go to Thunder Cay to make the deal, she would. She could stand a few more hours.

She said, 'If I could just use the bathroom?'

'Of course.' Boniface Hilliard waved a hand. 'Show her, Judy.'

Macy said an awkward 'Goodbye,' and followed the other girl reluctantly down the passage. The room she was shown was at the other end of the house, and obviously part of a little used guest suite. A deliberate choice, no doubt, she thought with irony.

Judy Ryan looked round with raised brows.

'I think everything's here—soap—towels.' From her tone, Macy suspected she would have liked to have added 'Polyfilla.'

She said neutrally, 'Thank you.'

'I presume you can find your own way downstairs? Good. Then I can return to my patient.' Nurse Ryan whisked herself away, leaving Macy wondering once again where and how she could possibly have seen her before.

That, however, was the least of her problems, she thought, turning on the cold tap in the basin and letting the water stream over the uneasy pulses in her wrists.

She supposed she'd just passed some unofficial vetting procedure, although Mr Hilliard clearly had no right to do any such thing. Presumably, he felt a strong involvement still with Thunder Cay, in spite of it belonging to someone else.

How on earth could we have missed such a thing? she wondered helplessly.

The last fifteen minutes had been no picnic by anyone's standards. In fact, she looked distinctly wan, she decided grimly, adding a touch of blusher to her cheekbones, and renewing the subdued coral on her mouth. If she was going to be forced to spend even more time in Ross's company, then she would do so with all flags flying.

She made her way back to the stairs, and was just about to begin her descent, when she glanced down into the hall below.

Ross was there, and Judy Ryan was with him, standing close enough to touch, her hand on his arm as she talked to him in a low voice, her face intense.

'So much for patient care,' Macy remarked under her breath, then paused. There was something hauntingly familiar about the little tableau. Something buried deep in her memory, now pushing its way again to the surface.

Photographs, she thought, spilling across a table, and her hand, pushing them away in revulsion, not wanting to look.

'See for yourself what he's like.' Her father's voice, ringing in her head, in grim triumph.

And her anguished gaze taking in at last the couple at the table. The girl's blonde head so close to Ross's dark one. The way her body leaned towards him, the tips of her full breasts brushing the sleeve of his jacket. The almost drugged sensuality in the kittenish face.

Then, she thought, watching the pair below her with curious detachment, as now.

And heard her own voice, choking on the words. 'Take them away. Isn't it bad enough that he's gone—that he's left me—without these? Couldn't you leave me with anything?'

Shock rooted her to the spot. She felt numb, and sick to her stomach at the same time.

Ross and Judy Ryan together in London all those years ago, she thought faintly. Ross and Judy Ryan here together now. It couldn't be possible. Her memory must be playing tricks.

It was all too much of a coincidence, unless, of course, it was no coincidence at all. Unless Ross had left Britain with the other girl, as well as his pay-off, and stayed with her all this time.

Carefully, Macy edged away from the pain beginning to build inside her.

Why should she care anyway? she flayed herself with angry bitterness. Her marriage was over long ago. Ross's relationship with the blonde nurse, or any other woman, was no concern of hers.

But as Judy Ryan's arms went up to draw Ross possessively down to her kiss, Macy snapped out of her trance and stepped backwards, so that the pair of them were hidden from her by the curve of the staircase.

Because, she realised with a commingling of fear and bewildered anguish, the sight of Ross in another woman's arms was still an agony she could not bear to endure.

And the implications of that she dared not even contemplate.

CHAPTER FIVE

As *Sweet Bird* cut effortlessly through the sparkling water, Macy stared rigidly ahead of her at the rocky bulk of Thunder Cay, getting closer with every minute that passed.

She was still in turmoil from that devastating moment of self-revelation in the hall at Trade Winds. Her impulse had been to cut and run. To let the deal on Thunder Cay go by default.

But she hadn't the physical means to leave, she realised tautly, as she waited at the head of the stairs, her nails scoring the palms of her hands, her mind trying to blot out the image of the two, below her, locked passionately in each other's arms. She was dependent on Ross for transport, so she was, to some extent, trapped.

Besides, the last thing she wanted was for Ross to know that anything he said or did had the power to affect her in any way. Pride, if not self-preservation, demanded that at least.

What she couldn't understand was why he hadn't ended their brief and secret marriage himself. If he'd been involved with another woman all this time, why hadn't he asked for a discreet divorce, instead of allowing things to drag on like this? Perhaps he was secretly ashamed of the way he'd treated her. If so, he was hiding it very well, she thought, anger slashing across the desolation inside her.

When she had eventually ventured downstairs, the hall was empty. From the open door, she could see Ross on the landing stage, loading some cartons and a couple of canvas bags on board the boat, helped by a tall black man in khaki shorts and shirt.

She didn't want Ross as a travelling companion again, but what choice did she have? And at least this time she wouldn't be alone with him, she tried to reassure herself.

She couldn't avoid flinching as he took her hand to help her on board, and saw his mouth set grimly as he absorbed her reaction.

But all he said was, 'Meet Sam, Mr Hilliard's right-hand man.'

'I thought that was you,' she returned coolly, returning Sam's smile as his big hand engulfed hers warmly.

'Far from it. I'm a comparative newcomer to the set-up.'

The fringe benefits were fantastic, she thought, as Sam started the engine. Use of a very expensive car, and now this boat, big, streamlined and reeking of money. Ross had certainly fallen on his feet.

'Here.' Ross handed her a dilapidated straw hat with a broad brim. 'You'll need this.'

'The sun doesn't bother me,' she dismissed, adding shortly. 'Please don't fuss.'

'As you wish. I just hope you don't regret it.' Ross tossed the hat down on to the cushioned seat.

I hope so too, she thought. I already have more regrets than I can handle.

It was largely a silent trip. Apart from asking her if she was comfortable, Ross seemed lost in his own thoughts. And Sam was content to hum gently under his breath at the wheel as he drove the powerful boat through the water.

For her part, Macy kept her attention fixed firmly on the approaching island, concentrating so hard that, in the end, her head began to ache.

Unobtrusively, she lifted her hands, and rubbed her temples gently with her fingertips.

'You should be wearing that hat,' Ross said flatly. So he'd noticed what she was doing.

'I'm fine,' she fibbed, not looking at him, but tinglingly aware of his proximity—altogether too close for comfort.

'Nice to know you're impervious to the elements as well as everything else,' Ross returned. His tone was silky, but there was an edge to it. 'But the fact remains, you aren't used to this kind of heat.' He nodded towards the island. 'Well, there you are—journey's end.'

But no lovers meeting. The words spun crazily in

and out of her mind. Macy Gilmour, she berated herself, you're pathetic.

'Yes, at last,' she returned shortly. 'I'll be glad to
get the deal sewn up.'

'You think your terms will be accepted?'

'I certainly hope so. It's a fair offer.'

'No doubt your father shares your ambition. I hear
Gilmour-Denys have been struggling of late.'

'You shouldn't listen to silly gossip.' She
stiffened. 'The company's in good shape.'

'Really?' he said politely. 'Then it hasn't over-
extended its borrowing on the strength of acquiring
Thunder Cay for the consortium?'

'Absolutely not.' Or has it? she wondered, remembering her father's edginess and unwonted anxiety.
But even if Gilmour-Denys had problems, she was
certainly not prepared to discuss them with Ross of
all people.

She hurried into speech. 'Are you going to tell me
something about the new owner?'

'What do you want to know?'

'Well, for one thing, how he got in ahead of the
field, and persuaded Mr Hilliard to sell to him.' She
paused. 'And how the sale was kept so quiet.'

'There was no actual sale,' he said. 'Thunder Cay
was made over to him by deed of gift.'

She turned sharply, aware of a jab of pain across
her forehead. 'What? But you don't give away a
valuable piece of property like that.'

'You do,' he said, 'if it's to your only son.'

Shock silenced her. Then she drew a breath. 'But that's nonsense,' she protested. 'Boniface Hilliard has no children. Everyone knows that.'

'Then everyone is wrong,' he said calmly. 'He has a son and heir, and presently you'll meet him.'

'But you can't keep something like that quiet. Why hasn't the Press got hold of it?'

His smile was tight-lipped. 'Boniface has never welcomed intrusion into his affairs—public or private. Don't let the laid-back attitude at Trade Winds fool you, darling. The place is a fortress. If you'd arrived uninvited, you wouldn't have got past the rickety gate.'

The engine note changed, as Sam throttled back.

'And now we have our own rickety gate to negotiate,' Ross added casually, pointing to the restless line of surf breaking just ahead of them. 'Quite a narrow gap in the reef. Something to bear in mind if Gilmour-Denys are planning a marina.'

It was certainly a delicate operation, getting *Sweet Bird* into the lagoon, and Macy winced as she heard the keel scraping across coral.

'Don't worry 'bout a thing.' Sam slanted a grin at her. 'We've got enough wrecks in these parts. I don't aim to add this beauty to them, no ma'am.'

'I'm glad to hear it.' She realised shamefacedly that she'd been holding her breath.

But any development carried out at Thunder Cay

would demand a better access than that, she thought. It might even be necessary to blast a bigger gap in the coral, although she dared not consider what damage that would do the myriad life-forms supported by the reef.

But that wasn't up to her, she reminded herself. That would be Cameron's ultimate decision, and if he'd ever been interested in green issues and the environment it was news to her.

She just had to conduct the preliminaries with the stranger who was waiting for them. Although why he should want to dispose of his father's gift was a mystery beyond her comprehension.

Safely inside the lagoon, she peered eagerly forward. The island was much greener than she'd anticipated, and not nearly as flat as Fortuna. The hinterland seemed almost rugged, by contrast. She could make out the house too, a solid wooden single-storey construction with a thatched roof, sheltered by the palm trees that fringed the wide crescent of silver sand. But no sign of life. She'd imagined the lone resident would have come down to meet them.

'Romantic, isn't it?' Ross came to stand beside her as Sam turned the boat towards the primitive landing stage. 'The perfect place for a honeymoon.'

'If you say so,' she returned shortly.

'Oh, I do,' he said softly. 'Imagine it, Macy—total seclusion to enjoy each other. No need to dress for dinner—or anything else. Nothing on your skin but the warmth of the sun, and the glory of the moon.'

His voice lingered over the words, creating tantalising sensuous images, and to her annoyance she felt a sudden betraying heat in her face.

Her voice was taut. 'We should let you write the brochure.'

He laughed. 'Always the businesswoman.'

Not always, she thought. Once I was trusting—vulnerable. Until you taught me differently...

Sam brought *Sweet Bird* gently to rest beside the small jetty. Ross jumped ashore to tie up, and Macy scrambled after him.

Without the noise of the engine, the island seemed not merely secluded, but suddenly, hauntingly quiet, she thought with a faint shiver.

She looked uncertainly at Ross, and found him watching her, his eyes intent, a faint smile playing about his mouth. He said quietly, 'Welcome to Thunder Cay.'

She glanced away hurriedly, aware her pulses had quickened, shading her eyes with her hand, her brows drawing together. 'There doesn't seem to be anyone around.'

'There will be. Go on up to the house,' Ross directed, as he and Sam began to unload the various cartons.

She hitched her bag on to her shoulder, and started up the beach, her feet sinking into the yielding sand.

She felt as if a heavy weight had been placed on her skull and was pressing her downwards. A cold drink, she thought longingly, and a seat in the shade. Then she'd be fighting fit again.

She was halfway up the beach when she heard *Sweet Bird*'s engine roar into life again. She swung round, and saw the boat reversing, then heading back towards the reef and the open sea beyond, while Ross stood on the jetty, waving goodbye.

For a moment Macy stood, open-mouthed in sheer disbelief, then she began to run back the way she'd come, yelling and waving her arms, screaming at Sam to come back.

Ross watched her, hands on hips, his face unsmiling.

He said, 'It's no use, Macy. He obeys my orders, not yours. And he'll return when I tell him, and not before.'

'And when will that be?' she demanded tautly.

'All in good time.' The aquamarine eyes studied her dispassionately. 'Relax, Macy. Enjoy the ambience. You're planning a resort where people can get away from it all. Test it for yourself.'

There was a sharp, tingling silence, and she was the first to look away.

She said, 'If this is a joke, it's in very poor taste.'

'It's all perfectly serious,' he returned. He slung the canvas bags over his shoulder, and walked towards her. 'You and I have a deal to negotiate.'

He paused. 'As well as the unfinished business I mentioned last night.'

'We have a deal?' In spite of the intense heat, she felt suddenly deathly cold. 'I don't understand.'

'Don't you? I thought you'd have put two and two together by now, and come up with an answer,' he said. 'But come up to the house and I'll explain in full.' He gave her a critical glance. 'In spite of your protests, you look as if you've had quite enough sun for one day.'

She said between her teeth, 'I'm not moving a step. You can explain right here, and it had better be good. You have no right to kidnap me and dump me here on someone else's property.'

'For the record,' he said slowly, 'I'm your husband, which gives me any rights I choose to assume.'

Her heart seemed to stop momentarily. She said thickly, 'It's a little late to remember that.'

'On the contrary, darling.' His voice slowed to a drawl. 'I've never forgotten it, even for a moment, during this long separation.' He paused, the cool blue gaze holding her—mesmerising her. 'And, also for the record,' he went on quietly, 'this is not someone else's property. Thunder Cay belongs to me.'

'That's nonsense.' Her voice wavered. 'You're lying—you have to be. You said on the boat that it belonged to Boniface Hilliard's son...'

'All perfectly true.' He made her a mock bow,

smiling at her sharp intake of breath. 'Ross Bannister Hilliard, at your service.'

'What?' Her voice rose. 'You're actually claiming to be his son? Since when?'

'Since the moment of conception, I presume.' He shrugged. 'Isn't that the biological norm?'

'Please don't equate yourself with any kind of normal behaviour,' she hit back at him. 'What is this? Some kind of confidence trick to get yourself yet another stack of unearned income?'

'No,' he said. 'I have all the documentation to prove what I say, and to confirm my ownership of this island. Now, come on up to the house and we'll talk.'

'Never,' she said. 'All deals are off. I'm going back to Fortuna right now.'

'It's a long swim,' he said. 'Watch out for barracuda. Or maybe they should watch out for you.'

'I am not joking.' Her voice was angry.

'Nor am I, Macy. Without a boat you're going nowhere.' He walked past her up the beach. 'Now, I'm going in the house for a cold beer. You, of course, can stay there and melt, if that's what you want.'

'I'm not moving until the boat comes back for me,' she said defiantly.

His brows lifted, and he began to laugh. 'In that case you certainly will melt. I told Sam to come back for us in a week.'

'Oh, God.' Her voice cracked. 'It can't be true…'

'Stay there and wait,' Ross advised crisply. 'You'll find out. I'll throw food to you at appropriate times, of course. If you plan to face seawards, the first thing to hit you in the back of the head will be dinner.'

He turned and went up the rickety steps to the veranda. After a long moment of indecision, she followed. She was scared, but standing on the beach in splendid isolation would solve nothing. Besides, the heat was making her feel swimmy and faintly sick.

She found herself confronted by a combined kitchen and living area. There was a shabby sofa, and an enormous table, its surface littered with papers.

Ross dropped the bags on the table then sauntered to the large refrigerator and extracted two bottles of beer. He offered her one, which she declined, in spite of her thirst, with a curt shake of the head.

She looked round slowly, assimilating her surroundings. There were only two rooms apparently leading off the living area. One of them, as she could see through its curtained archway, was a bedroom. The other preserved its privacy behind a solid-looking door. A lean-to extension at the rear housed the toilet and shower.

And that seemed to be it. The simple life, she thought, that all at once seemed incredibly complicated—even threatening.

Ross uncapped one of the bottles and swallowed

some beer, his aquamarine gaze coolly reflective as he studied her.

He said, 'You look stunned, darling. Take a seat before you fall down.'

'Is it any wonder?' She sat down at the table, glaring at him. 'I don't know what your game is, Ross, but I'm not taken in by it. I don't think you're related to Mr Hilliard in any way. You've just tricked your way into his affections somehow.' Just as you tricked me, she thought with anguish. 'He's old and ill,' she went on. 'An easy touch for a plausible story.'

'On the contrary, my sweet.' He drank some more beer, his eyes never leaving her face. 'Boniface may be physically frail, but mentally he could still buy and sell the world. I'm his son all right. And whether you accept it or not doesn't alter a thing.'

'You lied anyway,' she accused. 'You told me you didn't know who your father was.'

'No, Macy.' Ross shook his head. 'I said I didn't know him at all—a different thing from merely being aware of his identity.'

'Which you were?' she demanded, and, as he nodded silently. 'How long have you known it?'

'Since my mother's last illness,' he said quietly. 'The drugs they gave her made her ramble—say things she wasn't aware of—that she'd kept hidden all her life. When she died, I found letters that she'd kept. Photographs. A whole past locked away.'

'How convenient.'

'Not really. For a long time I didn't know what to do about it.'

'But you came up with the right answer in the end,' Macy said, with a bite. 'Tell me something. If you knew you were the only son of a multi-millionaire, why did you take the money to walk out of my life?'

'Call it a redundancy payment,' he said, his mouth curling. 'A fee for services rendered—anything you want.'

'Your golden handshake must have come as a pleasant surprise to him,' she said. 'A freelance photographer, living from hand to mouth, might not have been nearly so welcome.'

She paused. That earlier feeling of nausea had increased and intensified, and her head was throbbing, but she persevered. 'So when did you go for the jackpot—break the happy news to Daddy?'

'I didn't.' His tone was crisp. 'He found me. He'd promised my mother he would never come to look for her until he was free to marry her. Ironically, she and his wife died within weeks of each other, and I'd moved on, anyway, so the trail went cold.'

'Yet here you are—living happily ever after,' Macy said. 'What happened?'

'He became ill,' Ross said. 'Also frightened. And lonely.'

'You're breaking my heart.' A wave of giddiness

swept over her, and she leaned back, searching vainly for a breath of cool air from the open door.

'That I doubt.' There was sudden harshness in his voice.

'But your new-found wealth and status don't alter a thing,' she went on. 'I insist on going back to Fortuna.'

'And so you will,' he said softly. 'Eventually. When we've agreed our deal. I was short on bargaining power in the old days. Now I'm not. I have something you want, and you're going to pay for it.' He paused. 'In one way or another.'

'What are you talking about?' She could feel panic settling like a stone in her chest.

'Why, this desirable piece of real estate you've come so far to see—what else?' He was mocking her, and she knew it. There was more—far more going on here than a simple land deal.

'I refuse to discuss it here,' she said curtly. 'I prefer more civilised surroundings.'

He shook his head. 'Can't oblige. This is as civilised as it gets.'

She stared at him. 'You can't seriously intend to keep me here.'

'Ah, but I can,' he said softly. 'And I shall.'

'You bastard,' she said hoarsely.

His smile tautened. 'Ain't that the truth? If this is your idea of conducting negotiations, Macy, thank God you never joined the diplomatic service.'

'But what do you hope to gain?' she demanded hoarsely. 'Are you holding me to ransom—trying to force my father to pay more?'

'It always comes down to money with you, Macy.' The note of contempt in his voice stung her. 'No. This time it doesn't concern your father at all, but mine. Through circumstances beyond his control, he never held me as a baby, or played with me as a child, or talked to me as a boy growing up. We both missed out on a hell of a lot. Now, it seems there may be a limit on the amount of time he has left. And before he dies he wants to hold his grandchild— someone of his own flesh and blood—in his arms.'

The aquamarine eyes held hers inexorably. Impossible to resist—or even look away, Macy thought dazedly. Her own gaze was beginning to blur, putting him somehow out of focus. His voice too seemed to be coming from some far distance.

'That's why we're here, Macy. To take the honeymoon we never had. To give our marriage a second chance, and, perhaps, give my father the grandchild he longs for.'

She pushed her chair back, and got to her feet. She needed to speak, to tell him he was crazy, but the words wouldn't form on her dry lips. She wanted to turn and run, but it was as if she was anchored there.

The room was swinging round her, spinning faster and faster until it was out of control, drawing her down into some spiralling vortex where only darkness waited.

Her invisible bonds relaxed. She heard herself say, 'No,' her voice high and terrified like a child's. Then felt herself slip down, without haste, into the welcoming blackness.

CHAPTER SIX

THERE was fire in the darkness, a stifling heat which consumed her. She was lying on the burning sand, lifting her face to the pitiless sky in a futile search for rainclouds, knowing that the coolness of the sea was only yards away, yet unable to drag herself to it.

Faces swam on the borders of her consciousness. Her father's face, and Cameron's, their expressions intent as they assembled toy building blocks into a model of a hotel complex which spread and spread until it filled the room, pushing her aching body back against the wall.

Can't you see me? she screamed at them, as they began to blur and fade. Don't you know I'm here? Help me, please.

But all that emerged was a hoarse croak.

There was a girl's face too, pretty and petulant under curling blonde hair, with a look in her eyes which made Macy shrink inside her aching skin.

And there was the man, with eyes as pale as aquamarine, and a line of dark stubble along his tanned jaw. His was the face she saw most of all.

And he was her enemy. It was because of him

that she was hurting so badly. In some dim corner of her mind she knew this, and tried to struggle—to hide somewhere in the hot sand each time he swam into focus. She had to fight him—to escape at all costs.

From some long and aching distance, she heard her voice, small and exhausted, say, 'Don't leave me.'

He said brusquely, 'I'm going nowhere. Drink this.'

His shoulder was hard under her cheek, the cotton shirt he wore rasping against the fevered tenderness of her skin. But the fruit juice he made her swallow was like nectar in her parched throat.

Her eyelids felt drugged with heaviness, but she forced them open somehow, and stared round her. The first thing she realised was that she was alone. The second, that the room was totally unfamiliar with plain board walls, and uncurtained windows, shuttered against the sun. Apart from the bed, it contained a chest of drawers with a mirror above it and a chair.

And the third, and most startling realisation was that she was in the bed, and she was naked.

Macy sat up, galvanised into shocked reaction, despite the instant reproach of her still aching body. Remembrance began to return, slowly and equally painfully.

It was not all a bad dream, as she'd hoped. And

she was not safe in her bungalow at the Fortuna Bay hotel at all.

Far from it, in fact.

Ross, she thought, horrified, a faint film of sweat breaking out on her forehead. Oh, God—Ross.

As if she'd spoken his name aloud, he appeared in the doorway, leaning a negligent shoulder against the frame as he surveyed her. He was wearing faded red shorts and nothing else, and he looked devastating, she thought, her stomach lurching in swift, betraying acknowledgement.

'Welcome back to the real world,' he said silkily, the cool eyes travelling down her body.

Macey gasped, hurriedly dragging the sheet up to cover her bare breasts, a gesture which brought a faintly derisive smile to his mouth.

'It's a little late for that. And your body is hardly a mystery to me anyway.'

'What am I doing here?' she demanded huskily. 'What's happened to me?'

'Don't be silly, Macy,' he said. 'You remember perfectly well. You've had sunstroke, not amnesia.'

She swallowed. 'Is that what it was—just the sun?'

'Don't underestimate it,' he said. 'Your temperature was sky-high, and you were delirious. I had to sponge you down with cool water every few hours.'

To her annoyance, Macy found herself blushing.

'Was that strictly necessary?' She invested her voice with extra ice to compensate for her embarrassment.

'Entirely,' he said. 'I radioed Trade Winds for advice, and Judy told me what to do.'

'Of course,' she said tonelessly, cringing inwardly at the thought of the pair of them discussing her helplessness.

But a radio, she thought. Ross had a radio. On which she could transmit a message perhaps. Reach the authorities on Fortuna and make them send a boat to her rescue. Get her out of here at all costs.

'Don't raise your hopes, Macy,' Ross said, just as if she'd spoken the thought aloud. 'You'll never find it.'

'You can't keep me here against my will.' She glared at him, hating him for reading her so easily. 'I'll get out of here somehow.'

'Then you'd better start swimming,' he said pleasantly. 'The sharks will be delighted.'

She repressed a shudder, her hands tightening on the sheet. It was no good getting angry, she thought. Better by far to reason with him.

'Ross—you can't have meant all those foolish things you said—when was it?—yesterday?'

'Three days ago, actually,' he said, smiling ironically at her gasp of shock. 'And I meant every word.'

'But it's impossible—insane...' She heard her voice begin to shake, and controlled it with an effort. 'You're not thinking straight, Ross. I—I can understand why you want to provide your father with a grandchild—but not this way. You and I were finished long ago. We can divorce quietly as soon as you want—we don't need to worry about the grounds as it's past two years since we separated—and you can find someone else—marry her.' She tried to smile, crushing down the painful image of Judy Ryan. 'There won't be any shortage of potential brides.'

'Why? Because I'm a wealthy man now, instead of a struggling photographer?' His voice bit.

'No,' she said, in a low voice. 'I didn't mean that.'

'Not that it matters,' Ross went on almost casually. 'As I already have a wife.' The aquamarine eyes held hers making it impossible for her to look away. 'And no time to spare for a lengthy courtship, anyway. Boniface's health, as I've told you, isn't good.'

'Does he know?' she demanded rigidly. 'Have you told him who I am, and what you intend.'

'Naturally.'

'And he approves?'

Ross shrugged. 'Not entirely.'

'I'm relieved to hear it,' Macy said between her teeth.

'You decided his only son wasn't good enough

for you, Macy. You can hardly expect him to accept you with open arms.'

She gasped. 'That's not what I mean, and you know it.'

'But he's a pragmatist,' Ross continued as if she hadn't spoken. 'He recognises I have little choice. And anyway, you owe me.'

'In what possible way?' she demanded huskily.

'Four years ago we were married,' he said, almost dispassionately. 'It follows that, by now, we might already have had a child. Could even have been expecting another. You were keen on a family, if my memory serves. We both were. I can remember you clinging to me, while we were making love, telling me that you wanted my baby.'

'Stop it.' Macy put her hands to her ears. 'That was a long time ago. We're not the same people any more.'

'Having slept next to you for the past couple of nights,' he said, 'old times don't seem so far away. Except that you're even lovelier, if that's possible.'

Macy's heart missed a beat. 'I was ill,' she said slowly. 'You knew that, yet you actually slept— here—in this bed?'

'There wasn't much choice,' he said. 'As well as bathing, you needed constant drinks and attention.' He paused. 'And this is the only bed.'

'Is it now.' Macy fought the wave of heat threatening to engulf her. 'Well, from now on I shall sleep on the beach.'

'I don't recommend it,' he said. 'The no-seeums will eat you alive.'

'The what?' Her voice lifted to a squeak.

'They're a kind of sand-flea,' he explained. 'Bite like hell.'

'I don't care.' Her throat was tight. 'You can't make me stay here. You can't force me to do this. Rape is still a criminal offence, even if your fore-bears were pirates.'

He said gently, 'There's no question of rape, Macy, as we both know perfectly well. And as I shall take endless pleasure in reminding you.'

A shiver convulsed her. 'Don't,' she said huskily.

The cool eyes swept her mockingly. 'What's the matter, Macy,' he taunted. 'Am I rather too close to the truth?'

'No,' she said. 'You just disgust me, that's all.'

'That's not my intention,' he said. 'I want a re-awakening—a rekindling of all we used to feel for each other.'

'That's impossible.'

He shook his head. 'I don't think so. When I kissed you that night on Fortuna, you trembled in my arms.'

'That was rage,' Macy spat at him.

He laughed. 'Truly?' he drawled. 'Then you have

my permission to be as angry as you like whenever you wish.'

There was a silence. Then she said thickly, 'Ross—don't do this. Please.'

'Not a word I expected to hear from you, darling.' His voice was dry. 'That heatstroke must really have taken it out of you. Don't forget, you came here to do a deal. It's not quite the one you expected, that's all. But Thunder Cay can still be yours. A belated wedding gift, if you like.'

'But only if I—do what you want.' She forced the words from the tightness in her throat.

'Of course.' His tone was matter of fact.

'How can you live with yourself?' She lifted her chin, tried to stare him down.

Ross shrugged again. 'Isn't it a pre-divorce duty of couples to seek a reconciliation?' he challenged. 'That's what I'm asking, Macy. You won't be forced or rushed into anything, I give you my word. I can wait.'

'Very reassuring,' she said bitterly, and his mouth tightened.

'Nevertheless, that's the way it's going to be, my sweet. Gentle persuasion.' His voice was quiet, almost reminiscent. 'Just the two of us alone here together. No intrusive elements, or outside interference. I've told Sam that our stay here is going to be extended indefinitely, so you'll have plenty of time to think.' He pushed himself away from the door post.

'What about my own powers of persuasion,' Macy flung at him, as he turned away. 'Suppose I convince you that our marriage is a lost cause? That you should let me go?'

Ross slanted a brief smile at her. 'You can always try,' he said softly, and left her, slumped against the pillows, staring after him.

She felt as if she'd just taken part in the London marathon. But then, looking back, life with Ross had always been like that—lived at speed, sweeping her along, imbuing her with a feeling of reckless-ness—a sense of risk. Leaving her often breathless.

But she couldn't think like that, she reminded herself, her heart like a stone in her chest. There was not and never could be again any life with Ross.

This—abduction was sheer bluff. He didn't—couldn't intend to keep her here. Couldn't possibly think they could resurrect their dead marriage after what he had done.

It had to be a ploy, she told herself, a scheme to extract more money from Gilmour-Denys for Thunder Cay. Ross's way of revenging himself on the man responsible for his exposure.

Macy swallowed. Her father would be expecting to hear from her. What on earth would he say—and do, when he discovered where she was, and in what company? The truth about her marriage was bound to come out, and he would be hurt. And if the Press got wind of all this, there would be the kind of scandal and notoriety Gilmour-Denys had always avoided.

She hardly dared imagine what Cameron's reaction would be, she thought with foreboding. He was always so correct in his behaviour, so narrow in his expectations of others. That was why, in spite of his determined courtship, she had always known she could never marry him, even though she was going against her father's dearest wish by refusing.

Ross reappeared in the doorway. 'I'm getting lunch,' he said. 'Can you make it to the table, or would you prefer a tray?'

'I'd prefer to get up,' she said instantly. She was too vulnerable like this. She distrusted the enforced intimacy of the situation.

'Good,' he said. 'Later, if you feel up to it, I'll show you a little of this valuable piece of property—this hidden corner of the Garden of Eden.'

The words sank into a taut silence as Macy digested them—recognised them as part of the draft brochure Cameron had already prepared for the Thunder Cay development. There wasn't much he didn't know, she thought, seething. He'd been ahead of her every step of the way.

'You must want to see the island,' he went on. 'After all, that's why you agreed to come here.'

'And what a mistake that was.' She gave him a flat look. 'This may be Eden, but I have no plans to play Eve. I'd like my clothes back.'

'Certainly.' Ross grinned at her. 'Although the alternative has its appeal.'

He disappeared momentarily, and returned with an armful of garments which he dumped on the end of the bed. 'They've been washed and dried, but not ironed,' he added. 'I don't go in for those refinements.'

'You astonish me,' she said acidly.

After all the intimacies of the past few days, it was odd that she should find the idea of him doing her personal laundry a disturbing one.

We used to share trips to the launderette in the old days, she reminded herself. Why should this be different?

She said, 'I would also appreciate some privacy. Or do you intend to watch me.'

'That also has its appealing side,' he said. 'But, as I said, I can wait.'

He unlooped the door curtain and let it fall into place.

Macy realised she'd been holding her breath, and released it slowly, in a little nervous sigh.

She was being allowed to dress in peace, but that curtain only gave an illusion of privacy, and she knew it. She was in Ross's hands—under his control.

When he said 'I can wait', it wasn't just a warning. More a declaration of intent.

She'd never actually seen this ruthless side of him when they lived together, but of course it had always been there. It had surfaced when he'd left her like that. No goodbye. Just a cold-blooded receipt for the money signed 'with thanks'.

God, how that had hurt.

Yet it seemed he'd resented being recognised for what he was and bought off. Now, he was in a position to enjoy his revenge. Because that was all this was—all it could be, Macy told herself feverishly. He'd walked out. She owed him nothing. The days and nights when she'd given herself to him with joy and abandon were long past. Now her body was her own again, and it would stay that way. She'd learned too well the agony that passion could inflict in its wake.

Nor was she prepared to allow herself to be used as some kind of brood mare, she thought, with icy determination.

Ross could only keep her on Thunder Cay for a limited time. If she wasn't in contact with Gilmour-Denys very soon, her father, not to mention Cameron, would come looking for her. And a kidnapping scandal would damage the Hilliard name as well, or more.

'The food's ready.' Ross's voice reached from the other side of the curtain. 'Are you?'

'Nearly.' Macy scrambled out of bed, and stood for a moment fighting a slight light-headedness. After the fevered nightmares she'd been suffering, she was astounded she could feel so well.

I must have amazing powers of recuperation, she thought drily. And I'm going to need every last one of them.

Thanks to manmade fibres, her clothes were only a little creased, but Macy suspected she would be sick of the sight of them before her enforced stay came to an end.

There was a brush and comb on the chest of drawers. As well as undressing her, Ross must have unplaited her hair, she realised, as she dealt, wincing, with the tangled strands. He'd always liked her to wear it loose, stroking its burnished silkiness as it tumbled across the pillow...

She gave a vicious tug to a particularly recalcitrant knot, calling her thoughts to order. She had to be strong and single-minded if she was going to get out of this highly charged situation unscathed.

One moment of weakness, and she could be lost forever.

Not that she looked capable of punching her way out of a paper bag, she thought, grimacing. Her reflection showed her looking totally drained, her eyes enormous and her cheekbones far too prominent.

But maybe that wasn't such a bad thing, she thought with sudden excitement. Perhaps she could use the fragility of her appearance to her own advantage.

She put a hand to her head, as if warding off a dizzy spell, and studied the effect under her lashes. Not bad, she decided critically, but she must be careful not to overdo it, or Ross might get suspicious.

She'd go on this island tour with him, eking out the journey with frequent and prolonged rests. For which, of course, she would keep apologising. She might even allow herself a few angry tears at her own weakness.

She gave her pallid reflection a bracing grin, then took a deep breath and walked through to the living area.

Ross was standing at the stove, dishing omelettes on to two plates.

Macy's brows lifted as she sat down. 'Fresh bread?'

'Frozen and reheated. I run the freezer off the generator.'

'Of course,' she said. 'The simple life.'

'If by simple, you mean lacking in unnecessary complication, yes,' he retorted. 'Electricity's an essential.'

'And holding me to ransom isn't complicated?'

'Unavoidable,' he said. 'You'd hardly have accepted a direct invitation.'

'You're so right.'

He brought the plates to the table. The omelettes, she noticed bitterly, were perfect as usual, golden, succulent and moist. Like many men, Ross was impatient with housework, but a good, almost instinctive cook.

'Just like old times.' He sat down opposite her.

'Not in the slightest.' If her mouth hadn't been watering so frantically, she'd have thrown the plate at him.

'Be patient,' he said softly, cutting into the crusty loaf. 'You'll be surprised how easy it will be to turn the clock back.'

'You're wrong,' she said. 'Everything's changed. I'm not the same trusting, gullible fool I was when we first met.'

'Yet you're still involved with your father and dear old Cameron,' Ross drawled. 'Isn't that rather a contradiction in terms?'

She bit her lip. 'You've never had much time for Cameron, have you?'

'It's mutual,' he said laconically. 'No doubt the prospect of owning Thunder Cay and turning it into some glorified theme park will compensate him for missing out again with you.'

'You actually think he's that mercenary?' Her voice rose incredulously.

'Yes, I do. I always have. Your father and he had his marriage to you planned like some kind of merger years ago. And they had their sights set on this island in exactly the same way. All I had to do was drop a hint in the right quarter and they were sniffing round like rats with a piece of cheese.' He paused. 'I had to gamble they'd send you, of course. That's why I stressed negotiations had to be confidential. You've made quite a name for yourself in a quiet way. I'm impressed.'

'You really had it all sussed,' she said bitterly.

'I guessed they'd take the bait,' he returned. 'They must be getting desperate.'

'Not so desperate that they'd allow me to be part of some sordid transaction.'

'Grow up, sweetheart,' he said brusquely. 'In property circles, they reckon Cameron would sell his granny if someone offered the right price. You'd be a very small clause in a deal as potentially lucrative as Thunder Cay.'

'You're disgusting.'

Ross shrugged. 'You're not the only one who's abandoned a few illusions along the way,' he returned. 'You used me once. Now I'm repaying the compliment.'

'How dare you say that?'

'Because it's the truth. Face it.' His voice hardened. 'That's why our marriage had to be kept secret "until the right moment". That's what you kept telling me. Only there was never going to be one. I was good enough to have in your bed for a while, but not worth a lifetime commitment. Isn't that how it was?'

'Damn you,' she said unevenly. 'You walked out on me.'

'Did I have a choice?'

'I think so.' And her name was Judy Ryan, she added silently.

'We'll agree to differ on that. But now the world's moved on, and we're free to choose again.' His voice gentled, and his glance touched her like a caress. He stretched a hand to her across the table. 'Take a chance with me, Macy. I want you back in my life—back in my bed.'

The brush of his fingers was all it would take, she thought helplessly. The merest contact of skin against skin, and she would be lost for ever, drawn down into the dizzying sensual thrall he knew so well how to weave. If she took his hand, all the lonely, heated dreams would become magical reality—for a time. While she salved his damaged pride. Gave him, maybe, the child he wanted. But after that—what then? Her heart seemed to close. She clasped her hands together in her lap, forcing a cool smile.

'The world's full of willing women, Ross. Try your powers of persuasion on them instead. I'm afraid they don't work for me any more.'

His mouth twisted in a smile. 'Who said I was

really trying?' he asked, and went on with his meal as if nothing had happened.

And, after a bewildered pause, Macy did the same.

In spite of her emotional turmoil, she could have eaten every scrap on his plate as well as her own, yet with superhuman control she made herself pick at her eggs, as if her appetite was still minimal.

Accordingly, she refused the sliced mangoes Ross offered for dessert, but drank two cups of strong black coffee.

'Do you feel up to this walk?' Ross gave her a searching look, as he cleared the table.

If the alternative was remaining here with him, she was fit enough to scale the north face of the Eiger, she thought grimly.

'As long as it isn't too far.' She tried a brave smile.

'It's not a very big island. But then, you know that already.' He produced the straw hat again. 'And this time you'll wear it,' he added shortly.

She didn't argue. She couldn't afford any more moments of weakness. Not genuine ones, anyway, she thought as she followed him reluctantly out into the sunlight.

Those brief moments when she had yearned to touch him had taught her succinctly that she could not trust her senses, or the physical needs he himself had taught her. She was going to need every atom of strength she possessed to keep Ross at arm's length until this nightmare ended, and she was free again.

But, a small, cold voice inside seemed to be telling her, that freedom might cost her a harsh and bitter price.

CHAPTER SEVEN

THE track from the beach led uphill. The gradient was only slight, but half-buried rocks, loose stones and rampant undergrowth made the going hazardous. Macy soon found she didn't have to pretend to be breathless.

She was glad, too, of the need to concentrate. Ross walking ahead of her was a distraction she didn't need. She'd forgotten, or tried to, the lithe effortless stride, the sense of male power emanating from him.

'Want some help?' he asked when she hesitated at the broad bleached limb of a tree completely blocking their path.

In line with her role as semi-invalid, Macy forced a wan smile. 'Maybe.'

His hands closed on her waist, and, shocked, she found herself lifted bodily into the air. She was no featherweight, but the life he'd been leading since their separation had turned his muscles to tempered steel.

For an endless moment she was clamped against him, the half-naked warmth of his body penetrating her thin clothing as if it hadn't existed at all, making her potently aware of the clench of muscle and sinew as he lowered her gently to the ground on the other side of the tree.

It was a stark reminder of his physicality. A disturbing warning that if he chose to use his strength against her she would be helpless. A battle of wits seemed the only recourse she had, but so far Ross had appeared able to keep ahead of the game there too.

'Thank you,' she managed, dry-mouthed. He wasn't touching her any more. He wasn't even near her, for heaven's sake, but already walking on ahead, yet the sensation of being in his arms was as vivid as if she carried the imprint of his chest and loins superimposed upon her own.

A wave of heat, which had nothing to do with the afternoon sun, swept through her. She rallied herself fiercely.

'Sorry to be so feeble,' she tossed carelessly after him.

'I should keep it cut back, but I don't come this way that often.' Ross slashed with his hand at an intrusive clump of undergrowth.

'It'll all have to be completely cleared anyway.' Macy spoke the thought aloud, and received an ironic glance.

'I'm sure it will,' he said. 'Nature can be such an inconvenience for rich people who like their playgrounds tidy.'

She bit her lip. 'We're not out to ruin the island.

Just to use its natural resources to their best advantage.'

Keep to business—strictly business—she told herself as the pounding of her heart began to steady.

'You've been well-programmed, Macy,' Ross commented, his mouth twisting. 'Tell me, how did the Gilmour-Denys spies discover this place? It's been Hilliard private property for generations, and no one sets foot here without an invitation.'

'As I've discovered to my cost,' Macy muttered. 'As a matter of fact, Cameron saw it himself some years ago. He came down here and chartered a plane to look at a number of possibilities. What he saw of Thunder Cay seemed to inspire him, and as soon as he got back to Britain he commissioned plans and drawings. The whole thing became his dream.'

'And a dream with a high profit-margin,' he said softly. 'What could be better?'

'You'd know all about that, of course,' she returned evenly. 'Unfortunately for Cameron this particular dream isn't likely to come true. The cost is far too high.'

'How can you put a price on paradise? And is the decision yours to make anyway?'

'We won't argue about it,' she said shortly. 'The sooner this whole farcical situation comes to an end, the better.'

'Is that how you see my honest attempt to heal the breach between us?' he asked mockingly.

When was honesty ever part of our relationship? The question hovered unspoken on her lips. They were getting into deep water here.

She allowed her steps to falter, then stopped altogether, leaning against the trunk of a convenient tree, and fanning herself gently with her hat.

Ross stood watching her, hands on hips, a slight frown creasing his forehead.

'Are you all right.'

'Fine.' She tried a note of faintly quivering bravado. 'A route march is the best thing for anyone recovering from heatstroke.'

His frown deepened. 'We haven't much further to go. Unless you'd prefer to turn back.'

'No,' Macy said, smiling like a gallant little trouper. 'I'd much rather go on—really. What am I going to be shown—a secret cache of pirate gold that Old Bevis hid for a rainy day?'

He shook his head. 'A family treasure of a different kind.' He held out his hand. 'Come on.'

'I can manage.' She hung back. There was no way she could cope with the clasp of Ross's fingers round hers. Once they'd walked hand in hand together everywhere. For a moment she could almost smell the river mist on the Thames Embankment, feel the scuffle of dried leaves under her feet in Hyde Park.

I only had to reach out and he was there for me, she thought. Now his hand was outstretched again, and the evocation of that time of innocent happiness was too much pain to bear.

'As you wish.' He shrugged, and walked on.

After a pause, she followed, hugging her arms round her body.

The gradient had steeped perceptibly, and she kept her head down, taking each step with care. The last thing she wanted to risk was a twisted ankle.

The tangle of trees was thinning out, she realised, and ahead of them was a grassy knoll topped by an imposing house, built on two storeys. The thick stone walls were white, and the upper floor was encircled by a wrought-iron balcony.

So the beach shack wasn't the only habitation after all, Macy thought. But who occupied all this faded grandeur, which seemed so oddly familiar?

As they got closer, her throat closed with disappointment as she registered the peeling paintwork, the glassless windows, and the untended vines straggling over the walls.

'What is this place?'

'It's the original Hilliard house, built in the eighteenth century by Gervase Hilliard. He came here with a few slaves to try and establish a cotton plantation.'

'Slaves.' Macy wrinkled her nose. 'How appalling.'

'To us, yes,' Ross agreed levelly. 'To our ancestors, slavery was one of the economic facts of life. And Gervase was looking to make his fortune.'

'From cotton—here?' Macy's brows lifted.

'He wasn't the only one by any means. You'll find similar ruins throughout the islands. The Deveaux plantation on Cat Island was famous.'

'Why did he need the money?'

'He was a younger son, and he'd fallen in love with a rich man's daughter,' Ross explained. 'He grew good quality cotton, and for a while the plantation prospered. He was even able to build this house for his future wife, and when it was ready he went to Nassau to claim her.'

'And lived happily ever after? He deserved to, after all that hard work.' Macy kept her tone light.

'Alas, no,' Ross said softly. 'He arrived just in time to witness her marriage to another man—a wealthy Yankee.'

'Oh.' Macy digested this as they walked toward the bare rectangle which had once held the main door. She hoped Ross wasn't drawing any parallels. Not that there were any of course. 'Then I hope he soon found consolation.'

'No, he never did. He returned here, freed his slaves, and set fire to the cotton. He moved out of the house, too, and went to live on the beach in a kind of shelter built from palm fronds. It's supposed to be from him that the Hilliards get their capacity for solitude.' He paused. 'And possibly for falling in love with the wrong women,' he added levelly.

Macy moved hastily towards the door. 'Is it safe to go in?'

'Safe enough,' Ross said. 'And rather sad.'

She saw what he meant. In decay, the house had become a kind of conservatory. In places where the floor had rotted, shrubs grew freely, and in the former parlour, a small tree had forced its way through, its top branches reaching toward the open sky, clearly visible through the broken roof.

There was no staircase, but Macy could see the marks where it had once stood, like scars on the spotted walls of the square entrance hall.

The smell of vegetation was sharp, almost rank.

She shivered. 'Did it have to get like this? Couldn't it have been reclaimed—repaired in later years?'

'There were several unsuccessful attempts, but few people ever feel easy here. It's said Gervase still hangs around, hoping his lady will come to join him.'

'Oh.' Macy looked round, frowning. It had occurred to her why the house had seemed familiar. It was the basic design which Cameron had chosen for the central hotel block in the projected complex.

He must have glimpsed it from the plane that day—a gracious mansion crowning a hill. From that distance he wouldn't have noticed its dilapidation. But his plans for the complex were for luxury and upbeat hedonism. A resident ghost would hardly be a marketing plus for the clientele he had in mind.

'What happened to Gervase,' she asked eventually.

'He disappeared without trace one day. It was assumed that loneliness and disappointment got too much for him, and he simply walked into the sea.'

'Or maybe another boat came along, and he cut his losses, and sailed off to find another life and a new lady,' Macy said energetically.

Ross looked at her unsmilingly, 'Maybe. Is that the solution to everything, Macy—off with the old, and on with the new?'

'I try not to make sweeping judgements.' She turned towards the doorway.

'Yet you had no hesitation in judging me.' His hand descended on her shoulder, halting her, swinging her round to face him.

Colour rushed into her face. 'Stop that. I don't want…'

'I'm sure.' There was bitterness in his voice, a small flame blazing in the aquamarine eyes. 'But this is one time, Macy, when you don't get your own way.'

He pulled her against him, his hand lifting to twist in her hair, making it impossible to struggle. He said thickly, 'Don't fight me, Macy—just remember…'

For a moment, his dark face seemed to hover over her, like a hawk with its prey in sight. She tried to say, 'No' but the word emerged as a small incoherent sound. Then he swooped, his mouth closing on hers, making further protest impossible.

The heated intensity of his kiss took her by storm, the sensuous movement of his lips on hers melting her initial resistance like frost before a flame. Her lips parted helplessly to allow the more intimate access he was demanding. A slow, sweet trembling began in the pit of her stomach and spread through every fibre of her being.

This was what she had feared—had wanted so desperately to avoid. This sudden drowning in sensation—this obliteration of reason by the stark demands of her flesh.

Remember? she thought in despair, as she breathed the familiar scent of him. Oh, God, how could I forget?

His free hand lifted, encompassing one rounded breast through the thin top, his thumb moving almost hypnotically on the hardening nipple, creating a height of sensitivity that rapidly became a small agony, demanding surcease.

Whimpering silently, Macy felt herself push her hips forward, the molten core of her womanhood seeking the certainty of his erection.

'God.' The word rasped hoarsely from his taut throat. He propelled her back against the wall, crushing the ferns growing there, filling the air with their heady aroma. His hand dragged at her skirt, searching for her, all finesse—all gentleness suddenly dissipated under the driving force of a need as savage as it was mutual.

She wanted him to fill her—to make her complete—a whole woman once more. To wipe away the empty sterility of the past four years, and remember how it had been…

Remember. Suddenly all the passionate connotations of the word changed, and it rang in her head like a tocsin. Warning her. Making her realise where she was and what was happening to her. Dragging her back from the edge of the abyss.

'No.' The word tore out of her like a scream. Her hands balled into fists, belabouring furiously at his chest. Shoving him away from her, rocking him back on his heels by the suddenness of her attack. 'Leave me alone.' She dashed her hand across her mouth as if trying to wipe away the stain of his kiss.

He stared at her, dark colour along his cheekbones, his chest heaving as he dragged air into his lungs.

'Macy.' His voice cracked. 'In God's name—don't do this.'

'You started it,' she flung at him, her voice high and strained. 'No pressure. That's what you said, you bastard. I should have known I couldn't trust you.'

'I wanted you,' Ross retorted, his tone grim. 'And you wanted me. Or is that what you can't forgive, my beautiful uncaring wife? That you switched off the calculator in that icy little brain of yours and started behaving like a human being?'

There were tears perilously near the surface. But she couldn't afford to let them show. No sign of weakness. No surrender.

She said rawly, 'Damn you, Ross. Think what you like. But from now on, keep away from me.'

She turned, her head high, and walked away from him out of the empty, eyeless house, with its legacy of heartbreak and loneliness, and back down the track which led to the beach.

She'd gone about fifty yards when he came after her.

'Macy—slow down. You'll make yourself ill again careering off like this.'

'Much you care,' she said bitterly. 'It was your idea to—maroon me here.'

'If you're hoping I'll do the decent thing and let you go, you'll be disappointed.'

'Hardly. Decency has never featured very highly with you.'

'If that were true,' Ross said slowly, 'you'd be still at the house, on the floor, without your clothes, enjoying the re-consummation of our marriage.'

'Enjoying?' Macy shook her head. 'I think "enduring" would be more appropriate.'

'And "hypocrite" even more applicable.' Ross's tone bit.

Macy glared at him, and set off down the track, Ross keeping pace at her side. They maintained a frosty silence until they reached the fallen tree, which she scrambled over in undignified haste before Ross could offer his assistance. But her hurry cost her dear. As she swung herself to the ground, a protruding twig caught in her skirt and ripped a jagged tear, mid-thigh.

'Hell's bells.' Macy lifted a clenched fist to the sky. 'The only thing I have to wear and it's in rags.'

'Hardly.' Ross went on one knee to inspect the damage, and Macy recoiled.

'Just keep away from me,' she said between her teeth.

'If you can stop over-reacting for one moment,' Ross said wearily, 'there's a sewing kit at the shack. But if wearing a mended skirt offends your principles, I can offer a small selection of alternative clothes which will fit you.'

'Women's clothes?' Macy stared at him.

'As it happens,' he nodded.

Well, she didn't have to ask whose they were, Macy thought, pain commingling with anger deep within her. Naturally Judy Ryan would have stayed over on Thunder Cay—shared a meal at Ross's table—slept in his bed. The images ached on her inner vision. And the other girl was expecting to return, or she wouldn't have left a change of clothing there.

She said curtly, 'I think I'll opt for the needle and thread.'

Mouth compressed, he said, 'Just as you wish.' And this time it was his turn to walk away.

Macy followed at a resentful distance. Did he really think she'd be prepared to wear his mistress's clothes? Or did he imagine she was still unaware of the relationship?

Even if I hadn't been shown those photographs of them together in London, I'd have had to be blind and deaf to miss her performance in the hall at Trade Winds, she thought, seething.

When they arrived back at the beach house, Ross handed over the sewing kit unsmilingly.

'I'm going to catch some fish for dinner,' he said, adding with chill civility, 'Would you like to come with me?'

'Thank you, no.' Macy made a business of hunting out a spool of white thread. 'I'm going to do my mending, then have a rest,' she added, recollecting belatedly her role as semi-invalid. 'This afternoon has been tiring.'

He nodded. 'Unbridled stroppiness can have that effect.'

Macy stiffened. 'You feel I should meekly submit to being manhandled—sexually harassed?'

'On the contrary,' he returned. 'Meek submission is the last thing I want from you, darling. Start thinking in terms of unrestrained passion.'

He sent her a mocking salute, and left the shack whistling.

Macy called him a rude word under her breath, and instantly jabbed the needle into her finger.

Karma, she thought wearily, sucking away the bead of blood. The sting of the tiny, insignificant wound brought the lurking tears to the surface at last, and she sank down weakly on to the edge of the sagging sofa, and wept, until she could weep no more…

She couldn't believe, she thought, pressing her fists childishly against her wet eyes, how quickly— how fatally quickly her treacherous body had succumbed to Ross's lovemaking.

She had totally failed to gauge the depth of her own sensual hunger, or the fragility of the defences she could mount against him.

And he had let her go. That was the humiliating truth she now had to live with.

Because if he'd ignored her objections—mastered her protests—taken her in his arms again, she would have given herself with total, unreasoning abandon. And the realisation stunned her.

She shivered, tucking her legs protectively under her, and huddling into the cushions. She found herself thinking with a kind of panic, 'Where can I go? What can I do?'

She became aware of the scent almost at once, faint, elusive, and exotic as it tantalised her nostrils. She bent to sniff at the cushion, and as she did so caught sight of something white half-hidden down the side of the sofa.

She tugged it free. It was a woman's handkerchief, in good quality white linen, monogrammed with the single initial 'J'. The scent too was stronger, and quite unmistakable. 'Ysatis' she thought almost reflectively, as her fingers convulsively crushed the scrap of material into a tiny ball. The fragrance Judy Ryan had been wearing at Trade Winds.

Proof of the other girl's recent presence on the island, if proof were needed.

With a quiver of revulsion, she dropped the crumpled ball of material on to the floor.

What cruel game was Ross playing? she asked herself wretchedly. Why couldn't he be content with the woman who'd been his intimate companion for the past four years or more, instead of trying to force an unwilling wife back into his arms on his own outrageous terms.

Hurt pride, she thought wearily, or revenge. That was the only explanation. And no relationship could be built on such treacherous foundations.

'You used me once,' he'd told her. 'Now I'm repaying the compliment.'

It was as simple as that. And no amount of passion could ever make it acceptable.

Her head had started to ache again. She would go into the other room, she thought. Stretch out on the bed, and try and gain some oblivion in sleep.

She could only pray that this time there would be no heated, sensuous dreams to torment her.

She got up slowly, pushing her hair back from her tear-streaked face, staring ahead of her with pain-filled eyes. Life without Ross had been a desert of emptiness. But to live with him again, knowing she was merely being used, would break her heart.

She took a deep, steadying breath, then bent and retrieved Judy Ryan's handkerchief from the floor, stuffing it into the pocket of her torn skirt.

Another woman's scent, she told herself, to serve as a constant and potent reminder that Ross was another woman's man.

CHAPTER EIGHT

MACY must have slept, in spite of her emotional turmoil, because, when she opened her eyes, the room was filled with the strong rosy glow of sunset.

She became aware of other things too. A faint crackling noise, allied to a scent of woodsmoke, and another more savoury smell which made her mouth water suddenly.

And, also, that a thin blanket had been placed over her while she slept on top of the bed.

She bit her lip. It was an act of kindness on Ross's part, that was undeniable. But the knowledge that he'd been in the room while she was asleep and vulnerable was disturbing.

His room, she thought, looking round her. His bed.

She was thankful that she'd taken the trouble to shower away the marks of pain and distress, and mended the rent in her skirt before she took her rest. She'd have hated him to find her tear-stained and unkempt. She needed every scrap of self-possession and respect she could get.

She got up, smoothing the creases out of the much-tried white skirt, then went outside on to the small veranda.

A little way down the beach, Ross was kneeling beside a driftwood fire, above which, impaled on sticks, two fish were cooking. He was tending them, his expression intent, absorbed. Then, as if aware of her regard, he turned his head and smiled at her.

For a second, the years, and all else that had served to distance them, fell away, and she felt her heart lurch, suddenly and painfully. Be careful, she adjured herself, as she walked down the steps and began to cross the sand towards him.

'I hope you don't object to a barbecue,' he said as she reached his side.

'Not at all. Don't you ever get bored with this Robinson Crusoe act of yours.' Her voice was unnecessarily tart.

'Not yet,' Ross said cheerfully. 'Don't you get fed up with the rat race—even if you are involved with some of the chief rats?'

'Very funny,' she said stormily. 'However, I prefer their company to some I could mention.' She took a breath. 'Ross, isn't it time we called a stop to all this? I think you've amused yourself long enough at my expense, and now I'm getting annoyed.'

Ross gave her a laconic look. 'I'm sure the minions at Gilmour-Denys may jump when you snap your fingers, darling, but I don't. Go practise being imperious somewhere else.'

'Unfortunately, at the moment, there is nowhere

else,' she snarled. 'I'm asking you to send for the boat to take me off.'

'But the honeymoon's hardly begun, my sweet. And there's a lot more of the island to show you.'

'A pleasure I'd prefer to forgo.' She sank down on to one knee beside him. 'Ross, I'll make a deal with you.'

'That's what we're here for.'

'No.' She swallowed. 'Not that kind of deal. Let me go, now, and I won't say a word about what's happened to anyone. The last thing your father needs—or mine—is some monumental scandal.'

'What's so scandalous about a husband and wife reconciling under a tropic moon? All the world's supposed to love a lover, Macy.'

'We are not,' she said, 'lovers.'

'Not yet.'

'Not ever. We both have new lives—new relationships.'

His mouth twisted sardonically. 'Cameron Denys is hardly that. He's been there, waiting for your father to hand you over, gift-wrapped, since the day you left school. But Thunder Cay should be sufficient compensation.'

She said, 'I intend to tell the Gilmour-Denys board that it was all a mistake—that Thunder Cay was never for sale.'

He shook his head. 'Too late, darling. Ambrose Delancey will have told them by now that negotiations are under way.' He paused. 'Although not, of course, the actual form they're taking.'

He examined the grilling fish, nodded with satisfaction, and served them on to plates.

'Madam's dinner is served.' He pointed to a rug spread on the sand. 'Take a seat.'

Macy took the plate he handed her, and with one, sweeping gesture, tipped the fish back into the flames.

Ross watched its cremation without expression. 'You should have said you preferred it well done,' he remarked eventually, stretching out on the rug, and pulling a tray set with cutlery, glasses, and bottle of wine on ice towards him.

He uncorked the wine, filled both glasses, and began to eat with every evidence of enjoyment.

Macy watched sullenly. That had to be one of the most meaningless gestures of her life, she thought. And she was starving.

'Here.' Ross held out a glass of wine to her. 'Or have you decided on total abstinence as well?'

It was a Californian vintage she particularly liked, dry, but with a strong fruit base. There seemed little point in cutting her nose off a second time, so she sipped in inimical silence while Ross finished his meal.

Daylight was only a pale flush of memory in the sky, and the moon was climbing, golden and benign above the palm trees. The breeze that came from the sea was still warm, but Macy found she was shivering just the same.

'Cold?' he asked.

'No.' She was silent for a moment, feeling the wine caress her throat, and tingle through her veins. Then she said huskily, 'What do you want me to do, Ross? Go on my knees—beg you for mercy?'

'When you beg,' he said slowly, 'it certainly won't be for mercy. And it will be in my own good time, not yours. I've waited four years for you, so I can hold back till you decide to drop the pretence—and I don't mean your imitation of the Dying Swan this afternoon,' he added, with curt derision.

Macy flushed defensively, 'I didn't ask to get heatstroke…'

'To hell with that. I'm talking about a more fundamental dishonesty.'

'I don't know what you mean.' She stiffened.

'No? Then I'll be happy to give a brief demonstration.' He put down his glass and leaned over, detaching hers from her suddenly nerveless fingers.

'Ross…' Fright, and some less easily identified emotion, tightened her throat.

'Hush,' he said. 'It's all right. I'll make it all right.'

He moved beside, pressing her down without force on to the rug. Then his head and shoulders blotted out the moon, just as his kiss blotted out thought and reason.

This time, he was almost frighteningly gentle, allowing his lips and tongue to play with hers, until the taut rigidity of her mouth trembled into compliance. And as the moist, sensuous invasion continued, she felt a sigh of pleasure quiver through her body.

His lips placed a trail of tiny kisses along her jaw, and down the curve of her arched throat, finding every pulse, every sensitive area of delight.

He took the edge of the silken top between his teeth and tugged at it gently. She could feel the warmth of his breath through the thin fabric. Could feel her nipples firming in response, even before he bent and let his lips close round each tumescent peak in turn, laving them with his tongue through the clinging material.

Her arms lifted, almost of their own volition, to lock behind his head, and hold him to her. Later, she thought dazedly, she would hate herself for this. But now—ah, God—now…

With a stifled moan, she arched her whole body in offering—in surrender.

But Ross was moving too—rolling away from her, his breathing suddenly harsh.

She looked up startled, and saw him get to his feet.

'Ross.' It was a little cracked whisper. 'Don't leave me—please…'

In the gathering darkness, he was a tall shadow standing over her, but his voice had a cool and ruthless clarity.

'It wasn't so hard to make you beg, after all, Macy.

But I'm afraid the demonstration's over for tonight.
I said it would be brief.' He paused. 'Sleep well. I
give you my word you won't be disturbed.'

He turned and walked away down the beach
towards the silver ripple of the sea.

'Fool. Idiot. Imbecile.'

Macy muttered the words as she sat on the sofa,
staring sightlessly ahead of her.

So much for self-control, and all her good intentions. Without even trying, Ross had entangled her
in a fleeting web of tender sensuality.

The tenderness, of course, had been her undoing,
coupled with the sheer drenching sweetness of familiarity which had overwhelmed her in those
charged moments up at the Hilliard house.

Ross's mouth, she thought achingly. Ross's hands.

Her need for him had simply been dormant. Her
mind might deny him, but her body knew better.

What's the matter with me? she asked herself
wretchedly. What kind of woman could still want a
man who cynically and cold-bloodedly walked out
on her for money? A man, who now only wanted her
back for his own selfish and devious purposes.

A woman in love, of course. It was that simple.
That fundamental.

Even if she was able to escape from Thunder Cay
tomorrow, she would love him all her life. She could
admit that now—acknowledge it in the deepest part

of her soul. Not even the shame and heartbreak of his rejection had been able to change the way she felt about him.

The life she'd rebuilt had been a sham—a flimsy façade dragged together to shield her from self-knowledge.

One thing was certain. No matter how she might long for him, and for the fulfilment she would only ever know with him, she couldn't allow the bond of a child to tie her to a man who'd treated her with such heartless contempt.

Our child should have been conceived in love, she thought sadly. Not as a matter of expedience, or as compensation for imagined wrongs. After all, I was the one who was wronged.

Macy looked at the curtained entrance to the bedroom, her mouth tightening. His parting words had seemed to imply she could go to bed in safety tonight. But she knew the danger had never been more real. Not from Ross, but from her own weakness—her own desperate yearning.

She bit her lip, and focused her attention on the closed door next to the bedroom. Presumably it led to another room of sorts, but even if it was little more than a glorified cupboard she reckoned there'd be enough floor space to make up a bed for herself with the sofa cushions, and a blanket.

Unless, of course, it was locked. But to her relief, when she tried the heavy wooden handle, it turned easily, and the door opened towards her, with a faint squeak from its substantial hinges.

And inside was a compact and comprehensively equipped dark room.

Macy's brows snapped together. She supposed she should have guessed. He'd made no secret of the fact that he was still continuing his photographic career, and he'd said electricity was an essential.

The room didn't seem to be in use at the moment, although she noticed the radio he'd mentioned tucked into a corner. Her lips tightened. She knew nothing about sending transmissions, but she might have to do a crash course if all else failed.

There were several bulky folders on one of the work units, and Macy picked up the top one and opened it.

For a moment, she thought she was looking at some mysterious enchanted garden. Then she realised that the strange misshapen branches she saw were of coral, and the vivid splashes of gold, rust and orange weren't clumps of flowers at all, but sponges.

It was a wild, alluring underwater world confronting her, she realised with amazement.

She carried the folder back to the sofa, and leafed through the prints with mounting excitement.

Ross hadn't concentrated solely on coral, with its towering halls and bottomless caverns. There were detailed studies of other forms of marine life too. She recognised the exotic parrot fish, and the more homely grouper, as well as a shoal of angel fish.

And there were other, more sinister shapes, too. A moray eel, spotted like a leopard, and a hammerhead shark, with its distinctive blunted snout, and long streamlined body, dwarfing the girl diver, who swam below it like a miniaturised shadow.

She was in several of the shots, her hair streaming around her head like a blonde nimbus, and quite unmistakable.

Macy thought, Judy Ryan, and bit her lip till she tasted blood.

'Seen enough?' Ross's voice sounded harshly from the doorway.

Macy had been too absorbed to be aware of his approach. She started violently, but managed to retain her hold on the folder, as she got to her feet.

'I'm sorry,' she said awkwardly. 'I didn't mean to pry.' She forced a smile. 'I should have guessed why that door had to fit so well.'

'Probably.' He held out his hand for the folder, but she hesitated.

'They're very good. Did you take them locally?'

He nodded. 'Most of them off this island, and Fortuna. But we went down to the Abacos as well.'

Did we indeed? thought Macy. She indicated the photograph of the shark with its human counterpart. 'That took some guts.' She tried to keep her tone admiring, but impersonal.

'It isn't quite as hazardous as it seems. Sharks rarely bother divers unless provoked in some way. And Cliff Ryan was handling the security side of things, as always.'

'Cliff Ryan?' Macy's brows rose interrogatively as she relinquished the folder.

'Judy's brother. He runs a diving school and underwater exploration outfit on New Providence. He wouldn't let anything happen to either of us. Besides, Judy's very experienced. She was practically born in the water.'

'Yet she chose nursing instead.'

Ross nodded. 'She trained at one of the big teaching hospitals in London.'

So that's what she was doing there, thought Macy.

'When she qualified, she decided to come back to the Bahamas to do private nursing,' Ross went on. 'Her diving, these days, is purely recreational.' He paused. 'And, of course, she's very decorative.' His tone was bland. 'She photographs well, even in a wet suit, and as she works at Trade Winds she's always on hand.'

'Yes.' Macy put a hand in her pocket, and touched the tight ball of Judy Ryan's handkerchief. Always on hand. Always available.

She tried to smile. 'Are the photographs for a magazine spread—the *National Geographic* or something?'

Ross shook his head. 'They're for a book,' he said.

'The breakdown of coral is getting to be a serious environmental issue these days, and I was commissioned to write and take pictures about the life and death of a reef. The proceeds will be used for experimental work to try and halt the decline.'

'Being Ross Hilliard has its advantages,' she said.

He shrugged. 'Actually I was first offered the commission four years ago, when I was still relatively unknown.'

And when you were still with me, she thought numbly. So that was where you vanished to—sailing and diving in the Bahamas with your lady and her brother.

It could also explain why Ross had taken her father's money so readily. She wasn't sure what kind of publishing advance such a book could command, but if it was intended for an environmental charity it was unlikely to be high. Ross would have needed additional finance for his research.

She smiled resolutely, 'So you finally got to do what you wanted—make a record of one of the world's last wildernesses. Congratulations.'

'It was certainly fascinating,' he said quietly. 'The adventure of a lifetime.'

The lifetime that we planned, she thought in anguish. The adventure you promised me. Oh, Ross...

He frowned slightly, his eyes raking her face. 'You look tired,' he said abruptly. 'Go to bed.'

He took in the sudden hectic flush along her

cheekbones, the desperate clenching of her hands, and his expression gentled slightly. 'Macy, I said you were safe tonight, and I meant it. Go and get some rest.'

He turned towards the stove. 'I'm going to make some coffee before I turn in. Do you want some, or does it still keep you awake?'

Her heart ached at the accuracy of his memory. She said stiltedly, 'It—still does.'

'Need anything else?'

Only your arms around me. The words seemed to clamour in her head.

'No,' she said brightly. Maybe too brightly. 'No, thanks. Not a thing.'

She walked into the bedroom, and let the curtain fall into place behind her.

She could hear the sound of thunder in the distance. Macy grimaced, and turned up the collar of her trenchcoat. Storms always made her nervous. She hoped she'd get back to the flat before this one broke.

Perhaps it was the build-up in the weather which had made her edgy all day. Or maybe she was just looking forward to being home with Ross.

Things had been strained between them before she left.

'Do you have to spend the weekend at your father's?' he demanded.

'He's got a delegation of Japanese businessmen to entertain, Ross,' she tried to explain. 'He needs me.'

'I need you,' he said sombrely. 'Macy, you're my wife, not your father's tame hostess, and it's time he was told.'

'Yes,' she said. 'Yes, I know. But not yet. I want to get him accustomed to the idea, slowly.'

He said flatly, 'I don't think there'll be enough time in eternity for that. We should have told him right away, and to hell with the consequences.' He framed her face in his hands. 'There are things we need to discuss this weekend—important things.'

'That all sounds very dire,' she said lightly. 'But I have to go down to Caldecott. There's some paperwork to do with the Landin Trust I have to deal with as well. Won't your important things keep until Monday?'

He was silent for a moment, then he shrugged. 'It seems they'll have to,' he said, and kissed her.

It had been an odd weekend. Her father had seemed preoccupied, as if he was only going through the motions of being a genial host. Yet he was usually in his element, disguising business as pleasure at Caldecott Manor.

Nevertheless, a highly successful deal had been struck on Sunday morning, and by the time their visitors departed that evening Macy had been dropping with weariness, mingled with celebratory champagne.

She tried hard to listen attentively to Sir Edwin's painstaking explanations of the Trust documents she had to deal with, and had dutifully scribbled her signature where indicated, before crawling thankfully up to bed.

She usually had a lift with her father after these weekends, but to her astonishment when she woke on Monday morning, she found he'd left an hour earlier than usual. And then the housekeeper took advantage of her presence to bring a whole catalogue of queries to her attention—the kind of domestic trivia that Sir Edwin never heeded.

Accordingly it was lunchtime before she could get away and catch her train. And although she'd attempted to phone Ross several times to warn him she was going to be late, there was no reply from the flat.

Perhaps he'd been offered an assignment, she thought hopefully. They'd been thin on the ground lately, although she'd assured her father that everything was wonderful. She felt guilty each time she did so, knowing the secret she was harbouring. Perhaps Ross was right, and she should simply tell her father she'd been a wife for six months rather than wait for some ideal moment that might never come.

The front door of the flat was open, and she flew in, calling, 'I'm back. Have you missed me?' then stopped, because it wasn't Ross waiting in the living-room, but her father.

She checked, disconcerted. 'Daddy?'

After all, it was the first time he'd set foot in the place, and he looked grave, and rather pale, as if he found his presence there distasteful.

She thought, he knows—he's found out about the wedding.

He said heavily, 'You'd better sit down, my dear. I have some—bad news for you.'

He seemed to recede to a great distance. She heard herself saying very calmly and distinctly, 'There's been an accident, hasn't there and Ross is dead.'

'No,' Sir Edwin said bitterly. 'He's very much alive, or he was when I spoke to him earlier.'

'You and Ross have been together?' Macy moved bewilderedly to switch on a lamp. The sky was dark as slate outside.

'He came to the office by appointment,' Sir Edwin confirmed. 'He had what he called—a business proposition to put to me.'

She laughed. 'But Ross doesn't know anything about big business. He's a photographer.'

'Is he?' Sir Edwin said grimly. 'I'd say fortune-hunter and confidence trickster might be more accurate descriptions.'

'How dare you?' Blood burned in Macy's face. 'You've never even tried to like him—or to understand why I love him.'

'Do you blame me? When he stood in front of me only a few hours ago, and asked me how much I'd be prepared to pay him to get out of your life once and for all? He said he knew he'd never be acceptable in your world, and that your relationship wasn't working. However, he couldn't afford to just—fade out of the picture.' Her father's voice rose angrily. 'That's the man you love, Macy. A common shyster.'

She was very still. 'No,' she said. 'It can't be true. There must be some mistake.'

'Macy.' Her father took her icy hands, chafing them. 'I know what you must be feeling, how terrible this must seem. But believe me, it's all for the best. Illegitimate—penniless—living by his wits.' He snorted with contempt. 'Sweetheart, you're well rid of him.'

'He's gone?' Her reeling brain tried to make sense of what was happening. As if on cue, lightning flashed, to be followed almost at once by a long, low rumble of thunder. 'You—paid him to go.'

'It was what he wanted.' Sir Edwin spoke in a low, urgent voice. 'He must have had this planned from the start—from the moment he discovered who you were. He knew that I'd be thankful to get him out of your life, so he stayed just long enough to push the price up.'

'I see.' Her voice sounded like a stranger's. 'And exactly how much am I worth—in current market terms?'

'You'd better see this.' He took a folded paper from inside his coat, and handed it to her.

It was quite a simple document. It stated that, for the sum of one hundred and fifty thousand pounds, the undersigned, Ross Bannister, forfeited all claims, either financial or personal, on Macy Landin Gilmour.

The signature was unmistakably Ross's—an angry slash across the page, under the words 'Received with thanks.'

Another flash of lightning. Thunder—like the crack of some kind of doom.

Macy stared down at the paper. Macy Landin Gilmour, she thought. Not Macy Bannister. Nausea, bitter as gall, rose in her throat. She said, 'Is this all. He didn't say anything else about me—about our relationship?'

'No.' Sir Edwin stared at her, paling. 'Macy—you don't mean—surely there isn't a child on the way?'

She said quietly, 'No that isn't what I mean. I was wondering if he offered any explanation.'

There was a silence, then he said, 'There is an explanation. I hoped I wouldn't have to hurt you with it.'

Photographs—spilling across a table. She pushed them away and ran to the bedroom.

Ross's half of the wardrobe was bare; the drawers in the tallboy were empty; his suitcases had gone.

When the thunder roared again, Macy put her hands over her ears, and started to scream.

CHAPTER NINE

MACY sat bolt upright in bed, her heart hammering. Another dream, she thought dazedly. And its cause was not far to seek. Somewhere in the reaches of the night, there was a low, persistent growl of thunder.

She pressed her hand over her ears to blot out the sound, stifling the instinctive moan of distress which rose in her throat. Storms had this effect on her now. They brought back nightmares she wanted to remain buried in her unconscious mind forever.

She felt very hot. She hadn't undressed before she lay down, and her clothes were sticking to her clammy body. By morning, they'd be unwearable.

But at the time anything had seemed better than lying naked in Ross's bed, waiting for him to come to her.

In spite of his assurances, she was sure he would continue to sleep with her, as he'd done when she was ill, and the prospect of that dangerous proximity made her throat tighten in panic.

Only she was alone.

The thunder was still rumbling, steadily and monotonously, and although the sound was faint, it was there, and it made her feel as if she was stifling—

choking in this room. She had to get out—to breathe—to regain her equilibrium.

Ross was fast asleep on the sofa. In the moonlight, through the open door, the curve of his bronzed body was clearly outlined under the single sheet that he'd partly kicked away. Macy looked down at the width of his shoulders, the long, graceful line of his back, the smooth turn of his hip, and felt her mouth grow dry.

There was a time when she'd have woken him at a time like this, she thought. When she'd have asked for comfort, for reassurance, her fingers featherlight against his spine, her mouth pressing kisses on to his cool skin.

And even still half drugged with sleep he'd have turned to her, smiling, and pulled her into his arms, sheltering her with his body.

But that was long ago.

Tensely, she began to edge to the door, her eyes fixed on him, but he didn't stir, even when a floorboard creaked under her foot.

Outside, the breeze from the sea was stronger than it had been during the day, and Macy drew several deep, grateful breaths. She ran a hand round the nape of her neck, lifting the heavy fall of her hair away from her skin, easing her shoulders irritably beneath the clinging, sticky top. A shower would be ideal, she thought longingly, but she couldn't risk waking Ross.

The alternative, of course, was a swim. The gentle splash of the sea on the beach sounded beguiling, and she walked down the sand, shedding her clothes as she went.

The last few yards were wonderful, untrammelled and free. She'd often heard that skinny-dipping was the only way to bathe, she thought, as she waded out into the lagoon, but this was the first time she'd tried it.

The water felt cool and sharp on her heated skin, and when it reached mid-thigh level she lowered herself into it completely, with a little gasp of pleasurable shock.

She swam for a few yards, then turned on her back and floated, the water lapping her like silk.

The sea by night was full of movement, sound and colour undreamed of in daylight, she discovered, as long slow ripples lifted her, then let her subside gently.

The distant thunder was louder now, but she could see no flashes of lightning in the sky, only the gleam of spray along the reef, and a hint of phosphorescence in the calmer water of the lagoon.

And, nearer at hand, a steady splashing growing louder.

Macy turned her head to discover the source, and found Ross suddenly, startlingly, beside her. Her body jack-knifed in shock, and she swallowed a mouthful of sea and choked.

'Are you crazy—suicidal?' Even muffled by the water in her ears, his voice sounded molten with rage. 'Get out of here, now.'

'You're the one who's mad,' Macy flung at him, coughing, as he began to assist her none too gently towards the shore. 'The storm woke me, and I just wanted to cool off.'

'Storm?' Ross dumped her on the beach. 'What bloody storm?'

'Can't you hear the thunder?' She scrubbed at her stinging eyes. 'I hate thunder.'

He listened for a moment, then laughed harshly. 'That's no storm. It's the sea breaking on the reef. It makes that noise when the wind freshens and veers slightly. That's how this place got its name— Thunder Cay.'

'The reef?' she repeated. 'Is that all it was?'

'It's enough,' he said drily. 'Don't underestimate it, especially in a boat.' He paused to shake some of the water out of his hair. 'Now, listen, Macy. You don't swim at night off this island, or any other. Nor do you ever swim alone. You could get into difficulties.'

'I'm not a helpless child,' she said with dignity. 'Actually, I'm quite a strong swimmer.'

'You,' he said grimly, 'are not alone in that respect.'

He took her by the shoulders, turning her, and

pointing towards the reef, where those brief trails of phosphorescent light still glimmered.

'That's the wake of a big fish—probably more than one,' he said. 'Sometimes sharks come inshore at night looking for food.'

'Oh,' was all she could think of to say. Suddenly the velvet night had turned on her. It was full of danger, and a chill that penetrated to her bones, and her teeth were chattering.

In fact, she was trembling all over, but that wasn't because of the menace she'd unwittingly invited. She was suddenly, desperately conscious of her nakedness and his.

'I'm cold.' She tried to conceal the shake in her voice.

Ross muttered something rough and exasperated under his breath, then pulled her to him, and, before she could say or do anything to prevent it, he'd lifted her up in his arms as easily as if she'd been a child. Holding her, he began to walk back up the beach towards the shack.

'My clothes…' she began, but he shook his head.

'We'll look for them tomorrow. Let's get you warm and dry first.'

She let herself relax into the strength of his embrace, as the warmth of his body communicated itself to hers.

She should not be allowing this, a small voice in her head warned. But, dear God, it was good to be this close to him again. To feel safe—secure in his arms—even if that was an illusion.

Reality would return with the dawn, and she would face it then.

She turned her head, and buried her face in the curve between his throat and shoulder, feeling the strong pulse throb against her probing lips. She touched her tongue to his skin, licking away the salt. Reminding herself deliriously of the warm male essence which belonged to him alone. She was savouring him, anticipating all that was to come as she pressed herself against his bare chest, feeling her nipples peak in delicious excitement at the contact with his hair-roughened skin.

It was Ross's turn to shiver. 'Macy.' His voice was raw. 'For God's sake…'

He carried her straight into the bedroom, lowering her on to the bed, and detaching her clinging hands.

'Get under the covers.' His voice was strained. 'I'll make you a hot drink—something with rum in it.'

'No,' she said, watching him through half-closed lids. She reached out and touched him gently—recklessly. Stroked her hand down the flat plane of his hip. Let it linger. Watched his body's instinctive, involuntary response to her caress, and smiled. This time he would not find it so easy to walk away.

The bed was as soft as a pillow, and she was a siren, luring him to his doom and ultimately—

inevitably to her own as well. Only, she didn't care any more.

Nothing mattered. Only this night, and the two of them together again. Reunited after the long, barren years. Her need for him was as deep and elemental as the ocean itself.

Her voice was soft. 'Stay with me, Ross. Warm me. It's been cold for so long.'

Ross sighed, a harsh sound of capitulation.

'Too cold,' he muttered. 'And four endless years too long. Oh, God, Macy…'

He lay beside her, reaching for her, and she went into his arms as if she'd never been away. Their bodies moulded together in an aching, wrenching silence which spoke more loudly than any words. Their mouths touched, tentatively, questioningly at first, then with a burgeoning fierceness and certainty.

Ross's mouth began to explore her body, feathering across her breasts, before drawing the proud nipples into his mouth. The movement of his tongue across the aroused peaks sent desire, jagged as lightning, exploding across her nerve-endings.

Again, she could hear the thunder on the reef, but it was closer now, all around her, pounding in her pulses, echoing through her veins.

His thigh grazed hers, and she lifted herself against him in swift urgency, letting her body speak for her, making its own imperative demands. Showing him that she was more—more than ready for the culmination.

Ross threw his head back, a groan of acceptance escaping his taut throat. He entered her in one strong, fluid movement, and her body melted in welcome for him, closing around him, replying moistly and heatedly to each slow, lingering thrust.

Ross, she thought dizzily, had always made love as if there was all the time in the world. And nothing had changed. He would make this last to the edge of eternity—and beyond...

Her hands clung to his sweat-slicked shoulders. His damp chest hair rasped against her sensitised breasts, lancing them with a pleasure akin to pain.

Her slender legs enclosed him, drawing him deeper, holding him inside her forever. The rhythms of love, which he himself had taught her, lifted and dropped them like the ebb and flow of the sea lapping the shore only yards away from them.

She was the moon that drew the tide, and he was the high golden sun that flamed and glittered in every fibre of her being. Who gave her new substance and meaning in the shadows of her universe.

The slow, deep drive of his body into hers possessed her, controlled her totally, and she focused almost blindly on each new and intense sensation breaking over her.

Even so, the first dark spasms of rapture took her unawares. Then, utterly consumed, her body convulsed and shuddered against him—around him in the sweet violence of her release.

Macy heard herself cry out hoarsely at the beauty and power of it, and felt sudden grateful tears scald on her cheeks.

Ross's hands framed her face tenderly. He kissed her mouth, then licked the drops of salt away from her skin and lashes, waiting for the dizzying spiral of delight to abate.

Her return to earth was slow. Out of her languid, delicious euphoria, she tried to speak—to say his name, but he shook his head, placing a silencing finger on her parted lips.

Then, very gently, the union between them unbroken, he turned on to his back, holding her astride him.

Hands on her hips, he held her still for a moment like some creamy statue of a pagan goddess, a faint smile playing about his lips as he studied her.

Macy lifted her hands, flicking the sea-damp strands of mahogany hair back from her shoulders and breasts, watching the sudden flare in his eyes as she did so.

He began to touch her, running his hands easily and fluently over the planes and contours of her body. His fingers teased a pattern from the base of her scalp, down to the nape of her neck, then followed the delicate line of her back, questing, with a faint frown, her too-prominent shoulder-blades, tracing each vertebra as if it was precious to him. His hands stroked down to her flanks, making her arch sensuously, as he rediscovered her. Enjoyed her.

She was smiling too, now, pursuing an exact path through the mat of hair on his chest with her finger-tips, seeking the flat male nipples, making them stiffen and pucker under her touch, before she bent to brush them with the tips of her own breasts. Listening to the change in his breathing. Watching the aquamarine eyes blaze into hers like blue diamonds. Feeling him stir within her, telling her silently that he had waited long enough.

Now, it was her turn to make love to him, and she did so, moving slowly, sensually, erotically against him, her whole body attuned to his pleasure, obeying each intimate, unspoken signal, as they led each other once more into the warm labyrinth of passion, seeking the dark, secret core of ecstasy at its heart.

But this was for him—all for him, she told herself languorously, swaying backwards a little, cupping her breasts enticingly, smoothing her fingers down over her body to her thighs, and the dark, silky triangle at their apex.

Knowing that for him, watching her was part of the delight. Taking him gradually, inexorably to the knife-edge of release, then holding back. Tantalising him. Delaying the moment when his world would splinter into exaltation.

But when that moment came, when she heard him

cry out, his eyes glazed and unseeing in sublimation, when she felt him erupt like a flame inside her—then, to her astonishment, she found her own body clenched and quivering under its own new shock-wave of fulfilment.

'That was greedy of me.' Aeons, light years later, she murmured the words into his sweat-slicked shoulder.

'You were starving.' She felt his lips touch her hair, like a benediction. Then, cradled in his arms, Macy slept.

It was broad daylight when she woke, and she was alone. She lay quietly for a while, letting her mind drift back over the events of the night, in a kind of elated incredulity.

She had slept in Ross's arms for a while, then awoken to his kisses, turning to him in drowsy delight as they made love again, softly and tenderly.

No dream this time, she thought, stretching plea-surably. Just golden, glorious reality.

Except for one thing. She pondered it, frowning a little, her tongue soothing her faintly swollen lips. There'd been something missing—something not quite right...

Of course, she thought, suddenly. The words. 'My love. My sweet love.' He didn't say the words.

And now he wasn't here.

It was a troublous realisation, or maybe just part

of the tender melancholy which so often followed lovemaking.

She sat up determinedly. She wasn't going to lie here getting the blues. She was going to get on with the day.

The first day, perhaps, of the rest of their lives.

As she pushed the sheet back, she saw the pile of clothing stacked neatly on the end of the bed.

For a moment, she was motionless. Then slowly, stiffly, she began to turn the garments over. Underwear in crisp broderie anglaise. A pair of brief white shorts. A vest top, the colour of honey. Pretty, practical, and in pristine condition, she had to admit.

But not hers. Never hers.

Macy sank her teeth into her lip, as shock gave way to growing anger.

Presumably, as she'd slept with him—made love with him in the bed he shared with his mistress, Ross assumed she would have no compunction about borrowing Judy Ryan's clothes either.

She turned to the tallboy, dragging open the drawers until she found the ones she wanted.

There was plenty of choice, she realised, feeling sick. Everything from the latest beach and leisurewear to nightgowns and peignoirs like drifts of thistledown. A world of pleasure and seduction, wrapped in tissue.

Macy slammed the drawers shut again. Her whole body was cringing as if she'd turned over a stone, and found unnamed horrors scuttling underneath. As if she'd been slapped in the face.

But she couldn't say she hadn't been warned.

She sat down on the edge of the bed, wrapping her arms protectively round herself to stop the trembling. The hurt, like a stone inside her.

Oh, God, she whispered, her throat aching. What a fool I've been. What a blind, gullible fool.

She'd let her body betray her, deliver her bound and gagged into Ross's hands. In one night, he'd achieved everything he'd set out to do when he brought her here, she realised feverishly. She'd given herself to him, passionately and completely, but with no guarantees in return.

Ross wanted a figurehead in his life. A suitable wife at his side. A mother for his child. Those were the terms he'd laid down. The deal that was on the table.

But she—she wanted so much more.

She wanted Ross as the man she'd fallen in love with—the man she'd married, with such hope. But that was the dream. The reality was the unprincipled stranger who'd taken her father's bribe, and walked out on her. The man who'd used her cynically for his own behests, and who now offered nothing but the bleak façade of a marriage, while he pursued his own pleasures elsewhere.

Well, she could not—would not accept that, she told herself starkly. She could not exist in a relationship without love or trust, no matter how sexually beguiling.

And Ross only had to crook his little finger to bring her, quivering into his arms, she reminded herself with shame.

He must think she was such a pushover that she'd be prepared to settle for whatever crumbs of a liaison she could get.

But he was wrong. Whatever the personal cost to herself, the agony of another separation, she deserved better than second-best.

The water in the shower was cool, and she used it liberally, like a ritual cleansing, washing away the taste and touch of him.

Then she wrapped the towel round herself like a sarong, and set off down the beach to find her own clothes.

The sun still had some hours to reach its full power, but it was warm enough, nevertheless, to encourage Macy, after a brief hesitation, to discard the clammy folds of towelling altogether.

Eve after all, she thought, her mouth curling ironically. Eve, who'd tasted the forbidden fruit, and then been turned out of paradise forever.

And Ross, undeniably, came under the heading of forbidden fruit. Something she should have remembered last night. Instead, she'd practically thrown herself at him, given away her true feelings with every kiss, every caress.

And now she had to face the consequences.

Her hand touched her abdomen, delicately, questioningly, as it occurred to her what one of those consequences might be.

She lifted her chin. She would deal with that if and when she had to.

She found her bra and pants, then picked her designer top out of the sand and studied it ruefully. It would be like wearing a cheese grater, but what choice did she have?

She pulled on the top, and wriggled uncomfortably into her maltreated skirt. As she tugged up the zip, a prickle of awareness shivered down her spine, and she looked up to see Ross coming down the beach towards her.

He was covered minimally by another pair of disreputable shorts, and had a camera slung over his shoulder.

In spite of everything, Macy felt her heart lurch crazily and hopelessly.

'I left you some things. Didn't they fit?' There was no trace of last night's shared warmth and intimacy in the cool eyes that observed her. No particular triumph either.

'I wouldn't know.' She kept her voice equally impersonal. 'I prefer my own clothes.'

He said, after a pause, 'I see.' He turned away, and began to walk back towards the shack. 'I'm about to make some coffee,' he tossed over his shoulder. 'Unless you have qualms about accepting that too.'

He was actually behaving as if she was being unreasonable, Macy realised, seething as she followed.

She said shortly, 'It's hardly the same thing.'

'Oh?' Ross shrugged. 'I'm afraid your methods of discrimination are beyond me.'

I could say the same, she thought tautly, as he filled the kettle and set it on the stove.

'Anyway,' he went on, 'you won't have to wear those things much longer.' He fetched beakers, spooned granules into them, his attention concentrated on the task. 'I've sent for the boat. You're leaving—going back to Fortuna.'

She was leaning against the table. Behind her back, her fingers curled round the hard, wooden edge, gripping it until her knuckles turned white.

'What's made you decide that?' Her voice sounded as if it was coming from a distance.

He didn't look at her. 'Macy, don't let's pretend.' His voice was weary. 'I was wrong and I admit it. Our marriage won't work. It can't. Not without commitment and that doesn't exist. Maybe it never did.'

He swung round. The aquamarine eyes blazed at her. 'I should never have done this. It was madness, but it's not too late to salvage the situation. I'll take your offer—a quick divorce. Serve the papers, and I'll sign them.'

He threw his head back. She saw the veins taut in

his throat. 'Only make it soon,' he added curtly. 'I want this finished—over with, at last.' He brushed past her, and went out of the door, his long stride carrying him swiftly out of sight.

Out of her life for good, she thought numbly.

Yet that was what she wanted, she told herself rigidly. What had to be. And she should be thankful for it.

So, why was the desolation inside her enough to fill the world?

CHAPTER TEN

MACY sat on the floor in the parlour of the old Hilliard house, her back against the trunk of the little tree, staring sightlessly up through the broken roof at the sky.

She wasn't sure why she'd come here—except that it seemed like a refuge from the shack, and all its recent memories. Or, maybe, a place serving as a monument to a love affair that had gone wrong just suited her present mood, she thought wryly.

She'd waited half an hour for Ross to return, but there'd been no sign of him. She made the coffee when the kettle boiled, and threw it away cold and untasted.

Unhappily restive, she'd begun to prowl ridiculously up and down the beach before calling herself sternly to order. If she needed exercise she'd take a proper walk, she decided, and instinctively her steps had turned towards the track up to the house.

She looked around her with a sigh, wondering idly how much it would cost to restore the house to a habitable condition. Even in its present sad state, it had an undeniable charm. And it was a Hilliard family heirloom, however little that might concern her.

The house needed attention, she thought wistfully. It needed filling with love and laughter, and the rough and tumble of family life.

She lifted a hand, and patted the slender tree trunk behind her. 'I wouldn't cut you down,' she said. 'You'd be a feature.'

But it wasn't up to her, and never would be.

What she had to consider instead was what she would say when she got back to London, what explanations she could offer her father—and Cameron—about the failure of the deal.

The first thing she would have to reveal was the truth about her marriage. That it had existed. That it was now over—completely and finally.

Ross's words of rejection still seemed to be beating in her brain.

For the second time, he'd closed her out of his life and walked away, but this time no one had needed to pay him to do it. It was his own free choice, she thought, pain lancing through her.

Was this how Gervase Hilliard had felt when he returned here alone? she wondered. Had his life seemed a total desert, without happiness or even hope?

But she wouldn't become a recluse as he had done. For this time she might have something from the wreckage to console her.

But even if that crazy, ecstatic night had not given her Ross's child, her life would still change. She intended to resign from Gilmour-Denys, and become completely independent. If the Landin Trust couldn't provide enough to occupy her time, she might start some kind of business. Maybe even restoring old houses.

She got to her feet, dusting off her clothes. A token gesture, she supposed, considering the state of them, then paused to pick a small spray of leaves from the tree.

Something to keep, she thought. To remind her always, as if she needed any such prompting.

As she emerged from the front door, she saw Ross striding up the slope towards her. He halted abruptly when he saw her, his face set.

'What the hell are you doing here?'

'Just saying goodbye.' Macy lifted a shoulder. 'I hope that's permitted.'

'Of course.' For a moment, his usual incisiveness seemed to have left him. 'It's just—I didn't expect—I didn't know where you'd gone.'

'Not very far,' she said. 'Now this is a really small island.'

His smile was wintry. 'Yes.' He paused. 'The boat is almost here.'

The hours had gone, she thought. All she was left with now were minutes—even seconds. And they were ticking away.

She said quietly, 'I'll come at once.'

She collected her bag from the shack, and walked

down to the jetty where Ross was waiting, watching Sam manoeuvre *Sweet Bird* alongside.

And not alone either. Macy's steps faltered as she recognised a blonde head, surmounting a tanned body, provocatively displayed in a vivid blue halter top and clinging knee-length pants to match.

Judy Ryan—come no doubt to gloat over the spoils, she thought grimly.

From some undreamed of vat of courage she dredged up a smile, pinning it resolutely in place.

'Well, hello.' Judy's smile was cat-like as she jumped ashore. 'I thought I'd come along for the ride.' She looked Macy over critically as Ross, having greeted her quietly, began an low-voiced conversation with Sam. 'How's the recovery going? You still look rather—worn.'

'I'm fine, thanks,' Macy responded coolly. 'But I'll be glad to go home. I don't think the local climate suits me.'

'Actually you weren't all that ill,' Judy said. 'But like most men, Ross is inclined to panic a little.' She paused. 'I suppose he felt partly responsible for your being sick—having virtually kidnapped you.'

Macy looked at her levelly. 'I see there aren't many secrets at Trade Winds.'

Judy gave a little laugh. 'Well, it is a very close-knit household.' She paused again. 'And I do rather have a vested interest in Ross.'

'So I gather.' Macy forced herself to speak calmly,

when in reality she wanted to scratch her nails down the other's smug face.

'I wasn't very happy about his seeing you again,' Judy went on. 'I tried to warn him against it. But apparently it was something he needed to do—like a kind of exorcism, maybe.'

'Really?' Macy gritted her teeth. 'Well, if you're expecting my head to spin round, or for me to vomit live toads, you're going to be disappointed.'

'Oh, I don't think so.' Judy's eyes were limpid with satisfaction. 'In a way, I suppose I should be grateful to you—if it means that Ross is going to finish with his past, and give up being a hermit on this damned island for ninety per cent of the time. Maybe life can become normal at last.'

'You don't like Thunder Cay?' Macy ignored the implications in the other girl's words.

Judy's brows lifted. 'What is there to like about the back end of nowhere? A creepy old house in the middle of a few acres of nothing.' She gave a little artificial shudder. 'I hope your company does make something of it. We could do with some upbeat life round here.'

'I don't think that's likely to happen.'

'No? I presumed that was why your father had arrived at Trade Winds—to finalise the deal.'

Macy stared at her. 'My father?' she repeated dazedly. 'What do you mean?'

'Ross hasn't told you that he turned up earlier?'

Judy shrugged. 'Perhaps he was keeping it as a pleasant surprise.'

Macy felt hollow inside. A confrontation with her father was the last thing she needed. She'd hoped for a breathing space—some kind of brief respite to pull her life—her future together.

She said, quietly, 'No doubt,' and turned away.

Ross came over to her, his expression set. He said, 'You've heard you have a visitor?'

'Yes.' Macy shook her head in bewilderment. 'I can't think what he's doing here.'

Ross's swift smile was sardonic. 'He's come to find out what's happened to his precious deal,' he said. 'Not to mention his precious daughter.' He paused. 'I think I'll forgo the pleasure of a reunion with him.'

'I quite understand.'

'Now that,' he said, 'I doubt.' He took an envelope from the pocket of his shorts and gave it to her. 'A farewell gift.' His voice was suddenly harsh. 'To remind you of old times.'

'I don't need that...' she began.

'Take it anyway,' Ross said.

Macy made a business of pushing the envelope into her shoulder-bag. She didn't want to watch Ross walk away with Judy Ryan. It was not a final image she needed—the pair of them on Thunder Cay—together. But that was undoubtedly what the other girl had in mind.

Sam helped her on board *Sweet Bird*, his expansive smile slightly subdued. She took a seat in the bows, looking ahead of her.

As the boat moved off, she heard Judy laugh, softly but with a note of rising excitement.

It might as well have been a fanfare of victory.

Macy stared at the horizon—at the future—and found her vision oddly blurred. And frighteningly bleak.

Unlike most return journeys, it seemed endless. Sunk in her bitter thoughts, Macy forgot about Ross's envelope until they were nearly back at Fortuna.

She took it listlessly out of her bag. There was no message of greeting or explanation on the envelope. Just her name. A farewell gift. So, it was neither an apology or a love letter. But then, Ross had never been good at either of them, she recognised achingly. She was sorely tempted to throw it overboard, and let the wind and sea carry it away forever.

But curiosity triumphed in the end. As she opened the envelope, one swift glance told her what the contents were—a cheque drawn on a major London bank, and made out to Ross Bannister for one hundred and fifty thousand pounds.

Macy stared down at it in mingled incredulity and disbelief.

She thought, He kept it all this time without cash-ing it. But why? It makes no sense—no sense at all. To take a payment of this size, but never use it…

She swallowed. So he hadn't left her for money after all. That had just been an excuse. The real reason had been her inability to hold him—and his lack of commitment to her.

That, of course, was why he'd decided to let her go now. Because he didn't care enough, and never had. Never would. Because he'd been honest enough to recognise that a mere physical rapport was not sufficient basis for a lifetime's marriage.

Because he now had the woman he wanted, and was not prepared to settle for a convenient second-best either.

Macy sighed, and thrust the cheque, still in its envelope, back into her bag.

In a way, it was a relief to know that Ross's motivation hadn't been completely mercenary. On the other hand, it also served to deepen her feelings of hurt and rejection even further.

As Macy walked into Trade Winds, she met Ambrose Delancey coming down the stairs.

'Mrs Hilliard.' His greeting held a certain reserve.

Macy winced slightly. 'I don't think it's really appropriate to call me that any more,' she said quietly.

'No. Ross's message indicated the hoped-for *rapprochement* had not taken place.' His tone was kinder. 'It was not a course of action I advocated, of course. But he seemed to feel the situation called for desperate measures.'

'Yes.' Macy forced stiff lips into a smile. 'But I want you to know, Mr Delancey, that I won't make any waves—over anything. The important thing is for us both to be legally free, as soon as possible. Especially as there's someone else involved,' she added stiltedly.

'So I gather.' He nodded towards a door across the hall. 'You're aware that your father is waiting for you. He's in rather an agitated state.' He paused. 'Mr Hilliard senior's health doesn't permit him to have house guests, unfortunately, but I've been able to get an additional reservation at your own hotel.'

Macy shook her head. 'Thank you, but we'll be returning to the UK right away.'

'I hardly think so. Sir Edwin wants the Thunder Cay deal finalising before he leaves, and it will take a few days to draw up the necessary papers.'

Macy stared at him. 'You mean Ross is going ahead with the sale?' she asked incredulously.

Mr Delancey nodded. 'He radioed his instructions a short while ago.'

It hadn't taken Judy Ryan long to make her influence felt, Macey thought sadly. She forced a smile. 'In that case, I'll be flying home alone.' She held out her hand. 'Goodbye, Mr Delancey.'

'Good luck, Miss Gilmour. A car is at your disposal whenever you choose to return to Fortuna Town.'

'Thank you.' Clearly the sooner they left, the better, she thought drily. She lifted her chin. 'It's been—quite an experience.'

And it's not over yet, she added silently, as she prepared to face her father.

Sir Edwin was prowling restlessly round a large room, furnished predominantly in white. He was an incongruous even sombre figure in his dark suit. As Macy entered, he swung round, his brows snapping together as he surveyed her.

'My dearest child.' He sounded appalled. 'You look terrible. I've been beside myself.'

'Hello, Father.' Macy crossed the room, and kissed him on the cheek. 'I'm fine,' she went on carefully. 'What are you doing here?'

'I was informed that you'd been deliberately stranded on Thunder Cay with Ross Bannister.' His voice shook. 'Naturally, I came at once to put a stop to this outrage—to rescue you.'

Macy sighed. She could, she thought, make an educated guess as to his informant's identity. 'There was really no need,' she said, quietly. 'As you can see, I'm fine.'

'Fine?' Sir Edwin was scandalised. 'Macy—you can't have seen yourself. You're in rags. You look like some down-and-out.'

'Nevertheless, it's true,' she said firmly. 'And—

yes, I have been with Ross, but that's all over and finished with. There was no need for you to be involved.'

'Involved?' Sir Edwin echoed shakily. 'Are you mad? When that swine walks back into your life—has the gall to abduct you…'

Macy hunched a shoulder. 'He wanted us to have some privacy to discuss a possible reconciliation.' She tried to keep her voice matter-of-fact. 'But in the end, we agreed it wouldn't work.'

'I should think not.' Her father looked as if he'd been poleaxed. 'How dare that blackguard have the unmitigated gall to pester you again? Or does his supposed relationship to Boniface Hilliard set him outside the bounds of decent behaviour?'

Macy bit her lip. 'Well, at least he can't be accused of being after my money, this time,' she said wearily. 'Not that it matters. The fact remains that he still doesn't want me.'

'My poor sweet,' Sir Edwin said heavily. 'I shall never forgive myself for sending you here—subjecting you to this ordeal. Cameron, of course, is quite distraught.' He patted Macy's shoulder. 'As soon as you've got over all this—recovered your looks, we'll announce your engagement.'

'No,' Macy said forcefully. 'We will not. Not now. Not ever.'

'Macy.' Sir Edwin gave her a minatory look. 'You're upset. You don't know what you're saying.

Believe me, my dear, I know what's best for you. You need loving care, my dear, a stabilising influence in your life.' He smiled coaxingly at her rigid face. 'And you must see that Cameron's long devotion should be rewarded.'

'On the contrary,' Macy said flatly. 'I've never even considered marrying Cameron. I don't care for him, and I've not encouraged his so-called devotion.' She took a deep breath. 'In fact, I think it would be best—less embarrassing all round if I resigned from Gilmour-Denys when we get home.'

'No.' If her father's face had been florid before, it was ashen now. 'Macy—you can't do that.'

'Why not? I'm a free agent.' Or I will be very soon, she added silently, with a pang of anguish.

'Because you're going to marry Cameron,' he said energetically. 'It's always been an accepted thing. And he's been more than patient waiting for you to get over this—absurd infatuation.'

'Has he?' Macy lifted her brows. 'Well, that's unfortunate. Is Cameron also prepared to accept that my—infatuation could have repercussions?'

There was a silence. Sir Edwin was looking at her as if he'd never seen her before. 'Macy,' he said hoarsely. 'You don't—you can't mean...' He stopped. 'Oh, God.'

Macy said steadily. 'It's a possibility, but I didn't intend to break it to you like this. Let's go back to the hotel. We can talk there while I pack.'

Her father didn't seem to have heard her. 'My poor child,' he said, shaking his head. 'That it should come to this.' He squared his shoulders. 'But you mustn't worry. Everything can be taken care of. No young woman has to ruin her life these days.'

Macy stiffened. 'Stop right there. This is your own potential grandchild that you're talking about.'

'No.' His voice rose to a shout. 'I won't accept that. I can't. I won't allow you to give birth to an illegitimate child—bring shame on our family, after all my hopes—the plans I've made for you?' He drew a shuddering breath, trying to regain control. 'Dear God, I thought I'd got Ross Bannister out of your life forever. Now, you could be having his bastard. Are you quite mad?'

'If I am pregnant,' she countered quietly, 'I shall indeed be a single parent. But the baby won't be illegitimate.' She took a breath. 'There'll never be a right time to tell you this, Father. Ross was quite right about that.' She threw back her head. 'He and I are married.'

'You've married him?' Sir Edwin looked suddenly grey and old. 'Here—on Fortuna?'

Macy shook her head. 'No,' she said gently. 'Four and a half years ago—before he pretended to take the money and run.'

He sank down on the edge of a snowy-white sofa. 'No.' He sounded almost piteous. 'It can't be true.'

Macy sat beside him. 'I never intended you to

know,' she confessed. 'I'd planned a discreet divorce after five years' separation. But Ross had—other ideas,' she added with difficulty.

'Oh, yes.' The look her father sent her was almost manic. 'I suppose this is his idea of revenge. Of destroying me. And you, little fool, played right into his hands.'

Macy bowed her head. 'I can't deny that. But you won't be destroyed. Whether I'm pregnant or not, I'll move right away—out of London. Make my own life. You really don't have to worry.'

'Worry.' Her father's short laugh was harsh. 'My God, Macy, you don't know the half of it.'

'Well, at least you're going to get Thunder Cay.' She put her hand over his, but he shook it off.

'It will take more than that to save me now,' he muttered. 'My God, Macy, do you know what you've done?'

She said bitterly, 'I'm beginning to.' She got to her feet. 'We can't stay here, Father. We'll go back to the hotel, have a rest and talk again.' She forced an encouraging smile. 'Try and sort something out.' She paused. 'Give me a minute to arrange our transport.'

She went out of the room, closing the door behind her, then went quietly and quickly up the broad staircase to Boniface Hilliard's room.

She tapped on the door and entered before she could have second thoughts.

'So, it's you.' He was occupying his couch by the window, his face brooding. 'I thought you'd have been out of here by now.'

'I'm sure you did,' she returned levelly. 'But I wanted to say goodbye.'

'So, you've said it.' There was no softening in the pale eyes which were so like Ross's. 'I wasn't in favour of Ross's crazy idea to win you round, Miss Gilmour—or Landin or whatever you choose to call yourself. But when he sets his mind on something, it's hard to turn him round.'

'Yes.'

'When I found him, he was in a hell of a state,' he said harshly. 'I see no reason to forgive you for that, even if he can.'

'It was Ross who walked out on me.' Macy's eyes flashed. 'What about my feelings?'

'If you'd loved him, you'd have wanted to share his life. But you weren't prepared to give up a thing for his sake. What man—what real man is going to be his wife's lap-dog, dancing to her tune all the time?'

'You think I wanted that?' Macy shook her head. 'I'd have gone anywhere with him.'

'As long as it was five-star accommodation, and first-class travel all the way.' The blue eyes glinted fiercely at her. 'You should have hung on for a week or two, young woman. It might have made a difference.'

Macy shook her head, the image of Judy Ryan vivid in her mind. 'I don't think so,' she said huskily.

'That's what I thought.' Contempt rang in his voice. 'Did he give you the cheque back? He planned to.'

'Yes.' Macy was silent for a moment. 'If he didn't want the money, why didn't he just—tear it up?'

He smiled grimly. 'He wanted it as a souvenir. A permanent reminder of the biggest mistake he ever made in his life. If he's handed it back, I hope that means he's ready to start living again.'

She said quietly, 'I think his new life started a long time ago, Mr Hilliard. And I hope your new daughter-in-law is more to your taste. Goodbye to you.'

She would not cry, she vowed as she went downstairs. She would not give him that satisfaction.

But as Sam started the car that would take her away from Trade Winds forever, she was weeping inwardly.

And in her aching head, she seemed once again to hear the distant sound of thunder on the reef.

CHAPTER ELEVEN

IT WAS going to be a very long day.

Macy delivered her father to the bungalow adjoining hers at the hotel, adjuring him to rest. Then, in the privacy of her own room, she stripped off her clothes, throwing them into the waste bin in the bathroom. She would ask the maid to burn them, she thought, as she stepped under the shower.

She dried herself, pulling on one of the hotel's towelling robes, then stretched out on the bed, looking up at the ceiling fan as it slowly revolved.

This room—in fact, everything on Fortuna—only served to remind her of Ross, she realised bleakly. Four years had not been enough to effect a cure. How long, this time, would it take her to heal from the wound he'd made?

If she closed her eyes, he seemed to be imprinted on her eyelids. If she turned her face into the pillow, it seemed redolent of the warm male scent of him.

Imagination, she thought, was a dangerous thing.

The cool shower had refreshed her. It had also made her hungry. She reached for the bedside phone, and rang room service for a double order of coffee and club sandwiches.

'Is that instead of the bottle of whisky, Miz Gilmour?' came the cheerful query, and Macy bit her lip, as she realised who that must be meant for.

'No, as well as, please,' she said constrainedly.

She replaced the receiver and stood for a moment, frowning.

Sir Edwin had sat in a brooding silence throughout the car journey, his face haggard and like a stranger's. The last thing he needed was to drink himself into oblivion as she suspected he intended. On the other hand, a couple of snorts to relax him would do little harm.

In a way she was tempted to join him—try and find an alcohol-induced oblivion from pain and emotional hunger. But there were decisions to take and plans to be made, and she needed a clear head.

She swung herself off the bed, and dressed swiftly in cream cotton trousers, and a raspberry-pink top.

The first essential, of course, she thought, as she brushed her hair, was to get away from Fortuna altogether, and all its disturbing associations. With the finality of air miles between them, maybe she could begin to heal. And as soon as she got back, she would consult a doctor at an advisory clinic, and find out how soon a pregnancy test could be conducted. Her entire future, after all, hinged on the result, although she was aware life could never be the same again, regardless of whether the test was positive or negative.

As to where she would live, she supposed the world was her oyster. Except, of course, for the one place she really wanted to be.

When her food order arrived, she went next door and persuaded a patently reluctant Sir Edwin to join her on her terrace.

He drank some coffee, but only picked at his food, giving jet lag as an excuse, but Macy wasn't convinced.

She said gently, 'I'm going to ask Reception to call the airport for me, Father. You don't need me for the Thunder Cay negotiations, so I'm flying back.

His mouth tightened. 'No doubt your former husband will make us pay over the odds.'

'I hope not,' Macy said evenly. 'However, I don't think Ross will fail to cash your cheque this time around.'

Her father's cup clattered back into its saucer. 'What are you talking about?'

Macy sighed. 'The money you paid him four years ago,' she said. 'He never used it. He just kept the cheque with him all this time—as some kind of symbol of female perfidy, according to his father. Although why…' She stopped. 'Dad—are you all right?'

'It's the heat,' he said. He produced his handkerchief and wiped his forehead. 'I'm not used to it. He kept that cheque, you say?'

'Yes, until today.'

'Did he show it to you?'

'More than that—he gave it to me as a souvenir.' Macy gave a wintry little smile.

'That was very cruel.' Her father's voice shook. 'As if you needed any reminder of that terrible period in your life, or the way he treated you—betrayed you.' He held out his hand. 'Give me the cheque, darling, and I'll destroy it. You can't want to have a thing like that around you.'

'I'll get rid of it in my own good time.' Macy patted the bag hanging from the arm of her chair. 'It could prove a salutory lesson.' Then she frowned. 'But, dad, you must have known this all along. You must have realised the money hadn't left your account.'

'But naturally, I thought—I assumed...' He sounded totally at a loss. 'I didn't actually verify the transaction.'

What a word, Macy thought sadly, to describe the destruction of her marriage. The death of all her hopes and faith.

Her father was speaking again. 'I don't blame you for wanting to get out of this place, darling. I'll phone Cameron and ask him to meet you from the airport.'

'No.' Macy shook her head forcefully. 'I really don't want that.'

'Macy.' Sir Edwin leaned forward, his brow furrowed. 'This last week has unsettled you. I understand that. But when you get back to London, you'll feel differently, I'm sure.'

'If you mean my feelings for Cameron may change, Father, then you couldn't be more wrong,' she said gravely. 'I don't love him, I never have, and I never will. It's as simple as that.'

'That's the problem.' He was perspiring heavily again. 'I have certain commitments—certain guarantees…'

'Involving Cameron?' Macy found herself remembering some of the things Ross had said. She leaned back in her chair, with a small sigh. 'I'm sorry if you're in some kind of fix, but your arrangements with your partner are your own problem. I'm severing all connection with Gilmour-Denys, remember?'

'How could I forget.' His eyes were fixed on her urgently. 'Macy, Cameron's always wanted you.'

'I'm sorry it can't be mutual.' Her tone sharpened. 'What are you getting at.'

He dabbed at his mouth. 'I'm under a tremendous obligation to him, Macy. You could—help…'

There was a loaded silence.

She said slowly, 'I don't think I believe what I'm hearing. Are you intending I should be—some kind of pay-off for Cameron Denys?'

'I wouldn't put it as crudely as that.'

'I would,' she said grimly. 'Just how far has this gone, Father? What have you done to me?'

'Macy, I didn't have a choice. I've been in too

deep for years. And now Cameron is putting pressure on. This Thunder Cay deal is only part of it.'

'My God,' she said quietly. 'Let's have the whole truth, shall we? Ross never asked you for money to get out of my life, did he? It was all your idea, to leave the way clear for the charming Mr Denys. Isn't that the case?'

'Macy.' His face was agonised.

'My own father,' she said. 'You deliberately set out to manipulate—to ruin my life.'

'Ross Bannister was never right for you,' he defended himself. 'I wanted to save you from unhappiness.'

'You wanted to save me for Cameron,' she came back at him. 'Because what Cameron wants, he must have, even if he wants to change it—remodel it like Thunder Cay.' She gave a small mirthless laugh. 'How was I supposed to turn out, I wonder?'

Sir Edwin sagged back in his chair. 'Macy.' His voice pleaded. 'You must help me. Cameron could finish me.'

'No.' She shook her head gently but firmly. 'You've got yourself into this mess, Father, but you're not taking me down with you.'

'I don't recognise you any more,' he muttered. 'What's happened to you?'

'They call it desperation.' She nodded towards the adjoining bungalow as the telephone began to shrill. 'I think you're wanted. And please don't tell

Cameron I'm his for the asking,' she added icily. 'Because I wouldn't want to call you a liar as well as a fraud.'

As soon as he'd disappeared indoors, Macy snatched up her bag and headed for the car rental desk in the hotel foyer. She had no chance of getting on a flight that evening, she reasoned, so she might as well fill the remaining time by seeing the rest of Fortuna while she had the chance. After all, she would never be coming back.

This time, she headed north, putting as much distance between Trade Winds and its offshore island as she could.

She parked the car by the sea, and sat watching the faint creaming of the surf, remembering another crescent of silver sand. In her mind's eye, she saw a tall figure, lean and tanned, aquamarine eyes narrowed against the sun, his mouth curving in tender laughter. His hands gentle as he reached for her...

Oh, God, she thought unevenly. How can I bear it?

She had been shaken to the depth of her being by Sir Edwin's admission of his machinations. I never guessed, she berated herself. I never even questioned what he was telling me.

Yet what difference would it really have made? Ross hadn't come to her and told her what was going on, and that certainly wasn't because he held her father in affection or esteem. Or because he wanted to shelter her from the knowledge of Sir Edwin's deviousness.

He must have wanted out of the relationship. That was the only answer. Although it didn't explain why he'd been so bitter about the money he'd been offered. Or why he'd kept the cheque untouched.

She sighed. Perhaps there were some things she was fated never to know, she thought, trying to be philosophical. And she would do herself no good by endlessly chewing them over.

She had loved two men in her life, she thought drearily. Her father, and Ross. And she'd learned the hard way that she couldn't trust either of them. End of story.

She drove steadily, looking without seeing at the winding coast. And when evening came, she found a shoreside restaurant specialising in conch dishes, and ate there.

When she finally returned to the hotel, her father's bungalow was in darkness. She could only feel relieved. She didn't want to be badgered about Cameron, or to lose any more respect for her father by hearing further evidence of his wheeling and dealing.

She read for a while, then went to bed. But she couldn't sleep, or perhaps she was afraid to.

Afraid of what dreams might come in the night, she thought wryly, twisting restlessly on the mattress. Last night, her wildest fantasies had become glorious reality, and now her reawakened flesh was once more greedy for fulfilment. From now on her subconscious longings would have an added edge to them.

She pulled on her robe and went out on to the moonlit veranda, moving quietly so as not to disturb her father next door. She stood for a while, leaning on the rail, absorbing the sounds and scents of the darkness. Listening to the distant splash of the sea. Remembering how, only a few nights ago, she had wanted to follow the silver path of the moon down to the beach, and find Ross waiting for her there.

Madness, as she'd told herself at the time, but such sweet madness. And this time she didn't even try to resist, although she knew Ross would not be there. He was on Thunder Cay with Judy Ryan.

It's a stroll, she tried to placate herself, as she descended the shallow steps. Just a stroll to relax me. Some fresh air. That's all.

She moved without hurrying, breathing the fragrance in the air, pushing her way past the intrusive bushes and shrubs which lined the path and caught at her robe, showering her with pollen.

At last she emerged from the sheltering palms on to the sand, listening for the thunder on the reef, but hearing only the heavy beat of her own sad heart.

In the silver moonlight, the man's dark figure was clearly visible. He stood, his back towards her, at the edge of the sea.

For a moment she was motionless, then she began

to run, her bare feet sliding in the sand. She made no sound, but he turned instantly, as if alerted by some sixth sense to her presence.

They met halfway. Ross said huskily, 'Oh, my love. My sweet love.' His arms went round her, lifting her almost off her feet, as he kissed her with a deep and hungry passion.

'It's you. It's really you.' Half laughing, half crying, Macy touched his hair, his face, his chest through the half-unbuttoned shirt. 'I thought I was dreaming. What are you doing here?'

'I came to find you. To ask you to come back to me.' His voice was unsteady too. 'I was getting up the courage to walk up to your bungalow—to beg you on my knees if necessary.'

'You want me?' She lifted eyes wide with questioning to his face. 'But you can't—it isn't possible…'

Ross framed her face in his hands, his gaze tender but intense. 'I won't ask you for a lifetime commitment, Macy. You may not be ready for that. Perhaps you never will be, but that's a risk I'll have to take.'

He drew a deep, shaken breath. 'Come back to me on your own terms. If it only lasts weeks or months, then I'll survive it somehow. I'd rather have crumbs than no bread at all.'

'What crumbs?' Her arms went round him, hugging him fiercely in reply.

'Macy, don't fool with me,' he said huskily. 'You

did it to me four years ago—kissed me and smiled, then flung me to the wolves.'

'No.' She shook her head. 'I love you, Ross. I've always loved you. When you left me the first time, I died a little. Today, when you sent me away, I felt as if I was bleeding to death.'

'That was self-preservation.' His voice was raw. 'I thought I'd enjoy making you suffer. The thought had obsessed me since you threw me out. I swore I'd never let you get to me again. That I'd use you next time. But the longer we were together, the more I realised I couldn't do it. Whatever had happened in the past, this time I wanted your love, and nothing else would do.'

'I didn't throw you away,' she said in a low voice. 'It was my father. He told me everything today— how he wanted to split us up so that I could marry Cameron. He fooled both of us…'

'I know that,' Ross said quietly. 'But he didn't have to succeed, Macy. If you'd stood up to him— told him we were married, for a start—fought for me, we could have won. But you just obeyed orders and consigned me to hell. And that's what I thought I couldn't forgive. Your betrayal.'

'He was waiting for me at the flat,' she said. 'He said you'd asked for money, and showed me a receipt. I was devastated—destroyed.'

Ross sighed. 'Darling,' he said. 'If we're going to have a prayer this time around, we've got to be totally honest with each other. No more pretence. And you knew exactly what was going on, my love. You had to know. It was your money, for God's sake. That's what finished me—what drove me away. Your signature on the cheque.'

For a moment, she stood like a statue in his arms. Then she said, 'No, that's not true—not possible.'

'No more games, Macy.' His voice was imploring. 'Do you think I'm blind—or illiterate? Why do you think I kept the bloody cheque all this time—to be a thorn in my flesh, and keep my anger burning.'

'You think I'm capable of that,' she said slowly. 'And yet you still came here tonight?'

'Yes,' Ross said sombrely. 'Whatever kind of a fool that makes me. I was no saint, Macy. Our marriage wasn't perfect. Maybe you had your reasons for doing what you did. If it had been your father's money, I'd have torn the bloody cheque up in his face. I'd probably have torn him to shreds too. But when I realised you were selling me out, nothing seemed to matter any more.'

'I swear it's not true,' she said. 'There must be some terrible mistake.'

'Didn't you recognise your own signature?' he asked gravely.

She started. 'I never got that far. When I realised what it was, I felt sick. I just shoved it back in the envelope.'

'Where is it now?'

'In my bag, back at the bungalow.'

'Then we'll go and find it—get to the bottom of all this once and for all.'

She'd left the bungalow in darkness, but as they approached the veranda, Macy saw a lamp had been lit in the living area.

She tensed. 'Oh, God, I didn't lock the door. Someone's in there. We'd better call security.'

'No.' Ross halted her quietly. 'I think we can handle this ourselves.'

Something in his tone chilled her. She said, 'I don't think I want to.'

'We have no choice.' He opened the door, and ushered her gently into the room ahead of him.

Sir Edwin whirled round. 'Macy?' He swallowed. 'Hello, my dear. I was looking for you. Wanted to have a word. We should never let bad feelings fester overnight, eh?'

His voice was over-loud; too hearty.

Macy stared at him, a hand at her throat. She said, 'Father, what are you doing with my bag? Did you want something from it?'

She saw his face crumple. Watched the bag drop from his hand as if it had stung him suddenly. Ross's envelope slid out on to the floor, and Macy bent to retrieve it.

Ross had followed her silently in.

Edwin Gilmour's gaze went past his daughter, and

focused on his son-in-law. He said, 'You. Oh, dear God.'

Ross went over to the fridge and extracted a miniature brandy, which he poured into a glass and handed to the older man, motioning him towards a chair.

He said coolly, 'I think you have some explaining to do, Sir Edwin.'

Macy looked down at the cheque in her hand. Traced her own unmistakable signature with the tip of her nail.

She looked at her father. 'How did you trick me into signing this?' She was surprised how calm and unfazed she sounded.

'I put it among the trust documents that afternoon at Caldecott. I banked on your being too tired to look at things too closely, and anyway, I left it blank. I pointed out the dotted line, and you signed.'

'Because I trusted you.' Her voice cracked. 'Dad, how could you?'

'I had to do it. He'd never have taken money from me, but your signature was the clincher. It cut the ground from under him.' He put the glass down. 'I told him you were tired of playing house—of camping in a flat one remove from a slum. I said you wanted your old life back, but didn't know how to tell him. I said you didn't want him to leave empty-handed, but at the same time you had to be sure he wouldn't come back for more. That you'd never be content with the lifestyle he had to offer.'

'You were very convincing,' Ross said flatly.

'The money came from the Landin Trust, of course. I was going to explain the discrepancy as a number of donations to charity. But you never asked, and I presumed it had been overlooked somehow. I never dreamed that he would just keep the cheque.'

'If I hadn't,' Ross said in a voice like ice, 'Macy and I would have stayed at cross purposes all our lives. Each of us believing we'd been betrayed by the other.'

Sir Edwin nodded. 'I counted on that.'

'How could you?' Macy whispered. 'You took four years of our lives away from us.'

'But I wasn't completely to blame. He was having an affair, Macy.' Sir Edwin pointed a shaking hand at Ross. 'You saw the evidence.'

'What the hell are you talking about?' Ross demanded contemptuously.

Macy was very pale. 'Photographs,' she said. 'Of you and Judy Ryan—together in London.'

'We met a few times, yes,' he said, frowning. 'Boniface had managed to trace me, but I wasn't sure I wanted to know. I wasn't convinced that I could handle such a fundamental change in my life, so he asked Judy to make some preliminary approaches. Persuade me to meet him at least.' He touched

Macy's cheek gently. 'That's what I wanted to discuss with you that weekend.'

'But she's in love with you,' Macy protested. 'She came to Thunder Cay this afternoon to be with you.'

'That's news to me on both counts,' Ross said drily. 'I think she's quite in love with becoming a Hilliard. She made quite a play for Boniface himself at one time, and it amused him to point her in my direction instead. But he knew she hadn't a chance.'

'That's not what she thought,' Macy said. 'Besides, Ross, I saw her in your arms in the hall at Trade Winds.'

His grin was frankly sheepish. 'That's what I was hoping. I heard you on the stairs, and wondered what a spot of healthy jealousy might do.' He paused. 'But I didn't ask her to Thunder Cay today, or invite her to stay. That was all her own idea—and one that she now regrets. So much so, that my father will have to look for a new nurse.'

'You sent her away?' Macy gasped.

'She fired herself,' Ross said. 'I simply made it clear I didn't need consolation of any kind, and that if necessary I was going to spend the rest of my life winning my wife back to me.'

'That isn't very fair on her.'

'No,' Ross admitted. 'But there's nothing fair in love—or war. And sometimes non-combatants get hurt—if they interfere. She'll make out.'

There was a silence. Then Sir Edwin looked at Macy.

'You're going with him?' His voice was defeated.

'Yes,' she said. 'Wherever that takes us.'

He nodded, then rose from his chair, and walked to the door. He hesitated for a moment, looking at them as if they were both strangers.

He said, 'I'm sorry,' and went out.

Ross sighed, and some of the tension vanished from his shoulders. He said, 'I wish I could have spared you that.'

'It was horrible,' she admitted quietly. 'But necessary. Honesty can't be selective.'

'And now I've got to ask your forgiveness,' he said steadily. 'For misjudging you—for hurting you.'

'We're both guilty of that,' she said. 'But we were set up by experts, and we were no match for them.'

'And now?'

Macy walked smiling into his arms. 'I could take on the world,' she told him softly, then hesitated. 'Starting, I suppose with your father. He doesn't like me, Ross. And now I've caused him to lose his nurse as well.'

'Oh, I think he'll come round,' he said. 'When I told him earlier that I was coming after you—that I wanted you at any price, he ordered me to be gentle with you. He said you had wounded eyes.'

'Oh.' Macy swallowed, feeling the prick of tears

behind her eyelids. 'I thought he wanted you to divorce me and marry Judy.'

'Never in this world.' He shook his head. 'Judy was a good enough nurse, and an excellent diver, but the most I ever felt for her was gratitude.'

'But those clothes in the drawer in the bedroom—the underwear. They had to belong to someone.'

'They belonged to you.' Ross was rueful. 'Every single item, bought specially for our reunion. The trousseau, my love, you never had the first time around. And you rejected it,' he added in mock reproof.

'I was rejected too,' she reminded him, resting her head against his chest. 'You sent me away—told me it was over.'

'I was afraid,' he said. 'Frightened of being hurt—of losing you again when you got tired of playing house.' His mouth twisted. 'Whatever I may have implied, I knew if I took you again it would be for love. And if we made love, it would be forever, on my part anyway.

'But after we'd made love I realised that, however wonderful it had been, there'd been no commitment on your side at all. I'd given you pleasure, but that could be as far as it went. I couldn't take that. I told myself I'd rather be alone for the rest of my life.'

Ross shook his head. 'But, after you left, I felt as if I'd lost half of myself. I knew then that I couldn't let you go. That I'd pa_ any price to have you with me, even if it only turned out to be for a little while.'

His arms tightened fiercely round her. 'I hope you realise that if you come with me, you'll be giving yourself, heart, body and soul.'

'I know.' She planted a kiss on his chin. 'Will the rest of our lives be long enough?'

'We'll have to see,' he said solemnly. He looked round him, grimacing. 'Get dressed, my love. We're checking out. I'm taking you home.'

'To Trade Winds?'

'Indirectly. *Sweet Bird* is moored there. We're going back to Thunder Cay, to get on with our honeymoon.'

'Then you're not selling it?'

Ross snorted. 'Our own personal paradise? Not a chance. Although I pretended this afternoon that the deal was still on, it was only a ploy to keep you on Fortuna until I could reach you. I was terrified you'd leave—vanish out of my life before I could attempt to make it all right between us.'

He paused. 'But I must admit the shack isn't an ideal bridal suite. And it will never make a family home.'

'Oh, I agree.' Macy thought of the Hilliard house, and the empty rooms where one small tree stretched hopeful branches towards the sky. A living promise of regeneration.

She drew a deep happy breath. 'But I have a dream about that,' she said.

Cathy Williams is originally from Trinidad but has lived in England for a number of years. She currently has a house in Warwickshire which she shares with her husband Richard, her three daughters Charlotte, Olivia and Emma and their pet cat, Salem. She adores writing romantic fiction and would love one of her girls to become a writer although at the moment she is happy enough if they do their homework and agree not to bicker with one another.

CARIBBEAN DESIRE
by
Cathy Williams

CHAPTER ONE

EMMA had no idea who to look out for, and she didn't much care. She was at last at the tiny Tobago airport, only a few miles away from her destination, and that fluttering, panicky feeling of wondering whether she had done the right thing was back with her again.

This time, though, it was too late to do anything about it.

She collected her suitcases from the carousel, glancing interestedly around her, and then went to wait outside for her ride to the Jackson villa.

Even if the trip was a complete fiasco, she thought logically, at least it would give her the opportunity to sample something of the West Indies. How many of her friends would give their eye-teeth to be where she was now?

She looked around at the bustle of dark bodies standing in groups chatting, selling local fruit to the tourists, at the blindingly clear blue skies, at the Technicolor green of all the foliage. It was all a world apart from the grey, dismal skies of England which she had left behind.

She glanced across to the row of brightly dressed, ebony-skinned women standing behind their stalls of local sweets, lethargically fanning themselves with folded newspapers, and thought that it wasn't merely the scenery which provided such a contrast. Even the pace of life seemed slower, as though the warm, sweet breeze made people more easy-going, less in a frenetic rush to get somewhere.

Little snatches of their sing-song conversation reached her ears, and Emma made an effort to relax, to ignore that cramped, nervous feeling in the pit of her stomach which threatened to overwhelm her completely.

5

She had spent the last ten months weighing up the pros and cons of this trip, for heaven's sake; surely she should be feeling a little more confident about the whole thing?

It would help, of course, if the car would only come to collect her. If nothing else, it would give her less time to sit around feeling tense and queasy.

When all the flight arrangements had been made, she had been told that Alistair's gardener and houseboy would be there to meet her at the airport. Maybe, she thought hopefully, he was there and looking for her, although that didn't seem possible. It was hardly as though she blended into the background. With her long corn-blonde plait and pale complexion she stuck out like a sore thumb.

She dumped her suitcases on the ground and perched precariously on one of them, her slim arms clasped around her knees. All the doubts and indecisions that had plagued her ever since her decision to come to Tobago resurfaced with alarming force, and at the bottom of them all was the inevitable question: would it have been better to leave the past alone?

She was so absorbed in her thoughts that she was totally unaware of approaching footsteps.

'You must be Emma Belle. I'm here to meet you.' The man's voice was deep, with a lazy drawl and the merest hint of an English accent.

Emma looked up with a start and was struck by a fleeting impression of height and power. She clambered to her feet, feeling hot and distracted under his scrutiny, and inwardly thinking that the least he could do was offer to help her up instead of keeping his hands thrust firmly in his trouser pockets. She bent to retrieve her suitcase, and a tanned arm shot out, taking it from her.

'Allow me.'

'I can handle it myself,' Emma said, feeling peculiarly defensive.

'Fine.' Without another word, the man turned his back and began striding towards the car park, with Emma doing her best to keep pace with him.

'Could you slow down?' she panted in frustration. 'I happen to be lumbered with two suitcases and two hold-alls. You can hardly expect me to keep pace with you!'

The man stopped abruptly and turned towards her. 'You did say you could manage,' he said mildly. Emma looked up at him, taking in the hard planes of his face, the thick black hair, the vivid blue eyes which were staring at her with what seemed like more than a bit of superiority.

She flushed, immediately annoyed that someone whom she had met less than ten minutes ago was managing quite successfully to get underneath her normally calm, unshakeable exterior. Of course, she thought, he had caught her at a vulnerable time. She was tired, nervous and hot. Still, she was unused to being ruffled by members of the opposite sex, especially one whose sexuality was so blatantly obvious.

He was still staring at her, and she looked away hurriedly.

'Are you Alistair Jackson's gardener?' she asked suspiciously, thinking that she had never seen a gardener who looked as arrogant as this one before.

'No.'

'Who are you, then?' He could be anybody, she thought. There was a latent aggression to him that she didn't like one bit. And it didn't just stop at his physique, either. The man was either in a very bad mood, or else he was simply threatening by nature. Whatever, Emma decided that she wasn't going another step further until he explained himself.

She dropped her suitcases and folded her arms.

'Well?' she demanded. 'Who are you? I was told that I would be met here by Mr Jackson's gardener. I have no intention of going a step further until you tell me who you are and show me some sort of proof that you're authorised to collect me.'

'Proof? Authorised?' The man gave a short laugh, his blue eyes sweeping scornfully over her. 'You either follow me, or else you spend the rest of the day sweltering here in the sun.' He snatched her suitcases up as though they weighed nothing, and resumed his walking.

Emma hurried along behind him. She was not accustomed to being treated like this. Over the years she had cultivated a cool, aloof veneer that commanded respect. She liked being in control.

'You could at least tell me your name!' she panted furiously, noticing out of the corner of her eye that a few of the nearby locals were watching them, obviously amused.

This made her even more annoyed. Just who did he think he was? God knew what a fool she must look, stumbling behind this tall, raven-haired *barbarian*, her hair unravelling from its carefully woven plait, her fine features distorted with anger.

Not that he seemed to give a damn what sort of impression he was making on the people around them. He continued to stride purposefully away from the airport, obviously confident that she had no choice but to run behind him, making a complete spectacle of herself into the bargain.

'Your name?' she yelled furiously.

'Sorry,' the man said without turning around, and without sounding in the slightest bit apologetic, 'didn't I mention it?'

'No, you didn't!'

'I'm Conrad DeVere.' He stopped abruptly in front of a shiny but old Land Rover and began unlocking the boot.

Emma stared at him. Of course! She should have recognised him! In fact, she would have recognised him if the damned man hadn't been so rude and unforthcoming. He could have been King Kong and she probably wouldn't have known it.

The grainy grey newspaper print did nothing for him, she acknowledged reluctantly. He was not a man to be casually overlooked. She looked at him covertly as he slung her cases into the car boot.

Whizz kid in the financial world, heart-throb with women—just the sort of arrogant type she disliked. His attitude towards her only confirmed it. Any social graces the man had, he obviously wasn't wasting on her. Emma climbed into the passenger seat of the car and strapped herself in.

'I've heard of you,' she said, looking at his hard profile, the strong, tanned hands on the steering-wheel.

'No doubt you have,' Conrad replied drily. 'And what have you heard from my loyal band of tabloid reporters?'

She chose to ignore the lazy sarcasm in his voice.

'You handle all of Alistair Jackson's business interests, don't you? In addition to your own?' In fact, Conrad DeVere's interests were as extensive as Alistair's. Maybe even more so. He seemed to own everything, from hotels across Europe and America to property development companies; even, if she remembered correctly, several chemical plants.

His face appeared in the newspapers with nauseating regularity. She looked at that face now and decided that she didn't like it. Too sexy. Too confident. Too assured. The sort of face that belonged to a man who didn't really give a damn whose toes he trod on.

'Been doing your homework?' He switched on the engine, and began to manoeuvre the car out of the car park.

Something in his tone of voice made Emma's hackles rise.

'It's not exactly a trade secret,' she snapped. 'Besides, it's part of my job to find out as much as I can about the people I work with. It makes it easier to know what they're talking about when we begin working. Anyway,' she said coldly, 'what are you doing over here? Aren't Mr Jackson's head offices in America and London? Not to mention yours?'

She glanced out of the window at the picture-postcard scenery flashing past, glimpses of bright blue sea in strips against the horizon, whole tracts of land covered with tall, gently swaying coconut trees. It would have been much more enjoyable if she weren't stuck in a car next to someone to whom she had taken an instant dislike.

She didn't like his attitude, she didn't like his lack of politeness, and she certainly didn't like the way he had managed to shake her.

'I'm here because of you,' he said, taking his eyes off the road for an instant to glance at her.

'Me? Why?'

'I've wanted to meet you, to see what you're like.' His voice implied that he didn't particularly like what he saw, and Emma's mouth tightened.

'How flattering,' she said sarcastically. 'I didn't realise, when I accepted this job to help Alistair Jackson with his biography, that I would be privileged to the once-over by the great Conrad DeVere.'

His face hardened and Emma felt a quiver of alarm shoot through her. There was definitely something threatening about this man, but if he thought that he could intimidate her, for whatever reason, then he was in for a big surprise.

'I wanted to see for myself who would be working with Alistair. I hardly expected someone young and attractive.'

'Meaning?' Something about his tone of voice was making her uneasy.

'Meaning that I find it slightly surprising that a girl like you is willing to confine herself to life on a remote island, merely for the altruistic delights of working with an old man.'

'I don't know what you're getting at,' Emma said frigidly, knowing precisely what he was getting at and not liking it one bit.

'Oh, don't pretend you don't know what I'm talking about.'

'I'm not pretending anything,' Emma persisted stubbornly, 'and for your information my presence here is none of your business. You're not my employer. Thank God.'

The car slowed down and pulled over to the side of the road.

'What do you think you're doing?' Emma's green eyes flashed angrily. 'Could you please get this car going?'

He turned to face her, and Emma edged away from him, feeling a ridiculous prickle of heat rush to her face. Under the thick black lashes, his bright blue eyes were staring intently at her, totally devoid of expression.

'Let's get a few things straight right now,' he ground out. 'First of all, what you're doing here is my business because I say it is. Secondly, I don't appreciate your tone of voice.'

'You don't appreciate my tone of voice!' She laughed incredulously, 'I don't appreciate yours much, either! So we're quits! And as for my presence here being your business—well, excuse me for seeming dense, but I can't see what it has to do with you at all! Or do you normally take such an interest in every employee that Alistair recruits?'

He leaned towards her, and she could feel the warmth of his breath on her face. There was something disturbingly sensual about him. It confused her, and Emma didn't like being confused.

She inched away sharply and his hand flicked out, catching her by the wrist. Emma twisted uselessly, finally giving up the fight.

'All right,' she said tightly, 'so you're stronger than me.

But if you think that physical force is going to make me change my attitude towards you then you're wrong. You might be able to play the dictator with all those women who seem to have nothing better to do than flock around you, if the newspapers are anything to go by, but I'm not a member of your adoring flock, so I'll use any tone of voice I please with you. Now, if you'll kindly release me…'

He didn't release her, and Emma felt a swift stab of apprehension. Everything about Conrad DeVere was forbidding, from the taut, athletic grace of his body to the hard glint in his eyes. She wished that she hadn't argued with him. She should have just kept her big mouth shut and politely listened to whatever he had to say, and then just ignored him. It was what she would have done with any other man. She would have treated his words with contempt. But there was something about Conrad that sparked off all sorts of reactions in her.

'Are you going to listen to what I have to say, or do I have to resort to my own methods of persuasion?' His eyes roamed over her face and body, then back to her face.

Emma's eyes widened. She nodded. 'All right.' If he wanted to be a Nosy Parker, then who was she to argue? Nosy Parker, she thought, trying to derive some comfort from his diminished status. If only he were slightly less physically overpowering, she might just succeed in believing her description of him.

What, she wondered, did all those women see in him anyway? Personally, he was just the sort of man she loathed. She especially loathed the way that he was now examining her as though she were some distasteful species of insect under a microscope.

'I happen to be very fond of Alistair Jackson. He's been like a father to me for as long as I can remember, and I don't intend to see him fall prey to any potential gold-diggers.'

Emma's cheeks were burning. 'How dare you?'

'So, if that's what you have in mind, then you might just as well forget it, because you'll have me to contend with. He's already suffered at the hands of one woman after his bank balance; he doesn't need a repeat of the experience.'

His grip on her hand relaxed and Emma tugged it away, gently massaging the blood back into her veins.

So he thought she was a gold-digger! The idea would have been ludicrous if he weren't sitting there, inspecting her with menacing thoroughness.

'I don't know where you get your ideas from,' she said, controlling her temper with difficulty, 'but you're way off target. I heard of this job from a friend of a friend, and I applied. It's as simple as that. If you think I'm after Alistair Jackson's money, then you've got an overactive imagination.' She stopped to catch her breath, wishing she could sound more nonchalant and controlled.

'I help people write their biographies, Mr DeVere.' She uttered his name with exaggerated distaste and noticed with disappointment that he did not react. 'So I come into contact with the rich and famous quite a bit. I certainly wouldn't travel halfway across the globe to start my career as a gold-digger.' All right, so she didn't bump into the rich and famous on a daily basis, but the second half of her statement was the truth.

Conrad looked at her unhurriedly, his gaze starting from the top of her head and travelling slowly down her body. Then his eyes flicked back to hers.

'I made a point of doing a few checks on you when your application for this job was accepted,' he said smoothly. 'I found out some surprising facts.'

Emma's heart seemed to skip a beat. She licked her lips nervously, fighting to maintain some semblance of composure.

He couldn't have found out about her. Not that it wasn't

possible, but it was unlikely. Not unless he knew what he was looking for. So, she thought, there was no reason to be worried. Nevertheless, under the folds of her skirt her fists unconsciously clenched and unclenched.

'Really?' She tried to sound only marginally interested. She couldn't afford to let a flicker of emotion cross her face. This man was no fool. If she wasn't careful he would be able to sense her anxiety at his words, and then where would she be? Apart from being clever—too clever—he struck her as the persistent type. He would dig and dig until all her carefully arranged plans were unearthed and scattered in ruins around her feet.

She threw him what she hoped was a careless, sunny smile, although her mouth ached with the effort of doing it. Why, she thought, couldn't he just vanish on the next flight out?

'Yes,' he said conversationally, restarting the engine and slowly pulling away from the grass verge. 'Would you like to hear what I found out?'

Emma looked at the dark, ruthless set of his features and shrugged. 'Would I be able to stop you?'

'You could always tell me that you're not interested. Wasn't that your stand a few minutes ago?'

He laughed softly when she didn't say anything, and her teeth clamped together in anger. He was playing a cat-and-mouse game with her, and enjoying it.

She added 'sadist' to her list of descriptions of him.

'I wish you'd get to the point,' she said.

'Well, the point is, Emma—do you mind if I call you Emma? The point is,' he carried on, without waiting for an answer from her, 'that I know quite a few people in your line of work, and my contacts have informed me that over the past eight months you passed up three offers of a job, all working with some very prominent people. I was told that you had something else in the pipeline. To be specific, this job. So what I want to know is, why? If you're as free of any underhand motives as you claim to be, why turn down Rome and Hong Kong in favour of an island?'

Emma relaxed. He hadn't found out about her. She was stupid to have panicked at all.

'There you go,' she crowed triumphantly. 'If I were a gold-digger, I would have snapped up one of those offers.'

'Except that Alistair is the oldest, and by far the wealthiest.'

His vivid blue eyes met hers, and she could almost feel him trying to unlock her mind and unravel her most personal secrets.

No wonder, she thought, he was such a big deal in business. Even knowing that she was safe, she still felt a stab of wariness.

'That never even occurred to me,' Emma replied truthfully. 'I can't imagine what types you mix with, but you have a very jaded idea of women if you think that we're all after as much as we can get.'

'Are you normally so lippy?'

Emma flushed, feeling unreasonably offended by what she saw as an implied criticism of her. True, she always made a point of standing up for herself, but she had never seen it as a flaw in her character. Conrad made it seem as though it was a trait that wasn't particularly desirable in a woman. Just as well, she thought, that she couldn't care less what he thought.

'Is the interrogation finished?' she asked coldly.

'Doesn't the isolation of this island bother you?' Conrad continued as though she had not spoken. 'Don't you think that you might miss the bright lights?'

'I don't need the night life, if that's what you mean.' Unlike you, she added silently to herself. If the gossip columns were anything to go by, Conrad DeVere never slept.

A little voice told her that gossip columns did not exactly

adhere to the truth like glue to tissue paper, but she ignored it.

'Funny,' he mused with a sarcastic cut to his voice. 'You strike me as the sort of girl who would find the night life very exciting. After all, you're young, attractive…' He allowed the sentence to drift, the shrewd blue eyes glancing across at her.

Emma felt a twinge of alarm. She looked at him, suddenly oddly conscious of his masculinity. The heat, she thought, must be getting to her.

'And tired,' she finished hurriedly for him. 'How much longer before we get there?' He seemed to be driving abnormally slowly, although to be fair the roads were rough.

They had left the one and only stretch of highway behind, and were travelling across much smaller winding roads. On the one side, the dense mat of trees seemed intent on consuming the narrow strip of tarmac at the first opportunity; on the other the vista stretched across yet more thick forest until in the distance the water glimmered like sapphire.

'There's not much to do here,' Conrad persisted, treating her interruption with bland disregard. 'Won't you miss the theatres? And surely there's some young man waiting for you back in London?'

'That's none of your business.'

'As I told you, everything about you is my business.' His voice was soft and silky-smooth.

Emma didn't answer. She gazed through the window at the lush green panorama and wished that the man sitting beside her would simply evaporate in a puff of smoke.

While she had been arguing with Conrad she had had no time to feel apprehensive. Now that sick fluttering in her stomach was returning. They surely couldn't be very far away from Alistair Jackson's house now. Not that there was much evidence of civilisation around them.

Other cars were few and far between. There were no

buildings or high-rise houses, only the occasional scattering of villages where groups of dark-skinned children played by the side of the twisting road, or else bathed under standpipes. They were obviously self-sufficient for food, because chickens clustered around the wooden huts, and glimpses of back yards showed that they cultivated all their own vegetables and fruit.

'We're nearly there.' Conrad's voice broke into her silent appreciation of the scenery, bouncing her back to the present.

'Good,' she lied. She wished now that she had never boarded that plane at Heathrow. What if she discovered that Alistair Jackson was a disagreeable, cantankerous old man? Wouldn't it have been better to have remained in England and continued to visualise him through conveniently distant rose-coloured spectacles? Reality was so often poles apart from what you thought it was going to be.

'What did you mean when you said that Alistair Jackson had been taken in by a woman who was after his money?'

Emma would have preferred not to talk to Conrad at all, but the only option open to her, of remaining silent, was too full of uncomfortable worries for her liking.

'Nervous?' he asked with an aggravating guess at the truth.

'No.' Emma glared at him. On top of everything else, the man was a mind-reader. 'I was simply trying to be polite. If it's too much for you, though...'

Conrad smiled, his first genuine smile of amusement, and she glimpsed that notorious charm which the newspapers were always going on about. A ridiculous warmth swept over her.

'Lisa St Clair. Ever heard of her?'

Emma shook her head.

'No. The newspapers never managed to get hold of the story. They would have had a field day if they had. Happened years ago. She came to Alistair highly recommended as a nurse, a very beautiful nurse, and with her mind on doing a bit more than mere nursing. I was only a teenager when it all happened, but my father told me that Alistair escaped by the skin of his teeth. Apparently this lady had an accomplice, a good-for-nothing wastrel whom she kept conveniently in the background. Someone saw them together in a hotel somewhere in Trinidad, and word somehow got back to Alistair. He wasn't pleased.'

'I can imagine. From the newspaper clippings I've read of him,' she mused aloud, 'I wouldn't have thought him the sort to fall for someone like that. I guess all hard-nosed tycoons must have their soft spots.'

'I guess we do.' Conrad looked at her with wry amusement and Emma blushed.

It must have been exhaustion after the hours spent on the plane and at the various airports, because her rigid self-control seemed all haywire. She was responding to things Conrad said in a way that was so out of character for her that Emma could only blame it on nerves and exhaustion.

'He'd been through a prolonged bad patch,' Conrad was saying. 'I was only a boy at the time, but apparently his daughter, his only daughter, left home against his wishes. Eloped with some fellow.'

Conrad was concentrating on the road. He didn't see Emma's face whiten.

'What do you know about it?' she asked casually, toying with the leather strap of her bag. 'I mean, it's useful finding out as much as I can about Alistair, and as from as many angles as possible, if my input is to be relevant.'

It sounded good. Believable. Emma wondered whether to enlarge on the reasons for wanting to know why Caroline Jackson had left home, and decided against it. There was no point in arousing Conrad's curiosity unnecessarily.

Conrad shrugged. 'Not much more to tell. She eloped and

was never heard from again. Sank like the proverbial stone into a pond of water, and didn't leave a ripple behind her.'

Emma digested his summary of events in silence.

'Why didn't Alistair try to locate her?'

'How do you know that he didn't?' Conrad looked at her briefly through narrowed eyes.

'Just assumed,' Emma said hastily. 'I mean, if he had located her, they would be in contact now, wouldn't they?'

She made it sound like a statement of fact, rather than a question, and let the whole subject lapse into silence. Conrad was sharp enough to tune in to nuances of interest, and that was the last thing she needed.

The car was slowing down, turning away from the main road up an ever narrower side route, where the undergrowth, untamed and prolific on the main road, had here been trimmed back and given some semblance of order.

With a numb, prickly tension, Emma watched the large Jackson villa loom towards them.

It sat with majestic grandeur at the end of a long drive and an open courtyard, and in the middle of what Emma considered the finest gardens that she had ever seen.

The grass was trimmed to a crew-cut, and carefully land-scaped with all manner of tropical foliage, from the bright colours of bougainvillaea to tall hibiscus bushes, sprouting red and yellow open-petalled flowers.

It was so much more breathtaking than she had expected, and the photographs which she had seen of it were spectac-ular enough.

So here I am at last, she thought wonderingly. The present meets the past.

Her hand trembled as she slid open the car door, to find Conrad looking at her curiously.

'He doesn't bite.'

'What?' Emma blinked at him.

'Alistair. He doesn't bite. Or do you normally get an attack of stage-fright every time you start a new assignment?'

'Yes,' Emma said, agreeing with whatever he had said. Her mouth had dried up and all she seemed able to manage were monosyllables.

Conrad was staring at her thoughtfully, but he didn't say anything.

He collected her suitcases and hold-alls, and walked to the front door, chatting amiably to the plump dark woman who opened it.

Emma followed and with every step she took her palms felt more clammy. She should never have come. She should never have come, because there were some things better left alone. She looked around at the Land Rover with a sense of yearning.

Around her, she heard the rich sing-song tones of the house help, Conrad's laconic drawl, the ticking of a grandfather clock.

It all washed over her. She started when Conrad asked her whether she wanted to see Alistair now or else later, after she had bathed.

'Now,' she managed to say. When he began walking beside her, she turned to him politely. 'You can just tell me where to go,' she said. 'I'm sure I'll be able to find my way.'

'I'm sure you would,' he replied blandly.

He continued walking with her, and Emma stopped in her tracks. 'Why are you coming with me?'

'Because,' Conrad drawled with infuriating shrewdness, 'I want to be there when you meet Alistair. You may have half convinced me that you're not a gold-digger, but you're still hiding something from me, and I'd like to find out what it is. I'm not used to people having secrets, not from me, at any rate.'

For a second Emma forgot her nervousness, and rounded furiously on Conrad.

'If I wanted a chaperon, I would have asked for one!' she snapped. 'Shouldn't you be heading back somewhere, anyway, now that you're through cross-examining me? Don't you have work to do? Companies to run?'

Conrad was clearly amused by her display of anger. He smiled, and Emma resisted the temptation to knock out his front teeth.

'I'm touched by your concern for the welfare of my companies in my absence, but I think they can do without me for a few days.'

'A few days?'

Emma stared at him in dismay. The man unsettled her. She was in a delicate enough situation as it was; the last thing she either wanted or needed was to have him hovering around, making her feel things that she was not used to feeling and didn't much like.

'The study's just here at the end of the corridor.' He walked off, and Emma hurried after him. Since she'd arrived, she seemed to have spent most of her time hurrying after the damned man. With her mouth drawn in a tight line, she waited while he knocked and then pushed the door open.

'Alistair,' he said, 'I have your writer, Emma Belle.'

Alistair Jackson sat in his wheelchair, surrounded by shelves of books. Emma followed Conrad into the large room, her eyes fixed on Alistair's face.

He looked older than she had expected, somehow more frail. Had he really once been so tall and proud? The hair, full and dark in the faded photograph which she had inspected so many times, had given way in old age to a high balding dome. Under thick brows the eyes were still young, however, and were scrutinising her intently.

She was aware of Conrad lounging by the window, but

she could not prevent the curiosity from showing on her face.

Ever since her mother had told her about Alistair, when she had been very young, Emma had been curious about him, but it was only in the last few months, when the possibility of actually meeting him was on the horizon, that she had begun to build her careful, detailed picture of him.

She waited for him to speak, and when he did the depth of his voice surprised her. She listened to him as he shifted the conversation between Conrad and herself, chatting about generalities, and thought, He must have been quite something once. There was still an aura of command about him, even now.

Part of her responded to what he was now saying, asked the right questions, made all the right noises. The rest of her was slowly trying to reconcile him with the man whom her mother had feared and respected for so many years.

Slowly the tension began to ease out of her body. She could feel herself physically relax and begin to respond to his questions with less restraint.

When he asked her if the following morning would be too soon to start work, she responded enthusiastically, 'We could start this minute if you like!'

Alistair's firm mouth relaxed into a smile and he raised one restraining hand. 'I wouldn't hear of it. You've only just arrived. Spend the rest of the day unwinding. Believe me, you'll need some rest before we begin on my autobiography. The things I could tell you!'

His eyes clouded over and Emma remained silent. She wondered what was going through his mind. Was it her mother? The temptation to ask was almost irresistible, but she bit it back. Everything, she thought, would unfold in its own time and not a minute before.

'I'm sure,' Conrad drawled, 'that you're not the only one with stories to tell.' He looked at Emma with one raised eyebrow, and she scowled. She had almost managed to forget his presence.

'No,' she replied sweetly, 'I'm sure you have no end of stories that you could amuse us with.'

'Well, anyway—' Alistair looked at them narrowly, and then waved his hand '—no time for stories of any kind. An old man like me needs his beauty sleep.' He turned to Conrad with a grimace. 'You know how finicky that stupid doctor of mine is. He may even threaten to send that harridan of a nurse here again, and I don't think I could cope with the experience twice in a lifetime. It's bad enough that he sees fit to deprive me of my beloved whisky, and the occasional cigar, but—' and he turned to face Emma '—if you saw that battleaxe of a matron, then you'd really understand the meaning of suffering.'

He chuckled, but Emma suddenly noticed that he was looking tired. When he rang the bell for Esther to take him to his room, she stood up, realising with a start from a glance at her watch that they had been talking for far longer than she had thought.

'Conrad can show you around the house and grounds,' Alistair said from the door.

'I'd prefer to show myself around,' Emma began, but Alistair was already out of the room.

She turned to collect her handbag from where it was slung over the arm rest.

'No guided tour?' Conrad asked in a mocking voice.

'I'd rather go on a guided tour with a python.' To Emma's annoyance, he burst out laughing, and she reluctantly grinned. She looked at him and for a split second their eyes locked. Something in his expression made her turn away first, her heart pounding in her chest.

'I have unpacking to do anyway,' she said breathlessly, moving towards the door and keeping as much distance between them as she possibly could.

He moved towards her and Emma looked at him in dismay, her body responding with infuriating sensitivity to his nearness. She would have left the room, she had every intention of doing so, but her feet refused to obey the commands from her brain. They remained firmly planted on the ground until Conrad was so close to her that she could feel his warm breath on her face when he spoke.

'And I was hoping to find out what you're trying so desperately to hide.'

'Hide?' Emma laughed unconvincingly. 'I'm exhausted, that's all.'

'Well,' he said smoothly, 'I'm here for a couple of days more. Time enough for you to overcome your…exhaustion.'

This time Emma did flee, walking quickly towards the door and making sure that she shut it firmly behind her.

Esther showed her to her bedroom, but it was only when she was inside that she felt her body sag as all the nervousness and anxiety drained out of her.

Alistair, she thought, was at least not the cantankerous old man that she had dreaded. He was forceful but approachable, and with a biting but very witty sense of humour. In fact, Emma decided, he was endearing.

She sat on the bed, and pulled a sealed letter out of her bag, staring thoughtfully at the black, rounded writing on the front.

Eighteen months ago her mother had given her the letter, and told her to give it to Alistair, to hand-deliver it, to make peace for her as she couldn't do it herself.

Two days later she had died.

Emma carefully slotted the envelope underneath her make-up tray in the top drawer of the dressing table. She ran a bath, even though she knew that a shower would have been much quicker, and relaxed in the warm water for half an hour, turning over the events of the past few hours in her head.

Of course, Alistair was the only reason that she was here. Conrad had been right when he'd guessed that she did not need the job, but had taken it for a very specific reason.

With unwelcome obstinacy her mind threw into focus a graphic picture of him—raven-haired, arrogant, with the same caustic sense of humour as Alistair, except that there was an element of danger to him that was not there in the old man.

He was definitely a complication on the scene. Emma stood up and began rubbing herself vigorously with one of the towels.

She tried to squash all thoughts of Conrad DeVere, but they kept popping up with aggravating regularity.

In prospect, it had all been so straightforward. She would come to the island, with the very legitimate excuse of working for Alistair, and that way she would be able to find out all about him. It was what her mother had wanted.

Most importantly, she would be able to do it incognito.

She dressed slowly, her eyes wandering over the bedroom, appreciating the attention to detail of the décor, and the stunning view overlooking the gardens.

She reasoned that Conrad's appearance was nothing to worry about. He did not know who she was, and he was only going to be around for a couple of days at the most, anyway. She would simply avoid him, and concentrate all her energies on getting to know Alistair. That was why she had come in the first place, for heaven's sake.

She shuddered as she thought what Conrad would say if he found out her true identity. She had felt him trying to unravel her secret, using all his powers of hypnotic persuasiveness, but he had been way off target.

How could he possibly even begin to guess that Caroline Jackson, that shadowy figure who eloped with an undesirable man all those years ago—twenty-three to be exact—was her mother?

And what would he think if he found out? The worst. He was a formidable businessman. Hardly the sort who was overflowing with the milk of human kindness. She thought back to his attitude towards her and decided that he definitely was not the sort who was overflowing with the milk of human kindness. There was no question but that he would assume she had made this trip for her own ulterior motives. The man, she thought, was naturally suspicious and aggressive with it.

Emma lay on the bed and closed her eyes, the weariness of the last twenty-four hours catching up with her. She made a determined effort to shut Conrad DeVere out of her mind.

Alistair had at least been a pleasant surprise. Perhaps he had mellowed over the years. Her mother certainly had. Towards the end, she had spoken about her father with regret.

'It was all a mistake,' she had once told Emma. 'I ran away because I felt claustrophobic and I wanted adventure. Your father seemed to provide that adventure. He was everything Dad disliked. Wild, unstable, penniless. The worst part was that your grandfather was right. He was no good. He cleared off the minute I became pregnant with you.'

She had been too proud ever to return to the family home and admit that she had made a mistake. If she had, things might have been quite different.

If she had, Emma thought, I wouldn't be lying here trying to push unwelcome images of Conrad out of my mind.

She groaned in annoyance as her mind raced back to the unpleasant scene of him accusing her of being a gold-digger.

What on earth did all those women see in him, anyway? True, he had money and he was good-looking, but any fool could take one look at him and know that he was not the settling type.

So why did the mere thought of him make her feel hot and bothered? There were more important things at hand for her mind to become cluttered up with some man.

It was just a good thing that he wouldn't be around for much longer.

In the meantime, there was a lot for her to think about.

CHAPTER TWO

THE following two weeks were busy.

Because the days dawned earlier and brighter than in London, Emma found herself awakening before seven in the morning. Already at that hour the skies were blue and the sun was warming up in preparation for the intense heat which it would exude by midday.

She would normally have thought it a shame to waste the finest hours of the day cooped up in a study, but working with Alistair, apart from being of personal interest to her, was exciting as well. For an old man, Emma thought, with health problems, his dynamism was still formidable. He began the day at eight promptly and finished at one. Those five hours, Emma discovered, were utilised to the utmost.

'I'll be wizened and grey-haired at the end of this job,' she had laughingly told him on their second morning. 'I've met people a quarter of your age who haven't got your kind of stamina.'

Naturally the old man had been pleased and, to Emma's delight, tickled pink. Perhaps, she thought, her mother had found Alistair's energy and thirst for perfection simply too difficult to handle. As he described to her the dawnings of his rise from rags to riches, she glimpsed a man with a will of iron. There was little room in him for vulnerability, and maybe he saw the expression of love for his daughter as an area of weakness from which he shied instinctively.

All hypothesis. And anyway, Emma wondered, did it matter so much? She only knew that she was beginning to really like Alistair, to be fond of his ways and mannerisms.

He could be peculiarly thoughtful. It was a side to him

which Emma found strangely touching. Coffee was always brought through to them at least once, accompanied by a plate of home-made cakes, which he insisted that she partake of.

'We can't have you wasting away, can we?' he joked. 'Besides, you're much too slim.'

'I don't think there's any danger of my wasting away,' Emma replied, casting her mind back to Esther's superb cooking. 'I haven't eaten so well in months.'

'No one to look after you, then?'

From anyone else the question would have been too intrusive for Emma's liking. From Alistair she took it as something of a compliment. From what she read between the lines, he did not extend his friendship lightly.

When she responded with a laugh that she was all alone in the world, his eyes lit up for a split second, but he did not pursue the topic.

'I hope you don't find my pace of work too demanding?' he asked, as he gathered up his notes at the end of the morning.

Emma looked up at him. 'Just the opposite,' she replied truthfully; 'it's invigorating. On my last assignment, my employer had an unnerving habit of drifting off into hours of digression, and at the end of the day we would have a page or two of worthwhile substance to show for hours of work. I like the way you can concentrate on the important issues.'

'Flatterer.' He looked at her craftily. 'I taught Conrad everything I know. He's very much like me in a lot of respects. Works hard, that young man.'

'Mmm,' Emma murmured non-committally. She had managed to put Conrad to the back of her mind over the past few days.

As far as she was concerned, it was the best place for him, and she was determined that he would stay right there, and not intrude on her thoughts as he had done when they had first met.

'I suppose you know that he's quite a bigwig in the business world,' Alistair pursued.

'Mmm.' Emma obligingly altered the tone of her murmur, but she refused to be drawn into a discussion on him.

'Some say that he's relentless.'

'Do they?' I can think of quite a few other words to describe him, she thought to herself grimly.

'What did you think of him?' Alistair shot her another crafty look which he attempted to camouflage under the guise of guilelessness.

'I don't know him.'

'You know what they say about first impressions.'

Emma shrugged and said airily, 'He seemed the relentless sort.' And that's putting it mildly, she added to herself.

'Well, you'll get to know him a bit better,' Alistair informed her. 'He may have mentioned to you that he's going to be staying here for a while?'

'Well, he did say something of the sort, but...' But she had seen nothing of him for the past few days, and she had assumed that any such idea had been aborted. She had *hoped* that any such idea had been aborted. At the mere thought of him, she could feel her pulses begin to race. Damn man!

'But?'

'Well, he hasn't been around, so I thought that he'd decided against it. I thought he'd decided that someone with an empire to run couldn't afford the time off.'

'Everyone needs a rest now and then.'

'Do they?' Emma couldn't resist a touch of sarcasm. 'He struck me as the sort who ran on overdrive one hundred per cent of the time.'

Alistair chuckled delightedly. 'A girl with spunk. I like that. That's what...' He halted in mid-sentence and looked away. 'Those women Conrad goes out with—bubbleheads, the lot of them. I've met more animated Barbie dolls in my time.'

'Perhaps that's why he goes out with them,' Emma said coolly. 'Maybe he thinks that any woman with half a brain cell would be unfair competition for him.'

She was alarmed at the sudden twist in the conversation, and even more alarmed that the mere thought of Conrad DeVere and his love life was enough to make her ruffled.

Alistair laughed out loud with glee. 'I hope you tell that to him at the first possible opportunity!' he said.

'There won't be a first possible opportunity,' Emma informed him. 'I see no reason why our paths should cross, except possibly at mealtimes.' And even then, she thought, lengthy discussions won't be on the agenda. I'd rather chat to a boa constrictor.

She had begun stacking her work into piles for typing after lunch when Alistair interrupted her.

'Leave it.' He gestured magnanimously. 'Tomorrow's Saturday. You can deal with all that typing some time over the weekend. Why don't you go to the beach this afternoon. Have you been there yet?'

'Not for a swim, no.' She had walked along it in the evenings, paddling in the water and thinking that heaven must surely be a slice of this island. At dusk, the little private cove was so quiet that she could hear herself think.

'Tut, tut, tut. You must think me a slave-driver. I insist you go to the beach as soon as lunch is out of the way. In fact, I could get Esther to bring something down for you. There are coconut trees that you could eat under.'

'No, really, it's…'

'Nonsense.' He waved aside her objections. 'I'd accompany you for a short while, but my health—'

'I know,' Emma chipped in with a laugh, 'your doctor, his instructions. When is Conrad due here, then?' she asked with as much nonchalance as she could muster, her hand on the doorknob.

Alistair mumbled under his breath, 'Oh, some time over the weekend, I should think. Tomorrow, probably.'

Better make the most of the rest of today, Emma thought to herself as she slipped into her bikini.

She had brought over a selection of swimwear and chose the style which she thought was least unflattering to her still pale complexion. The thought of a few hours on the beach, with nothing but a paperback for company, was delicious. What with one thing and another, she had not been on holiday for quite some time, and she had not been outside Europe for even longer.

Her mother had tried to encourage her to take a trip to Florida some years ago, but Emma had refused. It had seemed such a lot of money which could have been used on other, less self-indulgent things.

How her mother would have relished the thought of her now in Tobago.

In fact, Emma thought, as she skipped down the rocky incline to the cove, her mother would have been pleased at how naturally she got along with her grandfather. It might have compensated for her own stubborn pride and refusal to see him for all those years.

She laid the towel close to some coconut trees and abandoned herself to the sheer bliss of lying prone under the sun.

With the heat at its height, she could feel it pricking against her skin. She half opened her eyes and, glancing around the deserted beach, carefully undid her bikini-top, resting it conveniently within arm's reach, although there was practically no danger of anyone else coming on to the beach. The house and grounds, Alistair had told her on their very first day, was simply too remote to invite casual passers-by. The actual cove itself was even more secluded, set as it was down an incline and totally hidden from prying eyes.

Emma looked lazily out at the sea, turquoise and clear. The soft lapping of the ripples along the sand was soporific and soothing. It would be easy to fall asleep, she thought, and emerge three hours later looking like a lobster. It wouldn't be a pretty sight. She slapped on another layer of suntan oil and ran down to the water-line, treading cautiously at first, then, as her body adjusted to the temperature of the sea, splashing in, swimming languorously away from the beach.

No wonder people came to islands such as these and never left. The hubbub of London city life seemed more than thousands of miles away. It seemed like light years away.

Emma lay back, floating on the water, her eyes half shut. The gentle swelling of the water under her was the closest thing she could imagine to lying on a vast water-bed. She folded her arms behind her head, delighted to find that she did not immediately sink to the bottom as she had expected.

A wet slap on her stomach made her eyes shoot open.

When Conrad resurfaced a moment later there was the lazy glint of enjoyment in his eyes.

'What the hell are you doing here?' Emma yelled furiously. With desperate, splashing movements she tried to shield her bare breasts from him without drowning at the same time. 'How long have you been around? Don't you have anything better to do than to prowl around scaring people?'

She was puffing and panting and all too aware that her face was probably blotchy and red as well. He, on the other hand, was calmly treading water, an amused smile on his lips.

'Did I disturb you?'

Emma felt her body burn as he lazily inspected her frantic movements.

'No! Of course not!' she shouted, her green eyes flashing with anger, 'I always enjoy people sneaking up on me and frightening me to death!'

She began swimming purposefully back to shore, realising with dismay that Conrad was keeping up with her, his bare brown arms cutting swiftly through the water.

'Shall I turn my back like a true gentleman?' he asked as they approached the beach, his mouth curving in what looked suspiciously like a grin.

'I'd appreciate it!' Emma snapped back. 'And if you're any kind of gentleman you'll swim right back out to sea and continue swimming until you reach some other island! And if I see you struggling, don't count on me to send help!'

She could hear him laughing as she walked towards her bundle of clothes. Her hands were trembling with anger as she slipped on her bikini-top, only managing to snap together the fastening clasp with difficulty.

She sat stiffly on her towel, watching him as he stood on the water's edge and ran his fingers through his wet hair. Damned if he was going to drive her off the beach and back up to the house. She had been enjoying herself until he came along, and she had every intention of continuing to do so. She would simply ignore him. She lay on her back, annoyed with herself for continuing to watch him as he walked towards her.

He moved with a lithe and curiously pleasing grace. Even from a distance there was something dangerously attractive about him. Emma firmly shut her eyes, trying to stifle a prickle of awareness.

'Mind if I join you?' she heard him ask from somewhere over her.

'Yes.'

He ignored her and tossed his towel alongside hers, stretching down slowly on to it.

Emma glanced at him covertly out of the corner of her eyes. Tiny droplets of water remained on his bronzed body, trickled from his hair on to his forehead. With his eyes half closed, she noticed, his eyelashes were long and black but, against the angular planes of his face, not in the slightest feminine. If anything, they emphasised his disconcerting physical sensuousness.

'You seem to have made quite a hit with Alistair,' he drawled without looking at her.

'We're getting along well, if that's what you mean,' Emma replied coolly, refusing to be drawn into an argument with him.

'I left him singing your praises.'

'He appreciates efficiency and my typing speeds are well above average.'

She turned round to find Conrad's fierce blue eyes fixed on her. As her eyes rested briefly on his mouth, alarm bells began ringing in her head and she looked away.

She would be stupid if she did not find Conrad attractive. Everything about him was put together in a way that almost screamed sexuality. But there was no way that she would allow herself to be attracted to him.

'I was under the impression that you weren't due here until tomorrow,' she said tersely.

'Were you? I told Alistair that I would be down today. In fact, Esther's already prepared my room for me.'

Emma wondered whether Alistair had forgotten. It wasn't like him, but everyone was allowed their fair share of memory-lapses.

'Disappointed?' he asked.

With a swift movement, he sat up and regarded her with cool eyes. Emma glared at him. She had had an unexpected thought. Perhaps his sudden craving for rest and relaxation at Alistair's house had its origins in a desire to keep his eye on her, to make sure that she didn't throw off her well-schooled and aloof front the minute his back was turned, and revert to the gold-digging vamp which he had assumed she was.

The thought was not pleasing, and Emma immediately began to feel her hackles rise. Why else would his opening remark be an observation on how well she got along with Alistair?

'I'm merely surprised that you decided to take a holiday when the world of big business is out there, no doubt struggling without you at the helm.'

Emma saw his mouth tighten with anger and was inexplicably ashamed of her sarcasm.

'You obviously have over-inflated ideas about my influence.'

Emma was silent for a while. 'I just thought that you were joking when you said you would be coming to stay with Alistair,' she finally admitted.

'I rarely say something unless I mean it.' Conrad's voice was smooth and razor-sharp. 'The world is already too full of people shooting their mouths off for no reason other than that they like the sound of their own voices. Alistair at least avoids that particular vice. When he speaks, he has something to say, something worth listening to.'

'Definitely,' Emma agreed.

She hoped that he would go away. Lying prone, she felt too conscious of his eyes on her and couldn't relax.

'Island life agrees with you,' Conrad said lazily. She felt his finger brush against her thigh and pulled away sharply.

'What are you doing?'

'There was a sandfly on your leg,' he said, with an expression of mock innocence. 'Do you normally jump a mile high when someone touches you?'

Emma glared at him. The spot where his finger had rested

still burned as though he had ignited a tiny flame underneath her skin. She looked at his fingers with disdain.

'Do you normally inflict your company on other people, when they clearly would rather be alone?' she asked coldly, ignoring his question.

'Most people don't view my company as a burden,' he said in a matter-of-fact voice, fixing his azure eyes on hers until Emma felt as though she was being mesmerised by a snake charmer.

Her heart was thumping in her chest and her mouth felt dry. What on earth is the matter with me? she thought. Could it be the heat? She didn't think she had been sitting in the sun for that long.

'Especially those of the opposite sex,' he continued, with a hint of lazy amusement in his voice.

'Well, there's no accounting for taste,' Emma bit out. His words had evoked an erotic picture of Conrad's lean, bronzed body and she tried to sweep it out of her mind like so much unwelcome dust under a carpet. Were there no limits to this man's ego? She was tempted to tell him that power and good looks had clearly gone to his head, but she resisted.

Instead she threw him a look of scorn, noticing that it did not diminish the half-languid smile playing on his lips.

'How about you?' he asked, lying on his side to face her, so closely that she was embarrassingly aware of his warm breath on her face.

'How about me?'

'You've told me that you're not interested in the bright lights. Is there some quiet, retiring young man patiently waiting back in England for you?'

'You already asked me that.'

'I know. You never answered.'

'Yes, I did. I told you that my private life is none of your business!' Emma faced him. Up close, she saw that the blue of his eyes was speckled with very dark grey. She felt unsteady for the briefest of moments, and looked away.

'I suppose that means that there is some forlorn fool awaiting your return. If I were your boyfriend, I'd make sure that you didn't stray too far. With a tongue like yours, you could land yourself in all sorts of trouble.'

'Well, you're not, and for your information there's no forlorn fool waiting for me either in England, or anywhere. Now could you find another spot on the beach to sit on?'

Conrad looked at her curiously, as though she were some new and different species of life which he had not run into before.

'How do you occupy your time when you're not working with Alistair?' he asked, changing the conversation, much to Emma's relief.

'I type,' she said abruptly. 'Alistair persuaded me to forget about work this afternoon and come down here instead.'

'Did he, now?' Conrad said thoughtfully. He stretched back on his towel, his hands clasped behind his head, and contemplated the sky. 'Alistair's always been fond of his games,' he muttered.

'I beg your pardon?'

'Nothing. Absolutely nothing.' He stood up, flexing his legs. 'I think I'll go up to the house now. Coming?'

'No. I'll stay down here for a while longer.' She looked at him pointedly. 'I might be able to enjoy the peace and quiet.'

'Suit yourself.' He looked down at her, his eyes casually running the length of her body. 'Be careful of the sun, though. Too much and you'll end up looking like something that's crawled out from the bottom of the sea.'

Emma sat up angrily as he turned and began walking off towards the rocky path that led back up to the gardens.

Dammit! Didn't that man have anything pleasant to say? True, he had only said what she herself had thought only a short while before, but nevertheless she resented his tone of voice. It was far too smug for her liking.

She hoped that he would trip over some of the rocks and come crashing back down to the beach. Nothing serious, just enough to wipe that clever, arrogant smile from his lips.

She followed his figure and saw him clamber lithely over the rocks and vanish towards the house.

Her serene enjoyment of the beach had evaporated. She lay on her towel for another fifteen minutes, her mind treacherously playing back images of Conrad and her own defensive, irrational response to him.

She fervently hoped that his little holiday on the island would be limited to a few days. She might be able to keep her temper in check for a few days, but, if he stayed much longer, then she would be bound to give way sooner or later. Something about him rubbed her up the wrong way, and, she acknowledged frankly, it had nothing to do with the fact that he probably still suspected her motives for being here in the first place.

No. It was something more fundamental than that. Everything about him nettled her.

Still, she thought with a twist of amusement, it must be quite a shock to his system to find that not every available female with twenty-twenty vision swooned at his feet.

She gathered up her belongings and headed for the house. Neither Alistair nor Conrad were to be seen. Alistair might possibly still be resting, but Conrad? Probably lurking around somewhere. He didn't seem the sort to be happy sitting still for too long.

Rather than take her usual shower, Emma ran a bath, copiously squirting bubble bath into the tub, and sank into the water with a sigh of bliss.

She was not looking forward to dinner in the evening. Normally she dined simply with Alistair, and they spent an hour or so afterwards conversing about ground that they had covered during the day, or whatever else came into their heads.

So far no mention had been made of her mother, and Emma was content to let the subject ride until the appropriate opportunity arose.

With Conrad now on the scene, she seriously doubted that such an opportunity was likely to arise, and that irritated her yet further.

She took her time dressing, slipping into an apricot sleeveless dress and her flat leather sandals. She had acquired the first golden shimmer of a tan and, against her pale gold colour and the apricot dress, her hair seemed startlingly blonde.

If blondes, she thought, staring at her reflection in the mirror, were supposed to be vivacious and giggly, then she certainly disproved the theory. Inside, she felt, was a brunette struggling to get out.

Her mother had been dark, her hair tinged with red, the colour of chestnut, and she had jokingly banned her daughter from ever taking a bottle of dye to her hair. A natural blonde, she had told Emma, was a rare species, and she should be thankful.

Emma wondered whether Conrad would have been so accusatory towards her if she had had dark hair. Maybe not. He might just have taken her more seriously from the start, or never even suspected her of anything in the first place.

She forced her thoughts away from him, and made her way slowly towards the living-room area, where a glass of sherry would be awaiting her. It had become a routine which she enjoyed.

Alistair was sitting in his usual position by the french doors which opened out on to the huge expanse of the garden.

Conrad, with his back to her, looked around as she walked in, meeting her stony glance with an ironic smile.

He was dressed in a pair of beige trousers and a short-sleeved grey-blue shirt which did very little to hide the broad width of his shoulders and his long, muscular legs.

'I see you took my advice about overstaying your welcome in the sun,' he remarked casually, inspecting her with the sort of slow thoroughness which had made Emma bristle on the very first day they had met.

'Actually, I had arrived at the same conclusion myself,' Emma said politely. 'It doesn't take a genius to work out that too much sun isn't a good idea.'

'Slowly but surely does it,' Alistair chipped in, his shrewd eyes glancing between them. 'You've acquired just the right shade of pale brown. You look quite fabulous. Doesn't she look fabulous, Conrad?' He looked ingenuously at Conrad, who seemed about to say something, only to have second thoughts.

'Fabulous,' he repeated drily, then switched his attention to Alistair, resuming the conversation which Emma supposed they had been having before she walked in.

Oh, charming, she thought, wondering why on earth she was disappointed to be excluded when to be excluded was better than to be subjected to a barrage of barely veiled criticisms.

She picked up her glass of sherry and sat on the sofa next to Alistair, listening to them and gradually becoming enthralled at their discussions.

When Conrad spoke, it was with a vigour and a command of knowledge which somehow came as no surprise. He discussed worldwide market trends, and their effect on Alistair's holdings, with a perception and shrewdness which she assumed had made him such a force in business.

Over the meal, a West Indian speciality of cooking bananas, Creole rice and fish stewed in coconut, the conversation switched to more general topics, and Emma found herself joining in.

Neither Conrad nor Alistair had been to London for several months, and they quizzed her about the theatres and the operas. Emma animatedly described as much as she could, from, she admitted, reviews and information gleaned from the newspapers rather than first-hand experience.

'The theatre I go to as often as I can,' she confessed, 'but the opera—well, that's quite a different matter. The prices tend to be way out of my league. I was invited a couple of times and I thoroughly enjoyed myself, but I have yet to make it on my own.'

'Who did you go with?' Conrad asked casually. 'An opera buff?'

'Oh, a friend,' Emma replied smoothly, steering the conversation away from herself and into less personal waters. Two glasses of sherry and a glass of port might have relaxed her a little, but certainly not enough to let slip anything revealing about herself.

She had always been careful about sharing confidences, preferring to keep her life to herself. Now it had become almost second nature, a habit to which she adhered almost without thinking.

Perhaps it was a character trait which she had somehow gleaned from her mother. When her mother had settled first in Coventry, then in London, she had always managed to keep her private life to herself, confessing to none of her friends anything about her background.

'They can take me as they find me,' she had once told Emma. 'My privacy is the one thing I cherish above all else.' She had laughed. 'Apart from you, my darling.'

Perhaps her obsession with privacy had stemmed first from her desire to conceal her whereabouts from her father.

There was no doubt that, as far as Alistair went, she had sunk without a trace.

Emma wondered whether he had ever tried to find her mother and thought not. Anger would have stopped him to start with, and then after that pride would have stepped in. Although, she thought honestly, her mother's pride, from what she had gleaned from Alistair's occasional throwaway remarks, had been far fiercer and deeper than his had ever been.

She had lived with the scars of her own mistakes, and had found it as impossible to forgive her father as she had to forgive herself. She would have erected enough barriers around her to have repelled the most insistent searcher.

Or maybe, she thought with a flash of intuition, Alistair *had* searched, and *had* found her, but had chosen not to intrude. In which case, he would have known about the existence of a granddaughter.

Did he? No, she convinced herself, although…although he treated her with the warmth of someone who delighted in her company far more than if she were merely his assistant. He could easily have checked her identity if he knew what he was looking for…

But no, she was just being over-imaginative. She frowned at him and brushed aside the thought, flicking it to the back of her mind like an irritating intrusion.

When she dragged herself back to the present, it was to find Alistair looking at her.

'Penny for your thoughts, my dear. We seemed to lose you there for a moment.'

Emma looked at him seriously. 'They're not worth a penny,' she said.

'What about a pound?' Conrad was staring at her, and Emma could almost see his brain clicking, trying to work out her secrets, trying to out-think her.

'Not much use on an island where dollars are the currency, is there?' She laughed awkwardly, suddenly feeling as though she were treading on quicksand.

The uncomfortable moment passed and Alistair was ringing his bell for Esther to take him to his bedroom.

'I'll leave you two to carry on,' he said, moving towards the door. 'Esther, bring through some more coffee for Emma and Conrad after you've taken me up.' He could already see Emma beginning to protest and waved aside her objections. 'You two have much more in common than you think,' he observed with a gesture. 'You should get to know each other better.'

'Alistair…' Conrad said in a warning voice, 'You're getting too old to play games.'

'Games? Son, I don't know what you're talking about. I merely feel obliged, as your host, to see that you get along and are enjoying yourselves.'

As he left the room, Emma heard him call over his shoulder, 'Besides, Conrad, I'm sure you'll want to tell Emma all about your fiancée. After all, they'll be thrown together soon enough, won't they?'

CHAPTER THREE

'YOUR fiancée?' Emma repeated incredulously. Why, she thought, was she so surprised, for heaven's sake? Wouldn't it be much more unusual if he *didn't* have a fiancée? She had read often enough about all those women who swarmed around him. A fiancée was the logical conclusion. In fact, it was surprising he wasn't married off by now.

Still, she felt a stab of pain and immediately composed her features into polite interest. She didn't like the man, wasn't interested in him at all apart from as a potential threat; she surely couldn't really give a damn if he was engaged, married, or widowed with ten children?

He was looking at her closely, his lips tightened into a grim line.

'Alistair has a knack of being indiscreet when he chooses.'

'Indiscreet? Why? Surely it's no big secret? I mean, isn't an engagement a cause for celebration?' She stared through the window behind him, not allowing a ripple of emotion to cross her face.

'For the moment, it's very much something of a secret. The newspapers would love to get their grubby little hands on a story like this, and that's the last thing I want.'

He ran his fingers distractedly through his hair, then sat heavily on the sofa, stretching his long legs out in front of him.

Emma tried not to look at him at all. She still had that funny feeling in the pit of her stomach, as though she had suddenly dropped one thousand feet in mid air, only to find herself safely on terra firma after all.

45

She wondered what his fiancée looked like, and the rush of jealousy that struck her almost left her gaping in surprise.

Of course, a shocked inner voice told her, it's not jealousy, simply the suddenness of the revelation.

'Alistair doesn't like her,' Conrad was saying. 'He thinks she's shallow and he thinks that I'm planning to marry her for totally the wrong reason.'

'And are you?' Emma felt compelled to ask, heartily wishing she could simply drop the subject rather than pursuing it with such tenacious interest.

'Well, I'm marrying her because it suits me to do so. It's more of a business arrangement. It's a matter of opinion as to whether or not that constitutes the wrong reason.'

He did not elaborate on what kind of business arrangement, and Emma allowed the words to sink in.

Fascinated, she watched as he clasped his hands behind his head, wondering how it would feel to have them caress her. She shook her head to get rid of the thought. What was happening to her? She had always been so level-headed.

'A business arrangement? You make it sound like some sort of company merger. And how does your fiancée feel about this?'

'Believe me, it's mutual. She thinks that marriage would enhance her career, and that I would provide the passport to all the right places. Which, of course, I would.'

'Of course,' Emma agreed cynically. 'A match made in heaven. You provide the passport and she provides the businesses. I'm surprised everyone doesn't jump on the bandwagon and start getting married for all those practical reasons. It would certainly do away with the candlelit dinners and courtship.'

Conrad was looking at her intently. 'I wouldn't have thought you were a firm believer in love at first sight and thunderbolts from the skies with violin music in the background.' His lips twisted cynically. 'Isn't that only the stuff of movies?'

'I wouldn't know,' Emma replied coolly.

'Meaning that you haven't been swept off your feet as yet?'

'Meaning nothing.' She felt a slow flush creep over her. It was beyond her why she was arguing the point with him. She had always thought that marriage could quite happily exist as a business arrangement. 'I simply think that you can't treat something as emotional as love and marriage with such detachment. As though you're going out to buy a car.'

'Love? Who ever mentioned love? Though she *is* very beautiful.'

Emma didn't answer.

'I wish I could see what went on behind that cool exterior of yours,' Conrad murmured, his eyes running over her body and finally resting on her face. 'You were vibrant enough at the dinner table, when you were discussing politics, but the minute the topic becomes too personal you close up like a clam.'

'Really?' Emma feigned indifference, but she could feel her heart pounding.

'Yes, really. Why are you so secretive? You've got some ulterior motive for being here. Why don't you just come out with it and tell me what it is? I'll find out sooner or later, you know.'

'Why do you keep trying to pry into what's no concern of yours?'

'If only it were that easy.' His words were spoken so softly that Emma barely caught them. There was a brief, electric silence broken only by the sounds outside of crickets and frogs.

'I'm surprised Alistair objects to the…to your arrangement,' she said hurriedly, 'when…'

'When what?'

Emma stared at him, realising that she had dug a hole for herself.

'When he opposed his own daughter's marriage for just the opposite reason, namely that it had not been thought out thoroughly, that it was solely an affair of the heart.'

'Did he say that?'

'Yes.' It was too late now for her to try and remember whether he had told her that or not. That watchful curiosity was back on Conrad's face and she turned away, not wanting to meet the questions in his sharp blue eyes.

'He's changed. Maybe that's the very reason he's against my engagement. Anyway, he's right about one thing. You'll be meeting Sophia soon enough. Her parents own a house on the golf course near here. She's coming to stay for three weeks.'

'How nice.'

Sophia, she thought. What a name. Hardly conjures up the picture of an ambitious career woman.

'Is she a model?'

Conrad looked at her in surprise. 'As a matter of fact, she is. She does a bit of acting as well, but from what I've seen she's hopeless.'

'That's charitable of you.'

Conrad's sensuous mouth curved into a smile and he raised one mocking eyebrow. 'I'll say this for you: you do have a certain dry wit that I haven't found in too many members of the opposite sex.'

'Maybe you've been hanging around with the wrong members of the opposite sex,' Emma said, trying to stifle the spurt of pleasure his compliment had given her.

'Maybe I have. Would you say it's too late to remedy that?' His voice was low and warm. Suddenly the room felt hot, too hot for comfort, and tiny needles were pricking under her skin.

'Far too late,' she replied crisply. Perhaps she was imagining the speculative intimacy behind his words, or maybe he was playing some kind of game. Whatever, she would do well to remember that she could not afford to let her guard drop. Not for an instant.

Anyway, she had no intention of being his victim. She rose abruptly, tossing her hair behind her shoulders.

'Well, I think I'll hit the sack.' She yawned and threw him a courteous, slightly dismissive look. 'I want to be up early to finish some work.'

'On a Saturday? No beach?' he asked with an air of feigned innocence.

The implication behind his words was blatant enough, and Emma replied more hotly than she intended, 'No, no beach! So you can find someone else to do your sneaking up behind!'

She slammed the door on his low chuckle.

Their conversation was still jarring on her nerves the following morning, and she made a deliberate point of avoiding him. There seemed little use in courting another battle of words, with her, she admitted, coming out the loser; and, besides, there was the typing to do.

As she settled in front of the word processor in Alistair's office she eyed the pile of notes, some scribbled, some astonishingly coherent, with an expression of reluctance.

Alistair had retired with his book to the pool at the back of the house. He had invited her to sit with him, but she had refused. She was not in the mood for lazing in the sunshine, even though the prospect of three hours' worth of typing did not do a great deal for her either.

She flicked through the sheets of paper, but her thoughts kept returning to Conrad.

She felt that she had guessed accurately enough at his character when she had first met him. A powerful man, aware of his own sexual attraction to women, and not against using it when it suited his purposes. The fact that he was almost frighteningly clever as well made his charm all the more lethal when he decided to use it.

She should have been prepared to meet him with the stony indifference which would have protected her against all his barbs, especially as he had had no qualms about telling her precisely what he thought of her when they first met.

It annoyed her that, after all that, he had still managed to get under her skin, like some wretched virus she couldn't quite manage to shake off.

A couple of throwaway compliments from him, a few ambiguous remarks which she had most probably imagined, and she had been squirming like a gawky teenager on her first date. Good grief! He probably acted precisely the same when he was talking to his sixty-year-old female employees. She frowned in self-disgust.

Shouldn't the fact that he was engaged have made him more reserved? she wanted to know.

He had disappeared to meet Sophia from the airport. When she saw them together, she would probably be able to put it all into perspective. They would be holding hands and whispering sweet nothings into each other's ears, even if he did profess to be cynical about love, and she would be able to relax and treat him as an almost married man. Easy. She would be able to harness her emotions and get her mind under control as it always had been.

She slipped the disk into the word processor and began clattering on the keyboard, sifting through the disorder until what appeared on the screen before her made sense.

The tiny dark grey print on the paler grey screen was soothing. After a while, Emma could feel the tension begin to ease out of her and her concentration take over.

Reading over what she had done, she saw Alistair in a more detached manner, the young Alistair at any rate, the boy still struggling to become a man and make his fortune in the world.

As yet, they had only covered his very early years, before he met her grandmother, and long before they'd had her mother and his story began to weave into hers.

He had been single-minded even as a young man, with the sort of blinkered drive that ground obstacles into dust. Emma could see how his ambition could have blighted any relationship he might have had with her mother. Her mother had been a sensitive woman. Incomprehensible to someone like the young Alistair, whose thirst for success had no time for the fine, subtle swings of emotion.

How he had changed, Emma thought. The old man with whom she now worked bore only a shadowy resemblance to the hard young boy about whom she was writing.

She become so absorbed in her work that it was nearly midday the next time she glanced at her watch.

She looked through the window at a perfectly clear blue sky. Even though the office was air-conditioned, she could almost feel the sun beating down outside. In weather like this it was no wonder everyone moved in slow motion. She did now, as well.

She stretched with a lazy, cat-like movement. The thought of lounging around the pool was beginning to look distinctly tempting, and she packed away her files quickly, flicking them into order as she did so.

Alistair was still by the pool when she emerged half an hour later, wearing a modest flowered one-piece and a pale blue beach coat. He was sitting in the shade, fully dressed in a shirt and cotton trousers and wearing a hat.

'Doctor's advice,' he said, pointing to the hat. 'He's managed to get me off the drink and the cigarettes, and now he even dictates my wardrobe. Pretty soon he'll be telling me what television programmes I can and can't watch.'

Emma laughed, her green eyes crinkling. Esther had prepared snacks for lunch, and Emma bit into one of the pasties, catching the crumbs with one hand.

In between mouthfuls of food, she chatted to Alistair about work. All the time she found herself watching for Conrad, almost disappointed when there was no sign of him.

Probably locked up in a bedroom somewhere, she thought, making up for lost time with Sophia.

The thought was so distasteful that Emma pushed it aside and concentrated on the surroundings, half listening to what Alistair was saying, half drowsing in the heat.

'Lying there, for a moment, my dear, you reminded me of someone, but I can't for the life of me think who. In fact, over the past few days, something about you…your mannerisms… It'll come to me in time, I expect. Old age. Dulls the memory, you know.'

Alistair's words cut through the haze of her drowsiness, and Emma sat up, trying not to let any surprise flicker across her face.

For the past few weeks she had been lulled into a sense of security, appreciating Alistair's company, almost forgetting the blood tie between them. Almost forgetting the letter lying in the drawer upstairs.

'I can't think why I should remind you of anyone,' she said warily, propping herself up on one elbow, and avoiding his speculative gaze. The niggling suspicions rose their heads, and she stamped them down resolutely. 'My goodness, you very nearly woke me up. I was beginning to fall asleep here. It's so peaceful and quiet. When will Conrad be making a reappearance?'

It was a line of conversation which she did not want to explore, but from experience Emma knew that Alistair could be distracted easily by the mention of Conrad's name. He seemed as proud of him as if he were his own son. If the alternative was a trip down memory lane, with Alistair trying to plumb his memory for a recollection of her, then far safer to stick to discussing Conrad DeVere, however unappealing the subject was.

'Some time this afternoon. He's gone to meet that wretched woman at the airport. He'll probably bring her back here with him, though thankfully she's not actually staying here. She'll be at her parents' house.'

'Yes, Conrad told me.'

'He's been discussing her with you?' Alistair's bright eyes looked at her slyly. 'I didn't realise you two were on such confidential terms already. Not that I mind in the least. On the contrary.'

'We're not on confidential terms,' Emma corrected him firmly. 'In fact, we're not on any kind of terms at all, confidential or otherwise. In fact, he didn't tell me a thing about his fiancée apart from her name and where she was staying.'

'Weren't you curious about her?' Alistair probed.

'No,' Emma lied.

Alistair shot her a disappointed look. 'Well, she's no competition for you at all, my dear.'

'Competition? I'm not in competition with anyone for that man's attention!' Emma responded hotly. She scowled at Alistair and he chuckled.

Alistair was needling her and clearly enjoying her discomfort. Emma resisted the urge to stick her tongue out at him. Instead, she turned over on to her stomach and let her arms fall on either side of the red and white sun lounger. Out of the corner of her eye, she looked at Alistair, who still wore the remnants of a grin on his face.

'Don't think much of Sophia. Nice enough, but I don't think they're suited. Don't approve of this engagement one jot. Never have.'

'So Conrad said.'

'Ah!' He sounded like the cat that had just discovered the pot of cream. 'So you *were* chatting about her! I thought you said that you hadn't been?'

'You're incorrigible!'

They both laughed. Emma stood up, bending her head forward and scooping up her hair, quickly braiding it and securing it with a coloured elastic.

'I,' she said, making a face at him, 'am going for a swim!'

'Not to get away from me, I hope?'

'You flatter yourself!'

With a lithe movement she stood poised on the edge of the pool for a few seconds, then dived cleanly into the water, gasping as she felt its coldness on her body.

She was a good swimmer and she enjoyed it. It was the closest thing to total freedom of movement that she could imagine. In England she had shied away from the public swimming baths, finding them overcrowded in the summer and too unappealing in the winter.

Here, she was making up for lost time. She held her breath and swam, using deep strokes to cover the length of the pool. When she re-emerged into the air, she threw her head back, her eyes shut, her face lifted towards the sun with an expression of hedonistic enjoyment.

Yes, swimming pools in England, she thought, had a long way to go.

She opened her eyes and turned towards Alistair, her mouth open to shout out her pleasure to him.

With a sensation of stunned surprise, she turned instead to face Conrad and Sophia, both staring at her, while in the background Alistair waved, gesticulating at Sophia's back and raising his eyes to heaven.

Emma reluctantly swam to the side of the pool and pulled herself out.

'Typing all done?' Conrad asked in a faintly mocking tone of voice. 'Not that I wouldn't have come to rescue you from the word processor if you had still been there.'

'How gallant.' Emma looked at his lean, muscular body with a shiver of unwelcome awareness, then she turned her attention to Sophia who had reached out and was holding Conrad at the elbow.

From behind them Alistair did the introductions. Emma barely heard him. She was looking at Sophia, thinking that, if her name did not conjure up the picture of a career woman, then her face and body certainly didn't.

She was tall and seemed to be tanned all over. Even her hair, cut fashionably short, was bronzed and so were her eyes, a peculiar shade of brown-gold. She was wearing five or six bangles on her wrist and every time she moved her hand they jangled like tiny bells.

Emma decided that she found the noise irritating. She herself possessed almost no jewellery at all and could never understand other people's fascination with it.

'You were working?' Sophia addressed her, raising her eyebrows in surprise. 'In weather like this?' She turned to Conrad. 'Darling, do you hate me too much because I wouldn't dream of being quite so industrious?'

Good grief! Emma thought, reaching for her towel and trying to ignore the indulgent smile on Conrad's face. She dried herself vigorously and then wrapped the towel around her, sarong-style. She stretched out on the sun lounger alongside Alistair. Through semi-closed eyes, she watched Sophia discard her silk wrap and twirl seductively in front of Conrad, showing him every possible angle of her body, scantily wrapped in what Emma estimated couldn't have been more than a few inches of white Lycra.

'Delightful,' Conrad commented, standing back to appreciate her. His eyes flicked across to Emma and she yawned widely. Pure coincidence, but, seeing him frown, she grinned back and stretched out for her book.

'Well, I'll see you lot later,' Alistair said, allowing Conrad to help him into his wheelchair. 'Sophia, dear, I can't imagine why you bother with a swimsuit. There's so little of it that you might just as well have spared yourself the expense and gone for the all-nude look instead. A lot cheaper.'

Sophia's teeth clamped together angrily and Emma stifled a laugh.

'Silly old man,' she muttered to Emma, sitting on the edge of her sun lounger.

'Anything but,' Emma disagreed coldly. 'He happens to be extremely clever.'

'Oh, I know,' Sophia agreed quickly, 'Still, brains aren't everything.' She threw Emma a knowing look which said it all.

They may not be all, Emma thought, but they help. Then she looked at Sophia and wondered whether they did after all.

Face it, she admitted to herself, the woman probably earns a thousand times more than you do, and she's certainly no Einstein.

'Conrad tells me that you're a model. I would have guessed,' Emma confessed honestly, 'if he hadn't said.'

Sophia looked pleased.

'You may have recognised me? I was on the cover of *Vogue* a couple of months ago.' She raised her chin slightly, her eyes narrowing against the sun, her movements poised and slightly artificial.

'I don't get much time for reading magazines,' Emma said, wondering what greater accolade there could be for a model than to appear on the front cover of such a reputable magazine. She thought with amusement that the only place her picture was ever likely to appear would be in a photo album.

'And what exactly do you do?' Sophia slipped a pair of large sunglasses over her eyes and directed her gaze to the flat surface of the pool.

'I type,' Emma replied succinctly, deciding that an elaborate job description would be guaranteed to bore someone like Sophia to tears.

'I once went to a secretarial college,' Sophia said off-handedly, 'I only lasted about a month and a half. The typing was all right, but the shorthand was too difficult. All those silly little symbols. I couldn't really get the hang of it at all. And I hated being surrounded by women! Anyway, I never could concentrate on anything for too long. Besides, modelling pays much more. Not that I need the money. I could quite adequately have kept going on my trust fund, and now that I'm about to marry Conrad, well…' She allowed the sentence to drift to a meaningful pause.

Emma wondered where the husband-to-be was. He seemed to have taken an inordinately long time dropping Alistair back to his room.

'You must be very excited about the wedding,' Emma volunteered, a little ashamed at the triteness of the remark. She was finding the conversation heavy going. For the first time, she wished desperately that Conrad would reappear.

'No, not really. I would quite happily have lived with Conrad, but he insisted on marriage. I think he's afraid that someone else might snap me up if we're not legally hitched.' She laughed, a deep, throaty laugh, and Emma thought sourly that even that sounded sexy. She could not have been a day over twenty, if that, but already with the self-confidence of someone quite accustomed to being the centre of attention. Every gesture she made proclaimed it.

She watched as Sophia delicately tested the water with one toe, then gradually eased herself into the pool. Why, she thought, did Alistair disapprove of the match? She, acidly, considered Conrad and Sophia to be perfectly suited.

'Well, what do you think?'

Conrad's deep voice behind her made her jump. He squatted down until his face was close to hers. Emma edged away and his blue eyes flickered with amusement.

'Think about what?' she countered icily, annoyed with him for the effect that he had on her. 'The weather? World politics? Religion?'

'Sophia.'

'Ah. As a matter of fact, she's not what I expected.'

'What did you expect? A gold-digger?'

'Like me?' Emma mocked.

'I never said that.'

'But you implied it.' For some reason she wanted an argument. She knew that she was being childishly aggravating, but something in her persisted.

'Let's get one thing straight, lady,' Conrad said grimly, 'OK, I admit I quizzed you when you first arrived, but you told me that you weren't after Alistair's money, and I believed you, if only in the absence of any evidence. It's obvious that you can't accept that.'

Emma looked at him dumbly. 'Sorry,' she muttered.

The sharp blue eyes raked over her face.

'I think you're being very unfair on Sophia. Are you sure that she knows that your idea of marriage to her is a business arrangement? A company merger?'

'Of course,' Conrad replied smoothly. 'As I said, it suits her as much as it suits me. Not that having her around wouldn't be a pleasure.' He shot Emma a quick, sideways glance. 'Isn't she most men's idea of physical perfection?'

'I wouldn't know!' Emma snapped, immediately regretting her burst of emotion, which she proceeded to cover under a veneer of indifference. 'But I'll take your word for it. You clearly have enough experience in that direction.'

Her fists clenched hard on the arms of the lounger. God, she thought, why on earth do I let this man bother me? She discarded the train of thought, because to pursue it might throw up a few questions to which she could not provide the answers.

She heard Sophia's lilting voice calling from the pool, and they both looked in her direction.

'I think you're being summoned,' Emma said sweetly.

'When it's by a beautiful creature like Sophia, I don't object,' Conrad replied with equal silkiness.

He moved with an almost mesmerising grace to the side of the pool, and then dived in. Emma watched his tanned body slice through the water and emerge alongside Sophia.

He said something to her, and she laughed, throwing back her head and exposing the slim column of her neck. Conrad's lips trailed across the fine skin and Emma looked away.

It doesn't take a thousand guesses to hit on what they'll be doing later on this evening, she thought acidly. They should keep that sort of thing for the bedroom. She shut the door firmly before her mind could start inventing images of them in bed and picked up her book, struggling to get past the one sentence which she re-read three times before giving up totally. She stuck the book over her eyes and tried to take no notice of Sophia's girlish laughter and Conrad's deeper chuckles.

They might be marrying for all the convenient reasons, but it was clear to Emma that there was no shortage of physical attraction between them.

She rarely thought about men and marriage, but for the first time she felt a sharp twang inside as she contemplated what she had missed out on.

True there had been men in her life, but none that aroused more than friendship. Certainly none that had ever tempted her virginity. In fact, when it came to sex, she could never imagine what all the fuss was about.

Still, a virgin at twenty-four! What an anachronism in the twentieth century!

She turned over on to her stomach. The sun was blisteringly hot and she felt like a piece of bread in a toaster, slowly being burnt. Water, water everywhere, she thought, and not a drop to swim in, because the last thing she wanted to do was jump into the pool and disturb whatever was going on.

She didn't have to look to know that Conrad was probably enjoying Sophia's company in more ways than one.

He had struck Emma as someone who worked hard, but who also played hard. The very last thing she needed to see was him playing hard with Sophia.

Alistair's wrong, she thought, Sophia is the ideal mate for a man like Conrad. He needed someone who didn't stretch his mind. His mind was stretched enough in his work.

She heard the splashing noises as they both emerged from the pool and remained rooted in her position with her back to them. It was rude, she knew, but something inside her had twisted with a feeling of sick pain when she had seen Conrad kiss Sophia's neck. Why on earth did her emotions keep failing her, when her head still remained screwed on and was telling her that she should be careful of Conrad DeVere in more ways than one?

When Sophia sat on the lounger next to her, Emma turned around, screwing her eyes against the sun.

'We thought you might like to come to a party at my folks' house tomorrow,' she said. Conrad's hand was resting on her shoulder, and Sophia touched it with her own.

It was a careless, intimate gesture which Emma deliberately ignored.

'It's a lunch party. There'll be tennis.'

'Tennis? I have to warn you that tennis isn't one of my strong points. It's been years since I held a racket, and even then what I did with it wouldn't have got me a place at Wimbledon.'

Sophia looked blankly at her, but out of the corner of her eye Emma could see an amused smile playing on Conrad's lips.

'You mean you can't play?'

'You hit the nail on the head.'

'Oh, that's no problem.' Sophia waved aside her objection with a flippant gesture, 'I'm pretty hopeless as well. Actually, I only ever play tennis for the exercise. I have to watch my shape—' she pouted, raising her face to Conrad '—or no one else will.'

Emma smiled politely and agreed to go.

She was curious to see who would be at this tennis party. She had been sightseeing briefly a couple of times, but on her own. She was beginning to miss the company of her friends, whose letters had been erratic but full of news about places and people who seemed a lifetime away.

She also managed to buy English newspapers once a week, which were at least one week out of date, but nevertheless fun to read. She sometimes read bits aloud to Alistair, and they discussed what was happening in England with the fervour of people isolated miles away from their native land. Alistair, though he had lived in Tobago longer than he cared to remember, and though it would never have occurred to him to leave it, still felt the need to know what was going on in London.

Maybe there would be Londoners at the party.

At any rate, from what Sophia had said, there would be enough people there for Emma to more or less lose herself in the crowd.

She was beginning to feel disproportionately tense in Conrad's presence. It would do her good to meet some other people and to readjust her emotional balance.

And of course, who knew? There might be someone there who would tell her a little bit more about Alistair.

CHAPTER FOUR

IT WAS late in the morning before Emma was finally dressed, made-up, and, she felt, trussed like a chicken for the party. Two hours late. Not bad going, she thought. She quickly scanned her reflection in the long mirror, wondering if her stretchy flowered dress was really suitable for a tennis party. It would have to do. Her wardrobe wasn't exactly crammed with tiny white skirts and matching tops. In fact, her only white pair of shorts was in the wash, and Emma had no intention of rinsing them especially for the occasion.

She tiptoed towards Alistair's bedroom and peered in. Asleep. Emma frowned as she looked at him. He was supposed to be accompanying her to the party, but at the very last moment had cried off ill.

'Nothing to worry about, my dear,' he had said, when Emma had begun fussing worriedly over him. 'And stop clucking like a mother hen. Anyone would think that…'

'That…?'

'That I'd never been ill before.'

'You never take to your bed if you don't have to,' she had said anxiously.

She had, in fact, been in two minds as to whether she ought to leave him, but the combined forces of Esther and Alistair had forestalled any last-minute cancellations on her part.

Her protests that it would be no bother to give it a miss had met with Alistair's dismissive wave of the hand, and a few mumbled words about never being one to spoil other people's fun.

Nevertheless as the chauffeur dropped Emma off at the villa she still felt a twinge of uneasiness.

In the space of a few weeks she had become more than a bit fond of the old man. In the privacy of her thoughts, she considered him her grandfather. He was her own flesh and blood. The thought that he might really be ill was surprisingly painful.

She tried to put her worries aside as she was ushered into the villa. The party was in full flow. She couldn't spot either Conrad or Sophia anywhere, and she absent-mindedly accepted a glass of fruit punch, liberally laced with rum.

Sophia's parents were a striking couple. They had lived in Tobago all their lives, as had their parents, and they couldn't understand why anyone would want to live anywhere else.

'England could certainly do with a sprucing up as far as the weather is concerned.' Emma laughed. 'I get letters from my friends and they always open with the words "it hasn't stopped raining for the past week". I miss London, though, even if it is grey most of the time.'

Sophia's mother tried to look sympathetic, but clearly found it difficult.

She took her elbow and shepherded her through the guests, introducing her, explaining Alistair's absence to his acquaintances with expressions of sympathy.

'The young people are outside.' She drew Emma through the open patio doors into the sprawling garden where a mixed doubles match was in full flow, watched by clusters of guests who were applauding with what seemed like much more exuberance than the game warranted.

The demon drink, Emma thought with a grin—doesn't it loosen up everyone? She gulped the remnants of her punch and took another glass from the bar, determined to make it last more or less until it was time for her to leave. She did not drink much as a rule, and she had no intention of starting now.

Conrad was playing with Sophia. Emma watched openly as he tossed the ball into the air and sent it spinning across the net to his opponents.

His well-tuned body was embarrassingly mesmerising and she felt her eyes dwelling on his movements with painful intensity.

He and Sophia won in straight sets, which met with wild applause. As he saluted his enthusiastic spectators with mock solemnity, his eyes caught Emma's and she carelessly raised her glass to him.

'You took your time getting here,' he said as he approached her, tossing his tennis racket on a chair. The perspiration was still damp on his face and he wiped it with the back of his hand. 'I see you dressed for the occasion.'

'It was the best I could do.'

She flushed as the smile left his lips and he looked at her through dark-fringed eyes.

'Where's Alistair?' he asked abruptly.

'He wasn't feeling too good so he took a raincheck.'

'Did he get in touch with his doctor?' The sharpness in his voice startled Emma.

'No, he didn't,' she said, confused. 'Should he have? He said that it was nothing to worry about, that he'd be fine if he took his tablets and went to bed.'

The uneasy feeling was back with her. Should she have insisted that he call Doctor Tompkins? She was tempted to phone him and find out whether everything was all right.

'I'll see him when I get back,' Conrad was saying. 'If I'm in the least bit doubtful, I'll get in touch with the doctor. Alistair has a habit of sweeping aside anything to do with his health, unless he thinks it's absolutely necessary.'

Maybe it was the authoritarian tone of his voice, but Emma immediately felt herself relax. He might have his objectionable traits, but she knew implicitly that he could be relied upon. If they constantly rubbed each other up the wrong way, then that was an unavoidable personality clash and did not detract from his in-built self-assurance.

'I see your tennis match was a walkover for you,' she remarked, realising that the one and a half drinks she had had were already beginning to have their effect. 'Is there anything that you can't do?' The question was uttered with a reckless disregard for its interpretation.

'You haven't seen the best of my accomplishments,' he murmured softly, the blue eyes gleaming with irony.

Emma knew that he was teasing her but it didn't make her feel any the less confused. Amazing how he could stir her emotions with a single sentence.

'Do you normally flirt with women, even though you're engaged?'

Conrad's lips tightened.

'Even with women you don't approve of?' she persisted.

'You flatter yourself if you think I'm flirting with you,' he muttered harshly, 'I call it trying to get a reaction.'

'What would your fiancée say?'

'You could always ask her and find out.' He gave her a mocking glance and Emma's fists clenched at her side. She summoned together her fast evaporating good humour and smiled at him.

'I can think of better things to discuss.'

Sophia was approaching, having changed out of her tennis outfit into a slinky gold trouser-suit, the bottom half of which looked as though it had been painted on to her body. The top was a mere strip of stretchy material that left little to the imagination.

She resembled some wild jungle animal, perhaps a puma, with her glowing bronzed skin and golden cat-like eyes. She linked her arm through Conrad's and Emma was struck at how physically well matched they were. There was something predatory about Conrad as well, but, in his case, latently dangerous.

Sophia looked at them and smiled, her yellow-gold eyes flickering invitingly over Conrad. 'Enjoying yourself?' she asked Emma.

'She's having a great time.' Conrad looked at her, one eyebrow raised in amusement, and Emma felt a strong urge to tip her drink over his head.

'I'll leave you to continue enjoying yourself without me.' He sauntered off and Sophia turned to Emma, chatting politely about the various people at the party, most of whom she had come into contact with in her line of work, one way or another.

All the while, her eyes skimmed the crowd, acknowledging the appreciative glances of some of the men with pouting approval.

She was like a flower, some rare and beautiful species which only blossomed in the company of men. They were her sun and water. It amused Emma to see that, although she talked to her, it was absent-mindedly, as though she was merely passing the time of day until something more exciting beckoned.

'I should really be on a shoot in Istanbul,' she explained in a low voice to Emma, 'but Conrad insisted that I come over here for a while. He never usually insists on my dropping my work to be with him, so I decided to come over. Anyway, at the last minute I managed to persuade the photographer, who's a friend of mine, to switch the shoot from Istanbul to here, hence this crowd.' She gesticulated broadly at the milling crowd and sipped from her glass.

Emma had stopped listening. Her thoughts were whirring in another direction.

So Conrad had insisted that Sophia fly to Tobago to be with him. What was it he had said about not believing in love? Obviously he couldn't bear to be apart from Sophia for too long. And you thought he was flirting with you, she reproved herself. The idea made her blush with shame.

Wishful thinking, she told herself, with punishing accuracy. True, there was something in his personality which made her feel defensive and angry, but why deny that he was a physically attractive man? He made no effort to deny it, for heaven's sake! He was fully aware of the effect that he had on women.

An alarming thought crossed her mind. What if he was aware of the effect he had on her? Emma shuddered.

She restlessly listened to Sophia's chatter, twirling her glass in her hand and inwardly cringing at what a fool she risked making of herself.

For starters, she was not his type any more than he was hers. Looking at it from that perspective was more to her liking and she dwelt on all the facets of his personality that she found disagreeable. His arrogance, his easy charm, that thread of ruthlessness which was sensed rather than seen.

Yes, he was not her type at all.

Anyway, he was the last person she should be attracted to anyway. He was engaged, for starters. Emma had always made a point of avoiding married men. An engaged man was more or less of the same ilk.

Besides, he had made his position quite clear on gold-diggers. She did not by any means fall into that category, but what if he were to find out about her connection with Alistair? Wouldn't he see her as the long-lost granddaughter who had travelled halfway across the world at the first possible opportunity, just to see what she could get out of an old, but extremely rich man?

True, he would find out in due course, but she had no intention of being around when he did.

So, she thought, reasons to avoid him.

She was feeling quite pleased with herself when Sophia

gestured towards a tall, fair-haired man whom she proudly introduced as her brother.

'I got all the looks,' he joked. 'As you can see, Sophia's only passable in comparison.'

He had the healthy, tanned look of a beachcomber, and Emma was surprised when he announced that he actually lived in Trinidad and ran a nightclub. She accepted another glass of punch and listened to him as he told her about what was involved in running a club. He was clearly enamoured of life in the tropics, had no intention of ever leaving, and good-humouredly tried to persuade her that England was no comparison to an island where even the rainfall was warm.

Emma found herself laughing in response to him, liking his easy manner. He was much more like the sort of men she was accustomed to dating. He didn't rouse her and he was no challenge. She could relax with him, speak to him on friendly terms. Most of all, he did not threaten her self-control. She smiled as he began describing the girl he was going out with and who had had to remain in Trinidad for the weekend because of work.

'What do you think of your sister's jet-setting,' she teased, 'if you're so adamant that there's no life beside island life? Don't you think that she might fall in love with Europe?'

'Youth,' he said airily, even though Emma suspected that he could not be more than twenty-five, 'will travel. Mind you, she'll be settling down soon enough when she marries Conrad.'

Emma nodded non-committally.

'Not,' he added, 'that she's too keen on the idea, although she assures me that she wants to have babies, and the sooner, the better. Fact is, though, she's only just twenty and she can't see herself in a mansion with only herself for company. Modelling's spoilt her somewhat. All that action. You know.'

Emma replied that she didn't really have a clue.

'Still,' he sighed, 'wedded bliss. It's got to happen some time. My number'll be up before I know it.'

She laughed sympathetically and, when he slipped his arm around her waist to walk with her to the bar, she relaxed against him.

A clipped, icy voice behind her made her swing around. Conrad was staring at her, his eyes cool and disdainful.

'Hope I'm not breaking anything up,' he said with no hint of apology in his voice. His hand snaked out, grasping her by the wrist and forcing her to face him. 'I've been looking for you,' he told her brusquely.

'What for? I'm managing perfectly well on my own!'

'So I see,' he muttered sarcastically. 'Do you normally find it so easy to mix with the crowd?'

'Yes!' Emma bit out angrily, yanking her hand away. 'Especially when "the crowd" happens to be someone as pleasant as Lloyd!'

'Well said, darling.' Lloyd grinned at her and winked. Out of sheer perversity she winked back, disregarding Conrad's thunderous look.

'Lighten up, Conrad.' Lloyd draped his arm around her neck and grinned disarmingly. 'Emma's not spoken for.'

Conrad ignored his remark. He looked at Emma and said, 'You. Follow me.' Then he turned away and began walking towards the house. Emma quickly and apologetically disengaged herself from Lloyd's stranglehold and followed Conrad's rapidly retreating back.

When she finally caught up with him, she rounded on him furiously. 'Just who do you think you are, dragging me away from a conversation like some kind of prisoner under arrest? Issuing orders for me to follow you, no less! If you want to throw your weight around, then I suggest you go do it with Sophia!'

'Call me your Guardian Angel,' he bit out, barely controlling his anger, 'I'm saving you from Lloyd, whose womanising reputation precedes him by several miles. From what I saw of him draped all over you, you were next on his list of conquests.'

'Well, thank you very much!' Emma said coldly, enunciating each word carefully. 'I can take care of myself, if it's all the same to you!'

She had no intention of telling him that the womanising Lloyd had in fact spent the last twenty minutes telling her about his girlfriend.

'Anyway, I'm not here to argue with you,' he told her tightly, 'I've just had a call from Esther. Alistair's taken a turn for the worse. She's calling the doctor. I'm going there now. I thought,' he added, emphasising the word, 'that you might like to come along with me, but if you're otherwise occupied…?'

'I'll get my bag,' Emma told him quickly, throwing over her shoulder as she walked away. 'You might have said that from the start, instead of beating about the bush. I'll meet you at the car in five minutes.'

She hastily apologised to Sophia's parents for her late arrival and early exit, nodding in frustration as they invited her to come again any time.

Her mind was racing ahead, praying that Alistair was all right and that it was all a false alarm. She knew that he was not well, but had never asked exactly how unwell he was. He had always been so alert with her that she'd never imagined it could be anything serious.

She, of all people, should have known that to rely on someone being alive indefinitely was to rely on an illusion. Hadn't her mother survived the car crash, told by doctors that she would be all right, only to die two weeks later?

Conrad was waiting by the car, his long fingers drumming impatiently on the bonnet. When he spotted her running towards him, he stepped into the driver's seat, reaching out to fling open the passenger door.

'What exactly did Esther say?' Emma wanted to know, as the engine throbbed into life and he carefully manoeuvred the car out of the drive. 'Did she give you any details? I mean, is it a heart attack?'

'She just said to come quickly. He's collapsed. She's put him to bed and he seemed to be getting his colour back, but…'

Conrad let the sentence hang in the air and Emma bit worriedly on her lip. But… That implied all sorts of things, and none of them pleasant.

And she hadn't even told him about her mother, about her relationship to him. She should have. She should have told him from the start instead of settling on some damn fool idea of keeping it to herself until she got to know him better.

Now she could only hope that it was not going to be too late.

'Hurry up,' she urged Conrad, only to be told that narrow, twisting roads did not encourage speed.

'Relax,' he told her grimly, 'And for God's sake put your seatbelt on.'

Emma obeyed without thinking.

She settled back against the seat, absent-mindedly watching the landscape roll past. Coconut trees, glimpses of some of the bluest sea she had ever seen, white sand shimmering under the heat.

'Don't think the worst,' Conrad said with maddening self-control. He placed his hand on her leg and Emma felt the warmth of his hand singe her flesh like fire. She flinched away and he immediately withdrew his hand.

'Sorry,' he drawled. 'Forgot. You're a lady who doesn't like too much physical contact. Not even, it would appear, contact of the innocent kind. You prefer Lloyd's brand of highly suspect fondling.'

'I never said that!' Emma protested angrily. 'And Lloyd's so-called "fondling" was not "highly suspect".'

She looked at him covertly, her eyes taking in his strong, tanned arms, the fine black hair curling around his watch-strap, the uncompromising lines of his face.

'As you like. Although I'm amazed you let him touch you. From the way that you recoil every time I accidentally brush against you, I would have thought that contact of any kind was to be avoided.'

Emma was stung by his assumption. 'Just because I'm not attracted to you, it doesn't mean I'm afraid of physical contact.' She lifted her chin defiantly. Conrad's eyes flicked away from the road for an instant, resting on her full lips.

Emma looked away in confusion. Wasn't it a good thing that he thought her some kind of ice maiden? If she had any sense at all, she would work on cultivating the image instead of seeing it as an accusation. Ice maidens didn't react to men like Conrad. She would do well to remember that.

'Is Lloyd more your type of man?' Conrad asked in a tone of mild interest.

He had slowed the car down to compensate for the narrowing of the roads. Every so often, he would have to swerve slightly to avoid ruts in the tarmac.

Emma's stomach tightened at his question. The air-conditioning in the car had been switched on, but she felt suddenly hot. She rolled down the window fractionally, but, feeling the blast of hot air, she immediately rolled it back up.

'I don't have a type,' she replied stiffly, folding her arms across her chest. She could feel her breasts hard under the soft fall of her dress, the nipples pressing against the thin material.

She had a wild yearning desire for him to reach out and

touch her. Her fingers tightened on the bare flesh of her arms, leaving red indentations.

'No,' Conrad agreed softly. At that moment he swerved to avoid a deep rut, sending the car jolting to one side. Emma's arm banged against the car door and she yelped.

'Are you all right?' Conrad asked, slowing the car to a standstill, but keeping the engine running.

'I can see why you insist on seatbelts.' Emma rubbed her arm and examined it.

'Let me have a look.'

'No!' she snapped, watching with consternation as he unfastened himself and stretched across her. She forced herself to appear calm. 'It's fine. Let's just get going and get this journey done with. Please. I want to see how Alistair is, and the sooner we get there, the better.'

Conrad shrugged and turned away. 'Suit yourself, but I'd rather not have two invalids on my hands.'

As the car pulled slowly away, Emma relaxed against the cushioned headrest and breathed a sigh of relief.

She closed her eyes and relinquished herself to the swaying of the car. She had over-reacted again, she realised. She had spent years erecting invisible barriers between herself and the opposite sex, only to discover that when she most needed them they were lying crumbled at her feet.

When she next opened her eyes the car was swinging into the drive to Alistair's house.

Emma sat up abruptly. All her previous anxiety had resettled like a knot in the pit of her stomach. Before the car had stopped, she was fumbling with the door-handle and unfastening her seatbelt.

She ran up to the front door and let herself in, aware that Conrad was following behind her but at a more leisurely pace.

'Where is he?' she asked Esther, who had appeared from the kitchen.

'Upstairs, with the doctor.'

Emma turned to Conrad. 'What shall we do? Do you think we ought to go up and see what's happening?'

'I think we can rely on Doctor Tompkins to emerge in due course and tell us what's happening,' he replied drily. 'There are no ambulances and he hasn't been taken to hospital, so I think we can assume that he's in a stable condition.'

'You're so practical!'

'Well, one of us has to be.' He smiled at her and his face was transformed.

'You should smile more often,' she said impulsively.

His smile broadened to a grin. 'I do. Quite often. You just spend so much time arguing with me that you don't get to see it.'

'Me?' Emma's green eyes looked at him incredulously, 'I never argue with you! It's always the other way around!'

'There you go again.'

She felt a sudden surge of warmth towards him. She knew instinctively what he was trying to do with his light-hearted bantering. He was trying to relieve some of her tension, to relax her, and it was working.

She heard Doctor Tompkins descending the staircase and raised her eyes to him with a sense of dread.

'Is he going to be all right?' Conrad strode towards the doctor, looking strangely incongruous in his shorts and T-shirt next to the doctor, who was more formally dressed, and carrying his black bag.

Doctor Tompkins was thin and dark, his curly hair almost completely grey, with a crisp, efficient manner. He looked reticently towards Emma, as if asking himself whether he should recognise her.

'She works for Alistair,' Conrad informed him in a clipped voice, correctly interpreting the question mark in his eyes. 'You can speak freely in front of her.'

The doctor nodded and said in a precise, professional tone that Alistair had expressed a desire not to have him discuss his condition with either Conrad or Emma.

Conrad looked at the doctor in surprise. 'Why not?'

Doctor Tompkins shrugged and looked at his watch. 'I'm running late for another appointment.' He glanced at them and his face softened. 'I've given Mr Jackson a prescription. Two tablets to be taken three times a day. He's to take it easy. Rest, relaxation and no drink whatsoever, not even a smell of whisky.'

'But he's going to be fine,' Emma interjected. 'Isn't he?'

'He wants to explain it to you himself. 'I really don't know why, but, as you are well aware, I'm duty-bound to adhere to a patient's wishes.'

Conrad nodded in silence.

'I'll be back in a couple of days' time to check him over.'

They both watched as the doctor shut the front door firmly behind him, and turned to each other. Coming hard on the heels of her anxiety of a few moments before, Emma had a feeling of bewildered let-down. What did the doctor mean that Alistair wanted to talk about his condition to them himself?

When they entered his room, it was to find the old man propped up in his bed, his face pale and subdued.

He looked at them both and gestured to Emma to sit next to him.

'I'm an old man,' he began pathetically. He looked at his hands and shook his head.

'What did the doctor say?' Conrad asked, breaking into what looked like a budding monologue on old age. He had his emotions under a tight rein, but even so Emma could detect in him the same worry that she was feeling.

Only, she guessed, he would not be the sort to rant and rave and tear at his hair. That strong, self-imposed discipline of his was too ingrained in his personality to ever give way like that.

'I'm to rest,' Alistair told them in a low voice. He turned to Emma and informed her sadly that he was not the man he used to be.

With an impulsive gesture, she reached out and slipped her hand into his. She looked up at Conrad and met cool, icy eyes.

'You still haven't told us what the doctor said, apart from that you need to rest. Which, incidentally, is what he's been saying for the last five years.'

Conrad approached the bed, his hands in his shorts pockets. 'What did the doctor say?'

'I'm sorry I dragged you both away from your party.'

'Never mind about the party,' Emma murmured reassuringly, receiving an affectionate pat on the hand.

Alistair sighed deeply, and was it her imagination or could she see tears pricking at the back of his eyes? She felt her heart constrict. All those feelings that had assailed her in the wake of her mother's death were with her again, and there was regret too. She had known Alistair for so short a time, too short.

She had still not recovered from the death of her mother. She still felt the loss that came when someone whose presence had been around from time beginning suddenly was no longer there. She did not want to think of the pain of having to endure a second loss.

'He doesn't know how much longer I've got,' Alistair said heavily. He pressed his fingers to his eyes as though wanting to shut out the seriousness of his words.

Emma gasped in shock. She had been expecting the worst, and now that it had been confirmed an icy chill settled on her.

Conrad was looking at him, his face controlled, his ex-

pression unreadable. He sat on the side of the bed, opposite
Emma, his vivid eyes resting on Alistair's face.

'Is there anything we can get for you?' he asked roughly.

'My children.' Alistair either didn't hear or else chose to
ignore Conrad's question. 'I've spent a long time acquiring
wealth, and at the end of the day I'm not sure if I've managed to acquire happiness. There are a lot of things in life
that I regret doing, and even more I regret not having done.
Now I'm an old man with not much longer left to live. I
want to speak my mind.'

He turned to Conrad, 'You might tell me that it's none
of my business, but you really musn't marry Sophia. She's
too young, and too…' He searched for the right word. 'Too
stupid for you. I know it's convenient and that you've
known her off and on for a long time, but that doesn't make
it right. I guess I'm the last person in the world to offer
advice about marriage, but you can forgive the frankness of
an old, dying man.'

'I know how you feel about this engagement, Alistair,'
Conrad said, with a touch of impatience in his voice.
'You've spoken to me about it frequently enough. What we
want to find out is exactly what the doctor said to you.'

Alistair ignored him. 'It would be different if you were
madly in love with her, but this plan of yours to commit
yourself for life to someone merely because it happens to
be convenient… Well, it can only end in tears.'

Conrad was wearing the caged, helpless look of someone
who wanted to argue a point, and was resisting through
sheer will-power.

He ran his fingers frustratedly through his black hair and
frowned heavily. 'We've been through this a thousand
times, Alistair, from every conceivable angle, and…'

'It would, of course, be my dying wish,' Alistair treated
Conrad's interjection with admirable nonchalance, 'to see
you married, but to the right girl. Someone with energy and

a mind of her own. Someone who could relate to you on an equal basis.' He glanced at Emma and smiled, absent-mindedly patting her hand.

Oh, no, she thought; oh, no. Matchmaking? He had just finished informing them that he was old and ill, and yet he still could find time for matchmaking?

A hundred little things suddenly slotted into place, like pieces of a jigsaw puzzle. She was torn between an aching compassion for Alistair—a sick man after all—and a strong desire to inform him that there was no way that Conrad was going to find someone with energy and a mind of her own, if that someone just happened to be her. They only just managed to tolerate each other, for heaven's sake! Besides, Emma was convinced that men did not suddenly change their tastes in women. They were drawn to variations of the same type, either physically or intellectually. And she had seen ample proof of the sort of women Conrad preferred.

For that matter, he was hardly to her liking.

She sat upright.

'I think we should leave you to rest now.' Conrad's words managed to rescue the silence which had threatened to become embarrassingly prolonged. 'There's no point in over-tiring yourself, that much the doctor did impart,' he added pointedly.

'Yes, perhaps you're right.' Alistair shut his eyes and sank lower into the bedclothes. 'Could you send Esther up with some lunch for me?' he asked in a weak, tired voice. 'A poached egg and some salmon, and perhaps just a piece of some of that coconut sweetbread she made yesterday. Also a cup of sweet tea and a slice of her ginger cake.'

'Salmon? Coconut sweetbread? Ginger cake, for heaven's sake? Should you be eating that sort of stuff?' Conrad stood up and looked down at Alistair through narrowed eyes.

'The doctor told me to rest, not to starve.'

'We understand,' Emma said hurriedly. She frowned

warningly at Conrad. 'I'll send her up with a tray in a moment. But first, I'd like to talk with you. Alone. If you're not too tired.'

She could sense that watchful air settle on Conrad like an invisible cloud.

'What's it in connection with?' he asked, staring at her, trying to read her mind.

'None of your business.'

'Alistair's ill,' Conrad said smoothly, 'I have to know whether what you have to say is going to upset him. He's supposed to rest, don't forget.'

You devious swine, Emma thought, playing on the situation for what it was worth. Typical.

'Will you two stop talking over my head as though I weren't here?' Alistair spoke, with a return to his former self. 'Go away, Conrad. I'll be fine.'

Emma grinned triumphantly at Conrad and met with a frowning response. Checkmate, she thought.

He walked towards the door, and stood there for a few seconds, staring at her as though he was trying to read her mind.

'Goodbye,' she said meaningfully, and was rewarded with a thunderous glare. He grunted something which she didn't catch, and shut the door gently. Emma turned to Alistair.

'There's something I think you should know,' she began hesitantly. 'I've been putting off this moment, but the time has come for me to tell you.'

CHAPTER FIVE

ALISTAIR looked at her with interest. All traces of illness seemed to have vanished and his colour had returned.

Emma twisted her hands nervously together on her lap. How to proceed from here? She had fleetingly considered this moment in the past few weeks, but she had had no idea that when it finally arrived it would find her so helpless.

'There's something I must go and get,' she eventually murmured. 'I won't be long.'

'I'll wait here,' Alistair promised. 'There's nowhere I can go.'

He was true to his word. When Emma returned, he seemed hardly to have shifted position. Without a word, she handed him the letter which she was carrying in her hand. Her mother had written it after the accident, even though she had been told by her doctor that she was on the road to recovery. Perhaps she had had forebodings of her own death.

'Give this to your grandfather,' she had instructed Emma. 'Even if you decide never to see him, make sure that he gets this. It's so late, too late now for me, but I must make my peace somehow.'

Emma had not known what was in the letter, and she still did not know.

As Alistair slit open the envelope and began to read, the room became so still that Emma could hear all the noises outside, the sound of the distant sea, the soft breeze stirring the grass and trees into rustling movement, almost as though magnified.

She waited patiently until Alistair had finished, not saying a word when he looked at her and then back to the letter, which he re-read three times.

'So,' he said.

There was a heavy silence. Alistair seemed wrapped up in his thoughts, and Emma did not want to disturb them.

Conflicting emotions surged through her. Painful memories of her mother, anxiety that her revelation might be such a shock to Alistair that he might suffer a relapse, relief that what she had come to do was finally done.

She studied Alistair's face carefully, pleased to see that he seemed to be handling the news well.

He folded the letter, stuck it into his top pocket and folded his hands on the blanket.

'I wondered when you would tell me,' he said gently.

'I wanted to find out about you for myself,' Emma began awkwardly, 'I needed to put everything in perspective. Only you fell ill…and then I was so worried that…' She stopped and shot him a surprised look. 'What do you mean, you wondered when I would tell you…?'

'I knew who you were, my dear, from the very first moment you walked through the front door.' He smiled delightedly at her confusion.

'You knew?' Emma's mouth dropped open in amazement. She didn't know whether to laugh, to cry, or to be angry. 'How?' she asked in astonishment. She sat on the edge of the bed.

'Well, my dear, believe it or not, I managed to trace your mother quite soon after she left Tobago with that man. But she refused to have anything to do with me, and after a while I thought it best to leave her alone until she had worked out her problems. But she never did.' He sighed, gesturing to Emma to pass him the box of tissues. 'I knew of her pregnancy, and of your existence, and I waited and hoped… What else could I do? Maybe more. I don't know. Maybe I should have forced a reconciliation.'

Emma shook her head dumbly, at a loss for words.

'I continued to keep tabs on her over the years, so that at least I could reassure myself that she was all right. When she died, a little of me died as well. But then you came along, like a breath of fresh air into my life. When you arrived here and didn't breathe a word of who you really were, I suspected that you wanted to find out about me in your own time, make up your own mind, and I respected that.'

'You naughty old man.' Emma smiled slowly. 'What must you have thought of me?'

'I loved you.' He patted her hand and pulled her towards him affectionately. 'Of course, now that it's out in the open, it'll be all the better, because I can call you granddaughter. I've been dying to call you that since you arrived.'

Emma laughed, feeling a rush of elation flood through her. 'You're crafty,' she accused him warmly.

'Well, craftier than you, little one.'

There was a sharp rap on the door, and they both jumped as Conrad walked into the room. He had changed out of his tennis shorts and T-shirt into a pair of faded jeans and a pale blue shirt. His eyes swept over them, resting quizzically on Emma.

'Have I interrupted something...?' he asked in a hard voice.

'As a matter of fact, you have, son,' Alistair replied, 'something wonderful.'

Emma looked in panic at Alistair. 'I don't think...'

Alistair was looking above her head to Conrad, and either genuinely didn't see or else chose not to see her mouthing the words, 'not now.'

'I'd like to introduce you to Emma Belle, my granddaughter.'

From behind her, Emma could feel Conrad's eyes on her

the coiled tension of his body, as he moved smoothly to the other side of the bed.

'Well, well, well,' he said softly, forcing her to meet his eyes. 'So this was your little secret.'

Alistair was looking at both of them, his eyes darting from one face to the other.

'Oh, dear,' he cut in, 'I feel quite weak all of a sudden. It must be the shock. Emma, dear, do pass me that cup of water on the table.'

She reached out for it, casually peering inside, and then suspiciously sniffing the contents. 'There's whisky in here!'

'Is there?' Alistair asked innocently. 'Oh, dear. Well, that'll just have to do, then.'

He plucked the cup out of her hands and swallowed a mouthful of the amber liquid, then lay back on the bed with his eyes shut. 'Much better. Even so, I do feel rather tired,' he murmured weakly. 'Perhaps you could leave me alone for a moment…?'

'Sure.' Conrad stood up and removed the cup from his hands. 'Get some sleep, Alistair, and no drink. Remember the doctor's orders.'

'Pah!'

'I'll see you later, Grandfather.' She kissed him on the forehead, ignoring his plea for just one more sip of the whisky before he settled down to sleep.

She knew that Conrad was staring at her, and she defiantly refused to meet the hard, questioning glint in his eyes.

She told herself firmly that she didn't give a damn what he thought of her now. Why on earth should she? He had thought the worst of her from the very beginning, and if this only served to cement his opinion of her, then so be it.

Conrad didn't say a word to her as they stepped out into the corridor, quietly shutting the bedroom door behind them. He turned away and walked quickly down the staircase, and Emma followed reluctantly.

She could just as easily have gone to her bedroom, in fact to any other room in the house which happened to be in the opposite direction to where Conrad was walking, but for some reason her feet refused to comply with reason. She found herself running behind him, until they were both in the sitting-room, and he had shut the door behind them.

Then he turned to face her. She watched the implacable set of his features with first dismay, and then anger. She didn't owe him an explanation, for heaven's sake! She wasn't going to let him intimidate her into thinking that she had somehow done something wrong!

'So you're the little granddaughter come home to roost,' he drawled, toying with one of the ornamental figurines which had been resting on the table, his long fingers twirling it around absent-mindedly.

'I'm Alistair's granddaughter, yes! Not that it has anything to do with you.'

His fingers tightened on the tiny statuette, and she watched in fascination, wondering whether he would snap it in two, but he replaced it on the table and stuck his hands in his pockets.

'As I told you before, everything you do is my business. Why did you come here? Why now?'

The blue eyes were cold and vaguely threatening.

'If you must know,' Emma said icily, 'it was the first opportunity I got after my mother's death. I couldn't come sooner, because Mum wouldn't have wanted me to.'

'She said so?'

'Not in so many words, no! I refuse to be put through this…'

She turned to walk away, and felt his hand clamp around her arm.

'Not so fast.'

'Let me go!' Emma wriggled uselessly against him, her rapid breathing making her breasts rise and fall quickly.

'How do I know that you haven't decided to come over here, suddenly full of granddaughterly love, because you know that Alistair is rich and his caring hand-outs could be very valuable to you?'

'You don't! But, just for the record, I haven't!'

His grip slackened, and she faced him, her mouth going dry as their eyes met. His head dipped down, and before she could pull away she felt his lips on her, savagely forcing open her mouth until his tongue was inside, probing her. A giddy excitement swept through her body, and her hands clenched his shirt convulsively as she returned his kiss, unable to fight the sudden, reckless yearning filling her.

This was madness. Part of her mind was screaming for her to stop, but the feverish pleasure she felt was so powerful. She could hardly catch her breath under the force of his kiss. How could she listen to reason?

He drew back with a lazy smile. 'Well, at least I know now that you won't be another Lisa St Clair.'

Emma looked at the devilish, dangerous face and ran out of the room, slamming the door behind her.

Her body was burning when she finally made it to her room and leaned against the door with her eyes shut. What had she been thinking when she'd let him kiss her? He didn't even like her, but even so he had managed to stir feelings in her that had risen from their slumbering depths like alarming, uncontrollable monsters.

Where had her common sense been when she had needed it? She breathed slowly, gradually feeling her body relax.

She had made a mistake. But mistakes could be rectified, and experiences, even incomprehensible ones, could be lessons. This one certainly would be.

When she descended the staircase next morning, she felt totally in control.

Conrad was in the kitchen, and he looked up as she came in.

His eyes flickered unhurriedly over her and Emma ignored him.

'Is this the ice maiden act?' he mocked.

'Has Esther made this bread for lunch?'

'Yes. Why don't you look me in the face when you're talking to me?'

'Because,' Emma said blandly, 'there's a host of other things I would rather look at. How's Sophia?'

'Ah! Reminding me that engaged men don't kiss other women, right?'

Emma flushed. That had been precisely her point, not that it seemed to have thrown him at all.

'She's fine. Actually, we'll be going to the beach after lunch. Pigeon Point. Would the ice maiden like to come along with us?'

'No.'

'Why not?'

'I have other things to do.' She bit into her sandwich and threw him a glacial stare.

'Like what?' Conrad leaned back in the chair and looked at her with a trace of amusement. 'Washing your hair? Painting your nails? It surely can't be work, because at the moment, without Alistair, you're a bit superfluous around here. I take it that you do intend to continue working, that your job here wasn't entirely a hoax to get into the family mansion?'

'You take it right!' Emma said, her pretence at calm giving way to anger.

'Then you'll be a bit bored here for a while. Alistair won't be back on his feet for at least a week, if not longer. So, come along to the beach with us.'

'A threesome?' Emma could have kicked herself for saying it, but it had been the first thing that had sprang to mind. Conrad, Sophia and…her.

'Does that bother you?' Conrad was looking at her intently and Emma felt the colour rise to her cheeks.

'No, of course not,' Emma said defensively. 'I just wouldn't want to get in the way of...'

'Of what? We won't be doing anything intimate on the beach, you know.'

He stared at her and laughed.

'I do think I've embarrassed you,' he said lazily, looking at her sideways.

Emma could feel her skin going a deeper shade of red and concentrated with unnecessary thoroughness on her sandwich. He was still wearing an infuriating half-smile on his face and she could quite easily have kicked him under the table.

'I'd love to come to the beach with you,' she said sweetly. 'Since I've been here, I haven't seen anything at all. Apart from the cove at the bottom of the garden.'

'Ah, yes, the cove.' He grinned and Emma regarded him with stony incomprehension. 'Pigeon Point, I have to tell you, isn't quite as private as that. But I think you'll find that the bathing more than compensates for any lack of privacy.'

He left the kitchen, whistling. I hope he gets stung by a jelly fish, Emma thought furiously.

Her nerves were still on edge when she left the house half an hour later to find both Sophia and Lloyd in the car waiting for her.

Conrad emerged from the house slightly behind her, his eyes raking over the occupants of the car.

'I didn't realise that you were coming, Lloyd,' he said in a voice which implied that if Lloyd's presence in the car was a surprise then it was an unpleasant one. 'Don't you have a nightclub to run in Trinidad? Or do you find the prospect of work in this weather a little off-putting at the moment?'

Emma stared at his cool expression in surprise. Personally, she was relieved that there was going to be a fourth person.

Lloyd smiled at her and she smiled back, disregarding Conrad's surly appraisal of them.

'We'll take the Range Rover, I think,' he said abruptly. 'There's more room.'

Without waiting for a response, he walked off towards Alistair's Range Rover, and they followed him, Lloyd with his arm around Emma's neck.

Conrad, Emma thought as she watched the angry pulse beating in his neck, was, on top of everything else, moody.

She looked from her position in the back seat at the unyielding set of his jaw, and wondered what could be eating him. He'd been fine when he had been laughing at her less than an hour before.

She decided to put all unwelcome thoughts of Conrad DeVere out of her mind, and sat back, lazily watching the scenery flash past, listening to Lloyd's chatter and laughing with ready amusement at some of his stories.

He was a social being, easy to be with, and ready with conversation to fill any potential gaps of silence.

Emma could quite easily lapse into a world of her own, and she did, thinking of Alistair and trying to ignore Sophia's proximity to Conrad in the front.

When the car slowed down and pulled up to the beach, Emma sat upright and gulped down the unbelievable picture postcard of the beach.

Of course, she had known that it would be beautiful, but she was still amazed at the turquoise clarity of the water and the feather softness of the white sands. The sea here was protected by a coral reef, which she could just see in the distance, and as a result the water was as calm as a swimming pool, the breeze barely causing it to ripple as it washed up on to the shoreline.

'Crowded,' Conrad said ruefully, pointing at another couple in the distance with two young children.

'You're kidding,' Emma remarked, gazing at the emptiness.

Sophia had run ahead and was already spreading out her towel and easing herself out of her skin-tight denim shorts and white vest. Lloyd had stripped off with slightly less aplomb and was splashing in the water, whooping with the enthusiasm of a ten-year-old.

Emma sauntered slowly with Conrad towards the patch of sand that Sophia had picked out. If I were Sophia, she thought, I would be reaching out right now to hold his hand. The idea was so silly that she speeded up and quickly slipped off her jersey top, acutely conscious that Conrad was doing the same.

What on earth does the man eat? she wondered, sneaking a sideways glance at him. There was not an ounce of fat on him; every inch seemed moulded to perfection. He lay down alongside Sophia, his head resting on his arm, and pulled a peaked cloth cap over his face so that he could see what was happening on the beach without being over-exposed to the sun.

'I can't stay too long in this heat,' Sophia observed, turning to face Emma. 'Can't risk any sunburn at all. Model's nightmare.' She yawned and Emma thought that it was just as well that she wasn't in any occupation like that, because she intended to get as much sun as possible.

'No sun and no food,' Conrad commented drily. 'Is it worth it?'

'You know I have to stay in shape.' Sophia pouted. 'You wouldn't love me if I didn't.'

He raised one eyebrow, but did not comment. Say it, Emma willed, tell her that you love her, isn't that why you asked her to come over specifically to join you in Tobago?

She squinted at Lloyd, who seemed to be a mere dot in

the distance, although she could see that he was still standing, with the water reaching him only slightly above the waist.

She stood up and walked slowly towards the water. It was beautifully warm. Emma paddled out to join Lloyd and immediately joined in a water fight with him, kicking away as he swam and tried to grab her legs. She lost herself in the sheer fun of it, lying on her back and floating alongside him when they had both exhausted themselves.

As they drifted to the motion of the current, she listened to him as he told her about his love-life, which, he said, was all over.

'I thought it was the real thing,' Emma commented with amusement.

'It was. At the time.'

She laughed, spluttering as he pulled her underneath the water. When she felt his lips brush against hers, she was surprised but didn't pull away.

'Is this the best you can offer to a heartbroken young man?' he asked with a grin.

'Heartbroken young men should be cooped up in a dark room, wondering how they're ever going to recover and finding relief in huge boxes of chocolates.'

'That's what heartbroken young women do,' Lloyd responded vigorously. 'We men are braver.'

'Ah.' Emma nodded sagely. 'By braver I take it you mean that you immediately find a replacement for the last girlfriend?'

This time Lloyd didn't answer. Instead, he grabbed her by the waist, and this time his kiss was harder, more demanding. His lips covered hers, and she could feel his tongue moving against hers, demanding a response.

Emma pushed him away to arm's length.

'Whoa. I don't intend to be the replacement,' she protested, but couldn't help laughing when he pulled a comic face. With Lloyd love and lovemaking was a game, one to be lost or won, but either way with the same degree of good humour.

He did not excite a response in her, but she could not find it in her heart to be severe. Besides, she had a feeling that severity was the last thing in the world that would deter Lloyd. He was too full of boyish enthusiasm to take it seriously.

His hands circled her waist and he said with an exaggerated French accent, 'We could make sweet music together.'

Emma giggled hysterically. 'With that phony French accent?'

'I have quite a large repertoire of accents. How about a Russian one?'

'No way.'

'Humphrey Bogart?'

Emma shook her head.

'I guess,' Lloyd said mournfully, 'you're telling me that we won't be making sweet music together after all.' He pretended to wipe a tear away from the side of his face. 'I'm crushed.'

'You will be in a minute if you don't stop acting the wounded animal.' She lunged at him, tickling him under his arms as he tried to escape by splashing her.

'Femme sans merci!' he yelped. 'Or whatever!'

They were still giggling as they headed back towards the beach. Lloyd threw his arm around her neck with brotherly affection.

'Look me up if you're ever in Trinidad,' he said soberly. 'I'll show you a good time, absolutely no strings attached.'

Emma promised. She would do it, as well. She liked Lloyd, and felt that they could become friends. She impulsively squeezed his hand and grinned up at him.

When she looked ahead, it was to find Conrad staring at her from underneath his cap with brooding intensity. Sophia waved at them. She had covered herself with a large white shirt and was wearing a wide-brimmed hat to shade her face.

'I think it's time we left,' Conrad said abruptly, as Emma sat down on the towel and prepared to smother her body with suntan oil.

'Already?' Sophia looked at him in surprise. 'We've only been here an hour. I'll have a quick dip, then,' she said, reading the cool, uncompromising expression on his face.

She walked gracefully towards the water, gently splashing her body with water as she submerged.

'We should have brought two cars,' Lloyd commented. 'Emma and I could have followed on.' He turned to her. 'Don't you agree, my little chickadee?'

Emma tried to stifle her giggle and failed.

'Shame, isn't it?' Conrad said in a frozen voice. His eyes were chips of ice.

What's eating him? Emma wondered. He had not glanced at her once, but she could feel the coldness emanating from his body in a wave. Maybe he had had an argument with Sophia, although the few times that she had spotted them from the water they had not seemed to be talking, far less having an argument.

Anyway, if he had argued with her, it was downright unfair to take it out on Lloyd, who had retreated into a bewildered silence.

'Perhaps we could come back here another day?' she remarked, turning to Lloyd.

This time Conrad did look at her and his expression was flint-hard. 'Have you forgotten why you're here?' he asked coldly. 'You're here to work. So you say. It's what you're being handsomely paid for. You're not here to frolic on the beach every day so that you can improve your suntan.'

'I have no intention of frolicking on the beach every day!' Emma spluttered angrily. 'To improve my suntan! For your information, this is about the first day I've taken off, and that's only because Alistair's ill and can't work at the moment! So don't you dare accuse me of shirking!'

She looked at him scathingly and a dark red flush crept up his face.

'I never accused you of anything,' he said harshly. 'You accused yourself. Perhaps it's a guilty conscience getting the better of you.'

Emma clenched her fists impotently at her sides.

She watched him as he strode towards the sea and muttered a few curt words to Sophia.

'You two seem to get along well,' Lloyd commented mildly.

'Does anyone get along with a cobra?'

'Oh, I don't know. Sophia tells me that all her friends find him wildly attractive and it's got nothing to do with the size of his bank balance. I think that half the thrill with Sophia is that she feels as if she's netted the biggest fish in the ocean.'

'Well, good luck to her,' Emma said darkly. 'I hope that she has the patience of Job. She'll need it if she's going to put up with Conrad DeVere for more than five minutes.'

They drove back in a silence broken only by the odd remark from Sophia, who seemed only mildly disconcerted by Conrad's terseness. She lay back with her head against the cushioned headrest, her eyes closed behind the large sunglasses, her face upraised to the sun which filtered through the glass into the air-conditioned car.

When they arrived back at the house, Lloyd drew her to one side, reiterating his offer to show her around Trinidad if she ever decided to pay it a visit. He was travelling back early the following morning.

'Can't stay away from my nightclub for too long,' he whispered conspiratorially in her ear. 'All those girls. I can't deprive them of my masterful company or else they start pining.'

'You live in a dream world, Lloyd,' Emma whispered back.

'I know, but it's fun, isn't it?'

Out of the corner of her eye Emma could see Conrad watching their brief parting exchange with a grim expression.

He nodded to them as they drove off, and Emma followed him into the house. In the sort of mood that he was in, avoidance was obviously the best policy. It had been an enjoyable afternoon, only marred by Conrad's ill temper. If he were less formidable a man, it could quite easily have been ignored, but his personality dominated everything and he had made no effort to hide his curtness.

Emma ran quickly up the staircase. Conrad was nowhere to be seen, which was just as well because he was about the last person she wanted to confront.

She mentally planned the rest of what remained of her day, deciding that she would sit with Alistair for as long as he wanted. They still had a lot to discuss, reminiscences which she would enjoy hearing about, if he did not find them too painful. There was much he could tell her and as much that she could tell him.

Her bedroom door was ajar when she reached her room. Emma wondered fleetingly whether Esther had been in to clean the room and forgotten to close it.

She pushed it open, her mind still racing ahead to all the things that Alistair and she had to say to each other.

Conrad was lying on the bed, in a pair of shorts and the same T-shirt which he had worn to the beach and which clung to his body in damp patches. His hands were clasped behind his head and he was surveying her through narrowed eyes.

Emma stopped in her tracks, feeling the adrenalin pumping quickly through her body. Her mouth went dry and the fine blonde hairs on her arms almost seemed to stand on end.

'What are you doing here?' she asked warily. 'What do you want?' She stopped where she was, not daring to take another step forwards. It would bring her too close to him.

She had already seen what he was capable of—worse, what she was capable of with him—and the prospect of a repeat performance of what had happened that morning frightened her.

The hooded blue eyes gazing at her sent little alarm bells ringing in her head, even though she told herself that she could control the situation.

But she didn't like the way he was looking at her. It was far too intense and far too stripping.

He's got a fiancée, she thought wildly, trying to compose her features into ordered calm.

She thought of Sophia, but the image was blurry.

'Would you mind leaving?' she said coolly. 'I want to change.'

'Feel free.' Conrad gestured expansively towards the en-suite bathroom, but did not budge.

'I'd feel freer if you left.'

They stared at each other for what seemed to Emma like decades. She could feel the heavy pounding of her heart, could almost hear it, and she wondered whether he could hear it too.

'You mean if someone else were here instead?'

Emma regarded him in frank puzzlement. 'Someone else?' she repeated. 'What are you talking about?'

'You know very well what I'm talking about,' Conrad replied roughly. He slung his legs over the side of the bed and was standing in front of her before Emma could even realise what was happening.

She looked around desperately at the half-opened door.

He followed the line of her gaze and closed it gently but firmly.

'You intrigue me. So cool and composed. I might have guessed that I was wrong. You proved that to me this morning. There's a fire burning in you. Were you hoping Lloyd would ignite it the way I did? You were all over each other. I'm surprised you managed to restrain yourself in the back seat of the car. Is he your sort of man?'

'More than you are, at any rate,' Emma bit out recklessly.

'How would you know? One kiss wasn't enough.'

Before she knew what was happening he bent his head towards her, his hand curling into her hair, drawing her face up to meet his.

With a muffled moan, Emma twisted her body to try and get away, but he gripped her closer to him, his lips devouring hers hungrily.

Emma felt herself sway. Her legs seemed to have suddenly turned to water. In fact, every nerve in her body seemed suddenly to have turned to water.

As his mouth moved over hers, the feverish greed of his kiss becoming more persuasive, she felt any semblance of self-control that she might have had slipping away from her, like grains of sand through an open hand. She closed her eyes and closed her mind from her normal processes of reasoning.

With a soft moan, half proclaiming her resistance, she succumbed to the searing intensity of his kiss, returning it with equal fervour.

Be reasonable, she thought wildly, but she couldn't because it felt as though this was what she had been waiting for. He had given her a taste of passion and she was thirsty for more. No man had ever sent these tremors through her body. Her tongue met his and she felt as if she was drowning in something over which she had no control.

Her hands met behind his neck, her fingers weaving into

his black hair. As his mouth bit against her neck she arched back, groaning softly as the spasms of pleasure tore through her.

She felt his hand move up her back, searing like red-hot embers through the thin material of her jersey. She was terrified by her loss of self-control. Was she so weak that she could abandon herself with such mindless oblivion to a man who was engaged? Someone whose opinion of her did not bear thinking about?

She should have been prepared for this. Her body, which she had always trusted to obey her commands, had forsaken her this morning, and the experience should have warned her. It should have shown her that his power to make her respond against her will was formidable.

She made an effort to pull away, but as their bodies disengaged slightly he slipped his hand over her breast, caressing it through the still damp swimsuit. With an impatient tug, he eased down the top, moaning as his hand came into contact with her naked skin. Her breasts hardened at his touch, her nipples taut as he rubbed them between his fingers.

Her eyes opened and she stared dazedly at him. He looked at her, and must have read the yearning on her face, because he eased her jersey off, his mouth trailing from her neck to her breasts.

His breathing was ragged, as ragged as her own was. She pushed him away from her, her mind finally engaging into gear. She thought of Sophia, and remembered where his allegiances lay. She must have been crazy to even let him touch her, far less to have responded with the hot excitement that she had.

'Let me go!' she muttered, pulling up her swimsuit so that it covered her breasts.

Conrad looked at her uncomprehendingly.

'Have you forgotten that you're engaged?' she asked, her

voice rising in self-disgust and anger. 'Get out of my room!'
She wished that the ground would just open and swallow
her up. In a minute she would burst into tears, and that was
the very last thing she wanted him to witness.

'God, Emma, I don't want to.' His hand stroked her thigh.
From under her lashes, Emma gazed at the warm curve of
his mouth. Her legs were dissolving. If she didn't do something soon, all thought of the rights and wrongs of what she
was doing would vanish like a puff of smoke. 'I want this
ice maiden to dissolve in my lovemaking.'

'You're engaged,' she said in a high, desperate voice.

'Engagements are made to be broken,' he whispered am-
biguously.

Emma didn't have a clue what he was talking about. His
words filtered into her brain and promptly evaporated under
the heated response of her body to his.

She held his wrist tightly, until she could feel her nails
biting into his skin.

'This isn't for me,' she said shakily. 'Please leave.'

'Don't make me.'

'If you don't let go of me now, right now, I'm going to
scream until you do.'

It took everything in her to say it, and she didn't feel any
better. His hand was warm and trembling slightly, and the
only thing she wanted to do was to feel it move over every
inch of her body.

The drowsy passion in Conrad's eyes was slowly being
replaced by incomprehension, as though she had thrown a
bucket of ice-cold water over his head.

'Are you telling me that you don't want me?' he muttered.

'I'm telling you to leave this room before I scream the
house down! Is this your ploy for getting me out of here?
If it is, then it's working, because there's no way that I'm

going to stay here if I have to be on the look-out for you all of the time!'

She thought of Sophia, and was relieved when she felt the anger building up inside of her. Anger was a safe emotion as far as Conrad was concerned. She could cope with that.

'Stop playing the innocent,' he bit out in a voice as furious as hers. 'I didn't exactly see you dashing for help.'

She had recovered completely now, and was rapidly gathering together the strands of her composure which had been scattered to the winds.

'And you dare call Lloyd a womaniser.' She spoke in a cold, calm voice. 'Well, you're a womaniser of the worst sort. Now get out of this room.'

He stared at her, speechless, and then turned on his heel. As the door closed behind him, Emma felt her body sag as though she had been held by strings which had suddenly been cut. She sank on to the bed and wondered what was happening to her.

She knew of course. Her subconscious had known for a long time. She was attracted to him. Why deny it? She had been attracted to him perhaps from the very first moment she clapped eyes on him. Seeing him with Sophia, knowing that he had most probably made love to her, had been agonising.

One of a queue, she thought cynically. She had hoped that his engagement would put things into perspective, show her what kind of fool she was being, but it hadn't. Admit it, she said to herself: you're a weak fool.

She relived the sensation of his body pressed against hers and his hands stroking her body with a shudder of disgust.

Sexual attraction, infatuation; call it what you want, she thought, it was an illness, a disease which she could overcome.

Or, if not overcome, then at least control. The man was a bastard, a dangerous, sexually mesmerising bastard. She had *thought* him a threat before. Now she knew that he was one.

CHAPTER SIX

EMMA'S body was still trembling when she stepped into the shower five minutes later. She numbly felt the hard jet of water streaming over her, cleaning everthing except what mattered, the part inside her which needed, as far as she was concerned, more than cleansing. It needed disinfecting.

Face it, she concluded miserably: the man was right when he said that she had let him do everything that he had. Worse, she had enjoyed it. She had relished the feel of him, all the sensations that had rippled through her as his hands and fingers had explored her body.

How long had she been waiting to touch him? She dressed slowly, deliberately choosing clothes in dull, muted colours, because that was how she felt inside.

It took a huge effort to pretend to Alistair, when she went to visit him, that there was nothing wrong.

'Are you sure?' he insisted, frowning. 'You look peaky.'

'I must have taken too much sun this afternoon,' Emma hedged vaguely, launching into an extended account of how she had spent the day, omitting all mention of Conrad. She knew from experience how Alistair responded to his name, and the last thing she needed was to spend an hour and a half talking about him. He had eaten away enough of her already.

By the end of the evening she felt totally drained and ready for bed. She had no idea where Conrad was, had asked no one, and was only grateful for his absence.

Coward, she told herself; you're going to have to face him some time, although every second that he was not around was a second more for her to reconstruct her barricade, her invisible protection.

Now that she knew what she was up against, maybe she could manage a little more successfully to slap down any wayward attraction, because there was no way that she had any intention of giving in furthur to her own frightening craving for him.

Had she learnt nothing at all from her mother? After her disastrous and brief marriage to her father, she had spent the rest of her life seemingly drawn to all those men from whom she should have been running as fast as she could. Towards the end, she had given up completely and resigned herself to the fact that stability and enduring love would always be beyond her grasp. It had only been her sense of humour that had saved her from becoming an embittered woman.

Emma had seen it and had learnt from it. Or, at least, she'd thought she had. Certainly if she had had any sense she would have left the island the minute she clapped eyes on Conrad DeVere. She had had too much faith in her own inner strength, and too little in his overwhelming and magnetic sex appeal.

It helped when Esther informed her in passing that she would be on her own that evening, as Conrad had gone to see Sophia and her parents.

It came as no surprise. Through the open kitchen window she had noticed that his car was missing, and it didn't take a fool to put two and two together. He had hardly decided to go for a drive to the beach so that he could look at the moonlight.

Oh, no. Not him. Not Conrad DeVere. Why look at the moonlight when he could take the quickest route to Sophia's house and finish what he had begun with Emma?

Something inside her whispered that he was not that type of man, but she paid no attention to it. It made things infinitely easier if she believed the very worst of him, and she needed all the help she could get.

For the first time since she had arrived on the island she slept badly, waking up several times to a feeling of disorientation in the inky blackness of the bedroom.

The face that stared back at her the following morning in the mirror was a true reflection of her state of mind. There were shadows underneath her eyes; even the tan seemed to have deserted her.

With grim determination, she carefully applied a layer of make-up, much more than she normally used, until she at least resembled something human. Her hair she drew back into a thick ponytail with a piece of black elastic.

She knew exactly how she would occupy herself for the morning. No beach, no relaxation, nothing so lazy and enjoyable. She did not want to enjoy herself at all. In some obscure way she thought that it would help if she punished herself, so after a light breakfast she quickly visited Alistair—who, although considerably brighter than he had been, now seemed to have developed the habit of pitifully referring to his advanced years—and then vanished into the study.

There was not much to do. She had finished all the typing which had been on her agenda a few days, so she painstakingly revised her work and then set about rooting through the books, devouring as much literature on Alistair's life as she could. There was a surprising amount of cuttings, some dating back further than she had expected. Emma read it all, slowly and carefully, making the time spin out as much as she could.

It was interesting reading about the man whom she was beginning to know so well, trying to fit together the pieces of his personality as seen in black and white against the flesh-and-blood old man lying in his bed upstairs. Wasn't there a wide variance? she mused. Only the factual side of his life could be relied upon as being the truth.

She was so engrossed in her detective work that when the phone clanged next to her Emma physically jumped and looked at it in surprise.

It was Sophia on the other end. She sounded breathless and slightly hesitant as she asked whether Conrad was back yet.

'I have no idea,' Emma replied truthfully.

There was a pause on the other end, 'Can you tell him that I called?'

Emma promised, glancing at her watch which showed that it had gone twelve o'clock. 'I could go and see whether I can find him for you,' she said reluctantly, relieved when the other girl told her not to bother.

'It's just that I'm flying out to Rome this afternoon,' Sophia explained.

'And you wanted to talk to him before you left.' Why wait for her to say it? Emma thought. If she volunteered the information herself, then it somehow made her feel more in control.

'Yes,' Sophia agreed, 'I wanted to tell him that I was sorry about how things ended.'

'I'll tell him.' Emma felt a thread of curiosity streak through her, but she was determined not to give in to it. She had already given in to too much as far as Conrad was concerned. Her first step in fighting off that desperate attraction towards him which threatened to engulf her, was to have as little to do with him, and as little to say about him, as possible.

'Don't you want to know what I'm talking about?' Sophia asked.

'Not really.'

'Well—' Sophia began, and Emma thought, Oh, no, here we go. She could recognise the lowered voice of someone who wanted to confess, to pour their heart out. Emma had been the confidante of her friends too many times for her not to see the signs.

This time, she did not want to be on the receiving end. There was too much locked up inside her which she would have liked to burden someone with, but couldn't. It wasn't simply that her friends were all thousands of miles away. The fact was that she had made too much of a habit of her aloofness, had cultivated her privacy for too long, for her to suddenly break it.

'You needn't talk to me about this,' she said with a hint of desperation in her voice.

'I know, but it's just that I haven't anyone else to tell. Besides, sometimes it's easier talking to a stranger than to a friend.' Sophia fell silent, as though she was trying to put her thoughts into some kind of sequence. 'It's just that I broke off the engagement and I wanted to make sure that we were still friends. I feel so badly about it, but I chatted to Lloyd about it when he was here, and I decided that I just wasn't ready for marriage. Besides, an important job came up.'

'An important job?' Wasn't marriage an important job? Emma wondered.

Sophia's tone relaxed, began to sound more confident and enthusiastic. 'A chance-in-a-lifetime opportunity, really. I got offered a contract to work for a cosmetic firm, and part of the agreement was no attachment to the opposite sex for a year. So you see, there was nothing really that I could do.'

'Of course,' Emma said with mild sarcasm. 'When exactly did you tell Conrad?'

'At the beach yesterday. Well, I sort of told him then. We talked about it properly yesterday evening—but it was while you and Lloyd were swimming that I sort of hinted...'

'Ah, I see.' And she did. No wonder he was in such a filthy mood on the drive back. It made sense.

'Of course,' Sophia said confidentially, and Emma could imagine her adopting a suitable pose by the telephone, 'I'll be missing out on all the security I would have had married to a man like Conrad. I mean, he's *the* catch around. Handsome, powerful, and of course rich, rich, rich. Not just his money, but he'll probably get all of Alistair's money as well. Still—' she sighed theatrically '—that's life, as my dearest brother would say.'

She chatted inconsequentially about Lloyd, but Emma didn't hear what she was saying. She felt faint. Alistair's money? Did he think he was going to inherit Alistair's money? He had never suggested anything of the kind, but if Sophia was as nonchalant about disclosing such information, then surely it must be based on fact. No smoke without fire.

Tiny, suspicious thoughts were buzzing in her head, irritating insects which refused to go away. Emma blinked and shook her head to clear it.

'Anyway, could you pass on the message?' Almost before Emma had had a chance to agree, the other girl had rung off, and Emma held the receiver away from her ear, absent-mindedly hearing the flat, purring dialling tone.

She replaced the receiver thoughtfully, no longer in any mood to pore over old journals and newspaper clippings.

The nagging uncertainties were becoming too persistent, the buzzing of one bee developing into a swarm. She didn't want to listen to them. After all, they were hardly based on fact, and Sophia might have been completely wrong in her assumptions—but then again, they answered a lot of questions.

For instance, was that the real reason for Conrad's initial reaction to her? Had he seen her as more than simply a potential threat to Alistair? Had he seen her as a potential threat to him as well?

She went out to the garden and looked admiringly at the flowers and plants, her mind somewhere else.

Anyway, she thought, it didn't matter one way or the other, because she really didn't care what the man thought of her.

She tried to relax and enjoy the warm, salty sea breeze rustling through the coconut trees and the hibiscus plants, but it was with a depressing feeling of inevitability that she saw Conrad's car pull up the long driveway. She had no intention of initiating a conversation with him. She watched him lever his long body out of the driver's seat and gave him a false, syrupy smile as he approached her.

He didn't smile back.

'Super garden,' Emma said conversationally, refusing to be rattled either by the hard set of his face or her disconcerting train of thoughts. It annoyed her that, however suspicious she was of him, she still could not prevent her physical awareness of him. 'Can you believe this variety of flowers? It's almost like being at the Chelsea Flower Show. I made an effort once to cultivate the small patch at the back of the house at home, but I soon discovered that I didn't have green fingers. Only when it came to the weeds, at any rate.' The small talk was dying on her lips, and she flashed him another brilliant smile.

She could feel the pulse in her neck throbbing with painful intensity and she kept her eyes riveted to his face. There was no way that she would let herself drink in the lean muscularity of his body. That would conjure up too many graphic images of it pressed against hers, his thighs hard and demanding, his hands feverishly raking her back and breasts.

'I've just seen the doctor,' he said bluntly. 'I passed him on the way back and stopped for a chat.'

Emma's eyes widened in surprise. She had had no idea that Doctor Tompkins had been to the house, but then she had been so absorbed in her work that she had not been aware of very much outside it.

'What did he say?' she asked quickly. 'I didn't even know that he had been. I was working all morning.'

'No change, and he still refuses to elaborate on the seriousness of Alistair's condition. I can't drag a thing out of him. He just keeps wittering on about the rights of the patient, and that it was Alistair's decision to tell us or not to tell us exactly what's going on.'

They had begun walking back to the house, Emma keeping a reasonable distance away from him.

She had wondered whether he would mention their lovemaking the day before, but apparently not. She thought bitterly that it meant so little to him that it was not even worth a passing word. He would put the whole thing down to experience, if he hadn't forgotten about it all already.

She had probably been no more than a trivial diversion for him. He would have willingly and expertly made love to her to take his mind off his rejection by Sophia and, when she had come to her senses and made him leave, would have put the whole episode out of his mind like an irksome dream.

How was he to know that every touch from him was now embedded in her heart, like some virulent stranglehold?

The women he dated, the women he made love to, she forced herself to think, were women of experience. He and they satiated themselves with each other and then moved on, like trains flashing past each other in the dead of night.

The fact that she could not forget just showed what a gullible fool she was.

Well, two could play at that game. She could be as cool as he was, even if it took everything out of her. There was no way that she would let him see how much he had affected her. She would cling on to the remnants of her pride if it was the last thing she did.

So she listened to him with a forced, tinny smile.

'What can we do?' she asked. 'If Alistair refuses to divulge exactly how serious his condition is, then we have no choice but to accept it.'

'You accept a lot, don't you?' he asked with a strange inflexion in his voice. 'All with that cool little face of yours.'

Emma felt her heart beating heavily against her ribcage and she said airily, 'I try.'

The atmosphere thickened between them and, to break it, Emma commented in a neutral voice that Sophia had called. 'To apologise about the engagement,' she added tonelessly.

'So she told you, did she?'

'She told me that she'd broken it off, yes.' And more. I hope, she thought silently, that it's wrecked your ego. She glanced across at him, but he did not look like a man whose ego had taken a beating.

He shrugged. 'It was mutual.'

'Was that why you were so abrupt and ill-humoured at the beach yesterday?' Emma could not resist asking coldly.

'At the beach?' He looked at her sharply. 'What are you talking about?'

You know what I'm talking about, she wanted to scream. Instead she said calmly, 'Sophia said that she began to tell you that she couldn't go through with the marriage yesterday at the beach.'

'Oh, yes, so she did,' he agreed.

'Faced with the choice of an offer from a cosmetics firm and an offer from you, she plumped for the better one,' Emma pressed. If she wanted to drive the point home and stir a reaction from him, she failed. He nodded agreeably but didn't seem in the least perturbed by the implication.

'She has her career to think of,' he said, pushing the front door open so that Emma could walk through. She brushed past him, feeling her pulses quicken at his proximity.

Didn't anything put a dent in this man's staggering self-confidence? And he talked about her coolness! Of course, he had mentioned that calling off the engagement had been mutual, but he had not elaborated. Maybe it was his own way of saving face, but he was not behaving like a man trying to justify a broken relationship.

'I think we should both go and see Alistair and try and figure out exactly what's going on,' Conrad said, relegating the whole subject of himself and Sophia to the past.

Emma nodded. She would have liked to have continued the discussion—she would have taken an almost masochistic pleasure in it—but she already knew him well enough to realise that he would divulge no more than he wanted to.

Alistair was in his wheelchair when they entered the bed-room, a book in one hand, a cup of coffee in the other. He had obviously not expected them and glanced sheepishly at the bed.

'You're looking better,' Conrad said drily, sitting on the old flowered sofa in the corner of the room. He patted the free seat next to him and Emma reluctantly sat down, primly crossing her legs at the ankles.

'I'm still a sick man,' Alistair mumbled, sipping out of his coffee-cup.

He glanced coyly at both of them, and said in a weak voice, 'I'm better for having my lovely granddaughter here, of course, but I'm still ill. The doctor tells me so, anyway.'

'Which brings us to the point in question,' Conrad said smoothly. 'The doctor. He refuses to say anything, leaving it up to you. Except that you haven't exactly been a fount of information either. So what's the story? How ill are you?'

'I've already told you,' Alistair complained evasively. He threw Emma a watery smile and asked her if she'd like Esther to bring up another tray with coffee and biscuits.

Conrad shook his head. 'You're avoiding the subject again, Alistair.'

'Perish the thought.'

'So, in words of one syllable, tell me what the doctor said. Is it your heart playing up again?'

Emma knew that Alistair had a heart condition. He had spoken to her about it, but he had not mentioned that that was at the bottom of his current problem. In retrospect, she realised that he had swept aside all mention of his illness with suave caginess.

'Something like that,' Alistair mumbled testily. 'I won't bore you with the details.'

'Please,' Conrad persisted, 'bore us.' He looked at Emma and glanced upwards. Without realising it, she dropped her mask and grinned.

'Well,' Alistair began, 'it's the old ticker. Not as strong as it used to be. The doctor said that I shouldn't get any shocks. A pleasant surprise might be nice, though—might revive me. I mean,' he added hastily, 'Emma's revelation was wonderful, a rush of spring air into an old man's bones, but as you can see I'm still very much under the weather. So the doctor tells me.'

'Very informative, Doctor Tompkins,' Conrad said wryly. 'His advice sounds very much like the sort of advice you'd prescribe for yourself.'

Alistair made an indeterminate sound.

'Well, no doubt you'll find this a pleasant surprise. Sophia and I are no longer an issue.'

Alistair's eyes gleamed under the bushy brows. 'All off, is it? Just as well, my boy. The two of you weren't suited at all, as I've told you often enough before. I'm just glad that you came to your senses in time. You know what they say: marry in haste, repent at leisure.'

He was smiling broadly.

'Still, you were right on one count, it's high time you settled down.'

'We've covered this ground already, Alistair. Don't tell me that you're growing repetitive in your old age.'

'It breaks an old man's heart to think that he might die without seeing you settled. Your father would have wanted it.'

Conrad frowned, a shadow of doubt crossing his face.

'We mustn't keep you. You're beginning to look tired.' Emma rose and walked towards the door.

When Conrad joined her a few minutes later, he looked unusually unsure.

'I just don't know what to make of him,' he said thoughtfully. 'If I didn't know better, I'd have said that there was nothing wrong with the old warrior, but there's no doubt that he did have a turn when we were at that damned party, and who's to tell how serious it was? The wily old devil's certainly not letting on.'

'But why shouldn't he?'

'Why indeed?'

Emma thought she knew why. He simply didn't want to worry either of them. He especially didn't want to upset her, knowing as he did that she was still suffering from the death of her mother, but there was no way that she was going to put forward this theory, not with that cynical glint in Conrad's eyes. He naturally wouldn't give her the benefit of the doubt, and the very last thing she wanted was an argument with him. In fact, the very last thing she wanted was to be with him at all, especially now.

When they reached the sitting-room, she branched out with the excuse that there was still some unfinished work left for her to do.

'Really?' Conrad said disbelievingly. 'You must be a much slower worker than I thought.'

He turned his back to walk away and as he did so Emma glimpsed a faint smile on his lips.

He never gave up, did he? she thought, simmering with anger. He obviously found his own sense of humour at her expense highly entertaining. She slammed into the study and through sheer perversity spent the next two hours doing what could quite easily have been done in twenty minutes.

She was relaxing back in the leather swivel chair, her eyes closed, when the door opened and Conrad walked into the study. He lightly swivelled her chair round, and Emma's eyes flew open.

'Thanks for knocking,' she muttered.

'I did.' Conrad's blue eyes mocked her.

'Well, it must have been very softly,' Emma snapped. 'I didn't hear a thing. What do you want, anyway?'

Conrad looked at her with mock hurt, but she could see from the twist of his lips that he still found it highly amusing to have burst in on her and found her half asleep in the chair.

It crossed her mind that he must really wonder what she was doing to justify her pay packet, and she immediately decided that, since he wasn't employing her, then it didn't matter.

'That's not very polite. Especially when I came to ask you out to dinner.'

'Dinner?' Emma eyed him in frank amazement.

'That's right. I know a very good restaurant not too far from here—close to the airport, believe it or not.'

'I can't make it,' Emma replied spontaneously. Dinner with Conrad spelt trouble.

'Why not? Don't tell me you've got other plans for the evening.'

'Esther will already have prepared something,' she fudged. 'It's after six o'clock.'

Conrad smiled, but his eyes were intent on her. 'I told her not to. She's going to do something light for Alistair.'

'How nice of you to arrange the evening for me on my behalf,' Emma commented coldly. She felt like a rabbit caught in a trap. The glint in Conrad's eyes told her plainly enough that he was not going to take no for an answer—not that she could come up with any kind of excuse, anyway.

'There's something I want to talk to you about,' he said flatly, 'so you can stop trying to wriggle out of it. I've booked a table for eight, so we'll have to leave by seven-thirty. I'll meet you downstairs, and be prompt. I have an aversion to being kept waiting.'

With that parting shot he let himself out of the room, and Emma regarded the closed door with a sinking feeling. She had no idea what he wanted to talk about but she resented his presumption that it overrode any plans that she might have made, even if her plans were only to wash her hair and retire early to bed with a good book.

She lingered over her bath, topping up the water three times until she felt that if she didn't get out she would emerge looking like a dried-out prune.

She was already beginning to feel slightly apprehensive about being so close to Conrad without any easy escape routes to hand. She didn't trust herself. Not after the last time.

With a sigh of resignation she picked out what she was going to wear. A full rose-coloured skirt with a snug-fitting matching bodice buttoned down the front, which revealed as little of her as possible. With a flash of inspiration, she tied her hair back with a bright scarf which she had picked up on one of her rare jaunts into Scarborough, the capital of the island, and made up with a little blusher and eye-shadow.

When she stood back from the mirror, she was pleased with the overall effect.

Conrad was waiting at the foot of the stairs for her. She saw him before he had a chance to look around, and in that brief moment she allowed herself the luxury of watching him unobserved.

He really was blatantly masculine. His face was turned away from her, his hands thrust into the pockets of his charcoal-grey trousers, but even in that attitude he was arresting.

He looked around as she began descending the stairs, carefully because she was wearing higher shoes than normal. From this distance, she couldn't make out the expression on his face but she was aware that he was staring at her, and this time there was no smile on his lips.

She wondered what was going through that head of his. He must have seen a million women descending flights of staircases to meet him, in hotels, in mansions, at clubs, but even so the way that he was looking at her made her nervously self-conscious.

He looked at her as though she filled his senses, but of course she wasn't completely dim. Wasn't that part and parcel of the inveterate charmer? To treat a woman with undivided attention, as though she was the only one in the world? She stared back into his brooding, black-fringed eyes politely.

'I'm not late,' she offered brightly.

Conrad's serious expression didn't alter. 'So I see,' he drawled, 'though it would have been well worth the wait.'

'Thank you,' Emma stammered. Out of sheer embarrassment she began chatting quickly, asking him questions about the restaurant, about Tobago in general. Anything to have the conversation flowing on a level which she found manageable.

Once in the car she relaxed in the darkness, and let her thoughts drift over Alistair, his illness, Conrad, and her own feelings towards them. Where would it all end? It was amazing to think that less than six months ago she had been in London, far away from all this. And before that...before that there had not even been any thoughts of Alistair at all, except as a shadowy figure whom her mother intermittently mentioned. Emma had no more expected to meet him than she had expected to meet Superman, even though she had speculated about him and the rift that had formed between her mother and him.

At least, from the point of view of Alistair, the journey had been worth it.

If in the process she had managed to ignite feelings which she had not even known existed, then it was something she would have to live with.

Besides, physical attraction didn't last. It was heady while it was there, but the effects wore off sooner or later, like the effects from drinking too much good wine. Conrad had succeeded in knocking her for six, but she would recover. It was no more than a sexual attraction, powerful though it might be.

The restaurant turned out to double as a small hotel as well, with guest quarters scattered among the creeping bougainvillaea and set back from the swimming pool.

They were shown to their table in what Emma conceded had to be the most charming setting imaginable. The restaurant was simply a small cluster of tables and chairs set in two circular, open spaces which were sheltered from the rain by thatched roofs supported on wooden beams.

The proprietor came over to them, delighting Emma when he told her that in the mornings the guests would breakfast to the accompaniment of the tropical birds which flew to the tables on the offchance of nipping some fallen crumbs of bread.

'It's idyllic,' Emma breathed to Conrad, when they were looking at their menus. 'So much nicer than those dreadful dark rooms in England that try and rake up a phony intimate atmosphere.' She wanted to add that intimacy was where they were now, sitting at tables from which she could see the stars and the moon, but she refrained.

'Glad you accepted my offer, then?' In the flickering light of the candle, she saw him smile drily at her, and her nerves raced.

'Did I have much choice?' she rejoined lightly. 'This place really is exquisite, though. And yes, I'm glad I came.'

She read the menu with interest, settling for the local dish of the day, and relaxed in her seat. The silence between them was comfortable and she had a brief, aching sensation of never having been so happy before.

Over the meal, Conrad talked to her about his business, about his interests and about a hundred other little things in a way that was amusing and informative.

As the proprietor brought them their coffee, he leaned back against the chair and looked at her leisurely through narrowed eyes.

'Aren't you going to get around to asking what it was I wanted to talk to you about?'

Emma looked at him, suddenly realising that she had completely forgotten the point of the evening. She had been so taken with the wine, the easy flow of conversation, the unreal atmosphere, that his question brought her sharply back down to earth.

'I was about to get around to it,' she lied, twirling the stem of her glass. For some reason she felt wary. Whatever he was about to say was serious. It was written on the sculptured contours of his face.

'It's about Alistair, actually,' he began, and Emma frowned, puzzled. Was that why he had brought her here? To talk about Alistair? She thought that they had covered all that already, and, even if they hadn't, surely it could have been discussed back at the villa?

'You mean his illness?' she asked, baffled.

Conrad nodded. 'Basically, yes,' he concurred. 'It doesn't appear that he's getting any better. True enough, he's not getting any worse, and it's undoubtedly helped knowing that you're his granddaughter, and having you around, but I would have thought that he'd be making more of an effort to get back into the swing of things by now. He's never been one to let his ill health get the better of him. He's a great believer in the power of the fighting spirit. How else would he ever have risen to where he was if he hadn't believed in his own strength of mind?' He paused as though rehearsing in his head what he was about to say.

'Maybe you'll believe me when I say that he's iller than he's letting on,' Emma interrupted. 'Isn't it like him to try and make light of something serious?'

'I've given it some thought,' Conrad agreed, 'and I think that maybe you're right.'

Now that he had said it, Emma felt a chill sweep through her. It made the seriousness of Alistair's condition all the more painful. She realised with a start that Conrad's confidence that he was going to be all right had influenced her reaction more than she had admitted. She had had an inexplicable faith in what he said, like a child who instinctively believed an adult.

Silly, of course, especially as he was now agreeing with what she had suspected all along.

'If the prospect of continuing with his work isn't enough to get him out of that bed,' Conrad stated bluntly, 'then there's only one thing that will.'

'There is?' Emma repeated sceptically. If there was, then she sure as hell couldn't think of it.

Conrad stared at her impatiently, like a detective waiting for his loyal assistant to arrive at the right conclusion. When she continued to look at him blankly, he said flatly, 'Yes.

You know what he wants so badly. Have all his none too subtle innuendoes gone completely over your head?'

Emma shook her head slowly. A nebulous thought was beginning to take shape, but it couldn't be…

'I can tell you see what I'm driving at. We're going to have to convince him that we're engaged and about to be married.'

CHAPTER SEVEN

'You're joking, aren't you.' It wasn't a question, it was a statement. Emma looked at Conrad, waiting for him to agree, to nod, to laugh, to do *anything* except sit there, unsmiling.

'I've never been more serious in my life.' He meant it, too, she could see that.

'But you can't be! It's the most ridiculous idea I've ever heard. It's ludicrous, absurd, downright stupid!' The words were tripping over each other. Emma gulped a mouthful of tepid coffee and made a face. On the few occasions that she had contemplated marriage, she had never once thought that it would be this way. Of course, men these days were practical; they proposed casually—going down on bended knee had been relegated to a thing of the past—but this was going too far.

She looked at him stubbornly, refusing to believe that he wasn't suddenly going to burst out laughing.

'Why is it ridiculous?' Conrad asked, his clever face scrutinising hers, almost as though *she* was the one who needed humouring.

'Why? I could think of a thousand reasons why!'

'Fine. Tell me about them.' He stretched back and looked at her patiently.

'All right,' she replied hotly, 'how's this for starters? He'll never in a month of Sundays believe us. I mean, it's hardly as though we hit it off from the start, is it? Don't you think he might just ask himself how come we've suddenly decided that we want to get married? One minute we're arguing with each other, the next minute we've decided that we'll celebrate our differences by getting engaged! Don't you think it's a bit extreme? Would you buy that if you were in his position? However much you wanted to believe it?'

It sounded convincing enough, and she sat back triumphantly. Her heart was beating fast, so fast that if she hadn't known better she would have thought that the mere idea of being married to Conrad, of pretending, for heaven's sake, was enough to excite her.

Of course, that in itself was ludicrous.

'Why wouldn't he believe us?' Conrad asked lazily. 'Don't you think we can convince him that we're madly in love? I do.'

Emma flushed. 'You must be a good actor, then.' When he didn't reply, she rushed on, 'Anyway, even if by some miracle of short-sightedness he *did* believe us, what then?'

'I don't follow you.'

'What makes you think that it'll make a scrap of difference to his health?'

She didn't know why she was even bothering to pursue this line of conversation, but now that she had started she realised with alarm that it was becoming increasingly difficult to back down. She should have laughed the whole thing off from the start and simply refused to consider it.

'Think about it,' Conrad said in a patient voice that made her want to scream. 'He's been going on about it in one way or another for ages. If he thinks that his dream is finally going to be realised, it would give him something to live for, something to start recuperating for.'

Put like that, it made sense in a weird sort of way. The sensation of sinking was getting stronger. Emma rooted around for more objections. People didn't *pretend* to be getting married, for God's sake. She didn't know anyone who had ever *pretended* to be getting married.

Trust him, she thought, to come up with a fool scheme

like that. His sharp mind was just the kind to bypass normal convention and settle on the quickest route possible, regardless of everyday scruples.

'I don't have to think about it. I can tell you without giving it any thought at all that I don't like the idea. He's my grandfather, and I just don't like the thought of deceiving him. It's underhand and it's dishonest.'

'You'd prefer to see him ill?'

Emma glared at him. Not only was he a dab hand at manipulating people, she thought sourly, he was pretty adept at manipulating words as well. He made her sound as though she was uncaring, merely because she had a few scruples!

'Of course I don't want to see him ill!' she retorted. 'I suffered enough when my mother died. Do you really think I don't feel scared stiff that I might suffer again if Alistair's condition worsens? It's just that what you're suggesting is unscrupulous.' In fact, typical.

'You don't think that the end justifies the means? If Alistair needs this push to recover, then I'm willing to do it.'

'Well,' Emma said sweetly, staring at Conrad's dark, brooding face, 'isn't that big of you? Of course, you're well used to arranged marriages, but have you thought that I might not be?'

'I would have thought,' he murmured equally smoothly, 'that you would have agreed to anything that might help him. You're his granddaughter, dammit. Naturally, I could be mistaken. Your great show of concern and affection might not be as genuine as you would have us all believe. It might just be a convincing little act, so that you can contrive to get some of Alistair's wealth to rub off on you.' His voice was soft, but he was watching her intently, his mouth set in a grim line.

Emma knew precisely what was going on in that head of his and she didn't like it. He had opted for the one argument that was guaranteed to squash any further disagreements from her, and had pulled it out like a card which he had been keeping up his sleeve.

'That's not fair,' she mumbled, staring defeat in the face.

He smiled, a slow, relaxed smile, like a tiger that had successfully cornered its prey. He signalled for the bill, not taking his eyes off her face.

'All right, and what if he recovers?'

'When.'

'Have it your way. What do we do *when* he recovers?'

'We can cross that bridge when we get to it. Is that it for your objections?'

Emma didn't answer.

'So that's settled, then?' he asked as they prepared to leave the restaurant.

Emma disgruntledly wondered why he even bothered to ask the question. He knew that her answer was no longer in the balance. 'So it seems,' she replied coolly.

'Good.'

They drove back in silence, Emma too preoccupied with her thoughts to have even the slightest interest in the dense, lush undergrowth darkly shifting around them.

When the car pulled up outside the house, Conrad switched off the engine and looked at her, his arm resting along the seat behind her head. Emma instinctively edged away.

'We'll see him tomorrow, first thing.'

Emma mumbled her agreement.

'And make it convincing.'

She forbore to comment, instead clanking open the car door and walking quickly towards the house. She waited while Conrad leisurely locked up the car and then sauntered to join her, taking much longer than necessary to open the front door.

He's enjoying this, she thought. He's enjoying knowing

that he's thrown me into an untenable position. The fact that she was angry was giving him the greatest of pleasure.

As soon as the door was open, she ran up the stairs towards her bedroom, ignoring Conrad's voice as he called out to her, 'No thanks for an enjoyable evening, then?'

The man was a sadist, she decided, once she was alone in the privacy of her bedroom. Fortune had definitely been having a laugh at her expense when the damned man had decided to take a break for some rest and relaxation. Why couldn't he have had a shorter break, as any normal person would have? Shouldn't he have realised that he missed his work?

For once she regretted the high standard of equipment in Alistair's office. It had made her job infinitely easier, and she had marvelled at all the gadgets and computers that kept him in touch with his companies, never once realising that they also managed to enable Conrad to more than keep in touch with his own companies as well.

She finally fell asleep with disgruntled reluctance, and awoke the following morning to a perfectly cloudless, still day. No refreshing breeze, only the sultry heaviness of relentless heat.

Through the opened window the heat was leaden and cloying, and Emma quickly shut the window, switching on the air-conditioning for the first time in days. There was no point getting a headache from the humidity when she needed all her wits about her.

When she got to Alistair's bedroom, it was to find Conrad already there, and in the relaxed attitude of someone who had probably been there for some time.

They both looked at her, Alistair unable to conceal the smug contentment on his face.

'Emma, darling, I've broken the news to Alistair.'

Conrad's eyes darkened as he came towards her, reaching to stroke the side of her face with his fingers. Emma fought down the melting feeling that swept over her, telling herself that it was all a sham and she had better not be foolish enough to forget it, even for one minute.

'Oh, good,' she said, forcing a smile.

'You'll have to do better than that,' Conrad whispered in her ear. 'Don't forget we're not playing games here. Alistair's health is at stake.'

He kissed her on the neck, sending a flood of colour to her face, and then slung his arm over her shoulders.

He drew her along to Alistair's bedside.

'My dear, congratulations.' Alistair beamed at her. 'It's an old man's dream come true. My beloved granddaughter, lost to me for years, now to be married to the young man who's always been as close to me as my own flesh and blood.'

'Not just an old man's dream,' Conrad murmured softly, 'ours too. Isn't that right, darling? I'm only sorry that it took us so long to find out.'

'Right,' Emma muttered, feeling a sickening wave of guilt wash over her. Why had she ever gone along with this damn fool scheme? She tried gracefully to disengage herself from Conrad's arms, but he pulled her tighter towards him. His fingers tangled in her long hair, ensuring that any further attempt to get away from him would be useless.

Talk about playing it to the hilt, she thought with desperation. She made herself relax against him, disturbingly aware of the steady beat of his heart and the warmth of his chest.

'I was telling Conrad a while back, before you came in, that I had hoped you two would hit it off, but when did you realise that you were in love?' Alistair looked interestedly at Emma's flushed face.

She turned to Conrad provocatively, her green eyes gleaming. 'When was it, darling?'

As far as she was concerned, if he was such a good actor,

then he could damn well do all the talking. She hadn't liked the scheme from the start and she would leave it to him to carry through as much as she could, even though she reluctantly had to admit that already Alistair was looking better.

'Oh, you explain,' Conrad murmured, stroking her hair but not releasing his grip. 'You women are so much more articulate at these things.'

The bastard, Emma thought, smiling sweetly at Alistair.

'I think I fell in love the minute I laid eyes on him,' she said, speaking with difficulty. In a minute she was going to choke. She only hoped that Conrad had been right, and that the end would justify all this, because right now she felt horribly trapped and deceitful.

His hand slipped to her waist, resting lightly underneath her breasts. She felt her body respond automatically and forced herself to ignore the melting feeling in her legs.

'So did I,' Conrad agreed. 'I didn't realise it at first, but isn't that always the way with true love?'

Emma chose not to reply to his question. She listened numbly while Alistair congratulated them, murmuring vaguely when he began discussing wedding plans.

'You'll make a beautiful bride, Emma,' Alistair beamed at her. 'You'll make up for the shambles over my own daughter's elopement. And you're both so perfectly suited. I could see it from the start.'

Conrad squeezed her waist lovingly and Emma tried not to stiffen. To do what she really wanted to do, which was to sink back into his embrace, would have been dangerous.

When they were finally outside and the door to Alistair's room firmly shut, Emma rounded on him.

'I thought you said that the possibility of Alistair bringing up the question of marriage wouldn't happen. And now that we're out of the bedroom, I'll thank you to keep your hands to yourself!' She stood back from him, impatiently sweeping her hair away from her face.

Conrad obediently stepped back, thrusting both hands into his pockets. 'And I thought that you enjoyed it.'

'Well, you thought wrong!'

'You're the first woman to say that to me.' His mouth was smiling, but the depths of his eyes were serious, and it flitted through Emma's head that he probably was telling the truth. Women for him had been conquered territory the moment he set eyes on them. His lazy sexuality, his power, would draw even the most hardened feminist. Women could not resist the sort of easy self-assurance that he possessed.

'You still haven't answered my question,' she snapped. 'How are we going to get Alistair off the subject of marriage?'

Conrad turned away and began walking slowly down the staircase. Emma hurried behind him.

'Why worry about it?' he asked with what Emma considered overwhelming naïveté. Couldn't he foresee the problems? She could. Now that they had embarked on this, she could foresee hundreds of them. How could he simply adopt such a *laissez-faire* attitude?

He was still striding ahead of her. She stood still and glared at him, her hands on her hips.

'No breakfast?' he called over his shoulder.

'I resent having to trot behind you like your pet dog!' Emma responded on a high note. 'This is serious, so if you wouldn't mind treating it as such…'

'Only on a full stomach.' He vanished towards the kitchen.

Emma's teeth clamped together and she followed him through, helping herself to coffee from the percolator.

'I didn't realise you meant it,' she said sarcastically, eyeing the plateful of fried bacon, sausage and eggs which he was preparing for himself. 'Do you think you have enough calories there, or perhaps you could set the whole thing off by simply melting lard over the lot?'

Through the kitchen window she could see Esther tending to the herb beds, clipping bunches of parsley and thyme which she used liberally in her food.

Conrad sat opposite her and began eating.

'Would you like some?' He gave her a concerned look which didn't fool her for an instant.

'Thanks, but I don't think my blood-pressure could stand it. And you still haven't answered my question.'

'Question?' he asked with polite interest.

'I was saying,' Emma repeated acidly, 'that this little game of yours is already beginning to have flaws. Alistair is talking about marriage as though we'll be walking up the aisle in a few days' time.'

'All the more reason for him to start his recuperating, then.'

As Esther bustled into the kitchen, Conrad stood up and stretched, throwing her a grin and moved to stand behind Emma's chair. He bent over, enfolding her in his arms.

'Congratulations,' Esther said with a broad smile. 'It'll be nice to have a wedding in the family.'

Emma gritted her teeth. She had thought that their little plan was not going to extend beyond Alistair. Clearly she had been wrong.

'I didn't think you knew,' she said lightly, feeling slightly dizzy as Conrad stroked her collarbone, his fingers moving dangerously close to the swell of her breasts.

'Of course, darling.' Conrad kissed her ear. 'Esther's like one of the family. After Alistair, she was the first person told.'

'Fine. Darling. And when shall we be putting the notice in *The Times*?'

She heard Conrad chuckle.

'So what you two up to today? You want me to prepare lunch for you?' Esther was sifting through the herbs, picking out the best clumps and laying them to one side.

'I don't think so,' Conrad said quickly, silencing Emma's protests that she was going to do some work and then relax in the cove. 'We're going to see something of the island. Maybe you could just cut some sandwiches for us.'

Esther nodded.

Sandwiches? Tours of the island? Emma felt as though her life was suddenly running away from her. In the past she had always been in control. She had friends, went to the theatre, to parties, let men take her out to dinner, but she had always been firmly in the driving seat, in charge of her own life.

She knew where she stood, and she liked that feeling of knowing that she could always extricate herself from any situation that proved difficult.

Now the driving seat had given way to a skateboard and most of the time she didn't even know what direction it was going to take. It was heady, and it was dangerous.

Decisions were swept out of her mouth before she even had the opportunity to utter them. By Conrad—a man whose motives, she constantly had to remind herself, were suspect, to say the least.

His hands were still resting on her shoulders and with a sudden move Emma stood up, relieved when he moved aside to accommodate her.

'Perhaps you should get ready,' he said mildly, his eyes running over her, taking in the curves of her body underneath the fine cotton layer of clothing.

'Can't I go as I am?'

'I suggest you bring a swimsuit. No need to put it on here—you can change into it if you need to.'

Where, Emma thought, in the car? She resolved to put it on the minute she went upstairs. But she would keep on what she was wearing. The heat had not abated; if anything it was becoming more claustrophobic, and thicker clothes would be unthinkable.

On the spur of the moment she packed a towel and a spare jersey, as well as her book, not that she had much hope of being able to read it. Even if they decided simply to find a beach somewhere, the thought of relaxing enough to enjoy a book with Conrad close by was a joke.

Her mind and body did funny things when he was around. He had a knack of throwing her off-key, although she thought as she looked at the hardback book that it could prove an ideal weapon if he decided to take their pretend engagement too far.

Alistair was delighted when Emma went to tell him what their plans were for the day.

'How very romantic,' he sighed, winking at her. He really was looking better. He had completely relinquished the bed, preferring to sit in his wheelchair by the window.

In fact, he was already talking about starting work again in a couple of days' time.

'It'll mean so much more now,' he informed her. 'I shall have to do some rethinking.'

'Why?' Emma asked ingenuously.

'To fit you in, of course. My granddaughter is part of my life, even though I missed out on a few years at the beginning. I want to incorporate all that's happened in these past few weeks into my autobiography. It's far more meaningful to me than all the wealth I've managed to accumulate over the years.'

Emma couldn't argue the point. She was just glad that her grandfather looked so well. Robust, even.

She was more than prepared to stay and marvel on his recovery with him, when the alternative was Conrad's company, but Alistair was having none of it. He shooed her towards the door, and seemed to be, she noticed disgruntledly, far more excited about the prospect of her touring the island with Conrad than she was.

'Are you sure you'll be all right here on your own fo

the whole day?' she asked as a last resort, not surprised when he threw aside her remark with a nonchalant wave of his hand.

'Esther's here,' he reminded her. 'So off you go.'

Conrad was waiting for her by the car, wearing a pair of denim shorts and a blue and white striped jersey. A picnic hamper had been packed for them by Esther, which, Conrad informed her as they were settled in the car, contained enough food to feed an army.

Emma laughed nervously and asked where they were going. She was already beginning to feel apprehensive at the thought of being isolated with him for several hours.

Outside the heat sat around them heavily, unrelieved by even the slightest hint of a breeze. The few people they passed, the animals, all seemed to be moving in sluggish slow motion.

They drove past a roadside stall, a makeshift affair of wooden boards groaning under the weight of fruit, all stacked into neat piles, and Emma was amused to see that the boy in charge was sound asleep in a hammock nearby. At least, she thought, she wasn't the only one affected by the thick, gluey heat today.

'I've decided to take us sailing,' Conrad said, half turning to see her reaction.

Emma received this doubtfully. 'I don't know how to sail,' she pointed out. 'In fact, I've only been on a sailing boat twice in my lifetime, and both times were disastrous. Maybe we could just go for a quick outing to Pigeon Point.'

She stressed the word quick, hoping that he would take the hint, which he didn't.

'I won't be of any help to you at all,' she persisted.

'It's not really a sailing boat, more of a small cabin cruiser. Just big enough for about four people, with two rooms, which should give us some protection from this sun. We can anchor out at sea and do some swimming.'

'Four people?' Emma asked hopefully. 'Will we have company?'

'Oh, no,' Conrad mocked. 'We are, after all, desperately in love and in no need of anyone else's company.' He began humming under his breath and Emma lapsed into silence, staring outside at the scorching countryside. Even the coconut trees seemed to be drooping, their heads hanging towards the earth.

Next to her, Conrad manoeuvred the car with precision to Store Bay, where their boat was waiting for them.

The sea was flat and calm and the sky perfectly cloudless. Emma climbed aboard before Conrad could help her up, determined to keep any physical contact between them to a minimum and for appearances only when Alistair was around.

The boat was exactly as Conrad had described: small, with a sheltered cabin area just large enough for two people, definitely a squeeze should there have been four.

'I hope you know how to handle one of these,' she said to him as he finished paying the boat owner and leapt on board.

'Don't you have any faith in me? Believe me, I've handled them more than once.'

'In similar circumstances, I suppose?' Emma threw at him, realising too late that she sounded at the very least childish, and at the very worst jealous.

'With women, yes, if that's what you mean.' He glanced at her as the engine throbbed into life and he began steering away from the shoreline.

'I meant with passengers on board,' Emma lied, scarlet. As the boat gathered speed, the salt air whipped her hair across her face and she fished an elastic band out of her pocket, carelessly tying it into a ponytail at the back.

'Leave it out.'

'What?'

'Your hair—leave it out. It looks sexier.'

Emma stared at him, her mouth suddenly dry. The shoreline was fast becoming a thin strip in the distance, and the realisation that soon she would be miles away from land, miles away from any escape route, hit her like a thunderbolt.

'I prefer it like this,' she told him warily, raising her voice to drown the sound of the motor. She turned away to put some distance between them and felt his hand from behind. Before she could protest he had pulled the elastic band from her hair and tossed it into the churning water.

'That's better.'

Better for whom? she thought. She retreated to the deck, cautiously peeled off her clothes down to her bikini, and sat down on her towel. When there was nothing around them but ocean she felt the boat slowing down and finally stopping.

This, she thought, was a bad idea. Conrad was easing himself to join her and she watched him surreptitiously, taking in his quick, lithe movements as he tossed the anchor overboard.

'Amazing, isn't it?' he asked, gesturing to the neverending stretch of water. 'Doesn't it make you feel insignificant?'

Emma nodded slowly. He was right, of course. They were no more than specks on the horizon. The solitude in the immense wilderness of sea around them was formidable.

The heat was sapping. They chatted lazily about any number of things, half drowsy in the intense warmth. When Conrad stood up and asked her whether she was going to join him for a swim, Emma peered dubiously down at the water.

'It doesn't look very inviting,' she said, looking at the black depths. 'Anything could be underneath there waiting for us to jump in.'

Conrad laughed, 'Anything like what? And what makes

you think that they're waiting for us? Don't you think that they've got better things to do than wait around for a couple of nondescript human beings to jump in the water for a swim?' He stretched out his hand for her and Emma grabbed hold of it, pulling herself up.

Immediately she was on her feet, she released him and went over to the side of the boat, watching in fascinated admiration as Conrad dived cleanly into the water, disappearing and resurfacing a minute later.

Did nothing frighten him? True, he was a strong swimmer, she had seen ample evidence of that, but this was different. The water was not transparent and blue but dark and deep and ominously still.

'Don't be such a coward!' he called, floating on his back with his feet crossed. 'Don't you ever take risks?'

There was enough of a taunt in his voice for Emma to throw caution to the winds and plunge into the water, gasping at the first cold impact. She swam over to Conrad, feeling peculiarly safe with him close to her. She had no idea why, since he could hardly fend off a school of sharks, or even one for that matter.

'What about sharks?' she asked in a low voice, glancing around her cautiously.

'What about them?'

'Are there any?'

He looked around, a wry smile curving his lips. 'None that I can see just at the moment. Don't worry, I'll keep my eyes open, and the minute I spot a wayward fin I'll let you know.'

'You know what I mean,' Emma accused him lightly liking him more than she wanted to admit, in this teasing easy mood, finding it too easy to forget that he should inspire caution and not camaraderie, 'Sharks like warm water There are bound to be a few, somewhere around us.'

'True,' Conrad agreed. 'But we'll just have to gamble that they can find more interesting things to do than attack us.'

'Mr Fearless,' Emma mocked, grinning.

He smiled back at her, his eyes darkening, and Emma swam away, circling the boat, her confidence increasing as she realised that she was as safe here as she would be crossing a busy street in London. Safer, probably.

By the time they climbed back on to the boat she was surprised to find that she was really enjoying herself. A few clouds were gathering on the horizon, but there was still no relief from the heat. It enveloped her the minute she was back on the deck, drying off her body in a matter of seconds, before she even had time to rub herself down with her towel.

They unpacked Esther's hamper in the shelter of the cabin, spreading the food out on the little table. There was crab, roast beef and chicken sandwiches, a potato salad, lots of tomatoes and a Thermos of coffee.

'And of course,' Conrad produced from the bottom of the basket, 'this.'

'Wine?' Emma laughed, 'Esther packed that?'

'No. That, I must confess, was entirely my own doing.'

Their eyes met and Emma looked away quickly, busying herself with the food, neatly serving out the sandwiches and salad on to paper plates.

The first warning they had of the storm was a sharp crack of thunder, as clear and as unexpected as the sound of a gunshot, and she heard Conrad swear under his breath. He left the cabin and returned seconds later wearing a grim expression.

Emma was standing at the tiny cabin window, staring at the rolling black clouds which seemed to be gathering momentum by the second.

'I should have known,' he muttered forcefully.

'Known? Known what?'

'Take a look outside.'

'I have. It's going to rain. We can always head back now in time.' She hastily began stacking the left-over food back into the basket.

'I can see you have no experience whatsoever of the tropics,' Conrad said cynically, 'Rain over here isn't like a downpour in England. And this isn't just going to be a light shower, over in fifteen minutes. We're in for something more severe than that. I should have known. All the signs were there. The heaviness in the air, the stillness. I asked that damned man who rented us the boat about it, but he said that there was nothing to worry about. The hurricane had swept through some of the islands further north, but Tobago was safe.'

Emma had gone white. 'What are we going to do?'

'Ride it through, what else?'

There was another crack of thunder and the stillness was replaced by a sudden, cool wind, churning the waters into a choppy black mass.

'But it was so sunny a minute ago.' She had instinctively edged closer to Conrad and slipped on her clothes.

'That's the nature of the beast,' he said drily, cramming anything that could move under the seat and securing them as fast as he could. 'The weather over here can change in a matter of seconds.'

As though to prove his point, the wind gathered force, gently buffeting the tiny cabin cruiser against the water.

'Where are you going?' Emma asked desperately, as Conrad prepared to go outside.

'I'll have to try and steer the boat into the waves.' He grimaced. 'Stay calm, whatever you do. The last thing I need is a hysterical female.' Before she could reply, he lowered his head, and she felt his lips brush against hers, then he was gone, and Emma retreated to the window, to a view of rain slashing against the water in a dense, black sheet and to the wind driving the water into a frenzied, seething mass.

Conrad had been right. She had no experience of weather like this. In England there was always a prolonged, polite warning of rain or snow. Here nature extended no such civilities. She released the full brunt of her displeasure with impressive speed.

Emma huddled against a wooden support, grasping it with one hand as the boat rocked furiously, like a matchbox tossed into rapids.

Every few minutes a gush of water would drench the window, blocking her view. She wanted desperately to go and see how Conrad was faring, but she knew without doubt that the last thing he needed was her presence behind the steering-wheel.

Hadn't he said so to her? No hysterical woman. She traced her lips where he had lightly kissed her, and tried to staunch the sudden, fierce need she felt for him, and the painful knowledge that what he was doing was necessary but highly dangerous.

Outside, the skies were black, as though night had prematurely fallen, even though it was only just two in the afternoon.

What if something happened to Conrad? Her blood froze as she considered the possibility. She had admitted her physical attraction to him, had argued that whatever she felt stopped there. It had to stop there because it would have been sheer folly for it to progress any further.

She was not his type, and anyway she couldn't trust him as far as she could throw him. That knowledge, bitter though it was, was her protection.

So why couldn't she simply follow the path pointed out to her by her head?

There was another roll of thunder and Emma covered her ears with her hands. If Conrad could ride out this storm, then she could ride out whatever it was that was slowly gnawing away at her insides.

Wasn't it all a question of time?

CHAPTER EIGHT

EMMA had no idea how much time had passed before the fierce pounding of the boat against the waves became more of a steady roll, and the wind gradually began to die away.

The rain was still falling heavily, but on to calmer waters. Emma stretched her legs, wincing in pain as she rested her weight on to her stiffened joints.

The first thought in her head was to check Conrad, to make sure that everything was all right. She balanced herself against the wooden side of the cabin, walking unsteadily towards the door when a sudden jolt sent her flying across the floor, crashing ungracefully against one of the benches.

She yelped in agony as an arrow of pain shot through her ankle. Gently she massaged the foot, hoping that nothing was broken. A sound from the cabin door made her raise her head and she saw Conrad framed against the grey sky, dripping wet.

A rush of relief swept over her, as powerful as anything she had felt before. She stared up at him, unable to speak, hardly able to think, simply ridiculously grateful that he was in one piece. She had a sudden chill of horror as she realised what might have happened to him out there. He could, for starters, have been swept out to sea. In violent weather like this, it wasn't an impossibility. If he had been, he would have vanished without a trace.

She felt her throat constrict and looked down hurriedly.

'I heard a noise,' he said, coming across to where she was still sitting on the floor.

'It's my ankle,' Emma said gruffly. 'I was trying to get outside and I fell.'

Conrad looked at her white face incredulously. 'Trying to get outside? What for? Did you think that you could help steer us to safety?'

Emma felt the prick of tears behind her eyes and swallowed painfully. 'Thanks for the sympathy!'

'Let me have a look,' he commanded, reaching out towards her.

'I'll be fine.'

'Dammit, Emma. This is no time for childish heroics. Let me see your ankle! Now!'

Reluctantly she stretched her leg out, biting her lip as his fingers pressed against her ankle, delicately trying to determine the seriousness of her fall.

'Sorry I tore into you like that,' he muttered, his head bent as he inspected her foot. 'It's been nightmarish out there for the past two hours, but thankfully we're out of the worst.'

'Two hours!'

'I told you it wouldn't be a fifteen-minute downpour. I'll need your T-shirt.'

'What for?' she asked, feeling embarrassingly undressed as she pulled the jersey over her head, even though her bikini top covered her.

Without answering, Conrad tore it into one long strip.

'What do you think you're doing?' She stood up, falling back in pain as her foot crumpled from under her.

'What does it look like? I'm doing my best to make a bandage for this ankle. I can hardly use my shirt, it's soaking wet. Looks like a sprain; I can't feel any broken bones.'

He carefully began to wind the cloth around her foot until the ankle was securely bandaged. 'Damn fool thing to have done,' he commented neutrally.

'Believe me, it wasn't premeditated! I don't normally hurl myself around boats on the offchance that I might break my ankle!' How could she have ever felt tearful relief that this man was back in the cabin with her?

She watched as he stripped to the waist and sat next to her.

'I've anchored the boat. The wind's gone, but it'll continue raining for at least another hour and there's no point our even thinking about making it back until it clears a bit more.'

'Alistair will be worried.'

'There's not much I can do about that. There's no radio transmitter on this boat, so we're uncontactable.'

Emma digested this information in silence.

He looked, she conceded sympathetically, tired. The wind and rain had whipped his black hair around his face, giving him a swarthy, unkempt appearance. In another era, she thought, he would have made a great pirate.

He gesticulated to the bottle of wine and Emma shook her head in refusal. The last thing she needed was alcohol, and he apparently agreed, pouring himself some coffee instead, which he swallowed in one quick gulp.

They hadn't spoken, and the bleakness outside, pressing on the small panes of glass, seemed to magnify the atmosphere of intimacy that descended on them.

When he beckoned her to sit next to him, she found herself complying.

Of course, it wouldn't do to forget that she was in dangerous waters, both outside and in; that they were only pretending to be engaged for Alistair's benefit and that Conrad couldn't give two hoots for her outside that. Even so...

The sea had calmed considerably. Only the occasional gust of wind shook the little cruiser as if to remind them that they could shelve any thought of heading back to land for the time being.

'Don't worry. It's over,' Conrad murmured soothingly.

He placed an arm around her shoulder and Emma leant against it, liking the warm, safe feeling that it gave her.

'Was it very bad up there?'

'I've spent more enjoyable afternoons, but fortunately I didn't have time to be afraid. When you're caught up in a situation like that, there's no room for fear.'

'Are you ever afraid?' Emma asked curiously. 'Of anything?'

'Oh, yes,' he said softly, 'but not what you'd expect.' He gave a short laugh, but didn't elaborate.

Instead, he looked down at her, his blue eyes warm, too warm for comfort. She really shouldn't be sprawled against him the way she was. She shifted slightly, and Conrad's arm curled further around her, so that his hand was right by her mouth.

She looked at it, seeing the way the dark hairs were silky-smooth on his wrist, the hands strong and not at all like a businessman's manicured hands.

She found herself raising her own to take it, linking her fingers through his. He stiffened slightly, then relaxed, and she felt his warmth infuse her like a heady fix.

She settled more comfortably. Her hair swept down across her face and she flicked it aside.

'I knew I should have tied it back.'

Conrad didn't answer. Instead he entwined his fingers in the long, tumbling mass, looping it around his fingers.

Outside, the rain continued to beat against the grimy window in the cabin, but inside the silence was deafening. A cold, sober awareness rushed over Emma, but she shut her mind to it, closing her eyes to enjoy the sensation of Conrad's fingers lightly stroking her hair.

'You're very tempting,' he murmured, and the look in his eyes made her nerves tingle with excitement.

She knew that she ought to protest, she half opened her mouth and he lowered his head to hers, his lips brushing over her upturned face. Emma could feel her whole body yearning for him with a desire over which she had lost control.

She smiled and moaned softly, her body shifting closer to his.

'I can smell the salt and the sea on you,' Conrad muttered unevenly, and he stretched out his arm so that her head was resting against it.

'It's as if I'm drunk with you,' he whispered against her neck. 'Do you feel the same way? Tell me you want me as badly as I want you.' She could see feverish passion in his eyes as he looked down at her and she felt herself drowning in it.

Oh, yes, she was drunk with him as well, intoxicated by the feel of him. She knew well enough what she was doing, but was powerless to stop. Everything in her, all of her cool, analytical practicality, was crumbling under the impact of the restless emotions surging through her.

She heard herself responding to him, telling him what he wanted to hear and what she felt, telling him that she wanted him. It was madness, but a delicious, persuasive madness, a delirium that filled her every nerve.

Conrad sighed heavily.

'You're the most provocative, stubborn woman I have ever met.' The words were muffled as his lips trailed across her neck.

Emma arched back, curling her hands in his hair, guiding his mouth to hers.

He kissed her with deepening force, his tongue exploring her mouth, and Emma responded with trembling hunger. She had fought so long against this, knowing that if she gave in again to him she would be lost, and she was. She didn't care. She was filled with a driving, suffocating need for him and all she wanted was to succumb to it.

His hands moved across her stomach and her nipples

hardened to meet his touch. His mouth, demanding, explored her breasts, and Emma shivered weakly. Tentatively she slipped her fingers underneath the elastic waistband of his trunks, feeling the hard curve of his buttocks under her hand.

Her face felt hot and flushed, as though she were gripped by a raging fever.

His movements now were urgent, his body covered in a fine film of perspiration to match her own. He gently eased her out of her shorts, murmuring as he caressed her naked thighs.

Restlessly he pulled her free of the remnants of her clothing. As he raised himself to strip, Emma stared at his hard body with greedy concentration, dwelling on the firm lines of his body, the fine dark hairs that spiralled down from his navel.

'Tell me you want me, Emma,' he commanded shakily, lowering his body against hers.

Emma stared drowsily at him, 'You know I do. More than anything.' With a fierceness, she thought, that engulfed her.

She felt a sharp stab as he thrust against her, and with her eyes closed did not realise that he was staring down at her in surprise. Her hands gripped his hips, pulling him to her.

'Emma,' he said huskily.

'I know. Please.' She lay back, her body suffused with mounting passion, moving with instinctive rhythm to him, plumbing the depths of a desire which she did not know existed.

The grey sheet of rain was fading away. Through the cabin window, she could actually see patches of blue sky struggling to peep through the dense pillows of black clouds. They lay back next to each other, Emma still in the crook of his arm.

'Silly, isn't it,' she said, more to herself than to Conrad, 'a virgin at my age?'

'Not silly at all. Rather special, in fact.' He seemed wrapped up in his own thoughts, and as Emma watched his face, resisting the urge to reach out and caress it, she could feel the first drops of cold reality begin to trickle over her, just as the sun began filtering into the cabin.

Of course, he didn't love her. He had made love to her because he fancied her, and because both their defences had been lowered. He had acted on instinct, touching her in a way that had left no room for doubt in her mind.

Not then, anyway. Now, the doubts which had been pushed to one side were becoming a steady, cold stream.

Why had he made love to her? He wanted her. She had felt it in his urgent moans as he thrust against her. But maybe there was more to it than that.

She looked at the handsome, clever face, a face designed to have its own way with the female sex.

He could have anyone he wanted, she thought. As Sophia said, he was the biggest and brightest catch in the ocean. So why her? Unless, a tiny insistent voice said, she had what he wanted. Namely, money.

Did he think that she was in line for Alistair's inheritance? Had that made her irresistible?

The palms of her hands were clammy and her head was spinning. All those thoughts rushing through her mind, gathering momentum even as she tried to banish them.

She groaned inwardly, hating him and hating herself even more because, despite everything, she had wanted him. She had needed him to touch her, like some fairy-tale Sleeping Beauty waiting for that single kiss that would revive her.

Except, she thought miserably, this was no fairy-tale.

If it were, then she would be able to at least gather her self-possession, and walk away from him with some dignity. But now she realised with horror that the attraction which she had labelled her private, physical obsession for him was much more than that. Perhaps that was how it had started. A tingling in her veins whenever he was near, the knowledge that he had managed to do what no one else had ever done, which was somehow to get under her skin until he filled her whole body and mind with his presence.

Oh, no, she was in love with him. All his little habits and expressions rushed over her, bombarding her with their profuseness. She had not realised just how much she had been taking in, details which she had stored away and which their act of lovemaking now released.

She drew away from him sharply, fumbling to get on her clothes with frantic, trembling hands. When he pulled her back against him, she looked at him with alarm and tugged away. How could she? How could she have made love to a man who cared nothing for her, and who quite probably had used her for his own ends? He was quite an expert at using people, she had seen that for herself.

He had used Sophia, hadn't he? He had been more than prepared to marry someone simply because it suited him, and he had made love to her for the same reason.

'What's the matter?' he asked lazily, making no effort to dress.

Emma grabbed his clothes and threw them on him.

'I think you should get dressed,' she said coldly, averting her eyes.

'You do, do you?' He stood up, his face clenched and hard. 'Don't you think it's a bit late to be putting on this puritan act?' He forced her to face him, and she controlled the pounding in her head, staring into his bright, glittering eyes with contempt.

'And you can wipe that expression off your face,' he said tightly.

'I'll look at you the way I want.'

He slipped back on his clothes, still soaking wet from the rain.

'You weren't looking at me like that a minute ago. Why the sudden change?'

'Has the weather cleared enough for us to leave?'

'Answer me, damn you!' He gripped her by her hair and Emma winced in pain.

'I want you to get this boat going. Now!'

'I asked you a question!'

'And when you ask a question,' she jeered, 'you get an answer, right? Just as you get whatever you want, right? Including women!'

'Right.'

'Well, not with me!' she shouted. He had released her, and she backed against the side of the cabin, until she was pressed against it and couldn't move any further back.

'Really? Are you going to try and convince me that I forced you to make love with me?'

'I don't have to try and convince you of anything!' Just as I don't have to answer your questions!'

The watery sun caught his hair and she looked away. It hurt too much to continue staring at him. It was like a test of strength, trying to fight against the insane love that she felt for him.

'You'll damn well talk to me, or else we'll stay right here for the rest of the evening, and longer if we have to!'

'Is that some kind of threat?'

'You're damn right, lady.'

He moved across to her, and her body froze as he placed his hands on either side of her, making any escape impossible.

'When all else fails, do you normally resort to threats?' she asked scornfully.

'No. Believe me, this is a first! I don't normally make

love, only to find that the first thing my woman wants to do is get out as quickly as she can!'

'I'm not your woman.'

'You were, not too long ago.'

'Only in the physical sense!'

He had left off his shirt, and the compulsion to place her hands on the flat, firm planes of his torso was so strong that she stuck them safely behind her back.

Why hadn't she listened to reason? Reason had told her from the very beginning to steer clear of him. If she had, she would never have fallen in love with him, and would never have found herself in the mess she was in.

'So what is it, then? Is it because you were a virgin? That's no reason to feel ashamed, you know. Just the opposite.'

A slow red flush crept up her cheeks.

'That's not the reason,' she said in a hard voice. 'If you want answers, then here they are. We should never have made love; it was a mistake. I think that I was just so relieved when you came through that door, so relieved that everything was going to be all right, that I gave in to some kind of temporary insanity.'

'In other words, let's just blame it on the heat of the moment.'

'That's right,' she said expressionlessly.

He didn't answer. He turned away, and when he faced her again it was to inform her that the journey back would probably only take forty minutes to an hour, and the sooner they got going, the better.

She watched him disappear through the cabin door, and then she collapsed heavily on one of the wooden benches, like a puppet whose strings had been suddenly cut.

Why dwell on what had happened? She had given in to him without restraint, she had ignored all the alarm bells sounding in her head.

She had swept all her suspicions tidily under the carpet, because, in the grip of her shaking passion, it had been simply more convenient to have them there, out of the way.

But, worse than all that, worse than her loss of control, her shameful, eager responses, was that she had fallen in love with him.

It did not bear thinking about.

She began tidying the cabin as quickly as she could, moving about slowly with her bandaged ankle.

She could feel the boat gathering speed, and reluctantly she made her way outside to the deck, joining him behind the steering-wheel, watching his hands with an inward shudder as she remembered how he had touched her, and politely made conversation about the journey back.

Conrad answered her questions with remote abstraction, barely acknowledging her presence.

She abandoned all attempt at conversation on the drive back, which they made in silence.

When they arrived back at the house, Esther was waiting for them by the front door, her face anxious and worried. She insisted that they go and see Alistair before changing, to put his mind at rest.

'He's been imagining the worst,' she confided, and Emma half smiled, thinking that the worst had happened, but not in the context that Esther meant.

Alistair was overjoyed to see them. He told them that they should really change into drier clothes, and then promptly insisted that they describe in detail what it had been like in the storm.

Conrad obligingly filled in the details, standing by the window with his arms folded, glancing perfunctorily at Emma when she chipped in with some remark of her own.

If Alistair noticed the coolness between them, he showed no sign of it. As they were leaving the room, Conrad slipped his arm over her shoulders, and she remembered with a stab of pain that they were supposed to be engaged. The loving couple. The situation was painfully farcical.

She forced the muscles of her face to smile at Alistair, looking away before he could see that the smile did not reach her eyes. He was shrewd enough to notice something like that, and whatever happened between herself and Conrad she would not jeopardise Alistair's visible recovery by aborting the charade, much as she wanted to. For better or for worse, they had embarked on this and she was quite determined to see it through to the end.

Once Alistair was better, and that looked to be sooner rather than later, she would leave the island.

As soon as they were outside the door, she shrugged Conrad's arm away from her.

'There's no one out here to impress,' she said coldly, tilting her chin upwards.

'Quite right,' Conrad came back quickly. 'There's no need to point out the obvious.'

She saw something flash through his eyes, something that she couldn't decipher, and immediately came to the conclusion that it was antipathy.

'Another thing,' she persevered. 'Alistair has more or less recovered. He's even talking about starting work tomorrow.'

'And you're wondering when we can call off this little game of ours,' Conrad finished for her.

'Yes.'

'We can break it to him within the next few days. I see no reason to prolong this.'

'Fine. That suits me perfectly.'

She swung round and began trotting down the stairs. The sharp staccato of his voice had cut her to the quick, but she would not let him see it.

She spent the remainder of the day cloistered in the study, preparing for work the following day, and returned there early the next morning. When the phone rang soon after lunch, which she'd had sent in, she almost ignored it, knowing that there was a good chance it would be for Conrad, and she did not want to have to go and look for him, and see that cold cynicism stamped on his face.

As it turned out it was Lloyd on the other end, over in Tobago because, he said, he could not get her out of his mind.

'Really?' Emma remarked drily. 'Now why do I find that a little difficult to believe?'

'Well, it could have been the truth. Actually, I have to see someone over here about some lighting equipment for the nightclub, but I also couldn't get you out of my mind.'

Emma laughed shortly, thinking how sweet those words would have sounded had they been uttered by someone else, in a different situation.

Still, it was nice hearing from Lloyd. His bantering lightened her mood, and when he suggested coming over for dinner Emma greeted the suggestion with enthusiasm. She had been dreading the ordeal of dinner alone with Conrad, if indeed he chose to make an appearance. Lloyd, at least, would do away with the necessity of even talking to Conrad, if she didn't want to.

'Eight all right?' he asked.

'The sooner, the better,' Emma responded fervently.

When evening came she took her time dressing, choosing a pale green dress which made her eyes gleam like emeralds and showed off her tan which, she thought, would be the envy of her friends back home. When she returned to England.

She made it down the stairs just in time to see Lloyd's car sweeping up the driveway. As she threw open the front door she was greeted with blaring pop music that was cut off abruptly when the engine was switched off.

Lloyd enfolded her in his arms and then presented her

with a bouquet of flowers which, he claimed, had been picked with his own fair hands.

She laughed, smelling the delicate blossoms and thinking that it was almost a shame that they had been picked at all. The wild, exotic flowers over here only seemed truly beautiful when they were nestled in their natural foliage. To see them in a vase was somewhat similar to seeing a lion caged at the zoo.

Lloyd was already regaling her with all the things which she had been missing out on by being in Tobago, instead of accepting his invitation to visit him in Trinidad. He stared at her in amazement when she began telling him about the storm, which, he informed her, had swept through Trinidad and had found him well and truly ensconced in his flat.

'A coward has a thousand lives, or something like that,' he grinned, 'Where's the lord of the manor, then?' He glanced around and Emma shrugged.

'Maybe his experiences in the boat have taken their toll and he's cooped up in bed with delayed shock.'

'I doubt that,' Emma commented cynically. 'If anything, he enjoyed the whole thing.'

She diverted the conversation, not wanting to discuss Conrad, and unsure as to whether she should mention her make-believe engagement. In the end she decided against it. It was much too involved, and would be over in a day or two anyway.

Over dinner, she let Lloyd set the conversation and they spent the evening discussing movies and records. She only half listened to what he was saying, however. At times she would find her concentration wandering altogether, and would have to pull herself up to control the crazy urge to look out for Conrad.

She had managed to project a suitable attitude of coldness towards him, but her mind was a little harder to control. It stubbornly continued to bombard her with sharp, strong images of him which made her blush. She never would have believed that she could close her eyes and feel a rush of sensation, but in the privacy of her bedroom the image of him was so strong that she could almost reach out and touch him. She closed her eyes, and could smell him, see the way his eyes crinkled when he laughed with genuine amusement.

When he finally did make an appearance, it was to find them settled comfortably on the sofa in the sitting-room, sipping coffee, and in Lloyd's case a glass of brandy.

Emma had switched on the stereo, and they were listening to a piece of classical music, which, she had informed Lloyd, would make a change from the pop music which he played every night in his club.

'Besides,' she had added, seeing him make a moue, 'there's not much choice. It's either this, or the pleasant sounds of nothing.'

She had hoped that Lloyd's company would put her in a more relaxed frame of mind, and she had been right. Lloyd did not burden himself with too many worries, not if he could avoid it, and he was blind to other people's worries as well. He was a free spirit and just exactly what Emma needed in the sort of mood that she was in.

Conrad stood at the door, the top buttons of his shirt undone, his hair tousled as though he had just stepped out of bed and had not been bothered to comb it.

Emma raised startled eyes to his.

'We wondered where you had got to,' Lloyd opened jovially.

Conrad walked slowly into the room, and Emma realised with shock that he had been drinking. As he stepped into the light, she could see that he had not shaved and a dark shadow of stubble roughened his face.

'Have you, now?' Conrad muttered through gritted teeth, his eyes not leaving Emma's face.

Lloyd shifted uneasily on the sofa and glanced across at Emma.

'Care to join us in a cup of coffee?' he persevered nervously. 'Or maybe in your case something stronger? The old boy may not have much by way of pop music, but he keeps a comprehensive line in alcohol. You look as if you need it.'

'Really,' Conrad snarled, turning to face him. 'How very observant of you. You clearly missed your calling. You should join the local detective force instead of doing whatever it is you do.'

'Nightclubbing.'

'Oh, yes. Forgot. Nightclubbing.' He dropped each word individually and with contempt.

Emma's initial shock gave way to a rush of anger. How dared he stride into the room and begin insulting her and her guest, who had done nothing to him?

He moved across to the stereo and picked up the Mozart album cover, staring at the record revolving on the turntable.

'Getting in the right mood?' he asked Lloyd sarcastically, then he spun round to Emma, his lips twisted in a sneer. 'I'm surprised you haven't gone the whole hog and dimmed the lights as well. Or did you think that that was just a little bit too passé? Still, I see you've dressed for the occasion.' He ran his eyes slowly over her, from her burning face to the tips of her feet, then back again to her face. 'No? Don't tell me, you always dress like that for dinner with a friend? Right?' He gave a mimicry of a laugh, running his fingers through his black hair.

Emma rounded on him. 'If you have a problem, then I wish you'd go and sort it out somewhere else!' she bit out. 'We'd been having a very pleasant time until you arrived on the scene.'

'Oh, I'm sure you had.'

Lloyd cleared his throat. 'Listen, old chap, why don't you

go to bed and sleep it off? You'll feel much better for it in the morning.'

'Yes,' Emma rejoined sweetly, 'why don't you disappear upstairs and sleep it off?' And I hope, she added silently, you feel anything but better in the morning.

'And leave you two down here?' Conrad looked at her with an expression of incredulity. 'Now that wouldn't be very polite of me, would it?'

'I think I can live with that.' The atmosphere between them was electric. Part of her felt very sorry for poor Lloyd, caught up in their private battle of wills, but it didn't manage to quell the anger inside her.

'No, I don't intend going anywhere. I may be many things, but I'm not impolite.' Conrad sat down heavily in between Lloyd and Emma, and folded his arms in the attitude of someone who had no intention of moving. His leg rested against Emma's and she shifted her position to avoid the contact.

Even in the state that he was in, and with her determination to treat him as part of the furniture, she still could not prevent herself from responding to him.

'Maybe I ought to leave,' Lloyd volunteered, gulping down the rest of his brandy and grimacing.

'Maybe you should,' Emma agreed, glaring at Conrad, who had a satisfied little smile playing on his lips.

She rose to see him out, and Conrad stood up as well.

'There's no need to see us to the door,' she said coldly. 'I know how to find my way there.'

'No bother.'

The three of them walked out in an uncomfortable silence. When they were at the front door, Lloyd turned to Emma and said in a low voice, 'It's been a nice evening.' His eyes flickered across to Conrad and then back to her. 'You know that my invitation for you to come and stay with me in Trinidad still stands. Any time. You're a good friend and I'd love to see you.'

'You might see me sooner than you expect.' Over her shoulder she could feel Conrad hovering, listening to every word that they were saying.

If he weren't a rich industrialist, Emma thought, he'd probably be a thug. He certainly had the makings of one, from the athletic, aggressive body to the air of threat that he could create whenever it suited him. It suited him now, and Lloyd almost ran to his car, only turning to wave at Emma when he was secure behind a locked door.

'Well, I hope you're satisfied!' Emma turned on Conrad, fighting to preserve some modicum of self-restraint.

'Very.' He leant against the door-frame and smiled.

'You ruined my evening!'

'So sorry.' He didn't sound in the least bit sorry. In fact, he sounded extremely smug.

'How much have you had to drink anyway?' Emma asked, walking back into the sitting-room to collect the dirty cups and glasses.

'Nothing.' He followed her, and she could almost feel his warm breath on her neck as she stacked the cups and saucers, balancing them precariously in one hand.

He made her edgy. She wished that he would just go to bed. In fact, she wished that he would just leave the island. He had managed to wreck her life and she needed to be a million miles away from him before she could start piecing it together again.

Instead here he was on her heels, watching as she dumped the dirty dishes in the kitchen sink.

'I think I'll go to bed now,' she said flatly, spinning round to find him standing much closer to her than she had expected. He stepped forward and she stepped back. It would have been amusing if her heart weren't doing nervous little somersaults in her chest.

'I wish that twerp wouldn't keep throwing himself at you.' Conrad was staring at her intently, refusing to step aside and let her pass him.

'Lloyd isn't a twerp.'

'He doesn't have a brain in his body.'

'He runs a nightclub! He can't be that brainless!'

'His partner runs the nightclub. Lloyd provides pretty backing; he doesn't actually make any decisions.'

'I'm not going to stand here discussing Lloyd with you,' Emma said coldly, hoping that he couldn't hear her heart thumping heavily in her chest.

'The most responsible decisions Lloyd makes,' Conrad continued as if he hadn't heard her, 'are what colour shirt he's going to put on in the morning. Does this blue shirt match OK with these checked grey socks? Should he go for the Paisley tie or the striped one?'

Emma didn't say anything. She couldn't deny that Lloyd didn't care overmuch for the grittier side of reality, that applying himself to anything serious would be anathema to him, and it infuriated her that Conrad was pointing out the truth, but in the most cynical way possible.

'I can't imagine what you see in him. Is it because he's pushy?'

'He's not pushy,' Emma defended Lloyd stoutly. 'I wanted to see him this evening, or else he would never have come. Not that it's any of your business, but he was over here for a couple of days and he got in touch. I invited him over to dinner.'

Not quite true, but it was plausible enough.

'Is that a fact?' Conrad caught her by the wrist, pinning her to the spot. He wasn't drunk. She could see that now. He was stone-cold sober, and she could also see that he was holding on to his self-control with difficulty. In the sort of mood he was in, she didn't trust him.

She tried to tug her hand away and instead Conrad pulled

her towards him so that her body was pressed against his. She could almost feel his heart beating under the fine cotton material of his shirt.

She twisted in panic.

'So,' Conrad rasped. 'You invited him here, did you?'

CHAPTER NINE

EMMA felt her skin tingle with alarm.

'Yes,' she muttered stubbornly, in answer to his question.

He was towering over her, his dark face alarmingly menacing. She knew that the best thing to do would be to try and laugh her way out of the situation, although, eyeing him from under her lashes, she wondered whether a forced humour might have just the opposite effect.

'Well, if he has any thoughts of trying on his juvenile charm with you, he'd better have a rethink.'

The unsteady smile died on her lips. She felt the blood rush to her hairline.

'Or else what?' she nearly shouted. 'I can do precisely as I please, and with whom. You may have made love to me but that's as far as it goes. I've already told you that it was a huge mistake anyway! Whatever I choose to do now is none of your business whatsoever.'

'I'm making it my business,' Conrad hissed, his hand tightening on her so that she winced in pain.

'You're hurting me!'

He slackened his grip, and she felt the blood flow back into her veins.

'You can forget about going to Trinidad to visit him,' he said in a low, harsh voice.

It was on the tip of her tongue to tell him that she had no intention of visiting him, but she bit back the words. Let him think the worst. Did she care? He had no right to act the tyrant with her.

'I'll do exactly as I please,' she said, enunciating every

syllable with cold precision. 'If you must know, I was thinking about flying out some time over the weekend.'

She wasn't, but that didn't matter. What mattered was her
need to assert her will.

'Not if I have any say in it.'

Emma's green eyes blazed. 'Stop trying to run my life
for me! Not only do you have me deceiving my grandfather,
but now you're trying to dictate who I see and when.' She
laughed bitterly. 'That might work with those women you
go out with, or sleep with, or even,' she added maliciously,
'get engaged to, but as far as I'm concerned you can just
take a running jump.'

'Would you have been surprised if I *had* had too much
to drink?' Conrad muttered through clenched teeth. 'You'd
drive any sane man to drink.'

'And you'd drive any sane woman right into a mental
asylum!' Emma yelled.

They looked at each other for what seemed like eternity.
In the dim background Emma was aware of the steady ticking of the kitchen clock, the night sounds drifting through
the closed windows, the hum of the refrigerator.

She was trembling all over. From the rage or from the
heady impact of his body against hers, she wasn't sure.
Then, as she opened her mouth to tell him to go to hell,
Conrad bent his head and his lips met hers fiercely, crushing
all attempts to push him away, under the sheer force of his
kiss.

Emma's fists closed uselessly against his chest as she
tried not to succumb to the mounting passion firing within
her.

His long fingers slid along her shoulders and down her
back, and she could feel them with an almost unbearable
intensity.

She heard the sound of her own voice telling him to stop,
but even to her ears it sounded weak with passion.

His teeth bit gently against the soft skin of her neck, and Emma's head dropped back, like a rag doll.

His hands moved to cup her breasts, and Emma's eyes flew open. If she didn't stop him now, if she didn't stop herself now, then there was no doubt that she would be pulled into her own dizzy need to feel him.

'Let me go,' she said, struggling against an aching want, as she felt his thumbs trace slow circular movements against her nipples. Under her hands, his skin was as hot as hers.

'No!' she said in a high, desperate voice, as his hands slid over her stomach. She pushed him fiercely, and he raised his feverish blue eyes to her.

'Leave me alone,' she said in a strangled tone.

'You want me, Emma.' He moved closer to her, and this time she pushed him away, with as much strength as she could muster. 'Don't retreat behind that wall of ice. You want me, I can feel it. When I touch you, you tremble, and when I kiss you I can feel your longing as strong as I can feel my own.'

There was no use in trying to deny it, and she didn't bother.

'I want you to leave me alone,' she whispered. 'I don't want anything to do with you. You can't give me anything, because you have nothing to give. You use people, and I refuse to be used.'

'What the hell are you talking about?'

'You know as well as I do! Don't think for a moment that I can't see you for what you are! Yes, I might be attracted to you, but that doesn't make me a blind fool!'

God, she thought, if only that were true.

She turned away, walking wordlessly out of the kitchen, and then running up the long staircase, taking the steps two by two, until she reached her bedroom door.

She slammed it behind her, leaning against it, shaking as though she had been through some terrible ordeal from which she had only just managed to escape. With quick movements she stripped off her dress, tossing it into a heap on the floor, and then stepped into the shower. She wanted to bathe away the perspiration covering her. Even under the cold, sharp water her body still burned where he had touched her, each touch erotic and tantalising, promising her the sort of fulfilment which she shamelessly craved.

She found it difficult to sleep that night. She would drift into a light doze, only to find some new image of Conrad leaping out at her when she least expected it. If this was love, then what, she thought with sharp agony, was the point? Every inch of her body seemed filled with pain.

She went over in her mind all the details of the evening, trying to read something behind his actions. All she could see was that he didn't want to give her up. She was valuable to him after all, she thought bitterly, in a very literal sense. She was his passport to Alistair's money.

God, and to think that despite all that, knowing what she did, she was still attracted to him. Not merely attracted, but desperately in love with his humorous, intelligent, caustic charm.

If her feelings hadn't been involved, if she had only been able to treat him as a fling, some kind of temporary aberration, then things would have been so easy. She could walk away and put the whole episode down to experience. Wasn't that how her friends reacted when they broke off from their lovers? They shrugged their shoulders, cried for a few days, and then moved on.

But on, no. Not her. Emma buried her face into the pillow to stifle her sobs. Why had she been stupid enough to fall in love with the man?

She cringed with embarrassment as she remembered how she had responded to his expert lovemaking, opening up to him with total abandon. At least, she thought, she had had the courage to run away from him last night, even though it had been the most difficult thing she had ever had to do.

She had listened to common sense, but she couldn't hide from the fact that every nerve in her body had wanted him then as much as she had wanted him on the boat. As much as she had wanted him from the moment she laid eyes on him.

She had hoped that Sophia would have been a deterrent, that seeing them together would help her to fight the weak-minded craving that threatened to suffocate her. But it hadn't. It had only served to make her more ashamed and confused.

She needed strength, and it was the one thing which he drained from her.

Even in the darkness of the bedroom, the mere thought of his strong brown hands exploring every inch of her was enough to make her tremble with desire.

There was no option left open to her now but to confess everything to Alistair, to tell him about their sham engagement and to try and make him see that she had no alternative but to leave the island on the first flight back to England.

She would return as soon as she had managed to pick up some of the pieces of her wrecked life. After all, they still had their book to finish.

She was pale and tense when she knocked on Alistair's bedroom door the following morning.

It was a cruel twist that he was looking better than she had seen him since he was taken ill. He hustled her into the chair closest to him, prattling on about everything from the weather to his health, fussing around her like a mother hen.

Emma bit her lip anxiously, feeling horribly guilty, and waited for a lull in the conversation before she began speaking.

Bit by slow bit she told him about Conrad's idea, about

her agreement, about how much it hurt her to know that they had done the wrong thing.

Alistair listened to her in complete silence, his hands folded on his lap.

'Whose idea was the engagement?' he asked interestedly.

'Conrad's, as a matter of fact.' Emma looked at him in surprise. He had not reacted as she had expected at all. In fact, he had not reacted. He did not seem in the least bit taken aback and she was at a loss to understand it.

'Ah.' Alistair flashed her an avuncular smile.

'Not that it matters,' Emma carried on. 'I agreed, so we're both to blame.'

'Of course,' Alistair soothed. 'It takes two to tango.'

'Aren't you in the least bit disappointed?' Curiosity got the better of her, and she stared at him with open puzzlement.

'These things happen. But why did you decide that now was the time to tell me the truth? Did you think that I had recuperated enough?' He chortled. 'Fancy the pair of you hoodwinking an old man like me. That's not happened to me from as far back as I can remember!'

'We thought that we were doing it for your own good,' Emma rushed in, apologetically. She hoped that he wasn't going to break down. He had taken the revelation so well, but of course it was all a façade.

He was probably going to dissolve into tears any minute now, or else turn away from her in disappointment. Quite possibly both. She looked anxiously at him, waiting for the inevitable.

Instead his sharp eyes returned her stare with equanimity.

'You still haven't answered my question.'

'Question?' Emma asked, bewildered. 'What question?'

'Why did you suddenly decide to tell me about it now?'

'I... Things have changed,' she stammered haltingly.

'Things?'

'Nothing went according to plan.'

'Meaning?'

Emma raised her shoulders helplessly. Why was he asking her this? She had the feeling that she was being kindly but efficiently cross-examined, except for what, she had no idea.

'I…I found out that I couldn't handle the situation.'

It was a flimsy answer, even to her own ears, but she just didn't know what else to say. Alistair had swept aside the whole explanation of their arrangement with a broad-minded wave, and seemed considerably more interested in quizzing her about tiny details which had no bearing on the case at all.

She knew precisely what he would say if she protested. Grandfatherly interest. She had come to realise that he was not without his fair share of tricks which he plucked from up his sleeve without a backward glance. There was no mistaking Conrad's mentor.

'What do you mean, you couldn't handle the situation?'

'Why are you asking me all these questions?' She looked at him with a trace of desperation.

'Grandfatherly interest.'

Emma couldn't hide a smile. 'I knew you'd say that. You're getting predictable in your old age.'

'And you're being evasive.'

'Oh, all right,' she said, giving up, 'I found myself getting too involved with Conrad for my own good.'

'Ah.'

Emma abruptly stood up and went across to the window, staring through it without seeing anything, only aware of feeling thoroughly miserable and horribly vulnerable.

'You've fallen in love with him?'

'More fool me,' she muttered. There was no point in expanding on the subject, and she threw him a look that said that the matter was closed.

'So what are we going to do about the book?' he said with bewildering good humour, changing the subject, much to Emma's relief. 'Not to mention the fact that I'm not going to let you out of my life now that you're here. I've made that stupid mistake once with your mother, and that was once too often. I've been given a second chance with you, and I won't lose you.'

'I'll be back,' Emma responded warmly. 'As soon as I've sorted myself out, I'll be back over. You'll see me before the year's out.'

'Well, you'd better go, then, for the moment. I feel a little tired. And no,' he assured her, reading her expression, 'I'll be quite all right. I just have some thinking to do.'

'Some thinking?' she asked suspiciously.

'Oh, yes, my love. A crossword puzzle I've been working on. I feel I may have solved the last clue.'

'Crossword puzzle? Clue? Grandfather,' she said helplessly, 'sometimes you lose me.'

She turned to leave the room, nodding as he called after her to send Esther up.

It was not yet midday, and already this was proving to be the longest day in her life. The thought of never seeing Conrad again was intolerable. In a way, it was almost better to continue feeling miserable, knowing that he was around, than to return to England and live in a void.

What would she do? The usual routine of theatres and dinners with her friends, some more freelance work although she had nothing lined up, and all the while she would hear the silent sound of the days as they ruthlessly ticked by, reminding her that nothing would ever change.

When she got back to her room, she disconsolately began throwing her clothes into a suitcase, not bothering to think about the horrendous ironing job she would have on her hands when it came to unpacking.

She phoned the airport, only to be told that there were

daily flights to Trinidad, but that all connecting flights from Trinidad to Heathrow were fully booked for the next two days.

'Two days!' Emma wailed. 'Is there nothing sooner than that? Like tomorrow?'

'Sorry,' the man automatically said in his businesslike voice. 'Perhaps you would like me to reserve a seat for you for the flight out this coming Thursday?'

'I… Yes, if you could, please.'

She dully gave details of her name, address and telephone number, mentally trying to work out what she was going to do.

Alistair, when she went to see him, had no solutions to the problem. He shook his head ruefully and gave her a brief lecture on the popularity of flights out of the island during the peak season.

He didn't sound in the least bit sorry that she would not be able to leave immediately. There was a distinct glint in his eyes when he told her that they would be able to do some work on the book after all.

'I can't stay indefinitely, Grandfather,' Emma interrupted him gently. 'It's too awkward.'

'Awkward?'

Emma looked at him impatiently. Hadn't she explained it all to him only a few hours before?

'With Conrad.'

'He'll be leaving by the weekend,' Alistair informed her. 'Going back to work. The business can't run without him forever, you know.'

'Of course not.'

Emma digested this bit of information with a sinking feeling. She hadn't given it much thought, but of course Conrad would be going back to run his companies. Companies didn't just run themselves. They needed someone at the helm. He had already had long enough on the island. Why hadn't she thought about it before? He wouldn't be around, even if she remained here.

Wasn't that just perfect? she told herself, fighting to look pleased with the news.

'Good. I'll cancel my provisional booking and we can get on with the book.'

The phrase 'take up where we left off' sprang to mind, but it seemed so pitifully inadequate that Emma refrained from saying it.

'Good.' Alistair smiled at her in a way that suggested that the conversation was over, and Emma left the room, dawdling on the way back, wondering whether the sun and sea would be so wonderful without Conrad somewhere in the background.

She realised with gloomy resignation that when he wasn't around she felt as though a piece of her was missing.

What a state of affairs for her to have become entangled in. She tried to console herself with the truism that time healed everything. Love would be no exception. In a year's time, she told herself, things mightn't look so bleak, and maybe there would even be someone else around, someone to take Conrad's place.

With a frustrated groan she acknowledged that he had probably spoilt the rest of mankind for her. He had given her something: the bitter-sweet taste of true, burning love. Who could ever provide any kind of replacement for that? One of those well-intentioned colourless men who formed part of her social set? Fat chance!

At least she was doing the right thing in not giving in to him. She told herself to start feeling a little more pleased with herself.

The sight of crumpled clothes, half packed, was just what she couldn't face. She shoved them out of sight on to the chest of drawers and lay down on the bed, covering her face with her hands.

There was a knock on the door, and without bothering to get up Emma mumbled, 'Come in.' Esther, she thought irritably. She didn't want to see anyone, not even kindly Esther. She just wanted to be on her own, to filter everyone else out until those thousands of images of Conrad that filled her mind had been subdued.

She uncovered her eyes, ready to ask Esther if she could come back later on to do the bed, and saw Conrad lounging against the door-frame, looking at her.

He looked alert and watchful, his black hair neatly combed away from his face. He was wearing a pair of faded jeans which emphasised the length of his legs and a pale short-sleeved shirt.

'What do you want?' Emma sprang out of the bed, flushing at the vulnerable position in which he had found her.

Didn't he know that she didn't want to see him? That he was the last person that she wanted to face? Obviously not. You did the right thing, she told herself sternly. He's untrustworthy, never mind how he looks.

'We have to talk.'

'What about?'

Her voice sounded cracked, and she cleared her throat, moving across to the dressing-table and perching on the stool. She would feel more composed the further away she was from the bed.

As though reading the train of her thoughts, Conrad raised one amused eyebrow and proceeded to take her place on the bed.

'About last night, and about what happened on the boat.'

Emma licked her lips which suddenly felt dry.

'We have talked,' she said as casually as she could. 'We talked about it then, and I don't see any point in rehashing the subject. There's nothing more to be said.'

'I think there is.'

'Well, we'll have to agree to differ.'

'Not if I can help it.' He was staring at her in a way that unsettled her. What was it she should remember? Why, she thought frantically, should she be feeling pleased with herself?

She stared back at him, not knowing what to say. A prickle of heat started at her toes and worked its way through her body, until she was burning all over.

'Anyway,' she said stiffly, 'I'd prefer it if you left my bedroom.'

'Why?'

'Because you're invading my privacy,' she said in a tight voice.

'Maybe that's my intention.'

Emma looked at him with alarm. 'That might well be *your* intention,' she said in a colourless, precise voice, 'but it's not mine. I don't want my privacy invaded, least of all by you.'

'Why not? Are you afraid of what you might do, despite all your good intentions?'

'No!'

'Methinks,' he said with wry accuracy, 'the lady doth protest too much.'

'I don't care what you think!'

'Come a bit closer and tell me that.'

Emma remained resolutely where she was. 'Go away. We have nothing to talk about.'

'All right, then, I'll come a bit closer to you. If the mountain won't come to Mahomet, et cetera, et cetera.' He edged himself off the bed, and moved across the room before she had time to take refuge somewhere a little further away.

'Don't try and escape,' he said, reading her mind, and gripping her wrist. Before she could find a suitable retort, he swept her off the stool and carried her struggling to the bed, depositing her ungracefully on it and lying next to her, his arms around her so that she had no room for manoeuvre.

'All right, Mr Strongman. Here I am. You've got me into a position that I can't escape from, and God knows what sort of satisfaction that gives you! If you want to talk, go ahead. Just so long as you leave this room when you're finished, because I don't want to have anything to do with you.'

'You don't mean that.'

'I do!'

'Then why,' he asked with frightening insight, 'are you shivering? If you meant that, you would be lying there as obedient as a mouse and about as responsive.'

Emma stared at him mutinously, hating her body for betraying her.

'Tell me why you don't want anything more to do with me. Answer me that, and I'll leave.'

'Fine!' He wanted to know, then she damn well would tell him. 'You accused me of being a gold-digger,' she said bitterly. 'You had the nerve to insinuate that I was only here for what I could get, when you are hardly an innocent in that area yourself!'

He looked at her with an impatient frown. The man's acting skills, she thought, were beyond compare.

'What the hell are you talking about?'

'Don't try and pretend with me!'

'For God's sake, woman,' he ground out, 'get to the point of this. I haven't got the faintest idea what you're on about. And I'm dying of curiosity.'

'When Sophia called that day to leave that message with you,' she said stiltedly, 'she filled me in on something that hadn't even crossed my mind.'

'Go on.' His voice was soft and menacing, and Emma looked at him warily, wondering whether her confession was such a hot idea. Somewhere at the back of her mind, a vague doubt flitted across. What if Sophia had been wrong?

What if Conrad had no interest in Alistair's money? She ignored it.

'Alistair's money,' she muttered grudgingly. 'She told me that it was common knowledge that you stood to inherit Alistair's money…' Her voice wavered, as the puzzled frown gave way to one of derisive comprehension.

He was beginning to follow the gist of what was about to come, and from the looks of it it didn't thrill him.

'Common knowledge with whom?'

'She said…'

'And you believed her.' He looked at her with disgust and stood up.

'Wouldn't you, if you had been in my place?' she asked defensively.

'No. Because I would have used my little grey cells and worked out that any such suggestion was preposterous.'

'It's not preposterous! It makes sense.'

'Oh, yes? Then perhaps you could fill me in on your line of reasoning.'

The nagging doubts about the validity of Sophia's statement were getting stronger, especially when she looked at the thunderous expression on Conrad's face. Anger and scorn blended together, neither of which were doing anything at all for her confidence.

'Why else would you have been so angry at the thought of my being here?' she asked feebly. 'And after you knew about me, why did you make love to me? You were trying to seduce your way into Alistair's money because… because…'

The words died on her lips. Now that she had spoken them, she was overcome with a desire to take them all back.

It was too late for that, of course. The distaste stamped on his face filled her with the growing horror that not only had she been wrong, but also totally off target.

She looked at him bleakly, wishing that the ground would

suddenly open and swallow her up. She could cope with his anger, his teasing, his insinuations, but his loathing was unbearable.

'You stupid little bitch,' he said in a cold voice. 'Did it ever occur to you that I was angry at the prospect of your being a gold-digger because I had seen it happen once before to Alistair, and because I love him and feel protective about him? And did it ever occur to you that I made love to you because I wanted you? Not,' he bit out, 'that you can possibly accuse me of seducing you, because the feeling at the time, if I recall, was entirely mutual!'

His words lashed her like invisible whips, hurting her in a way she would not have thought possible.

'Also,' he continued relentlessly, 'if you had used that brain of yours, you might have realised that I don't *need* Alistair's money. I have quite enough of my own!'

'Yes, I guess so, but...' She looked away miserably.

'But nothing! You jumped to all the wrong conclusions because it suited you!' He turned towards the door, glancing around when his hand was on the knob. 'If it's of any interest to you,' he said scathingly from over his shoulder, 'I knew that Alistair had a granddaughter anyway. He told me years ago. I never suspected that the granddaughter was you when you showed up here, but I knew of your existence. I've always known where Alistair's money would go, and I've never given it a thought.'

'Why didn't you say?'

'Believe it or not, I didn't think it was relevant. I didn't think that that narrow little mind of yours would work in that direction anyway.'

'You're hardly pure, driven snow yourself!' Emma said in a high, shaky voice. 'You had no qualms about accusing me of something I wasn't guilty of!'

'Don't try and justify yourself by using that argument.' He looked at her with distaste. 'All I can say is that if you believed that of me, then, lady, I was way off target with you. As far as I'm concerned, you're now in the past tense, and my only regret is that I ever had anything to do with you in the first place!'

He left the room, closing the door quietly behind him, and she could hear the sound of his steps echoing on the wooden floor before he descended the stairs.

Then a dead feeling seeped through her, leaving her too numb to cry, too numb to do anything except stare at the ceiling.

She had misjudged him, and he was right, there was no way she could justify her distrust. She had been an utter fool to have ever listened to what Sophia had told her.

She had believed it because she had wanted to. She had used the knowledge to try and shore up her own defences against him because she had been frightened by the power of her love and by her vulnerability to it.

He didn't love her, and in some weird way she'd thought that she might fight her own love for him by believing the worst of him.

God, how wrong she had been! She still loved him with every ounce of her being, and now not only did he not like her, but his lasting memories of her would be ones of loathing.

She buried her face into the pillow and began to cry.

CHAPTER TEN

EMMA awoke to a feeling of disorientation. The room was in blackness, and she realised that she must have fallen asleep.

She didn't have the energy to get out of bed, even though the clock reminded her that it was nearly seven and only thirty minutes away from dinnertime. She didn't much feel like eating either.

She remained lying where she was, making no effort to fight off the misery gnawing away at her insides.

Conrad detested her. That one thought filled her head and beat away in her mind like the repeated throbbing of a drum. He had left her room with the stamp of disgust on his face, and she had no doubt that she would never lay eyes on him again.

The prospect filled her with anguish, and the anguish glued her to the bed, because all incentive seemed to have left her.

She should be relieved at his decision, she knew that. He might have left, she told herself, believing the worst of her, but at least he had left and she would no longer have to fight the feelings that assailed her every time she looked at him or was in his presence.

Hadn't she convinced herself time and again that her love for him would never be returned? In which case it was much better that he was out of sight, because out of sight might one day be out of mind.

Even if she had not believed a word of what Sophia had told her, even if that disastrous conversation between herself

175

and Conrad had never taken place, things would not have been so dramatically altered.

After all, the fact still remained that she was in love with him, fiercely, passionately and hopelessly in love with him. And he wanted her because he fancied her. The two feelings were poles apart and she had always only been the one who stood to lose.

The truth was, if she was going to be honest with herself, that she would not have been satisfied with lust instead of love, and he had no responsibilities towards her. He was as free as a bird, and any fool knew that birds didn't stay in one place for very long.

He might not have been in love with Sophia, but he had been engaged to her. She, for heaven's sake, had had more of a hold over him.

No, things had worked out for the best. That sour taste in her mouth and the gaping despondency in her soul might try and convince her otherwise, but her head would always protest.

She gazed mournfully at the clock, watching the time tick by, knowing that she should rouse herself and go down stairs, but her body felt like lead, and she could feel her eyelids beginning to droop again.

She reluctantly yielded once more to the panacea of sleep.

She awoke suddenly, with the feeling that someone or something had awakened her.

Her eyes took a while to adjust to the darkness, and then she made out the shadowy form of Conrad, sitting on the bed, looking down at her with an expression which she couldn't quite make out.

She sat up hurriedly, rubbing the sleep out of her eyes.

'You!'

'Yes, me,' he said drily.

'What are you doing here?'

'You brought me back.'

He smiled a slow, wry smile and Emma felt her heart skip a beat, then another as he raised his eyebrows and looked at her ruefully.

'Me?'

'Yes, you. You're a witch, I know that now. You cast a spell over me and I found that, however angry you made me, I couldn't leave.'

She looked at him, her eyes wide and questioning.

'But you had left!' she protested, the lingering smile on his lips bringing a flush of colour to her cheeks. 'When you walked out of this room you told me that you were sorry you ever met me, and that you didn't want anything more to do with me!'

'I guess I made a mistake.'

He stroked her hair, and leaned forward to kiss her on her forehead. Emma sank back with a dizzy feeling against the pillows.

Nothing changed the fact that, whatever he was saying to her now, and however appealingly he said it, he still only wanted her. But as his lips descended to meet her own she closed her eyes and decided just to savour this one kiss. The battle would wait until after that.

She kissed him with restless passion, enjoying his low moanings as he moistened her neck with his mouth.

His hand slipped smoothly underneath her white T-shirt to caress the full soft swell of her breasts.

With a mammoth effort, she pulled away from him, and said in a low voice, 'I can't. You may think me silly and gauche, but I can't make love to you when I know that you don't love me in return.'

Conrad gave a soft, delighted chuckle. 'In return?'

'Well, yes.'

'Are you saying that you love me, Emma Belle?'

She flushed and looked away. What was the point of trying to deny it? She had fallen into her own trap, and maybe it was better that she told him anyway.

'I love you, Conrad,' she muttered under her breath.

'I beg your pardon? I didn't quite catch what you said just then. Something about love…?'

She glared at him, and said in a loud voice, 'I love you! You annoy me, you bewilder me, you make me feel as though I have no control over myself, and I love you for it! Is that loud enough for you?'

'Loud and clear.'

She had thrown all caution to the winds, and she didn't much care any longer. She didn't care if he didn't return her love, it only mattered that he knew how she felt, that she had been honest with him.

She braced herself for the pain that would fill her when he told her that he desired her but that, well, as far as love went, now that was a horse of a different colour.

When he did not say anything, she finally raised her eyes to his. He turned away and switched on the bedside light. All at once the room was suffused in an orange glow, and Emma blinked rapidly.

'I want us to see each other,' he said.

Emma didn't want that at all. The darkness at least provided some shield for her. To have her hurt exposed in the brightness of the room was not what she wanted at all.

She lowered her head, and her hair fell in a gold curtain across her face.

'Look at me,' he murmured, tilting her chin up.

Their eyes met, and he said unhurriedly, 'I love you.'

'What?'

'I love you, Emma. What I do for you is exactly what you do for me, and I adore you for it.'

The blood rushed to her head.

'You're joking!' she whispered incredulously.

Conrad shot her a disapproving glance. 'Now, now, m

ittle witch, why do you insist on believing the worst of me? t's a habit you're going to break out of, you know. It loesn't do my confidence any good at all. Still, we've got lifetime of trying to cure that particu-lar—'

'What?'

'Don't tell me you didn't hear. I said we've got a lifetime)—'

'Is that a proposal?' she asked tremulously.

'Oh, haven't I said? Will you, Emma Belle, marry me?' This time the silence was complete. She nodded.

'Yes! Yes, yes, yes!'

'I prayed you might say that.' With a stifled moan, he issed her face, her eyes, her nose, her mouth.

She felt a wonderful release, as though she had spent the ist few weeks balancing precariously on the edge of a cliff, id had now finally found solid ground.

And it felt wonderful.

She sighed with pleasure as he slowly stripped and then roceeded to do the same to her, removing each article of othing with agonising leisure.

Her body was aching for him, and when they were freed their clothing she pulled him towards her, delighting in e feel of his naked flesh against hers.

But he was not rushing things. His lips teased her nipples to arousal, and she felt the warmth of his mouth sucking em, nuzzling her breasts, while he stroked her thighs and omach with his hand.

'I want,' he said huskily, 'to enjoy every inch of you. aking love on the floor of a rocking boat has taught me at I'm too old for that.'

'You seemed to manage all right to me,' she responded nguidly.

'Just all right?'

Her laugh was low and throaty. 'Immodest beast. I knew from the start.'

They made love slowly, as though they had all the time in the world. His mouth caressed the flat planes of her stomach and Emma parted her thighs, drowning in intoxicating need. His tongue delicately circled her navel, and she arched back in pleasure. It was unimaginable that anyone else could arouse her like this. All the men she had been out with were boys in comparison, hollowed-out shells, incapable of exciting her.

When he slid into her, she groaned and moved agitatedly against him.

'God, I've waited for this,' he muttered into her hair.

Emma didn't respond. The waves of pleasure rolling over her had silenced her, had drowned out everything but the delicious fire burning in her.

Was it hours or days later when he lay next to her on the bed, his hand tracing the delicate planes of her face? Emma didn't know. She smiled at him.

'So, Miss Belle, what are you thinking?'

'I'm thinking that another woman might have had all this.' She looked at him from under her lashes, loving the way that his eyes seemed able to darken depending on his mood. They were a deep, drowsy blue now, and she felt her heart quicken.

'Sophia?'

'You were engaged to her! I hate even thinking about it'

'You have yourself to blame for my breaking off the engagement.'

'You? You little liar!' she teased. 'Sophia told me that she broke it off. Some modelling contract.'

'Well, she simply beat me to it, that's all. Thanks to you all my well-ordered plans were scattered to the four winds, hard as I tried to hold them together and pretend that nothing had changed. Sophia's modelling contract was a gift from above.'

His hand circled her waist, gently caressing her stomach, moving up to cup a breast.

She rolled to lie on top of him, sighing as his fingers pressed against the length of her spine. Her hair fell, forming a curtain around his face, and she kissed him hard, feeling the rough stubble on his chin where he hadn't yet shaved.

His body moved under her, and he gripped her from behind until they were moving together rhythmically, as one.

For the first time, she understood how people could lock themselves behind closed doors, and spend days in bed. The idea, which she had used to find incomprehensible, now made sense.

She rolled off, holding him against her, feeling his long, lean legs warm against her own.

'Do you know,' he said, 'that I never imagined, when I was waiting for your plane to land, that the woman who got off would turn out to be a stubborn, outspoken she-devil like you who would open up my eyes to something I'd never experienced before?'

'I could be insulted at that description!'

'But you're not.'

'No, because most of those adjectives happen to fit you as well. When I met you, I thought you were the most arrogant, pig-headed person I had ever laid eyes on.'

Conrad threw her a loving glance of mock hurt.

'Now that's really wounding!'

'You're too immodest ever to be wounded!'

'Not true,' he said soberly. 'I would have been more than wounded if I had had to face the prospect of life without you. Just the thought of ever being apart from you makes me sick.'

They looked at each other in silence for a while, then Conrad murmured, 'I can't live without you, my darling. Do you know that, that night when I came back here looking like something the cat brought in, I'd spent the whole time staring at the sea, trying to work out how I had managed to fall so utterly under your spell. When I got back here to find you and Lloyd like a couple of lovebirds on the sofa…'

His voice hardened, and Emma giggled contentedly.

'We were not like a couple of lovebirds,' she protested. 'We were just chatting about cinema shows and his love-life, of all things.'

'Well, you may not have been cuddling up to him,' Conrad agreed, 'but there was no way that I was going to chance anything happening by vanishing upstairs to bed. Which is what you asked me to do, if I recall.'

'So I gathered. Lloyd was very embarrassed. So far you've been in a foul mood every time you've seen him.'

'You mean the beach?' Conrad said wryly.

'The beach. When I saw you in such an evil temper, I thought that you had had a falling out with Sophia, and then later on she rang and told me that the engagement was off. I guessed that you had taken the news badly.'

'Were you jealous?'

'A bit,' Emma admitted, thinking that that was the un-derstatement of the year.

'You needn't have been. Actually, like everything else since I met you, you were the cause of that.'

Emma looked at him mockingly, feeling his body stir under her.

'Don't play the wide-eyed innocent with me. You can guess why I was in a bad mood.'

'Tell me anyway,' she said lazily, moving closer to him.

'You and that damned Lloyd. That boy has a lot to answer for. When I saw the two of you frolicking together at the beach, I saw red. Never mind about the engagement. That was trifling next to the rage that came over me—he was all over you. I had half a mind to find some excuse to come and drag you forcibly out of the water and bring you back home where I could safely keep my eye on you.'

Emma tried to imagine the scene that would have occurred, and almost wished that he had done just that, although she had no doubt that she would have protested as loudly as she could.

'Why did you ask Sophia to come over here?' Emma asked, suddenly remembering what Sophia had told her at the party.

'Oh, she told you, did she?'

'Not nastily. Just by way of conversation. She said that you insisted that she join you here, and that she came because it was so out of keeping with you.'

'And you put two and two together and came up with five.'

'I thought that you couldn't do without her, if that's what you mean.'

'Precisely what I mean.' He looked at her sideways and she blushed. 'As a matter of fact, I did ask her to come over. To protect me from you.'

Emma stared at him in disbelief. If there was one person in the world who looked less in need of protection, it was Conrad. She could well imagine other people needing protection from him, but not the other way round.

'I was already starting to realise the effect that you had on me,' he continued. 'I thought that it was just my imagination, but just in case I decided to get Sophia over to help put things into perspective. I never believed in love; I certainly never believed that it would hit me like the proverbial thunderbolt. I was wrong.'

'I'd never have guessed,' Emma commented. She remembered thinking how jealous she had been of Sophia. Just seeing them within a foot of each other had been enough to spark off a depth of misery which she had not known herself capable of feeling. If he had not believed in love, then she certainly had likewise thought herself immune to it. When the virus had attacked her, she'd been knocked for six.

'You weren't supposed to,' Conrad remarked drily. 'Falling for you was something I couldn't handle. I could cope with the prospect of an arranged marriage, for all the convenient reasons, but you made me see fast enough that I would have to scrap that idea. Even then, I didn't want to let on to myself what was happening. I kept thinking that I ought to return to work, but somehow I carried on finding reasons to stay.'

Emma watched his dark, striking face and wondered what would have happened if he had called it a day and flown back to London. Would she have recovered? She shuddered at the mere thought of it.

'I did think that your short break for a bit of rest and relaxation was dragging on a bit,' she said pensively.

'So did Gregory Palin at Head Office. I remember him phoning not once but three times, and at last I could use the truthful excuse of telling him that Alistair was ill and I couldn't leave the island until he had recovered. Funny, but I've never suffered from nerves. I could face a hall of stockholders and talk to them without the slightest twinge.'

He looked at her accusingly before continuing, 'From as far back as I can remember, I've made decisions, tackled trade unions, and relished every moment of it. I thought that I was immune to anything remotely resembling uncertainty. I never dreamt that I would meet a woman who could make me a wreck all in a matter of a few weeks.'

He grimaced and Emma laughed softly.

'You might well laugh,' Conrad said drily, 'but I've never had to put myself out for any woman until you waltzed into my life, and then all of a sudden I found myself acting totally out of character. I started being irritated by all kinds of doubts about marrying simply because it was a suitable arrangement, even if Sophia was quite prepared to do the same, and then, even worse, I discovered that I was shying away from the thought of having to leave the island.'

Emma looked at him with amusement, and saw from the flicker of expression on his face that he was still amazed at it.

'I'm glad you stayed,' she whispered, thinking that that was the understatement of her life.

'You didn't give me much choice. You argued with me, gave me sleepless nights, laughed at me. I hope you're satisfied.'

'I couldn't be more satisfied. And, if it's any consolation, you did the same.'

'Good.'

They laughed, and he kissed her gently and lingeringly.

'I only hope that you're not too much of a distraction when we get married.'

'Who, me?' Emma looked at him innocently and grinned. 'This,' she said, 'should ensure that Alistair's back on form in no time at all. I was worried when I told him that the engagement had all been a sham, and that I had fallen in love with you but that it was one way.'

She tried to remember it, but it seemed like a million years away. 'I knew he would have to have found out eventually about us, about the fact that it was all a clever idea on your part to help him recuperate more quickly, but I still hated telling him. I felt like a traitor.'

Conrad shot her an amused glance.

'What's so funny?' Emma asked curiously.

'You are.'

'Me?'

'The situation. What did Alistair say to you when you told him?'

Emma thought back. 'He didn't seem as upset about it as I had thought he was going to be,' she said. 'In fact, he hardly seemed upset at all.'

'The wily old so-and-so.'

Emma looked at Conrad in surprise. 'Why do you say that?'

'Because, my beauty, we weren't the only ones playing the pretend game. Alistair was at it as well.'

Emma propped herself up on her elbow and stared at Conrad, trying to figure out what on earth he was talking about.

'What do you mean, he was at it as well?' she asked, rubbing her ankle against his leg.

Conrad pulled her down to him. 'Don't do that,' he said with a wicked smile.

'What?'

'Slide your foot against my leg. Not when I'm trying to tell you something serious. It throws me off course.'

Emma continued, liking the power of being able to throw Conrad off course. It gave her a satisfying tickle of delight

'Where was I?' he asked.

'Alistair.'

'Oh, yes. He confessed all to me when I went to see him after I had stormed out of your bedroom. Apparently, he wasn't ill at all.'

'What?' Emma stared at Conrad's face in astonishment.

'The day we rushed back from the party, imagining the worst, it had all been a false alarm, only Alistair decided not to enlighten us.'

'You mean we worried in vain?'

Conrad nodded in amused resignation.

'Alistair was apologetic about the whole thing, but he said that he saw it as a golden opportunity to throw us together. He didn't imagine that we would get engaged, I think he saw that as a bonus from heaven, but he did think that wouldn't have done any harm if we were united over our concern for him.'

'But what about the doctor?' Emma asked, beginning to see the humorous side of it all.

'Ah. Well, Alistair was ill when he called the doctor out, but it turned out to be only an acute attack of indigestion. Hence his insistence that the doctor not breathe a word to us about his condition.'

It was beginning to slot together. 'But he told us that the doctor said that he didn't know how much longer Alistair had got to live.'

'Poetic licence there. Alistair unconvincingly argued with me that he never told us that he only had a short while left. He said that he told us that the doctor didn't know how much longer, but that it could be decades. Who was to tell? Can anyone predict the length of life given to them? We, he pointed out, merely put the wrong interpretation on his sentence.'

'Well, I never…' Emma settled comfortably against Conrad, feeling the bristle of hair against her breasts.

She was glad that she had worried in vain, and in a way Alistair's ploy had worked. It had thrown them together, even if the method had been a little devious. She would have to have stern words to him about that. Maybe.

She smiled to herself and kissed Conrad's neck, her tongue tracing little patterns on it.

With a low moan, his hand slid around her waist, and he pulled her close to him.

'So all's well that ends well,' he said huskily.

'Are you going to spend the rest of the day talking,' Emma asked wickedly, 'when there's so much more we could be doing?'

'Like what?' Conrad's blue eyes met hers and he raised his eyebrows questioningly.

'You're right. Let's carry on the conversation.'

'We will, you little vixen,' he murmured warmly, 'but later.'

Emma sighed happily. There would be a lot of 'later's from now on.

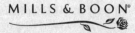

MILLS & BOON®

Live the emotion

PENNINGTON

Catherine George
PENNINGTON
Bargaining with the Boss

BOOK TEN

Available from 2nd April 2004

*Available at most branches of WHSmith, Tesco, Martins, Borders,
Eason, Sainsbury's and most good paperback bookshops.*

PENN/RTL/10

THE
LITTLE NUT
BOOK

Rosamond Richardson

PIATKUS

Other titles in the series

The Little Green Avocado Book
The Little Garlic Book
The Little Pepper Book
The Little Apple Book
The Little Strawberry Book
The Little Lemon Book
The Little Mushroom Book
The Little Bean Book

© 1983 Judy Piatkus (Publishers) Limited

First published in 1983 by Judy Piatkus
(Publishers) Limited of Loughton, Essex

British Library Cataloguing in Publication Data

Richardson, Rosamond
The little nut book.
1. Nuts
I. Title
641.3′4′5   TX399

ISBN 0-86188-406-X

Drawings by Linda Broad
Designed by Ken Leeder
Cover photograph by John Lee

Typeset by V & M Graphics Ltd, Aylesbury, Bucks
Printed and bound by The Pitman Press, Bath

CONTENTS

I had a little nut tree
Nothing would it bear
But a silver nutmeg
And a golden pear.
The King of Spain's daughter
Came to visit me
And all for the sake
Of my little nut tree.

Traditional

WHAT IS A NUT?

By definition a nut is a fruit which consists of an edible, usually single, kernel enclosed in a hard shell; often 'nut' means just the kernel itself. But a nut has come to mean much more than just a kernel. Your nut is your head, and when you go off your nut you go mad; in a nutshell, you are a nutcase! A hard nut to crack is a difficult problem or person; you can be nuts about somebody; or you can't cook for nuts. At the beginning of this century a 'knut' was a swell or dandy. And the rounded shape of the nut has given its name to the doughnut. Nuts have spawned a verb 'to go a nutting'; and Nut-Monday, the first Monday in August, used to be observed as a holiday.

NUTS AND NUT TREES

THE ALMOND TREE

The almond tree (*Prunus dulcis*) is very like a peach tree in appearance, but longer-lived and larger – it can reach about 30 feet in height. The crop is of great importance in the Mediterranean basin, in California and in Australia.

There are two kinds of almond, sweet and bitter: the former is grown for its crop of nuts, the latter for the oil in the kernel which is an important source of

Prussic acid. These kernels should *not*, therefore, be eaten raw – not that their bitterness is at all appetizing. The sweet almond rarely bears mature fruit in Britain, and both species are grown chiefly for their astonishing beauty in flower.

The fruit resembles an immature peach, but does not become fleshy and juicy, splitting open early to reveal the ripening nut within. The nut has a hard, woody shell harbouring one white seed in a brown skin – very occasionally there are two seeds in one shell. They are used in confectionery for nougat, sugared almonds and macaroons, and are an important source of almond oil. Over one half of the weight of the nut is oil, which is used in the manufacture of flavouring extracts, and for cosmetics, perfumery and pharmaceutical products. Almonds are harvested by knocking and gathering, or by jarring from the tree with the use of long poles.

'With many a bud if flowering Almonds bloom,
And arch their gay festoons that breathe perfume,
So shall thy harvest like profusion yield,
And cloudless suns mature the fertile fields.'

Virgil

2

THE SWEET CHESTNUT TREE

Castanea sativa, known as sweet chestnut, European Chestnut and Spanish Chestnut, grows all over Southern Europe, North Africa and South Asia east to the Caucacus. In Britain they are planted mainly for decorative purposes, for the nuts seldom ripen to full size in an unsympathetic climate. It is a prolific seeder; the burr-like fruits each contain two or three nuts inside a leathery, spiny husk.

The wood and bark of the sweet chestnut are rich in tannin, which is used to convert raw hides into leather. The timber is firm and durable, and has been used over the centuries for furniture, dimension timbers, panelling, joinery and fencing. It makes good charcoal and is used for paper pulp.

The sweet chestnut has played a part in folk medicine: a tincture of the leaves cured chilblains, eczema and rheumatism. An infusion of the bark was a remedy for fevers and ulcer pain; chestnut powder relieved colic and intestinal disorders, and an essence of chestnuts boiled in water, added to the bath water, soothed skin troubles.

* Keep a chestnut, begged or stolen, in your pocket as a charm against rheumatism.

THE COCONUT PALM

This best-known of palms (*Cocos nucifera*) is a native of Indo-Malaya and grows near to the sea on low-lying areas a few feet above high water. It acquires about twelve new leaves each year, and sports 10,000 male flowers and 30 female on its compound flower-stalks, which mature at different times to ensure cross-pollination. It first flowers when five years old, and reaches full fruit-bearing in 15 years. The fruits take one year to ripen, and the annual yield of a mature coconut palm is between 50 and 100 nuts. The tree lives for about 50 years.

The hard, woody nutshell, covered with sandy-brown fibrous hairs, has three 'eyes': from one of these a young tree shoots, from the other two its roots. Harvesting takes place five or six times a year, either by collecting fallen nuts, or by picking by human climbers, the most expert of whom can deal with 25 palms in a day.

Copra, the dried nut-mead from which coconut oil is expressed, is produced in huge quantities in the Philippines and Indonesia. The Indonesians have a saying that there are as many uses for the coconut palm as there are days in the year. The oil is used to make soaps, shampoos, detergents, cooking oils, margarines, vegetable shortenings, synthetic rubber, glycerine, hydraulic brake-fluid and platicizers for safety-glass. Purified and de-odorized it becomes cocoa-butter for use in cosmetics. Copra meal is fed to livestock and used in fertilizers. A drink called toddy is made from fermented coconut milk, which, when distilled, becomes a kind of brandy called 'arrack'. The fibrous husk, or coir, is used to make ropes, mats, cables, baskets, brushes, brooms and furniture stuffing. The young buds are eaten in salads or as a vegetable known as 'palm cabbage'. The mature leaves are used in thatching and basketry, the timber in constructing native huts as well as being exported as cabinet wood under the name of 'porcupine wood'. All these uses have been known for centuries.

'The Indian nut alone
Is clothing, meat and trencher, drink and can,
Boat, cable, sail, mast, needle, all in one.'

George Herbert (1593–1633)

THE HAZEL TREE

The hazel or filbert (*Corylus avellana*) is cultivated throughout Europe, Turkey and the US for its nuts. It is a familiar hedgerow shrub or small tree in England, bearing its bright tassels of 'lambs' tails' in February, and offering our bleak winter landscape its first touch of colour. These catkins are the male flowers, and the female flowers are smaller, tiny buds with protruding red tassels.

The nuts grow in clusters of usually four, but sometimes three or two, and are partly encased in overlapping bracts. They are rich in oil (as much as 65% of the nut's weight is oil), small and enclosed in a hard smooth golden-brown shell.

The hazel has traditionally been coppiced for its tough and pliable wood, from which, over the centuries, countrymen have made hurdles, fencing, wattle and daub, and basketwork. It makes an excellent laid hedge and is the proverbial twig for a divining rod. The oil from the nut is used in the preparation of cosmetics and perfumes.

THE PEANUT PLANT

The peanut (*Arachis hypogaea*) is not a true nut. It is really the seed from the pod of an annual leguminous plant. However, it is universally called and accepted as a nut.

The peanut is a native of tropical South America, and is now cultivated in Asia, Africa, Australia and the Americas. To mature properly peanuts need five months' warm weather with a growing season rainfall of anything between 24 and 40 inches. They are prized for their edible oil as well as for their nuts, which have been used in oriental cooking for centuries, and which are now enjoying a world-wide boom in the snack-market. The peanut plant has many other uses, too: the discarded plant can be used for hay, and some farmers give their swine peanut plants as fodder. The oil, which constitutes half the weight of the nut, is used in soaps, margarines, ink, lipstick, paint, explosives, paper, flour, milk, shaving cream, washing powder, metal polish, bleach, axle-grease, lino, rubber, cosmetics, shampoo, ice cream and cheese. The nuts are made into peanut butter and various types of confectionery like caramel, marshmallows, peanut brittle and chocolate-coated peanuts. The shells are used in wallboard, kindling and cat-litter; the skins in the manufacture of paper.

Many Africans regard the peanut as being one of several plants possessing a soul.

THE WALNUT TREE

A handsome, spreading tree, the English or Persian Walnut (*Juglans regia*) can live for several centuries and grow to between 100 and 150 feet tall. The nut-hulls or 'shucks' are smooth, green and glossy and about ⅓ inch thick. The nuts themselves are straw-coloured with a bony shell. One single tree can yield 150 lbs nut in a year.

The exact origin of the walnut tree is uncertain, but it is thought to have come from Asia Minor and spread east from Persia to Afghanistan, through the Himalayas to China.

Apart from its harvest of nuts, the walnut tree has a variety of uses: its fine, hard timber has been prized by cabinet-makers for centuries, and has also been much used for gunstocks. A liqueur called 'brou' is made from the shucks, and the fragrant leaves are an aromatic addition to a pot-pourri. The juice from the leaves stains skin brown, and was even used by gypsies to make their faces darker. John Loudon's *Suburban Gardener* claims that a decoction of walnut leaves kills slugs!

* At one time in the stableyards of all country houses and farms a walnut tree was to be found as it keeps flies away from the horses.

SOME MINOR NUTS

BEECHNUT

Although it has relatively little importance as human food, the mast of the common beech tree (*Fagus sylvatica*) has been used in times of famine and shortage, and in parts of Europe is used to make a pleasant-tasting salad oil. The principal use of the nuts however is as a source of food for game and swine, and the French used them for feeding their pheasants and fattening domestic poultry.

BETELNUT

This is the fruit of the Areca or Betel Palm, a native of Malaysia. It is a maritime species, widely cultivated in India and Ceylon, Malaysia and the Philippines. The nut is a mottled grey and brown colour, nestling in the centre of a fruit which is about the size of a hen's egg. These bright orange fruits are gathered before they are quite ripe, and the husks are removed. The seeds are then boiled and either dried in the sun until they are almost black, or cured. They measure about 1 – 1½ inches in diameter, have a high carbohydrate content and are lowish in protein.

It is calculated that one-tenth of the world's population indulges in betel-chewing: a small piece of the seed is wrapped in a leaf of the betel-vine, and sometimes other spices are added. The chewing stimulates a flow of saliva which temporarily dyes the mouth, lips and gums brick-red. Contrary to popular belief, the teeth of habitual chewers are not permanently blackened by the betel juice – and indeed it is supposed to prevent dental decay – but continued use can cause oral carcinoma. The fresh nuts have intoxicating properties and can cause dizziness. The husks are used in tanning, and the nuts contain an alkaloid called arecoline, which is used as a vermifuge.

BRAZIL NUTS

The Brazil nut is the large seed of *Bertholletia excelsa*, a majestic tree which grows up to 144 feet in height. It is a native of Central America and northern South America, and is especially common in Brazil and Paraguay. The firm, round fruit of the tree contains between eight and 24 nuts which are arranged like orange segments. These are harvested between January and June, and with some considerable difficulty, because of the height of the tree and the weight of the fruit. The shell of the nut has three sharp edges and is brown and hard.

CASHEW NUT

The cashew tree is a native of Brazil. The tree bears a pear-shaped 'cashew-apple' which has a thin, glossy skin and juicy edible flesh. It varies in colour from red to yellow, and it is to the end of this apple that the cashew nut is attached, sunk into the calyx end like a kind of exterior seed. It turns greyish-brown when ripe, is between $\frac{1}{2}$ – 1 inch long and is shaped like a thick letter C. It has two shells: the outer one is slightly elastic, the inner one hard enough to require cracking. Between the two is a brown oil which can cause severe blistering, but if removed with care can be used in industry as a lubricant, a waterproofing agent, a preservative on light woodwork and in the production of plastics. Tannin from the leaves and bark is used as a dye, the sap is used as indelible ink for marking linen, and the tree produces a gum which is insecticidal. The timber is used for packing cases, boatbuilding and charcoal.

Cashew nuts have a fine flavour and an appetizing creamy texture, not to mention a high food value. The nuts, dried and roasted, are rich in protein and have a calorific value of about 200 calories to the ounce. India is the largest exporter of cashews in the world, the US the largest importer.

The cashew apple is eaten throughout South America and has a pleasant, slightly sharp taste. It is eaten not only fresh, but made into delicious jams and jellies, as well as a refreshing drink. Fermented, it makes a wine very popular with the Brazilians, and also a vinegar known as 'anacard'.

COCO DE MER

The Coco de Mer, or Double Coconut, is the fruit of a palm native to the Seychelles. The fruits, or nuts, among the largest known, take ten years to ripen and are two-lobed, suggesting a double coconut. A fleshy, fibrous envelope surrounds the hard nut-like part, whose contents are edible. The empty fruits, freed of their germinated seed, are found floating in the Indian Ocean – hence the name 'coco de mer'.

MACADAMIA NUT

This lovely, round, white, skinless kernel is the fruit of an Australian tree whose aboriginal name is *kindal kindal*. It is a difficult nut to penetrate, being surrounded by a tough brown shell about ½ inch thick, and then a husk. It has been cultivated commercially in Hawaii ever since its introduction there in 1892. It is a delicious dessert nut, lovely in fruit salads, and is also delectable with meat and fish. It has a low protein content but is high in calories since it contains a large percentage of oil.

PECAN NUT

The Pecan is the most important nut-producer of the genus *Carya*, commonly called Hickory. To produce good kernels pecans need high summer temperatures both day and night, so it is seldom found in Europe, although some trees around Bordeaux bear ripened fruit. It grows well in the central and southern states of America.

The Hickory is mostly valued for its timber, although several hickory nuts are important food crops, of which the pecan is the sweetest and most sought-after. The nuts have mottled brown shells of a long cylindrical shape, and their size can vary from 45 to 200 nuts to the lb. The nuts are high in fat content and contain valuable protein, provide 180 calories to the ounce, and are a valuable source of food. The Spanish explorer de Vaca tells us in his log of Indians who survived two months of the year by eating these nuts alone, which they stored like squirrels for the leanest days of winter.

PINE NUTS

Pine nuts are the seeds of several species of pine trees found in the Americas, Europe and parts of Asia. Two in particular, *Pinus edulis* or Nut Pine, and *Pinus pinea* or Stone Pine, yield the tastiest nuts, and they have been prized as protein-rich food since the days of ancient Rome. The seeds from other species produce a fine oil used in cooking and also for lamps.

PISTACHIO

The Queen of Sheba is said to have eaten pistachios with pleasure, and they are an ancient symbol of happiness. The tree guaranteed joy and plenty to lovers who met beneath its branches.

The fruits of this deciduous tree, *Pistacia vera*, are extensively used for food as well as food-colouring, and the tree is now widely cultivated from Afghanistan to the Mediterranean, in West Africa, and to a small degree in California. The nuts, which look like olives and grow in grape-like clusters, are from ¼ inch to ¾ inch long, whitish and with a tendency to split open down one side. Each nut is enclosed by a wrinkled, reddish skin, and the outer shell is bony. The pistachio has a subtle and pleasing flavour and is fairly rich in fat. The husks contain tannin which is used for dyeing and tanning.

WATERCHESTNUT

A member of the Evening Primrose family, the waterchestnut is an annual, floating aquatic plant found from Europe to the Middle East, and in the Asiatic sub-tropics. It grows abundantly in the slow-moving waters of the Yangtze river, and since it multiples rapidly it can cause blockages, as in the Potomac river below Washington, where it has naturalized.

The fruit is relatively large, about ¾ inch long, and either conical or a flattened triangular shape. It has a leathery skin and four spiny horns. It is an important source of human food, and is so-called after its slight resemblance to the sweet chestnut and the similar use to which it is put. It is rich in starch, like the chestnut, and contains nitrogen compounds and mineral salts.

THE NAMES OF NUTS

Almond (Prunus dulcis): Prunis dulcis means 'sweet plum-tree', and the almond is its seed. This latter name derives from the Old French 'amande' and Low Latin *amandula*, which word gave to Italian its *mandorla*, the familiar almond shape in medieval art which encloses God, Christ and the Virgin Mary in a symbolic intersection of the spheres of heaven and earth, spirit and matter.

Betelnut (Areca cathecu): This is a 17th-century name from the Portuguese *betel*, the plant *piper betel*. A 1813 edition of a Dictionary of the Portuguese and English Languages says: 'The leaf is the delight of the Asiatics; for men and women, from the prince to the peasant, have no greater pleasure than to chew it all day in company; and no visit begins or ends without this herb. The "betel" makes the lips so fine, red and beautiful, that if the European ladies could they would purchase it for the weight in gold.'

Cashew (Anacardium occidentale): Cashew is an 18th-century name for a nut called by eastern Brazilian tribesmen *acaju*. The Portuguese knew it and called it *caju*, from which we have the English 'cashew'. Sixteenth-century botanists called it 'elephanten lause', elephant louse, a name highly descriptive of its fat, curved, smooth 'C' shape.

Chestnut (Castanea sativa): The chestnut gets its name from an ancient city Castanea, in what is now Turkey, where it grew in profusion and was much admired for its beautiful foliage and nourishing nut. It is also known as Spanish Chestnut because Britain has imported chestnuts from Spain for centuries.

Coconut (Cocos nucifera): In the 16th century, when the Portuguese were bringing coconuts back in quantity from the Maldive Islands, they gave them the name 'cocus' or 'coco' from their word *macaco*, meaning a monkey's grinning face, or a bogeyman.

This association has stayed with us to this day, as Coco the Clown illustrates: there is a strong resemblance between his face and the 'face' of the coconut with its shaggy hair and round depressions which look like eyes and mouth. By the 17th century the name 'coconut' was in popular use.

Hazel, Filbert or Cobnut (Corylus avellana): Hazel gets its generic name *Corylus* from the Greek *korus*, a cap, describing the shape of its husks. Its specific name, *avellana*, is said to have come from Abella, a town in ancient Campania where, according to Pliny, it originated. The popular name 'Cobnut', in the 15th century 'cobill nut', describes a rounded cobble-shape. Children used to play conkers using hazelnuts, and the winning nut was the 'cob'.

The three common names – Hazel, Filbert and Cobnut – are based on the relative length of the husk compared with the nut: filberts are those with husks distinctly longer than the nuts; cobs are those with nuts and husks of equal lengths; and hazels have husks shorter than the nuts. So filberts were long nuts, cobs of medium length and hazels short and roundish. In 1942 the American Joint Committee on Horticultural Nomenclature officially recognized 'filbert' as the one name which should be applied to this genus.

Hickory (Carya spp.): This very English-sounding name is short for the American-Indian *pawcohiccora*, or *pokahickory* as the pioneer settlers pronounced it. It was the name given to the milk from pounded hickory nuts and the word was recorded by a Virginia settler, Captain John Smith (1580 – 1631).

Peanut (Arachis hypogaea): A 19th-century name describing the podded fruit so reminiscent of the pea, it is also known as Groundnut and Earthnut because it grows beneath the surface of the soil. Its specific name *hypogaea* comes from two Greek words meaning beneath the ground. Monkey-Nut describes what people felt about its value as food before the present upsurge in its popularity.

Pecan (Carya illinoiensis): The 18th-century name for this nut was 'paccan', from American-Indian meaning a nut which is difficult to crack.

Pistachio (Pistacia vera): Pistachio gets its name from the Greek *pistake* meaning pistachio tree.

Walnut (Juglans regia): The Old English for this nut tree was 'walhknutu', a foreign nut, because it was the nut from Gaul, the land of foreigners, brought here by the Romans. *Juglans* comes from the Latin *Jovis glans*, Jupiter's acorn, evidently food for the gods. *Regia* means royal, fit for a king, and it has been known in the past as Royal Nut, and also as Persian Nut, a name which reflects its suspected origin, although it may originally have come from China.

THE HISTORY OF NUTS

ALMOND

Well over a thousand years ago the Phrygians of Asia
Minor regarded the almond as the sacred tree of life,
and even further back in time the Ancient Greeks
created a lyrical legend about its origin. Phyllis, a
beautiful Thracian queen, fell in love with Demophoon, the son of Theseus and Phaedra, and they
were married. Soon after, he was shipwrecked on the
coast of Thrace while returning from the Trojan
Wars, and immediately afterwards was recalled to
Athens on the death of his father. He promised his
royal bride faithfully to return within a month, but
failed to do so. Phyllis, distracted at his absence,
pined away and died of grief, and was transformed
into an almond tree. When eventually Demophoon
returned and heard what had happened, he ran to the
tree and clasped it in his sorrow, and, although it was
bare of leaves, the branches suddenly burst forth
with beautiful blossoms, as if the queen were

acknowledging his repentance and showing him the unchangeability of her love.

Traces go back even further. The almond tree is mentioned frequently in the Book of Genesis. It may have been one of the fruits of the Tree of Knowledge, and almonds were among the fruits offered to Joseph. Aaron's magic rod, which budded and bore fruit in the Tabernacle in the course of one day, was an almond branch. 'It budded and brought forth buds, and bloomed blossoms, and yielded almonds' (Numbers XVII 8). The seven-branched candlestick in the Temple Sanctuary in Jerusalem had its sconces in the form of almonds in a representation of Aaron's rod when it budded. It was this branch that Jeremiah was shown as a visionary token that God had granted him prophetic wisdom. There is a legend that the original Aaron's rod was kept safe and finally came to Rome to become the staff of the Pope. Today, sugared almonds are the traditional gift exchanged at baptisms in the Catholic church.

Rich in legend, the flowering almond is the tree of the Madonna, symbolizing fruitfulness on the one hand and purity on the other, because of its beautiful blossoms borne on bare branches. If the sweet almond is a harbinger of Spring, the bitter almond is an emblem of grief.

The almond has been grown in England since the 16th century or earlier, principally for the loveliness of its rosy pink blossoms. It was transported to the Americas from Spain by Franciscan fathers in 1769.

SWEET CHESTNUT

The majestic beauty of the sweet chestnut has been an inspiration to artists since the days of the Greeks and Romans, and it has also provided a rich source of food to man and animals alike. Indeed, the chestnuts of Asia Minor supplied Xenophon's entire army with food during one of his campaigns.

The tree has been known to grow to immense proportions and to a great age: the largest chestnut on record, growing at the foot of Mount Etna in the last century, was reputed to have a girth of 204 feet and to be over 2000 years old – so Plato would have known it as an old tree when he lived nearby in Syracuse! Tradition has it that this giant supported a colony of nut-gatherers who gradually destroyed the tree by cutting off its branches to stoke the fires on which they were cooking the nuts. Other sources say that it was destroyed by volcanic action.

The sweet chestnut ranges through much Mediterranean woodland, and is found in Asia Minor and North Africa as well. It has been successfully propagated in England, India and Australia, and in the 19th century it was established in the eastern United States as well as on the Pacific coast. At the turn of 20th century, however, disaster struck: sweet chestnuts became infested with a fungus disease, inadvertently introduced on stock from the east. It spread rapidly from Long Island across the North American continent, and within 35 years countless thousands of dead trees stood silent witness to one of the world's greatest forest tragedies. The Americans have now introduced two different species of chestnut to replace the dead ones, so gradually new plantations will replace the decimated trees.

It is probable that it was the Romans who introduced the sweet chestnut into Britain, very likely as a food plant. Chestnuts are eaten raw or boiled or roasted, and the smaller ones are dried and milled into a flour with a sweetish flavour and agreeable smell. This 'flour' has been used for centuries, especially in Corsica, for making a kind of porridge, a polenta, a yeast-cake and thick fritters. The flour also makes a non-elastic paste when mixed with water, and the smaller nuts make fodder for swine. John Evelyn (1620–1706) reckoned that in his time this use of the chestnut for peasant food had led it to be underrated by the British:

'But we give that fruit to our Swine in England, which is amongst the delicacies of Princes in other Countries; and being of the larger Nut, is a lusty, and masculine food for Rustics at all times. The best Tables in France and Italy make them a service, eating them with Salt, in Wine, being first *rosted* on the Chapplet; and doubtless we might propagate their use, amongst our common people, at *lest* being a Food so cheap, and so lasting.'

COCONUT

Famed as one of the world's most important crop-trees, coconuts have been dispersed all over the tropics, partly by ocean currents but mostly by man. It is the natives' 'king of plants', being a primary source of food and a major cash-crop. The Sanskrit for coconut, *kalpa vriska*, means a tree which gives all that is necessary for living, describing the many uses to which the fruit, leaves and timber are put. Marco Polo was one of the first Europeans to describe coconuts, and the later great voyages of discovery such as that of the navigator-cum-pirate-cum-Royal Navy Commander William Dampier (1652–1715) brought the coconut to its long-established familiarity in the West.

HAZEL

The many ancient traditions associated with hazel have elevated it to a status approaching the sacred. The holy family rested under a hazel tree during their flight from Egypt, and a hazel tree offered shelter to the Blessed Virgin Mary when she was caught in a storm on her way to visit her cousin Elizabeth, who was also with child. There is a Hebrew legend that Eve hid herself in the foliage of a hazel bush after eating the forbidden fruit.

The Ancient Greeks had a story that when the gods were on a mission to redeem the barbarous state of mankind, Apollo gave Mercury a hazel rod endowed with the power of imparting the love of virtue, of calming the passions and of banishing hatred. Mercury moved among the peoples of the earth and, touching them with it, taught them patriotism, filial love and reverence for the gods. The hazel rod of Mercury has ever since been the emblem of peace, and mercredi, Wednesday, is the day of the hazel. The month of wisdom, August 6 to September 2, is hazel's month.

Hazel was one of the sacred seven trees of the Irish grove in early Celtic mythology, and the nuts, sweet and sustaining and enclosed within a small, hard shell, were considered to encapsulate perfect wisdom. So the hazel is the tree of wisdom, the poet's tree, and to the early Celts the wanton felling of this sacred plant was punishable by death.

The hazel is thought to have reached Britain about 10,000 years ago, and it soon became established in pre-historic forests. There is evidence that Neolithic people living in the Somerset marshes 4,500 years ago used bundles of hazel-rods to make pathways to

help them to carry heavy loads over soft ground, and ever since then its pliable, tough timber has been put to many uses. It has been woven, for example, into the primitive coracle, the basket-like framed boat stretched with animal hide and still used today (covered with canvas) by Welsh and Irish fishermen. It was widely planted in Southern England from around 1400 BC onwards, and woven into panels for the 'wattle and daub' method of house-construction.

Its most famed use, perhaps, is as the mystical divining rod, known in this country since the days of Agricola, used not only by water-diviners and treasure-seekers, but up until the 17th century for searching out murderers and thieves. Hazel rods were also used by pilgrims as walking sticks, and then either left in the churches of their destination, or kept as a precious relic to be buried with them when they died.

Right back in the 9th century, in the heroic poetry of the Edda, a hazel rod was a symbol of authority, and in Scandinavian mythology it was dedicated to Thor. Ancient kings used it as a sceptre-staff, and they say that it was of wattled hazel hurdles that St. Joseph of Arimathaea raised the first English Christian church at Glastonbury. During the Second World War millions of hazel-stakes played a vital role in the naval landings on the beaches of northern France.

The hazel is dedicated to St. Phillibert who was born in Gascony, became an abbot, and died in 684 AD. His feast day is August 22nd, when the first ripe hazelnuts, or filberts, can be found.

PEANUT

Although the peanut has been known to man for over 3000 years, it is only recently that the plant has become a feature of our Western diet. Peanuts probably originated in Brazil, where ancient potters made jars in the shape of peanut pods, and decorated them with peanuts embedded into the clay. Graves of Incas often contained jars of peanuts, left there to provide the dead with food for the afterlife.

By the time the Spaniards reached South America in the 16th century, peanuts were being grown as far north as Mexico, and the Conquistadores took some back with them to Spain, where they are still grown, and from where they travelled to Africa and Asia. Peanuts were known to the North American Indians (it is said that they invented peanut butter), and were eaten by the Pilgrim Fathers during the lean winter of 1623. However, it was as a result of the slave trade with Africa that peanuts came to be an important crop in the southern states of America. In the 18th century they were thought of simply as swine-fodder – or at the most food for the very poor. As time went on peanut crops were grown for oil as well as for food, and soldiers in the Civil War used them to supplement their diet. By the 19th century peanuts were a moderately popular snack-food, and were roasted and sold by street-vendors, but the total production was very small.

In the 1920s, however, farmers in the south found themselves unable to grow cotton on boll-weevil infested land, so they turned to peanuts, a new cash-crop which adapted well to the cropping and harvesting system previously used for cotton. New machines were then invented for commercial farming, and since then there has been a 'peanut revolution' in the West. In the East, peanuts have long been a characteristic element of the cuisine, and today India and China are the biggest growers.

WALNUT

The Greeks knew the 'Royal Nut' or 'Persian Nut' – our English walnut – centuries before the birth of Christ. They dedicated it to Proserpine and all infernal deities, because of a legend surrounding Carya, youngest daughter of Dion, King of Laconia. She and her two elder sisters were given the gift of prophecy from Apollo as a reward for their father's hospitality to him, on the condition that they would not misuse it. Bacchus fell in love with Carya and convinced her of his passion, and the jealous elder sisters tried, with their newly-acquired powers, to prevent their meetings, so abusing the gift and breaking the promise. Bacchus, in revenge, turned the two sisters into stones, and his beloved into a walnut tree. Consequently, the fruit of the walnut tree was believed to increase the powers of love.

Magic powers of healing were attributed to the oils and elixirs made from the leaves, shells and kernels.

The Romans imported the walnut from Greece in about 100 BC. Ovid tells us that, during Roman wedding ceremonies, the bride and groom threw walnuts amongst children to symbolize their leave-taking of childish amusements. The first written record of the walnut's presence in Britain dates from about 1562. The Pilgrim Fathers took it to America in the 17th century but it failed to thrive. The strain that has succeeded there is a hardy cultivar carefully selected to survive the conditions, and now California leads the world in the production of walnuts.

The great palaces of Europe have long been graced with elegant furniture made from the fine-grained and beautifully-coloured walnut wood. Its qualities as cabinet-wood have been unequalled by any other hardwood for the past 500 years.

Walnut trees can live to a great age. A famous tree once grew in the churchyard on the north side of St. Joseph's Chapel at Glastonbury. It never budded before St. Barnabas' Day, June 11th, when it would burst into leaf and flourish like the rest of the species. Queen Anne, King James II and many influential noblemen are said to have given large sums for cuttings off the original tree.

'Oh God! I could be bounded in a nut shell, and count myself king of infinite space, were it not that I have bad dreams.'

Hamlet

THE NUTRITIONAL VALUE OF NUTS

Nuts are a highly concentrated source of nutrition and energy. Each type has a distinctive taste. They are nice to eat on their own; they add crunchiness to soups, salads and garnishes; they provide protein, dietary fibre, vitamins and minerals; and they are a valuable and inexpensive form of nourishment, since small quantities contain high percentages of these constituents. Nuts make a pleasing addition to chop suey or a salad, a risotto or a sandwich, a fruit pie or cakes and breads; and a packet of nuts in a picnic basket will boost its nutritional value enormously. They are a versatile and valuable source of food, and excellent as a fast energy snack.

Almonds are high in proteins and fats, low in sugars and carbohydrates, and have a good quantity of dietary fibre. They contain iron, zinc and calcium, provide 160 calories to the ounce, and are a good source of vitamins B_1, B_2, B_6 and E.

Brazil nuts are very high in fat content and rich in protein, contain medium amounts of dietary fibre and are low in sugars and carbohydrates. They are rich in zinc and vitamin B_1, and also contain B_2, B_6, and E. They provide 175 calories to the ounce.

Chestnuts are rich in starch, sugars and carbohydrates, and low in fats and proteins. They contain less dietary fibre than other nuts and provide 48 calories to the ounce when peeled. They have quite a high water content, and contain vitamins B_1, B_2, B_6 and E.

Coconuts, when fresh, are very high in fats and dietary fibre, and low in sugars, carbohydrades and protein. They contain no starch and have a high water content. As well as vitamins B_1, and B_2, they contain B_6 and C, and provide 100 calories to the ounce.

Desiccated coconut is even higher in dietary fibre, very rich in fat and contains a little more protein and sugars. It provides 171 calories to the ounce.

Hazelnuts have a moderately high fat content, and provide 108 calories to the ounce, a medium amount of protein and carbohydrates, and low sugar and starch. They contain a small amount of dietary fibre, vitamins B_1 and B_6. The vitamin E content is exceptionally high.

Peanuts are very high in protein, (26%, which is higher than eggs), and they are extremely rich in fats. They are low in sugars, starch and carbohydrates. They contain vitamins B_1, B_2, B_6 and E, and are rich in iron, calcium and zinc. They provide 162 calories to the ounce.

Walnuts are very high in fat, contain a good amount of protein and a little dietary fibre. They are low in sugars, starch and carbohydrates and contain vitamins A, B_1, B_2, B_6 and E. They provide 149 calories to the ounce.

HARVESTING AND STORING NUTS

Always gather your nuts when they are fully mature, and then if you store them properly you should be able to keep them fresh during the winter. It is best to store them in their shells rather than shelling and drying them.

Almonds: The only almonds to ripen at all in Britain are bitter almonds, which in small quantities can be used to flavour cakes and puddings. Do not, however, eat the fresh kernels or put them whole into a dessert – they have a high prussic-acid content and can be dangerous. When you want to use sweet almonds, place them in a warm oven for a few minutes to help crack the shells.

Chestnuts: Remove the husks from around the outside of the nuts, wipe them clean and put in alternate layers with dry sand in a box. This is how they store them in the Périgord, covered with a lid. Alternatively, hang them in loosely-woven bags or sacks in a cool place. If they start to shrivel it means that they are too dry, so put them in slightly damp sand for a few days – no longer, or they will go mouldy.

Walnuts: Pick up fallen walnuts as soon as possible after they have dropped, and beat any other ripe nuts off the branches with a long pole. Remove the husk so that the shell is free from any trace of fibre, to eliminate the possibility of mould. 'Put the husky ones into a long coarse sack and let two people take an end each and shake the nuts from end to end with a rolling movement, backwards and forwards. Throw them out on to the clean grass, and you should be able to pick them up fairly clean. If not, leave till dry and do it again.' (Dorothy Hartley: *Food in England*.)

Scrub the walnuts quickly in water with a soft nailbrush, not allowing them to soak in case they crack along the seam. Dry the nuts in a single layer at room temperature, with a draught if possible.

To store, you can either hang them in a net bag in a cool dry place, or fill an earthenware crock with layers of nuts alternating with a mixture of half salt and half coconut-fibre refuse. The salt prevents mould from growing, the fibre absorbs any moisture. Store the crock in a cool place and the nuts should keep fresh until the following May.

SALTING NUTS

If space is at a premium one of the best and tastiest ways to keep nuts is to salt them. Shell your nuts and grill them lightly all over. Heat some oil in a pan and shake them in the oil until well coated and slightly browned. Drain on kitchen paper and sprinkle with salt. Cool, and store in airtight jars indefinitely.

This method is particularly good with almonds, hazelnuts, pinenuts and brazils.

NUT RECIPES

ALMONDS

Almonds have a fine taste and have been used in gastronomic cuisine for centuries.

STUFFED COURGETTES

Although there are many versions of stuffed courgettes, this recipe takes top marks for delicacy and originality.

3 large courgettes
1 large onion
oil
2½ oz almonds, skinned
salt, pepper and ground mace
1 egg, beaten
1 oz each Parmesan and breadcrumbs

Halve the courgettes lengthways and scoop out the flesh, leaving little hollow boats. Chop the onion and soften it in some oil, and then add the chopped courgette flesh and cook for a few minutes. Grind the nuts coarsely and stir in, then season to taste with salt, pepper and mace. Bind with the beaten egg. Heap the stuffing into the courgette boats, and cover with the cheese and breadcrumbs mixed together. Bake at 400°F, 200°C, gas 6 for 25 minutes.

For 6

ALMOND SAUCE FOR RICE

This is incredible. It is either a meal in itself, or a side dish for a light meal.

3 oz almonds
½ pint stock
1 clove garlic, crushed
a large bunch of parsley, finely chopped
salt and pepper
lemon juice and Tabasco
8 oz Basmati rice

Grind the almonds fairly finely and mix them with the stock. Bring to the boil and add the crushed garlic and finely chopped parsley. Season to taste with salt, pepper, lemon juice and Tabasco. Simmer for 20 minutes over a very low heat.

Meanwhile, cook the rice. Pour the sauce over the cooked rice and serve hot.

For 2

ALMOND AND WALNUT PUFFS

Serve these with coffee after a meal.

Grind 2 oz blanched almonds and 2 oz walnut pieces, then add 4 oz icing sugar, grated peel of ½ lemon and 1 egg white. Liquidize thoroughly. Form into little balls, roll in more icing sugar and place on rice paper on a baking sheet. Bake at 325°F, 160°C, gas 3 for 20 minutes. Quite delicious.

BRAZIL NUTS

Brazil nuts are almost synonymous with Christmas. Their creamy texture and coconut flavour make them a delicious ingredient of any cooked dish, and it is worth experimenting with them as a substitute for more common nuts.

CURRIED BRAZIL NUTS

These make a lovely change from plain nuts at Christmas – they are warmly spicy, and delicious with mulled wine on cold evenings.

2 oz butter
2 tablespoons olive oil
2 teaspoons garam masala
1 teaspoon each ground coriander, cardamom and cumin
8 oz shelled brazil nuts

Heat the butter and the oil with the spices, and allow to bubble for a minute. Add the nuts and simmer for 3 minutes, tossing and stirring so that they are well-coated. Then put the nuts in a baking tray and cook at 400°F, 200°C, gas 6 for 20 – 25 minutes until they are well-browned.

Drain on kitchen paper, sprinkle with salt and leave to cool. Store in airtight jars.

APRICOT AND BRAZIL NUT MALT LOAF

This classic bread improves with keeping: wrap it in cling-film and keep it in the fridge for a day or two. Serve it sliced and spread generously with butter. It will vanish!

1 x 15 oz can apricots
2 oz shelled brazil nuts
4 tablespoons malt extract
4 tablespoons black treacle
2 oz butter
2 oz brown sugar
8 oz plain flour
3 teaspoons baking powder
$\frac{1}{4}$ teaspoon salt
1 egg
6 tablespoons milk

Drain and chop the apricots and coarsely chop the nuts. Melt the malt extract, treacle, butter and sugar together. Sift the flour with the baking powder and salt and make a well in the centre. Into this pour the malt mixture, the well-beaten egg, the milk, the apricots and the nuts. Mix thoroughly with a wooden spoon and pour into a loaf tin lined with greaseproof paper. Cook at 325°F, 160°C, gas 3 for 1 – 1$\frac{1}{4}$ hours until a knife comes out clean from the middle. Cool on a rack.

CASHEWS

Personally I rate the cashew nut as tops: whether roasted and salted, or plain as in these recipes, its soft texture and subtle taste are unbeatable.

CHICKEN WITH CASHEW NUTS

Chinese in origin, this delicious dish is simple to prepare and takes only a short time to cook.

2 chicken pieces
salt and pepper
sesame oil
butter
4 spring onions
½ green pepper
4 oz canned bamboo shoots
4 oz unsalted cashews
1 tablespoon soy sauce

Season the chicken pieces with salt and pepper and fry gently in the sesame oil and butter until golden and cooked through, about 20 minutes. Chop the spring onions, dice the seeded pepper, slice the bamboo shoots and add them all, with the nuts and the soy sauce, to the juices in the pan. Stir and heat through for about 2 – 3 minutes.

Serve immediately, spooned over the chicken pieces on a bed of soft noodles.

For 2

CASHEW BRITTLE

Don't bother with this recipe if you are worried about your waistline: it is hopelessly, deliciously, more-ish.

8 oz sugar
3 tablespoons water
2 teaspoons vinegar
6 oz roasted cashews

Combine the sugar, water and vinegar and cook in a thick pan over a gentle heat until the sugar has dissolved. Then simmer until the syrup goes a light caramel colour. Chop the cashews and stir them in quickly, and spread on to a greased baking sheet. Press down as thinly as possible with the back of a spoon, and mark into squares while still warm. Allow to cool, then break into pieces and store in airtight jars.

CHESTNUTS

Chestnut vendors on winter streets popping their nuts over the coals is a part of our past that has not changed for centuries. The best way to cook and peel chestnuts is to slit the surface on the domed face of the nuts, put them in a baking tin with a little water and roast in a hot oven for about 10 minutes. Peel them while still hot.

CHESTNUT SOUP

A wonderful soup for winter – rich and warming.

8 oz chestnut purée unsweetened
¾ pint good stock
1 onion
2 sticks celery
1½ oz butter
cream
salt, mace and cayenne

Mix the purée with the stock and simmer gently.
Slice the onion and the celery and cook gently in the butter until soft. Add the chestnut mixture gradually, stirring well, and finish with the cream. Season to taste and serve hot.

For 4

RED CABBAGE WITH CHESTNUTS

I cook this to go with goose at Christmas.

1 small red cabbage
3 tablespoons each vinegar and water
salt and pepper
8 oz peeled chestnuts

Chop the cabbage coarsely and put into a casserole dish with the vinegar and water. Season with salt and pepper. Cook, covered with a lid, for 2 hours at 325°F, 160°C, gas 3. Stir in the chestnuts and stand on one side for 20 minutes before serving.

For 4

MONT BLANC

This is my humble version of a French classic.

¼ pint water
2 oz sugar
1 lb chestnut purée, unsweetened
6 small sponge cakes
rum
½ pint double cream, whipped
vanilla essence and icing sugar to taste
grated chocolate

Boil the water with the sugar until a thick syrup is formed. Add to the chestnut purée and mix well.

Place the halved sponge cakes in the bottom of a large flat dish and sprinkle with rum. Pipe the purée around the edge of the dish to form a nest, and fill the middle with the whipped cream, flavoured with vanilla and icing sugar. Dust with grated chocolate and serve chilled.

For 6

COCONUTS

Desiccated coconut is now a world-wide commodity, which is easily stored and always adds flavour and texture to sweet and savoury dishes alike.

COCONUT KISSES

Delectably light and delicately flavoured, they are a perfect teatime treat.

4 oz butter
4 oz sugar
1 egg
1 teaspoon vanilla essence
8 oz plain flour
1 teaspoon baking powder
a pinch of salt
4 oz desiccated coconut
desiccated coconut for coating
12 glacé cherries, quartered

Cream the butter and sugar until light and fluffy. Add the egg, beating lightly, and stir in the vanilla essence. Fold in the flour, sifted with the baking powder and salt, and then the desiccated coconut. Form into a light dough and shape the mixture into small balls. Roll in desiccated coconut and top each ball with a piece of glacé cherry. Place on a greased tray and bake at 325°F, 160°C, gas 3 for 30 minutes, until golden. Cool on a rack.

Makes 48

COCONUT AND PINEAPPLE CORDIAL

A tasty and summery drink with an individual flavour, which is popular with children and adults alike. It makes an exotic soft drink for a cocktail party.

½ pint coconut milk, made by pouring ½ pint boiling water over 2 oz desiccated coconut and leaving to stand until cold
8 oz coarsely chopped pineapple
2 tablespoons caster sugar
1 drop almond extract

Combine the coconut milk, pineapple, sugar and almond extract in a blender until very smooth; the pineapple should be completely liquidized. Strain, pour into a jug and chill.

Serve in tumblers with ice.

For 2

'If a man were placed on earth with nothing else but the coconut tree, he could live in happiness and contentment.'

Syrian saying

HAZELNUTS

I think that hazelnuts are fantastic in fine desserts –
in meringue bases particularly, filled with exciting
fruit mixtures and topped with cream.

HAZELNUT GÂTEAU

This makes one of the very best of all desserts – it is
light and moist. One of my favourite fillings is fresh
fruit jelly flavoured with lemon juice.

6 oz butter
4 large eggs
8 oz sugar
4 oz flour sifted with a pinch of salt
8 oz hazelnuts ⎫
6 tablespoons caster sugar ⎬ *ground finely*
1 oz plain chocolate, grated ⎭

Cream the butter. Beat the eggs with the sugar until
thick and pale. Add this alternately with the flour to
the butter, finally stir in the nuts and sugar.

Pour the mixture into two sandwich cake tins and
bake at 350°F, 180°C, gas 4 for 40 minutes. Cool,
remove from the tins and fill with your chosen
filling. Decorate with grated chocolate and serve
chilled, with crème anglaise (page 46) or cream.

For 6

Hazelnut Macaroons

3 oz hazelnuts
2 egg whites
3 oz caster sugar

Toast the nuts in a very hot oven, shaking occasionally until they are browned and the skins are beginning to flake off. Grind them finely.

Whisk the egg whites until they are stiff. Beat in half of the sugar and then fold in the nuts with the rest of the sugar. Put tablespoons of the mixture on to rice paper on a baking tray and cook at 325°F, 160°C, gas 3 for 30 – 40 minutes until set and slightly browned. Cool on a rack.

Makes 15

Spiced Hazelnuts

Heavenly morsels to serve instead of petit fours.

1 egg white
2 oz sugar
1 tablespoon cinnamon
⅛ teaspoon each ground cloves and nutmeg
8 oz hazelnuts

Beat the egg white until it is stiff and fold in the sugar and the spices. Toss the nuts in this mixture until well-coated and place on a greased baking tray. Bake for 30 minutes at 325°F, 160°C, gas 3.

HAZELNUT ICE CREAM

A sophisticated ice cream, in which the great taste of the hazelnut is exploited to its fullest potential.

Crème anglaise:
3 egg yolks
4 oz caster sugar
1 tablespoon flour
⅔ pint hot milk

4 oz hazelnuts
¼ pint double cream
caster sugar

To make the crème anglaise, beat the egg yolks with the sugar until thick and creamy. Beat in the flour and then gradually add the hot milk, stirring all the time. Cook over a gentle heat, stirring until the custard thickens. Remove from the heat.

Grind the nuts fairly coarsely and fold half of them into the custard and add the cream. Freeze.

Sprinkle the rest of the nuts liberally with sugar and cook in a baking tray at 425°F, 210°C, gas 7 for 20 – 30 minutes until the sugar caramelizes. Turn out on to a flat surface to cool. Then fold into the freezing cream. Re-freeze, and stir again 1 hour later. Leave to freeze completely.

For 6

PEANUTS

Here are three of the recipes which lead me regularly into temptation.

PEANUT SOUP

4 oz roasted peanuts
¾ pint stock
pepper and Tabasco to taste
¼ pint double cream

Liquidize the peanuts with a little stock until completely smooth. Add the rest of the stock and stir over a gentle heat. Season to taste with pepper and Tabasco. Add the cream, heat through, and serve with croûtons.

For 4

PEANUT AND CHEESE BALLS

4 oz cream cheese
salad cream to moisten
salt and Tabasco
4 oz peanuts

Mash the cream cheese with the salad cream and season to taste with the salt and Tabasco. Form into little balls. Grind the nuts coarsely. Roll the cream cheese balls in the nuts. Pierce on cocktail sticks and serve with drinks.

PEANUT BUTTER COOKIES

Home-made crunchy peanut butter is completely different from the commercial variety. It makes some of the best sandwiches in the world, and these cookies are scrumptious.

Crunchy Peanut Butter:
2 oz roasted peanuts
2 oz melted butter

Grind the nuts coarsely and stir into the melted butter. Leave to cool and set.

For the Cookies:
4 oz softened butter
4 oz sugar
1 egg
1 teaspoon vanilla essence
6 oz plain flour
½ teaspoon salt
1 teaspoon soda bicarbonate
4 oz crunchy peanut butter (see above)

Cream the butter with the sugar and beat in the egg and vanilla. Fold in the flour, sifted with the salt and soda, and then beat in the peanut butter. Place teaspoons of the mixture on a greased baking sheet and cook at 400°F, 200°C, gas 6 for about 8 minutes until browned a little at the edges. Cool on a rack.

Makes 36

PECANS

Very common in the United States, the pecan is a somewhat specialist nut in the United Kingdom. It is worth hunting out however, even if only to make the notorious pecan pie!

PECAN PIE

America's famous recipe, given to me by a Transatlantic friend. This makes the best pecan pie I have ever tasted.

2 oz butter
4 oz brown sugar
2 eggs, beaten
1 tablespoon flour
¼ pint golden syrup
⅛ pint milk
¼ teaspoon vanilla essence
6 oz shelled pecans
1 x 8-inch flan dish, lined with sweet crust pastry
*   and baked blind*

Melt the butter and beat in all the other ingredients except the pecans. Sprinkle the nuts over the pastry shell, and pour the mixture over.

Bake at 375°F, 190°C, gas 5 for 15 minutes, then turn the heat down to 325°F, 160°C, gas 3 and cook until a knife comes out clean from the centre, about 30 minutes. Serve warm or cold with thick cream.

For 6

PINE NUTS

Pine nuts are misnamed: they should have been called Divine Nuts. They are out of this world, and unfortunately very expensive.

PAMELA HARLECH'S PINE NUTS AND TAGLIATELLE

This dish is sublime. It is also a weekend dish (look at the amount of garlic!). But the gentle heat of the chillis and the flavour of the nuts heightened by good olive oil makes this a sensational sauce for pasta.

¼ pint good olive oil
3–4 dried chillis
1 lb tagliatelle
4 cloves of garlic
6 tablespoons roasted pine nuts
4 tablespoons fresh chopped basil or parsley

Heat the oil gently and break the chillis into it. Infuse over a very low heat for 5 minutes. Set aside.

Cook the tagliatelle 'al dente'. Just before it is ready, strain the oil into another pan, crush the garlic into it and add the pine nuts. Cook them over a gentle heat for a minute or two, and then mix into the drained tagliatelle.

Serve immediately, sprinkled with the chopped herbs.

For 4

WALNUTS

Walnuts have been used in cooking for so many centuries that there are hundreds of great recipes to be found for them: soups, salads, jams, and cakes, meat dishes, fish dishes and vegetable dishes. They are immensely versatile: here is one of my favourites.

WALNUT SAUCE FOR SMOKED FISH

This is a rich and pungently tasty cold sauce which goes beautifully with smoked mackerel and is positively Epicurean with smoked trout.

2 oz walnuts
1 large bunch of parsley
1 oz breadcrumbs
olive oil
2 cloves garlic, chopped
salt and pepper
¼ pint cream

Grind the nuts finely and chop the parsley. Add the breadcrumbs and then gradually stir in the olive oil until it reaches the consistency of thick cream. Season to taste with finely chopped garlic and salt and pepper, and thin out with the cream. Serve chilled.

For 4

Nuts In Beauty Products

Coconut Oil

Pure coconut oil comes in the form of a pearly-white, greasy mass, either odourless or with a slight and pleasant smell of coconut. Store it in well-filled and tightly-closed jars because when exposed to the air it becomes rancid. This oil or ointment is easily absorbed and is much-used in preparations for the scalp; coconut shampoo gives hair a healthy lustre. The coconut oil bought at the chemist will be thinned down with other oils. Coconut oil is used commercially in the preparation of soaps, detergents, skin-cleansers and creams. 'Cocoa butter', the purified and deodorized product of coconut oil, makes a thick, oily face cream which softens the skin.

Peanut Oil

Otherwise known as 'arachis oil', this is pale yellow with a faintly nutty odour and a bland and nutty taste. It must be stored in well-filled and tightly-closed jars. Its uses in beauty preparations are much the same as those of olive oil – as a skin-softener – and it is a cheap substitute for almond oil in cosmetics. Its extra bonus is that it contains vitamin E. Peanut oil is also used as drops for softening ear wax.

ALMOND OIL

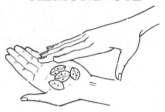

Pale yellow and with a faint smell, almond oil has a bland and nutty taste and must be stored in a well-filled and tightly-closed container. Not only does it nourish the skin, it soothes and softens it and is used in the preparation of cold creams, brilliantines, hair-lotions and other beauty preparations.

Rub a few drops of almond oil into your scalp a few hours before washing your hair and it will give it a wonderful shine. The oil can also be used to soften chapped hands, and is used in the commercial manufacture of essential oils.

AROMATIC BATH OIL

4 oz fresh herbs, such as marjoram, thyme, rosemary
1 pint sweet almond oil
1 tablespoon cider vinegar

Pulverize the herbs in a blender and stir in the oil and vinegar. Put into a jar and seal tightly. Shake every day for about a month, and then strain and re-bottle. It makes a lovely bath oil which softens the water and gives out a delicious aroma.

Nut Decorations

A Christmas Nut Bowl

Take whole almonds, walnuts, brazil nuts and peanuts – all with their shells on – and spray them with gold and silver glitter spray paint. Spray a few pink, pale green and mauve if the colours are available. Allow them to dry and then heap the coloured nuts high in a pretty china bowl.

Mouse In A Nutshell

An appealing idea for little Christmas presents or stocking-fillers. Halve a walnut very carefully so that each half-shell is intact. Remove the nut part and scrub clean gently. Make a little felt mouse as illustrated below, stuff him with kapok, and use beads for his nose and eyes, and fine wire for his whiskers. Tuck him up with a pretty scrap of fabric for his bedcover.

NUTTY FOLKLORE

ALMONDS

* The Czechs distribute almonds, symbols of fruitfulness, to wedding guests at marriage ceremonies; whereas Germans present the bride and groom with nuts.

* To dream of eating almonds means that you will have a long journey ahead. If they taste sweet it will be a properous one; if bitter, it will not.

* Pliny considered almonds to be a potent remedy for drunkenness, and Plutarch tells the story of a notorious wine-bibber who used to take bitter almonds as a prophylactic against the after-effects of his hobby! Gerard supports this in his *Herball* of 1597: 'It is reported that five or six [bitter almonds] being taken fasting do keepe a man from being drunke.'

* There used to be a fortune-telling game where you named a row of chestnuts set along the top bar of a hot grate. The first 'name' to pop was the first lover to pop the question. If the nut jumped into your lap, you won him; if it popped into the fire and was burnt up, you didn't!

* In Venice there is a custom that on St. Martin's Day (11th November) the poor women in the city gather beneath the windows of those more fortunate than themselves, and they sing a long ballad. After expressing their good wishes towards the occupants they ask them for chestnuts to appease their hunger. Chestnuts were distributed to the poor on this day, and chestnut sweetmeats were traditionally eaten on St. Simon's Day (28th October).

HAZELNUTS

* The hazelnut is a symbol of happy marriages, because its nuts grow united in pairs.

* A hazel rod has the power to frighten serpents. St. Patrick held one in his hand when he gathered all the poisonous reptiles of Ireland on the promontory of Cruachan Phadraig and cast them into the sea.

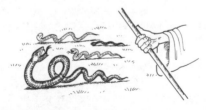

* To dream of finding hidden hazelnuts predicts the discovery of treasure.

WALNUTS

'A woman, a spaniel, and a walnut tree,
The more you beat them, the better they be.'

* If your walnut tree is not bearing fruit, beat it with a bill-hook in March while the sap is rising.

* The walnut tree is a tree of ill-omen, and a favourite haunt of witches. Nothing will grow in its shade, and if planted in an orchard it will kill off all the neighbouring apple trees.

* The nut of the walnut, on the other hand, is propitious and a symbol of fecundity and abundance, so it is favourable to marriage. It was scattered or distributed at weddings in Ancient Greece and Rome.

* Barren women were sometimes fed a boiled mixture of crushed black walnuts and a little water, mixed with fine cornmeal, to improve their fertility.

* To dream of walnuts means difficulties and misfortune ahead. In love, it implies infidelity and disappointment.

* The resemblance of the peeled walnut to the human brain led to the medieval belief that, by the Doctrine of Signatures, the nuts could cure mental illness.

GROW YOUR OWN NUT TREE

WALNUT

If in the Spring you sow a whole walnut which has been carefully stored (see page 33), you may succeed in growing your own tree. The 'nut meats' are in fact seed-leaves, and these remain inside the shell while a stout shoot will appear through the soil, bearing at first small scale-like leaves. As time goes on proper leaves will develop, and slowly a little tree emerges.

Plant the seed, or nut, in a potting compost mixture in a medium-sized pot. Keep it indoors or in a greenhouse, well-drained and moist. When the tree is about 1 foot tall, plant it out in the Spring – and hope for the best.

GROW YOUR OWN PEANUTS

This is not a serious exercise but it is great fun for children because the results are dramatically quick and very attractive. Because of our climate, you are in fact only growing the plant, not the nut, but it is still worth it for its decorative leguminous leaves.

Plant a whole peanut, with its shell on, in potting compost in a well-drained container. You can do it any time of the year as long as you keep the pot in a warm place indoors, and make sure that it is well watered. Shoots, then stems and leaves, are quick to appear, and soon you will have a rampant peanut-plant!

A HAZEL SHRUB

You can buy small young hazel bushes from garden nurseries. The main stem will have been pruned back to about 18 inches. Plant out your young bush in October or November, in a position which gets open sun or partial shade, and which is sheltered from N and NE winds. It likes a well-drained soil, and does particularly well on chalk.

For two to three subsequent autumns cut back the previous season's wood by a half – down to two or three buds – to build up the bush. When flowering starts, after four or five years, shorten old growths in March after flowering (because the hazel is self-pollinating) and this will stimulate new shoots. In August cut out any strong growth in the centre of the bush to increase its spread, and remove all suckers. Eventually your hazel will reach about 20 feet.

ACKNOWLEDGEMENTS

My thanks for their friendly assistance to the Fruit
and Vegetable Information Bureau; the National
Institute of Fresh Produce; Marilyn Burbage at the
Tropical Products Institute; Suzanne Kew and
Sigrid Barber at the Ministry of Agriculture,
Fisheries and Food; Rod Smith of K.P. Nuts Ltd.;
and to Mrs Margaret Wilson of the W.I.